Santa Baby

Santa Baby

Katie Price

x

C̄

Century · London

Published by Century 2011

2 4 6 8 10 9 7 5 3 1

Copyright © Katie Price 2011; Rebecca Farnworth 2011

Katie Price and Rebecca Farnworth have asserted their right under
the Copyright, Designs and Patents Act 1988 to be identified as the
authors of this work.

First published in Great Britain in 2011 by
Century
Random House, 20 Vauxhall Bridge Road,
London SW1V 2SA

www.randomhouse.co.uk

Addresses for companies within The Random House Group Limited can be
found at: www.randomhouse.co.uk

The Random House Group Limited Reg. No. 954009

A CIP catalogue record for this book
is available from the British Library

ISBN 978-1-846-05963-6 (HB)
ISBN 978-1-846-05964-3 (TPB)

The Random House Group Limited supports The Forest Stewardship
Council (FSC®), the leading international forest certification organisation. Our
books carrying the FSC label are printed on FSC® certified paper. FSC is the
only forest certification scheme endorsed by the leading environmental
organisations, including Greenpeace. Our paper procurement policy can be
found at www.randomhouse.co.uk/environment

Typeset by SX Composing DTP, Rayleigh, Essex
Printed and bound by CPI Group (UK) Ltd, Croydon, CR0 4YY

Chapter 1

Tiffany Taylor shivered in the cool night air and hopped from foot to foot to keep warm. It was meant to be June but it felt more like March, and she was seriously under-dressed in a black tutu-style skirt, silver sandals, bare legs, fingerless lace gloves, and a black tuxedo jacket. She stood out from the other girls in the line snaking outside the West End club who were all in a uniform of brightly coloured, revealing body-con dresses and fake tan, and could have given the girls from *TOWIE* a run for their money. Tiffany's style was more quirky and individual.

She checked her watch again. She might have guessed that her best friend Kara would be late. It was after midnight. Tiffany, or Tiff as all her friends called her, stifled a yawn. She had been up since seven this morning and had only stopped working an hour ago at her waitress job in a busy pizza restaurant.

An icy wind whipped her long chestnut-brown hair into her face, plastering it against her glossed lips. Great. She attempted to smooth it back, hoping that she didn't smell of pizza dough or, worse still, garlic bread. She'd sprayed on masses of Coco Mademoiselle, even though she was down to the last dregs and who knew when she would be able to afford a new bottle. Usually, before a night out clubbing, she would have showered and washed her hair, but tonight she'd had no time. It had been a quick freshen up in the Ladies with wet wipes. Oh, the glamour . . .

'Hiya, Tiff. You haven't been waiting long, have you?' It was Kara, looking glossy and gorgeous in a turquoise, one-shoulder dress. As usual her accessories matched perfectly – a satin clutch bag and heels, and a turquoise stone necklace. Tiffany, who had studied Fashion and Textiles and wanted to be a stylist, had given up trying to point out to her that sometimes you could be a little too 'matchy matchy'.

'Ages!' she exclaimed.

'I don't know why you're standing out here . . . I'm on the guest list.' A man in his mid-twenties, suited and booted, and standing next to Kara's boyfriend Harley, spoke up. He must be Tiffany's blind date courtesy of Kara, even though she had begged her friend not to set her up.

'Oh, yes, this is Gavin, who I was telling you about. Gavin – Tiffany . . . Tiffany – Gavin,' Kara babbled away.

'Hiya,' Tiffany said, instantly deciding that Gavin was not her type. Kara had gone on about how fit he was. And he was good-looking, but he did nothing for her because he seemed so full of himself. She could tell that his clothes were expensive – the designer suit and shirt, the show-off watch – but those kinds of things never impressed her. Style wasn't about how much money you spent. And Tiffany especially didn't like the way he looked her up and down, blatantly assessing her attractiveness.

'Cheer up,' Harley whispered as they trailed behind Kara and Gavin to the front of the queue. 'If he's that bad, we'll make an excuse and leave.'

Harley was the nicest, most easy-going man that

2

Tiffany knew. Kara, who was a bit of a stunner with her petite body, huge brown eyes, long blonde hair and pretty face, could have taken her pick of the fit-looking blokes who worked out at her dad's North London gym which she helped manage, but she had fallen in love with Harley. He was by no means plain, with a pleasant face, the sort you felt you could trust, short brown hair and grey-blue eyes, but you wouldn't have put him in Kara's league. Though he did have two killer cards in his pack – he had a fantastic body, and he was a fireman. Way to go, Kara! She was the envy of all her female friends except Tiffany, who could only ever see Harley as Kara's boyfriend.

By now Gavin had reached the head of the queue and was remonstrating with the girl in charge of the guest list. She was flanked by two tall bouncers in long black overcoats. Tiffany envied them their coats; if she didn't get inside soon, there was a strong possibility that she would get hypothermia and end the night wrapped up in Bacofoil or whatever they used. *So* not a good look. Now she had met Gavin she had a very strong desire to go home. She was knackered; her feet were killing her after her ten-hour waitress shift. She didn't fancy Gavin, and she wasn't going to pretend to fancy him. She decided that she would make that clear as politely as possible and give him the chance to go off and find himself another date. Then at least she would be free to enjoy herself with Kara and Harley.

'Well check it again! I know I'm on the fucking list . . . I'm a friend of the fucking owner!' Gavin exclaimed. Tiffany bridled at his tone. She'd had enough experience of obnoxious customers to know how it felt to be on the receiving end of their tirades.

'Less of the attitude, mate,' one of the bouncers spoke up. A Geordie from the sound of him.

'And why don't you fuck off back to the North?'

What a charmer! Tiffany looked at Kara who grimaced and mouthed, 'Sorry.'

Tiffany fully expected to be refused entry after that but the girl found their names on the list and the thick red rope was unclipped from the stand to allow them in. As Tiffany walked past the bouncers, one of them, the Geordie, caught her eye. He was strikingly handsome but his dark brown eyes were full of scorn and she burned with embarrassment at being associated with a foul-mouthed tosser like Gavin.

Things didn't improve once they were inside the club. Gavin insisted on ordering champagne, even though there was no way Tiffany would be able to pay for another round. She sat on one of the low-slung black velvet sofas and wondered how soon she would be able to make her escape from him. Kara had spotted someone she knew and was deep in conversation some distance away, so could not be relied upon to rescue her. Gavin sat down next to Tiffany and draped his arm along the back of the sofa, as if he already had a claim on her. Well, he could dream on!

For the next twenty minutes, though it felt far, far longer, Gavin talked at her. He ran his own business selling second-hand computers. His talk was all about the money he had made and how great he was at selling, of his flash new flat, his top-of-the-range car. Big wow, thought Tiffany who had zero interest in the business world, or properties, or cars. She was on the verge of nodding off when he moved further along the sofa, so close to her that their thighs touched. She tried to inch away from him, but was already pressed against the arm of the sofa on the other side.

'So, Kara tells me you want to do something in fashion. I don't know much about it myself. I just know what I like.' He gestured at his own clothes. 'Suit by Dolce & Gabbana, shirt by Ted Baker, shoes by Ralph

4

Lauren.' He grinned at her. 'Boxers by – well, I'll leave you to find that out for yourself.'

Or not, Tiffany thought. She couldn't even bring herself to laugh. He was so arrogant and vile.

'You remind me of someone,' Gavin continued, seeming not to notice that Tiffany had failed to respond to his chat-up line. 'It's the eyes . . . Yeah, I know, it's that glamour bird, Angel Summer. You look a bit like her.' His eyes leered at her. 'Though you haven't got all her other assets, have you?'

It wasn't the first time that someone had pointed out the resemblance she bore to the famous former glamour model. Tiffany had never been able to see it herself. But if Gavin had intended the comment to be a compliment, it hadn't worked. She took a deep breath. There was no way she could sit here and listen to him a minute longer, especially as he clearly thought a shag was on the cards.

'Gavin, mate, can I be honest? It's not going to work out between us.'

He looked at her as if he hadn't understood. So he was thick as well as arrogant? What a perfect combination. Time to be direct. 'I don't fancy you. I'm not going to sleep with you tonight. So why don't you take your bottle of champagne and find some other girl?'

Anger made him ugly and hard, showing the bully always waiting to come out from behind the designer clothes. 'Who the fuck do you think you are? What is it you do again? Oh, yeah, you're a waitress. A nobody. What makes you think I wanted to shag you anyway? I could do way better than you, darling.'

And reaching for the bottle of champagne, he stood up and strode away.

While Tiffany was heartily glad to be rid of Gavin, his aggression had shaken her. The level of hostility he had directed at her had been horrible; he seemed to have a real loathing for women. She hated men who thought they could treat women like dirt, just because they could splash the cash. She looked around the club and was relieved to see Kara and Harley returning from the dance floor.

'I've just seen Gavin. He was all over some blonde,' Kara said. 'Sorry, babe, I had no idea he was such a wanker. I've only met him a couple of times and he seemed OK.'

Tiffany resisted the temptation to say that 'wanker' was written all over him. You only had to look at him to know that. She adored Kara but her friend was a little ditzy, and also had a tendency to see only the good in people. Harley raised his eyebrows at Tiffany. He had seen exactly what kind of man Gavin was from the off.

'Let's have a drink and a dance, and maybe you'll find someone else,' Kara added hopefully. She had been trying to line up Tiffany with another man for the last six months, since she'd split up from Billy, her on/off boyfriend of the last two years. Kara didn't get it that actually Tiffany was perfectly happy being single for a while.

She managed to raise a smile, though. She would try and enjoy herself, for the sake of her friend.

And after she'd had a couple of Mojitos and danced to some of her favourite tracks, Tiffany felt a whole lot better. She had almost forgotten about the vile Gavin. But unfortunately she and her friends found themselves leaving the club at the same time as he was and bumped into him in the foyer. He was alone and very drunk. He had spilled his drink down his expensive shirt. Clearly things hadn't worked out with the blonde.

'Oh, look who it is. Little Miss Frigid! As if I'd want to shag *you*.'

He stepped towards Tiffany who edged back, not liking the mean look in his eyes.

'Come on, there's no need for that, mate,' Harley said reasonably. 'Why don't I get you a taxi?'

But Gavin carried on advancing towards Tiffany, while she backed away nervously. And when Harley reached out to put a restraining hand on Gavin, he swung out wildly with his left fist and punched Harley in the face. All hell broke loose then as Kara screamed, 'You bastard! Don't you touch my Harley!' and launched herself at Gavin, battering him over the head with her turquoise clutch bag, which was probably more painful than it sounded as Kara packed a lot of cosmetics. Within seconds the bouncers had raced into the foyer and pulled her away from Gavin, struggling to restrain him.

'Don't you fucking touch me!' he yelled, elbowing the two men. 'Fucking low-life scum! I bet you've just come out of prison and this is the only job you could get.'

Tiffany couldn't believe what she was witnessing. Gavin was a complete psycho!

'Actually, mate, I was in army,' one of the bouncers said, the one who had looked at Tiffany so scornfully.

'Couldn't get a proper job, eh?' Gavin spat. 'And now you're out and most likely pretending you've got that Post Traumatic Stress bullshit.'

For a moment a look of pure rage flared up in the other man's eyes and Tiffany was certain he was going to deck Gavin. Not that the idiot didn't deserve it. Instead he turned to her, the look of scorn back in his eyes. 'Nice boyfriend you've got. Now get him out of here before I call the police.'

Tiffany was about to protest that Gavin wasn't her boyfriend, but the man had already turned away to talk to his colleague. Gavin's bravado had crumbled at the mention of the boys in blue and he was practically sprinting out of the club. Tiffany looked at Kara who simply said, 'Taxi. Now.'

An hour later Tiffany was home. Never had the rundown studio flat she rented just off the Archway Road in North London seemed so inviting, even though it was cold and damp. Tiffany made a quick dash into the shower then piled on layers of clothes: a vest, her pink brushed-cotton PJs patterned with pawprints, her fluffy dressing gown and socks. The cold here prevented Tiffany from being stylish in bed. Gavin didn't know what he was missing, she managed to joke to herself. She curled up in bed with a hot water bottle, but even then she was shivering. She had turned down her step-mum's offer to buy her an electric blanket for Christmas, saying that she was twenty-two, thank you very much, and not sixty! She had regretted that decision every time she'd subsequently got into bed and shivered under the duvet. Tonight had been shit! She was never going to let Kara set her up with anyone else *ever* again. She winced as she recalled how the bouncer had thought that Gavin was her boyfriend. As if!

Tiffany could have done without the whole experience. It had been a nightmare couple of weeks as it was. She had recently got in touch with her birth mother, with whom she hadn't had any contact since she was a baby. It had been a total disaster. She had wanted to meet her real mother for years. Had expected to feel something for the woman who had given birth to her, some kind of connection. Instead the woman she had met had been a hard-faced junkie who didn't appear to have any feelings for her daughter at all. It had been a crushing experience. Fortunately Tiffany had a great relationship with her dad, who had brought her up, and with her step-mum Marie. But it was hard not to feel unwanted and rejected after the experience.

And then there was her job as a waitress, which Tiffany hated. She had finished college over a year ago and had been trying so hard to make it as a stylist, working for free wherever she could. But she had got nowhere and, as she couldn't carry on working for free, had been forced to take on the waitressing shifts. Her dreams of being a stylist seemed to be slipping further and further away from her. But hey, she tried to cheer herself up as she burrowed further under the duvet, at least she had not ended up with that loathsome Gavin!

Chapter 2

Sunday lunchtime, Tiffany arrived at her dad's terraced house in Faversham, a small town in Kent. She was about to put her key in the door when it was swung open by Lily-Rose, her beaming eight-year-old step-sister.

'Hiya, Tiff! Can I show you my dance routine to Lady Gaga? I've been practising all morning.' She twirled round in her pale pink leotard and matching skirt. *Britain's Got Talent* had a lot to answer for, Tiffany thought. Right now all she wanted to do was tuck in to her dad's famous roast, and collapse on the sofa.

'Give Tiff a chance to come in,' shouted Marie from upstairs. 'She was probably up all last night, living it large and doing shout-outs to all her homies.'

'Giving it large,' Tiffany shouted back. 'And no one says that any more. It's *so* 2000.'

'Whatevs, babes,' Marie retorted.

Tiffany followed a pirouetting Lily-Rose into the kitchen where her dad was already hard at work, slaving over his roast potatoes. He was wearing an apron with a picture of a frilly bra and pants set on the front, a cheeky present from Marie, who never cooked. Tiffany was so used to seeing him in it that she didn't bat an eyelid.

'Tiffany, how are you?' Her dad was one of the few people who ever called her that. He turned away from the oven and hugged her. It was so nice to see him, her solid, dependable dad, Chris, who had always been there for her.

'I need coffee,' she replied, sitting down at the kitchen table. The caffeine might make the performance of 'Born This Way', a little more bearable. She could only hope that Lily-Rose had not taken things to extremes and been incubating in an egg, or fashioning an outfit out of meat. Chris would go mad if she'd been at his organic beef.

'I'll get you one, love,' said Marie, coming into the kitchen. She was thirty-seven, with wild auburn curls, freckles, green eyes and the warmest smile in the world, Tiffany always thought. She kissed her step-daughter on the cheek and Tiffany received a reassuring waft of her perfume, Clinique's Happy. Lily-Rose completed her pirouttes and ended in deep plié. Then she jumped up and exclaimed gleefully, 'I've got a joke about Lady Gaga.'

'Go on then,' Tiffany replied, knowing full well that she was bound to have heard it many times before.

'How do you wake Lady Gaga up in the morning?'

'I've no idea.' Tiffany played her part.

'Poke her face!' Lily-Rose squealed. 'Geddit?'

And even though it was the tenth time Tiffany had heard it, she still smiled. It actually wasn't a bad joke for an eight-year-old.

'So will you come and watch me now?' Lily-Rose put her hands together in prayer. *'Please.'*

'You know she won't give up asking until you do,' Marie said, handing Tiffany a mug of coffee.

Tiffany had come up against Lily-Rose's iron will many times in the past, and so she took the coffee and followed her sister into the living room.

Thankfully there was no giant egg or meat dress in sight. With one flick of the stereo remote, Lily-Rose was off, strutting her stuff, performing a series of complicated arm movements, turning this way and that, miming to the words, with an assurance that was beyond her years. Tiffany clapped away and smiled; her sister was so happy, so confident in the love of both her parents. Tiffany remembered how she herself had always felt there was something missing from her own life. Her dad had been a fantastic single parent, but Tiffany had wanted a mum too. It was only when Chris had met Marie that Tiffany finally felt her family was complete.

Marie wandered into the living room as Lily-Rose was coming to the end of her routine. 'I was just remembering what I was like at her age,' Tiffany commented.

'You were so bossy, always telling me what I should wear. You had such strong views.'

'It never worked though, did it?' Tiffany laughed. Marie wore a uniform of jeans and slouchy tee-shirts and nothing could make her part from that, even though Tiffany constantly tried to get her to wear dresses and heels.

'So how's it going? Any luck on getting any stylist work?'

Tiffany shook her head. She'd emailed, phoned, gone in person to see a number of magazines . . . and no one could offer her anything, even working for free.

'I'm doomed to work at that pizza restaurant for the rest of my life,' she said gloomily. 'I'll be buried in a coffin made of pizza dough.'

'Of course you're not! You're very talented, and one day soon I'm sure you'll get a break. You deserve it. Now come on through, girls, Dad's about to serve lunch and you know how he hates people being late.'

'That was fab, Dad,' Tiffany declared, putting her knife and fork together on her empty plate. Her dad was a

12

brilliant cook; in fact, it was his dream to open his own restaurant or gastro pub, but he had always been too worried about money, wanting to provide security for his family. Marie didn't earn very much as a teaching assistant at the local primary school. So instead Chris worked as a carpenter and cooking was his hobby.

'I hope you saved some room for dessert. I've made poached pears in red wine. Ice cream for you, Lily-Rose.'

'I'll have some in a minute, I need to check on Justin Bieber,' Lily-Rose declared, sliding off her chair.

'That's the name of her new dwarf hamster,' Marie interpreted. 'He's cute but also annoying.'

'Kind of like his namesake then,' Tiffany replied, as she got up and cleared away the plates from the table. She paused at the work surface to admire the pears in red wine, marvelling again at her dad's culinary skill.

'I don't know why I ever moved out,' she commented. Of course the commute to London had been a killer and so expensive that it was cheaper for her to rent the grotty flat. But maybe she could have a change? She sat back down. 'Come to think of it, maybe I could move back in for a few months while I work at getting a stylist job? I could babysit Lily-Rose for you by way of rent.' She was voicing an idea she'd had for a while now. It would mean sleeping in the tiny box room, but at least she wouldn't be scrabbling round to pay bills at the end of every month and she could give up working at the restaurant. Both her dad and Marie were looking awkward, however.

'Er, you know we'd love to have you back, Tiffany,' her dad said, 'but we haven't really got the space.'

'It's OK, I could have the box room and I'll streamline my clothes. Less is more.' She felt a little hurt that he wasn't welcoming her back with open arms.

'We should tell her, Chris,' Marie said quietly. 'I know we wanted to wait a bit longer, but it's only fair.'

'Tell me what?' They were making her feel anxious.

'Well, Tiffany, the thing is . . . the box room is going to be a nursery.' Her dad smiled broadly as he put his arms round Marie. 'We're having a baby.'

Instantly Tiffany shot up from her chair and hugged them both. 'That is such fantastic news!' She thought they had given up on their dream of having another child after Marie suffered three devastating miscarriages.

'We're being cautiously optimistic,' her step-mum said. 'I've just had the sixteen-week scan and every-thing seems to be fine.' She had tears in her eyes and Tiffany had tears in her own; she knew how much Marie wanted this baby.

'If there's anything I can do to help . . . if you need me to come and look after Lily-Rose, anything . . . just let me know.'

'I know you'll help me, Tiff, and I don't want you to feel left out because of what happened with your real mum. You know that I see you as my daughter, just as much as Lily-Rose and the baby.' It was an emotional moment. Tiffany had a lump in her throat as Marie hugged her, because thrilled as she was for Marie, she couldn't help thinking yet again of her real mum who hadn't wanted her . . .

'God, it's like East bloody Enders!' Chris tried to joke, but Tiffany knew that he found it emotional too. 'I'm going to serve out pudding.'

Marie had a rest after lunch and Tiffany and Chris went out with Lily-Rose who was itching to go rollerskating around the local park. 'You don't mind about the baby, do you?' Chris asked as they watched Lily-Rose skate confidently ahead of them, her blonde hair blowing out behind her like a banner. 'Like Marie said, we don't want you to feel left out.'

'Of course I don't mind!' Tiffany exclaimed. 'Though you're going to be a well old dad!'

'Cheek! I'm only forty-two. In my prime.'

'Yeah, whatevah!' Tiffany teased back.

'And I'm sorry about the room. Perhaps you could move in until the baby's born?'

'No, Dad, thanks anyway. I'll work something out, you've got enough going on.'

By the time they got back to the house, it was late-afternoon and Tiffany had to head off as she had agreed to fill in for a couple of hours at the restaurant. It was drizzling, the sky was grey, and the thought of work was depressing. Marie sensed her mood. 'Chin up, Tiff. You'll be OK, I see great things ahead for you.'

'But in the meantime, it's garlic bread, dough balls and pizza all the way,' Tiffany replied as she zipped up her black biker jacket.

She was halfway down the street when Chris came running after her, waving a letter. 'I meant to give this to you.'

'Thanks.' Tiffany looked at the official brown envelope. Knowing her luck, it was a reminder for a bill she hadn't paid. She gave her dad another quick hug, stuffed the letter in her pocket and promptly forgot all about it.

Chapter 3

Angel considered her reflection in the dressing-room mirror. Yet again she felt that her stylist, Claudia, had dressed her in completely the wrong outfit for the TV makeover show she presented. She wanted to look approachable and sassy, ideally wearing clothes from the high street mixed in with the odd designer label. Instead Claudia had given her a purple, fitted designer dress, which made Angel look as if she was trotting off to a cocktail party. And the dress didn't even fit properly – being too tight across the bust and too loose around the waist. Sometimes she had a sneaking suspicion that Claudia wanted her to look bad . . .

'Can I be honest?' Jez, her hairdresser and one of her closest friends, piped up.

'I've never known you not to be,' Angel replied dryly, guessing that he would be giving the dress a big thumbs-down. She spun round and faced him. He had his sucked-on-a-lemon expression firmly in place on his perma-tanned face.

'In a word – frightful.' He walked over and tugged at the loose fabric at her waist. 'It doesn't even fit!' he hissed. 'God almighty, if I did your hair as badly as she dresses you, I'd be out on my ear, even though we've been friends for over twelve years!'

Angel groaned. She hated confrontation, but knew she had to square up to the situation. 'I know. I'm going to have to speak to her. She doesn't seem to have

16

any idea what the show is about, even though she's been working on it for four months.'

Angel had an hour's slot in the ITV breakfast show, twice a week, where she gave women makeovers and acted as a sort of agony aunt. It was Gok Wan meets *Ten Years Younger*, but what saved it from being just another style show was Angel's warm personality. She had a great gift for making the contributors feel completely relaxed with her and open up about their lives, which was quite something seeing as how Angel herself was so breathtakingly beautiful.

She had only been presenting the show since January as she sought to develop her career in new directions. She had once been Britain's most famous and beautiful glamour model, but had stopped that a few years ago, though she still modelled every now and then, mainly to promote her perfume and clothing ranges. Topless was out of the question, though every few months she would get a cheeky request from a lads' mag. She was also famous for being married to Cal Bailey, the stunningly handsome former Chelsea and England footballer, and together husband and wife formed one of the UK's most well-known celebrity couples.

The door opened and Claudia sashayed in, a vision in a pale cream lace dress that was definitely not from the high street. 'Oh, Angel, you look delish!' she exclaimed in the cut-glass accent that always set Angel's teeth on edge.

'Do you really think so?' she asked uncertainly.

'I really, really think so!' Claudia drawled, walking round her. 'We likey very much.'

Sensing that Claudia was swaying Angel and that his best friend was going to end up looking atrocious on national TV and be featured in all the 'what were you thinking' pages in the celeb mags, Jez nudged her in the ribs. Subtlety was never his strong point. Angel pulled herself together.

'Actually, Claudia, I don't likey,' she replied. 'It doesn't fit me, and the colour looks tarty. As I've said before, I need to wear more casual clothes. The women we're styling have to be able to relate to me.'

Claudia shook her head. 'There is no way I'm letting you wear one of your trackies on TV. It would be career suicide, for you and for me. Never mind the UGGs!' She shuddered as she said the word.

Angel loved her tracksuits and UGGs. They were what she changed into the moment she came off air and she knew Claudia thought they were too chavvy for words – even her hugely expensive beige Chanel tracksuit.

'I'm not talking about wearing tracksuits, they're my chill-out home outfits. I'm suggesting something like red skinny jeans – coloured jeans are in, aren't they? Some kind of tee-shirt maybe and my red suede wedges. Something that says summer and fun! Not . . . I'm wearing a dress that you couldn't possibly afford.'

Claudia flared her nostrils in disdain and tossed back her honey-blonde hair. 'If that's what you want,' she said tightly, 'I'll go and find a tee-shirt now.' And she flounced out of the room.

'I sometimes wonder if she's getting back-handers from the designers whose dresses she tries to force you into,' Jez mused. 'I can honestly say that I have never met a stylist with such a total inability to style anyone.'

'She always looks good though, doesn't she?' Angel replied, wriggling out of the hateful purple dress.

'That's because all her clothes are high-end designer.' He paused. 'She's running out of chances. Seriously, when are you going to get rid of her? I don't think she even likes us. I can tell that she thinks we're dead common. A bit too doors-to-manual for her.' He grinned. 'And I can understand her not liking you for that, because you are a bit common, but me?' Jez struck a pose, one hand on his forehead, one on his hip. 'I'm class all the way!'

'Oh, shut up and do my hair!' Angel ordered him jokingly. 'And I'm going to speak to Oscar after the show and explain about our problem with Claudia.'

Oscar was the producer who had been responsible for appointing Claudia, but given that Angel was the star, she was hoping that she might be able to convince him the stylist had to go.

Two and a half hours later the show had gone out and Angel was free to leave. And much as she loved her work, she loved the feeling of a job being done and knowing that she had some free time ahead of her. She walked out of the TV studios arm in arm with Jez, and then stopped in reception when she saw a handsome dark-haired man, dressed in a leather jacket and jeans. Sometimes Angel forgot just how incredible-looking her husband Cal was. At thirty-four he was more handsome than ever, with his jet black hair turning slightly grey at the sides. He was going to be the kind of man, like gorgeous George Clooney, who just got better-looking with age.

Jez gave a wolf whistle. 'Well, hello, someone looks hot to trot.'

Cal walked over and kissed Angel on the lips.

'I didn't expect to see you,' she said.

'I thought I'd surprise you. It feels like I haven't seen you for ages and so your mum's looking after Honey and we're spending the rest of the day and night together in a hotel.'

'How romantic!' Jez exclaimed. 'I'm jealous! D'you know what I've got to look forward to this afternoon? Back-to-back appointments doing highlights. And then

I have to go to the flat to let someone in to check out our drains as we've got a noxious smell. And *then* I guess I'll have a low-fat ready meal and watch *America's Next Top Model* as Rufus is working late.' Jez flung open his arms. 'Just kill me now, I can't take any more of this mediocrity!'

Cal smiled at him, well used to his dramatics. Reaching into his jacket pocket he pulled out an envelope and handed it to Jez. 'Or . . . you and Rufus can go to the premiere of *The Fast and The Furious Six*. I have the tickets here, and Rufus is finishing work early.'

The Fast and The Furious film series, with hunky Vin Diesel, was one of Jez's guilty secrets, as the block-busting macho car action movies didn't exactly fit in with his camper than a row of pink tents, trimmed with maribou feathers, image.

Jez checked around to make sure no one had over-heard. Then he reached for the envelope and slipped it into his black Mulberry messenger man bag, and planted a kiss on Cal's cheek. 'Thank you, thank you, thank you! Right, I'm going to leave you lovers to it.' And with that he exited the studio with an extra spring in his step.

Cal slid his arm round Angel's shoulders. 'Shall we go to the hotel?'

'Right away!' she declared, putting her arm round his waist. 'I was feeling knackered, but now I'm up for anything.'

'Good,' he murmured kissing her neck. 'That's what I'd hoped.'

Angel sleepily surveyed the hotel room. The expensive La Perla underwear Cal had bought her was scattered across it, along with his clothes. There was an empty bottle of champagne in the ice bucket. The thick silk curtains were closed and the scented candles were giving off a soft glow.

As soon as they had got to the hotel – the very exclusive May Fair – she and Cal had spent the most wonderful afternoon in bed, reminding each other of all the many reasons why they were still crazily in love with each other after over ten years. She still desired him more than any other man, and knew that he desired her more than any other woman. She had revelled in that knowledge as he kissed and caressed her body, made love to her slowly at first, then fast and hard, whipping them both up into a frenzy of passion . . .

'Love you,' Cal said, turning to her. 'You're still the most beautiful woman I have ever seen.' He traced a finger round her lips, then kissed her softly.

'Love you too, more and more,' she replied, then rested her head on his chest so that she could hear his heart beating. 'We're so lucky, aren't we?' And she meant it. The afternoon had been perfect but now she felt an edge of sadness creeping in, as she hoped, prayed, that this might be the time she got pregnant. And then she tried to block the thoughts, which always led to her feeling blue.

The couple had been trying for the last six months. Cal had wanted another baby pretty much since their daughter, Honey, had turned one. It had taken Angel more time but now she too longed to have another baby . . . but it just wasn't happening. They'd both had a series of fertility tests and everything seemed to be fine. The doctor had told them to leave it another six months before they started any fertility treatment. But it had left Angel feeling anxious. What if she couldn't have another baby?

It was as if Cal sensed her anxious thoughts as he stroked her hair and said, 'I know what you're

21

thinking, but you have to remember what the doctor said. There's no reason why we shouldn't be able to have another baby.'

She raised her head and looked at Cal, who smiled as he said, 'Maybe we need to have more afternoons like this.'

Not for the first time she wondered what she would ever do without him. Her lover, her soul mate – always her rock.

She managed to smile back and said, 'And now I must have something to eat!'

Cal reached for the room-service menu. 'Let me guess . . . fish and chips with salad, for your guilty conscience. Followed by white chocolate cheesecake.'

'Hah! You know me so well.'

It was exactly what Angel was planning on having. She had never been one of those celebrities who starves themselves to a size zero. Lucky she didn't really need to diet – horse riding, swimming, good genes, and a husband who cooked healthy delicious meals kept her enviably slim. 'And I bet you're having grilled sea bass, no chips and salad?'

'Yep. Next you can decide what movie we watch, and then around half-nine I've booked us both massages. Oh, and this is for you.'

Cal reached down by the side of the bed and handed her a pink velvet jewellery box.

Could her husband be any more perfect?

Angel opened it up to discover the most adorable necklace. Two hearts linked together – one in diamonds, one in pink sapphires – and a diamond arrow through both.

'That is gorgeous!' Angel exclaimed, immediately putting it round her neck and holding up her hair so Cal could fasten it.

'Glad you like it, I wanted to treat you.'

'I feel bad I haven't got you anything.'

'I'm sure you can think of something,' he teased.

'Hmm.' Angel began kissing Cal's chest, and just as she was about to continue her exploration further down his body, looked up and said, 'You can order room service, can't you? I'm going to be a little bit busy.'

Cal lay back on the pillow and reached for the phone, a smile playing across his mouth as he somehow managed to make the call . . .

Chapter 4

Mamma Mia's was heaving. Tiffany was practically running between tables, taking orders, picking up the heavy plates of pizza from the pass, where Vincent, the bad-tempered head chef, was shouting at everyone for not being quick enough. It was the pre-theatre rush and the place was full of people wanting a meal before they trotted off to see *The Lion King*, which was on round the corner, or one of the many other West End musical extravaganzas that were a short distance away.

Tiffany was not feeling her best as she had stayed up drinking with Kara the night before. She had received yet another brush-off from a magazine, even though she had offered to work for free. Home-made cocktails had seemed like the only answer but, boy, was she paying for it today. Her head was pounding and the smell of the food was making her feel nauseous. Wearily she went over to check on table number nine.

'We wanted a thick-crust Four Seasons,' moaned a disgruntled middle-aged man, with an appalling comb-over, who was sitting with his equally disgruntled-looking wife and two children.

He jabbed at the half-eaten pizza with his fork. 'This is thin crust.'

'I'm so sorry, sir, you should have said and I would

have replaced it,' Tiffany replied, while thinking, *D'oh!* Why had he eaten it if it had been the wrong order? Customers never ceased to amaze her.

'Well, I'm not paying for it, it's not what I ordered.'

Rule number one: *never* get into an argument with customers. Smile sweetly and make a quick exit. Leave it for Ruthless Vera to deal with. The Polish manageress had a way with the difficult male customers, mainly down to her impressive breasts, which she was not afraid to flaunt. But today Tiffany was not in the mood for smiling sweetly. 'I'm sorry, sir, but you *have* eaten half the pizza.' The temptation to do a loser hand signal and tell him that his combover wasn't fooling anyone was powerful.

'And there was hardly any mozzarella or avocado in my tricolore salad.' Now the wife was piping up. Again, she had scoffed half of it.

'What do you expect? You're in the heart of London, and you're paying bugger all for your meal,' Tiffany thought. Except, by the look on the woman's face, it was clear that she had, in fact, said it out loud.

Oh, shit.

'Can I assist you with anything?' It was Vera. Like a shark sensing blood in the water, she had come over to see what all the fuss was about.

'We're not at all happy with the service we've had. We've had the wrong pizza; the salad is inadequate. And it's just not good enough.'

'I see, sir. Well, you have eaten the pizza, but perhaps we could bring you another salad and, say, drinks on the house.' Vera held up a bottle of white wine, which Tiffany knew from bitter experience was so acidic it set your teeth on edge and no doubt stripped away your stomach lining. But the man and his wife clearly were not connoisseurs as they nodded enthusiastically at the prospect of the free bottle.

Vera looked meaningfully at Tiffany. 'Please go and get the wine glasses.'

She did as she was told and wondered when Vera would choose to give her the bollocking that she knew was bound to come her way.

Tiffany knew that Vera didn't like her because she was younger and prettier. And she knew that Vera resented the way that she had stood up for the other waitresses and waiters, many of whom were from Eastern Europe, when Vera had tried to pull a fast one by claiming they were not entitled to sickness or holiday pay, which in fact they were. But because Tiffany's dad knew the owner of Mamma Mia's, Vera had to play nice. But not that nice.

Tiffany was just putting on her coat at the end of her very long shift when Vera called her in to the tiny office at the back of the restaurant. She sat down behind the desk while Tiffany had to perch on the small stool. The office was so small that Vera's large breasts seemed to dominate the room, encased as they were in a purple, shiny wrap dress. Like two giant Quality Streets, Tiffany thought, trying to cheer herself up. It was quite a combination set against Vera's aquamarine eyes – coloured contact lenses, Tiffany was sure, though the manageress claimed they were naturally that colour.

'I know how you like everything to be official and above the board,' said Vera in her strongly accented English.

'You just say above board,' Tiffany couldn't stop herself from saying.

Vera smiled. 'So clever, Tiffany. I wonder why you are still waitressing?'

Tiffany's stomach lurched. Was she going to be fired? She owed rent and needed to pay her phone bill. Why hadn't she been nicer to the irritating couple?

'So, this is a formal warning.' Vera drummed her

purple acrylic nails against the desk for emphasis. 'If we have any more instances of poor service from you, then I shall have no choice but to let you go.'

Tiffany opened her mouth, all set to defend herself, then closed it. She didn't want to say anything she might regret, anything that might give Vera the chance to get rid of her on the spot.

'Do you understand?' the manageress demanded, fixing her with a beady unnaturally blue glare.

'I understand, Vera.'

For a week, Tiffany managed to keep her head down and stayed out of Vera's bad books. But on Friday night, at eight o'clock, the customer at table fifteen proved to be her undoing. She was taking over from one of the other waitresses whose shift had finished. As she walked over to table fifteen, she was so busy avoiding other waiters who were rushing to tables with orders of food that she didn't see who was sitting there until she was right in front of him. To her dismay, she saw it was the tosser from the nightclub, Gavin. Of all the people she had hoped she would never have to see again, he was high on her list. Number one, in fact. But maybe he wouldn't recognise her? Customers often only saw the black waitress uniform and didn't notice the face at all. Unfortunately, not Gavin.

'Hello, Tiffany.' He did his gross-out thing of looking her up and down.

'I've just signed another big deal and was in the area and fancied pizza. I'm slumming it a bit, to be honest. Usually I'd go to Nobu or J. Sheekey's. But you know when you get that urge for something really cheap?' He put extra emphasis on 'cheap'.

'Well, here's your starter.' Tiffany tried to sound casual, even though every inch of her was screaming: 'Wanker alert!' Was it pure chance that he had ended up in her restaurant or had the creep planned it?

She placed the garlic bread with melted mozzarella in front of him, trying to manoeuvre her body so as to put the maximum amount of distance between them. But all the time she was aware of Gavin's arrogant gaze raking over her.

'Black pepper?' she asked, reaching for the tall pepper grinder.

He nodded. As she twisted the wooden grinder, he said, 'I see you're good with your hands. Is that how you supplement the pathetic wages you get here?'

She managed to put the grinder back on the table without decking him across the head with it. 'Can I get you anything else?'

'I'll have a bottle of wine. The best one the restaurant does, even though I'm prepared for it to taste like shite.' He gave a nasty little smile. 'I don't suppose you can tell the difference.'

What was he playing at? Had she really dented his ego that much that he wanted to seek her out and wind her up? He was a bully, she decided as she went to fetch his wine, as well as being a wanker.

Carlo was behind the bar. 'Tough night?' he asked sympathetically. Lovely Carlo, whose wife had just had a baby so he was having to work extra shifts. Vera was always especially mean to him as he showed no interest in her and she fancied him.

'Tough customer,' Tiffany muttered.

'Do you want me to serve him? I saw him looking at you in a way I don't like. If ever a man looks at my daughter like that, I will punch him.'

It was probably not a good idea if Carlo went anywhere near Gavin.

'I'll be OK, thanks, Carlo.' And Tiffany picked up the bottle of Montepulciano which was actually a very good bottle of wine, not that Gavin would realise.

'Is it worth me tasting it first?' he asked sneeringly.

'It's entirely up to you.'

'Oh, just pour it.'

Tiffany carefully poured out a glass. Gavin took a sip, wincing as he did so. 'It's rougher than I'm used to.'

'I'll go and get your pizza,' Tiffany said, itching to get away from him.

She could feel her cheeks burning with suppressed anger as she walked away. She longed to go and let off steam with one of her fellow waiters but Vera was on the war-path. Instead she served another couple of tables, but all too soon Gavin's American Hot was ready.

As she approached she could hear him talking to Zena, a young Polish waitress.

'You ought to get yourself down a lap dancing club. Great figure like yours, you'd be raking it in. Lots of Poles there . . . pole dancing. Get it?'

Zena blushed and looked embarrassed. 'I'm happy here, thank you very much,' she said in her sweet broken English.

'Seriously, what time do you finish here? I could take you to a club . . .'

'Thank you, no, I cannot.'

Realising that he wasn't going to get anywhere with Zena, Gavin turned nasty. 'Expect you've got a cleaning job to go to. Good scrubber are you?'

Zena had tears in her eyes as she walked away from him.

He really was a piece of work. Racist, sexist and a total wanker! He was the gift that kept on giving.

'Ah, here's my pizza girl. Hey, pizza girl, why can't you smile like that pretty waitress? Don't you want to get a nice fat tip from me? I don't suppose you earn anything here.'

Something snapped in Tiffany. She'd had more than enough of him. And she'd had enough of being treated

29

like shit, not just by Gavin but by a long line of customers, so many of whom had been rude, talked to her as if she didn't matter, as if she was nothing. Six months of pent-up rage boiled over in her. Before Gavin knew what had hit him, she dumped the piping hot pizza on to his lap. And, as he yelled in protest she picked up the bottle of wine. 'Bit hot for you, sir, is it? Here . . . have this.' And she poured half the contents over his head, the red wine running down his arrogant face like blood. 'Enjoy your meal, sir. It's been a pleasure serving you.'

She swung round in time to see Vera advancing towards her, breasts jutting like torpedoes, an almost gleeful expression on her face as if she was relishing the prospect of a scene.

'You don't need to say anything, Vera, I quit.' And to the cheers of the other waiters and some of the customers, Tiffany took off her apron, flung it to the ground and marched off.

Vera was still fussing over Gavin as she passed them. 'I'll sue!' Gavin shouted after her.

'So will I . . . for harassment, you dickhead!'

Tiffany was buoyed up on a wave of anger and righteous indignation all the way to Leicester Square tube station. It was only when she realised that she had run out of credit on her Oyster card and had barely enough change for her tube ticket home that the enormity of what she'd just done hit her. She had quit her job! And, yes, she had hated it, but the people she'd worked with were nice, apart from evil Vera, and she didn't have to think too hard about what she was doing. Now she was going to have to get another job . . . another shit job.

She scrabbled around in her jacket pocket, needing just ten pence more for her fare, and her fingers touched an envelope. She pulled it out. It was the letter her dad had given her the other week. *Oh, well*, she thought, *I may as well see the damage*. She ripped it open, and as she read the letter it was as if everything and everyone around her faded away into the distance. The people rushing to get their trains, the thwack of the ticket barriers opening and closing, the announce-ments, all vanished. The letter was from her real mum, Tanya, and she had sent it to the social worker first, asking her to pass it on to Tiffany. The writing was barely legible and the spelling pretty bad, but the meaning was clear enough.

> I thought Tiffany should know that she has a half-sister. She's Angel Summer – the famous model. I don't know if Angel will want to know her. She came and saw me once but didn't do nothing for me, and didn't want to know me after. But maybe she could do something for Tiffany. And I wanted to say sorry to both of them, to Angel and Tiffany. Sorry I couldn't be a mum to them.

As if in a daze Tiffany looked up from the letter. Someone bashed into her in their haste to reach the ticket barrier, but she hardly noticed. Angel Summer, the former glamour model now turned TV presenter, famous for her beauty and for being married to the gorgeous England footballer, Cal Bailey . . . she was Tiffany's half-sister! It seemed too incredible to be true, the plot of of a Hollywood movie. It couldn't possibly be true, could it? And yet why would Tanya lie about such a thing?

Tiffany made her way to the platform, feeling as if her world had just been turned upside down and inside out. And in a twist of fate, staring right at her from across the track, on a massive billboard advertising her new TV show, was Angel.

31

Chapter 5

Tiffany chewed the end of her pen as she tried to come up with a letter to her sister that would make her sound sane and not like some loony-tune stalker. But it was proving so difficult. How should you break the news that out of the blue you have found out you are some-one's long-lost sister? You couldn't exactly Google tips from the internet. For her fifth attempt – the last four had ended up in the bin – she got straight to the point:

Dear Angel,
    You don't know me but I am writing to let you know that I have just found out that you could be my half-sister. I know how mad that must sound but it's true. I recently got in contact with Tanya, our 'real' mum, and afterwards she wrote and told me about our connection. I don't want anything from you; the chance to see you is all I ask. My meeting with Tanya didn't exactly go well . . .
    So here's some stuff about me: I'm twenty-two, I live in London. I'm Aquarius. My favourite colour is red. My favourite book is *Wuthering Heights*. My favourite film is *Little Miss Sunshine* – I always cry at the ending. I've got a tattoo of a dolphin on my ankle. My dad is a carpenter, but wants to be a chef,

my step-mum is a classroom assistant, and I have a half-sister, Lily-Rose, who wants to be Lady Gaga. I studied Fashion and Textiles at college and I'm trying to get my career as a stylist off the ground – at the moment it's a case of Tiffany Taylor, stylist to no one but herself. I love going to the cinema, clubbing and girlie nights in. And I'll stop there in case you think I really am a stalker – I'm not.

Tiffany sighed after she'd read through her letter, having no idea whether she had got it right. It was probably the best she could come up with in the circumstances.

After some research she had tracked down Angel's agent and planned to send the letter to them. Kara had been all for her writing to Angel; in fact, was wildly excited about it. However, Tiffany hadn't yet told her dad and Marie, as she didn't want to give them anything to worry about. She sealed the letter in the envelope and wrote Angel's name on the front, c/o The Carrie Rose Agency, and stuck on a stamp. Then she quickly grabbed her jacket and ran out of the flat to post the letter, before she could change her mind. As she shoved the envelope into the letter-box she wondered if she would ever hear back from Angel.

That night she went round to Kara's flat in Camden. Her dad had bought it as a rental investment, but Kara had begged him for it, and as she could pretty much twist her dad round her little finger he'd agreed. Harley had moved in as well but Kara's mum and dad didn't know that so every time they came over she had to remove all traces of her boyfriend. Harley had got used to living out of a suitcase.

'Harley's out playing football so we can have a total girlie time. We can watch Angel's TV show, I recorded it this morning,' Kara declared as she let Tiffany in. 'I've got fizzy wine from M&S and a chicken Caesar salad.'

Even when she was relaxing at home Kara always looked as if she had made an effort, with perfect make-up and freshly washed and blow-dried hair. Tonight she was wearing a pink Juicy Couture tracksuit, co-ordinated with pink nail varnish and pink UGGs, and a necklace with a pink diamante K hanging from it. Tiffany couldn't help wondering if it was in fact Kara who was related to Angel. Style-wise they were a perfect match, both sharing a passion for pink, trackies and UGGs, none of which Tiffany cared for one little bit. In fact, it was a running joke between her and Kara that she wouldn't be seen dead in a pair of UGGs and Kara was always trying to persuade her to try some on, telling her that once she did there would be no going back. She too would be hooked on the ridiculously comfortable boots.

Tiffany slipped off her very un-UGG-like leopard-print high courts and followed Kara into the small but beautifully decorated flat. Everything was cream or white, except the bedroom which was a girlie girl's paradise of pink. The curtains had love hearts on them, there were pink flower-shaped fairy lights decorating the mirror, a bright pink duvet cover, a pale pink sheepskin rug. Tiffany often wondered how Harley felt about sleeping in such a room, where even the sheets were pink. She figured he was man enough to cope.

'I still can't believe that you're Angel Summer's half-sister!' Kara exclaimed, pouring out two glasses of cava. Tiffany flopped back on the cream leather sofa.

'Maybe I'm not. Maybe Tanya is just saying it to wind me up,' Tiffany said gloomily. She shuddered inside as she remembered the grotty flat she had met her mum in. It had been so dirty and cheerless, not a single photograph of her children anywhere to be seen. Tanya was in her late-forties but looked considerably older, with her grey complexion, sunken cheeks and decayed teeth. She had shown little interest in Tiffany other than wanting to know what her job was. She had seemed disappointed when Tiffany told her that she was a waitress but that she wanted to be a stylist. Maybe she had wanted her daughter to give her some money? The reunion had left Tiffany feeling utterly depressed and wishing she had never contacted her in the first place. But Tanya had said sorry in the letter . . . that was something, Tiffany supposed. And much as she wanted to close the door on all thoughts of her mother, she felt a spark of sympathy for her and her wretched life. Her dad had always brought her up to think of Tanya as someone who needed help, who hadn't intended to be a bad mother.

Kara pulled her back to the present. 'I don't think she would do that. There would be nothing in it for her – and from what you told me, she only sems to care about herself. Stop obsessing. Let's watch the show.'

She pressed Play on the remote control and Angel's beautiful face appeared on screen as the opening credits rolled.

'OMG! I can see a resemblance now!' Kara said excitedly, looking from Angel to Tiffany.

'Can you? I can't at all.'

'It's the eyes and the mouth. Yeah, you have the same-shaped mouth as Angel . . . I can't believe I didn't notice it before. You jammy cow to have those lips!' Kara, who had a perfectly sweet mouth, suffered from lip envy and was constantly trying to find the perfect pout-boosting lip-gloss. She reached for her latest purchase and slicked it on to her already glossed lips.

'I'm not so sure about the styling this week,' Tiffany

commented as a young mum who had got stuck in the rut of jeans and hoodies was styled to within an inch of her life in a pencil skirt, cripplingly high platform shoes and a tight-fitting jacket. 'It doesn't exactly say school run, does it? They should be finding things that will fit with her lifestyle.'

'Babes, you would be so good on a show like this. Imagine, you could work with Angel. You'd become famous! And I could come on as your PA slash manager!'

Suddenly Tiffany had a horrible thought. She had mentioned her ambition to become a stylist in her letter to Angel with no intention other than that of giving some background about herself. But perhaps Angel would see it differently and think that Tiffany was after something. She did a mental head-slap. She should have steered clear of the whole stylist thing. Chances were that she was *never* going to hear from Angel now.

After the girls had watched the show, Harley returned from football. He was so tall and broad that he made the flat seem even tinier.

'So have you told Tiff our news?' he said, sitting down on the sofa with a beer.

'You're getting married? Kara's pregnant?'

Harley smiled. 'Not quite there yet.'

'I finally told Mum and Dad that Harley and me were living together,' Kara put in.

'Welcome to the twenty-first century, Kara!' Tiffany teased. She had always thought that her friend should come clean with her folks and that they would most likely survive the shock of their only daughter, 'their princess', living with her boyfriend. 'And? How did they take it?'

'They were completely cool. I wish I'd told them ages ago.'

'Except Kara's mum went round singing from "Single Ladies (Put A Ring On It)", so I could hear,' Harley said dryly.

'God! Who wants to get married anyway?' Tiffany said, folding her arms.

'One day you'll want to,' Kara said knowingly. Tiffany didn't bother to reply.

'Billy was asking after you tonight.'

Billy and Harley played football together. Billy was *always* asking Harley about Tiffany. 'I told him you still weren't seeing anyone. Nor is he.'

'He still loves you!' Kara chanted. Tiffany threw a chocolate-brown fake-fur cushion at her.

'Crap! He just wants to be friends with extras,' Tiffany said cynically.

Kara shook her head. 'Nope, it's more than that.' But Tiffany didn't believe her.

They chatted on for a couple of hours until eleven but Tiffany turned down Kara's offer for her to stay over. As she stood shivering at the bus stop she wondered when Angel last had to get on public transport. Her whole life must be one of wealth and privilege now, where she could buy anything she wanted, do anything she wanted, go anywhere she wanted . . . The world was her oyster, whereas Tiffany just had an Oyster card . . . an out-of-credit one at that. Though she knew from the celeb mags and tabloids, who were obsessed with Angel and Cal, that the couple had gone through a very rough patch. He had an affair while Angel was battling post-natal depression and then she had left him for Ethan Turner, an American baseball player. She and Cal had actually got divorced and it had looked as though Angel was going to marry Ethan. But she had jilted him at the altar because she had realised that she was still in love with Cal, and the couple had reunited and got married again. Their story was so dramatic and so romantic!

Tiffany thought of her own disastrous love life: a two-year on/off relationship with Billy which had eventually fizzled out. Kara could say that Billy loved her all she liked – Tiffany knew he just wanted to be friends, or rather friends with extras. And yes, every now and then Tiffany gave in to his booty call. The thing about sex with an ex was that she knew what she was getting; it was an itch she could scratch. But she never felt good about herself afterwards. And cute as Billy undoubtedly was, he was not the love of her life. Tiffany didn't even know if she believed that she would one day meet the love of her life. Was there really 'the one' who was out there, just for her? She wasn't sure. All she did know was if the bus didn't come soon she was going to have to go into the kebab shop and buy some chips to keep her warm. What was the betting Angel Summer hadn't done that in a very long while?

Chapter 6

'How come you even look good in the morning?' Angel demanded, as she padded into the kitchen. Cal was making Honey her breakfast before he took her to school, and looked glowing with health. She planted a kiss on her daughter's head and went to check her own appearance in the mirror in the hallway. This was her first day off in ages, and as far as she was concerned being on TV three days a week and having to wear make up under the studio lights was playing havoc with her skin.

'I look so rough, I'm getting lines,' she wailed. 'Now I'm thirty, you'll be trading me in for a younger model soon, I just know it.'

Honey and Cal exchanged eye rolls. Angel dragged herself away from scrutinising her reflection and sat down next to Honey. She swiped a piece of her daughter's toast, which Honey promptly swiped back.

Cal came over and put his arms round Angel. 'Even in those ridiculous slippers, you're still the most beautiful woman I know.'

Angel held up one pink fake-fur-slippered foot and said defensively, 'I get cold feet. I can't be glam twenty-four/seven.'

'Don't I know it!' Cal shot back. 'You put them on my legs every night.'

'I knew you had your uses,' Angel teased.

'I'm good for other things as well,' he murmured in her ear. 'How about I show you tonight?'

Angel considered her husband's tip-top physique. 'How about you do?'

And then there was no time for further conversation as it was the usual morning whirlwind of making Honey's packed lunch, plaiting her daughter's hair, cleaning her teeth and making sure she had her book bag and water bottle.

After hugging her daughter and Cal goodbye, Angel sat back down at the breakfast table with a bowl of porridge and a cup of tea. She intended to have a lazy morning, then meet her best friend Gemma for lunch in their favourite Italian – though how relaxing that would be she wasn't sure as going out with Gemma and eight-month-old baby Milo felt like being part of a military campaign. Gemma wanted everything to be perfect all the time.

She flicked through the pile of post on the large glass-topped kitchen table, pausing when she came to a letter from her new agent Susie. Carrie, the woman who had first discovered her as a model when Angel was just seventeen, had recently retired from the business and had moved to Spain with her husband to run a bar on the Costa del Sol. Dave the husband would be doing most of the work, Angel was pretty sure, while Carrie would be very good at telling him what to do. Still she had to hand it to Carrie; she'd never thought their marriage would last as Dave was considerably younger and Carrie's previous relationships had always been short-lived, but they seemed happier than ever, and Carrie, who had been the toughest businesswoman Angel had ever come across, had completely mellowed. Now the Carrie Rose Agency was run by Susie, who was much more laid-back than her former boss.

Angel ripped open the envelope, expecting to find a cheque or contract in it, and was entirely thrown when she discovered the letter from Tiffany. Her first reaction was one of complete shock, followed by a flash of excitement that maybe it was true and she did have a half-sister. Then disbelief followed. Maybe this Tiffany Taylor was just trying it on. Over the years she and Cal had received more than their fair share of letters from nutters. Maybe Tiffany Taylor was a stalker-nutter? She read the letter again. It seemed reasonable. Tiffany didn't sound like a nutter; she sounded down-to-earth and funny. Though you never could tell. Cal's ex-girlfriend Simone hadn't seemed like a nutter either, and then she had revealed herself to be a complete psycho bitch when she had stalked Angel and tried to stab her with a kitchen knife.

She reached for her phone. As always in moments of crisis, Angel had to know what Cal thought. He was typically calm and measured in his reaction. He didn't even sound too surprised.

'I always wondered if you might have a half-sister or -brother, but I thought your mum just mentioned a half-brother?'

'God knows how many children Tanya gave away,' Angel said grimly. 'Do you think this Tiffany Taylor could be my half-sister then?'

'It's possible, isn't it? But don't rush into contacting her. I'll get Sean to check her out. See what he reckons. Then if you do go ahead and meet her, we could always do a DNA test to know for certain.'

'But what should I do now?' Angel asked him. The letter had shaken her up, reminded her of Tanya whom she would rather forget. She couldn't forgive the woman who had abandoned her, and becoming a mother herself had only hardened that feeling.

'Shall I tell Mum and Dad?' Angel had a good

41

relationship with her adoptive parents Frank and Michelle, which had grown stronger over the years. But she didn't want to do anything to upset them, especially Frank who'd had a heart attack three years ago.

'I wouldn't say anything to them just now. And, babe, don't stress about it. Meet Gemma and we'll talk about it later. Love you.'

'Love you.'

It was all very well Cal telling her not to stress about it, but Angel couldn't help it. Meeting her birth mother had been such a disaster. There had been no connection between the two of them. Tanya had expressed no regret for giving Angel away, nor did she seem to care about her daughter at all. Halfway through the meeting, her aggressive boyfriend had turned up and demanded money from Angel. And that had been the last she had heard of Tanya. She was only surprised that she hadn't received more begging letters from her mum over the years or that she hadn't sold her story. Angel wondered what had prompted Tanya to make this revelation to Tiffany now.

Angel padded upstairs to have a shower and paused on the landing to look at one of the many photographs of Honey that adorned the walls. Her beautiful daughter was smiling away for the camera as she sat proudly on her pony. Angel didn't think it was possible to love her any more than she did. Honey meant everything to her; she loved her daughter with all her heart, would have laid down her life for her, could not imagine living without her. How sad that Tanya had never felt that overwhelming love for her own children . . .

'I've got your usual table, Angel,' Alonzo told her as she walked into the cosy Italian restaurant in the Brighton

Lanes. She and Gemma had been coming to the family-run restaurant for years and loved the food and the friendly atmosphere. Angel could afford to eat at the most expensive restaurants but she never liked anything too fancy – she liked keeping it real.

She sat down at the table by the window and Alonzo brought her over a glass of champagne – well, she didn't like keeping it that real! And as she watched the world go by, she wondered where Tiffany Taylor was, wondered what she was like as a person. Would they have anything in common? Would there be some kind of connection between them? Or would it be an upsetting re-run of her meeting with Tanya, when she'd felt nothing but sadness and rejection?

She was lost in thought when Gemma arrived, pushing the bright red Bugaboo into the restaurant. Instantly Angel got up and hugged her friend but Gemma was distracted, worrying about getting Milo out of the buggy as she thought he should still have been sleeping. Gemma was following a baby-care book that advocated a strict routine, whereas Angel had always been more relaxed – at least when she had fully recovered from the post-natal depression that had blighted the first six months after she'd had Honey.

'Can you get the antiseptic wipes out of the bag and clean the high chair?' Gemma asked as she unclipped Milo from the harness and picked him up.

'I'm sure it's clean,' Angel replied, but the look on Gemma's face told her she had better do what was asked or she wouldn't hear the last of it during lunch. Once Gemma was satisfied it had been given the anti-bacterial treatment, she carefully manoeuvred Milo into it. He beamed away, showing off a new tooth. Thankfully he was a very chilled-out baby. He must take after his dad.

'So what's new with you?' Gemma asked, sitting down and flicking back her long black hair.

Angel took a deep breath. 'I had a letter from someone who claimed to be my half-sister this morning.' She thought she may as well come straight out with her bombshell news as she never knew how long she would have Gemma's attention before it strayed back to Milo. But her friend was already distracted and busy opening up a pot of puréed baby food, 'I wonder if Alonzo will microwave this sweet potato for me . . . Milo loves it. Did Honey like it? It's packed with vitamins and is so good for them . . .' She looked over at Angel. 'Sorry, what were you saying?'

Angel grabbed her friend's perfectly manicured hands. 'Look at me and I'll tell you! But I need your full concentration first.'

'OK,' Gemma promised. And when Angel repeated her comment, her friend was suitably shocked.

'Do you think she really is your half-sister? I mean, it would be a great scam, wouldn't it?'

'Not that great,' Angel replied. 'As soon as we'd had the DNA test, we would know the truth.' She paused and for a second looked wistful. 'It would be good if there was someone decent I was actually related to.'

'Even if she is your half-sister, she might still be a raving nutter,' Gemma said darkly.

'Cal's going to get Sean to check her out. And then we'll take it from there. It's not like I'm going to arrange to meet her on my own or anything. I haven't told Mum and Dad yet.'

Gemma arched one of her beautifully shaped eyebrows. That was one thing that hadn't changed since she'd had Milo – she was still the most immaculately groomed woman Angel knew. 'Never let it be said that your life isn't full of drama.'

'I could do without it,' Angel replied. 'This year is

supposed to be about me and Cal trying for a baby. I don't need any drama.'

Gemma smiled at her friend sympathetically. 'Don't worry, I'm sure you'll get pregnant soon.' It had taken Gemma several years herself, during which time she'd had a miscarriage, so she knew what she was talking about.

After that their conversation turned to Angel's TV show. Gemma was a beautician by profession but had always been a fashionista and had strong views about the styling on Angel's show.

'I think you need to get rid of Claudia. She has no idea how to style the women you have on the show. She makes them all look the same, in pencil skirts and heels, even the women who are only going to be able to wear heels for special occasions, not every day.'

'You wear heels every day,' Angel replied, but she knew Gemma was right.

'I've *always* worn heels. It's one of my trademarks.'

It certainly was. Angel was only surprised that Gemma hadn't given birth in a pair of Louboutins.

'I bet if you went back and interviewed those women a couple of months after they'd had the makeover, you would find them back in their old clothes. Jez does a good job with the hair, though.' He was a complete natural in front of the camera as Angel had known he would be when she had pressed to have him on the show. She kept asking Gemma to come on as the make-up artist, but her friend kept making excuses, even though Angel knew that she would be brilliant.

Angel sighed. She really was going to have to do something about Claudia, even though she hated the thought that she might be responsible for someone losing their job.

Their main courses arrived. Angel had what she always did at the restaurant – tortelloni Aurora, pasta filled with ricotta cheese in a delicious tomato and cream sauce – while Gemma went for a salade Niçoise, and picked out all the potatoes. Along with her drive to be the perfect mother, she had also been pushing herself to lose the baby weight in record time. But if anything, Angel thought that Gemma had lost too much weight. Her pretty heart-shaped face looked a little gaunt. She had tried tactfully to suggest that maybe her friend should ease up on the diet, but Gemma had been very defensive.

After lunch the two friends headed off to the beauty salon round the corner which was owned by Gemma's mum Jeanie, where Gemma worked part-time as a beautician. Angel loved the relaxed vibe of the salon and adored Jeanie, who was her mum's best friend. She wished she could confide in her about the letter from Tiffany – she had always valued Jeanie's down-to-earth, no-nonsense approach, but she felt bad about telling her before she had told her mum Michelle.

'Nice lunch, ladies?' Jeanie asked, as Angel and Gemma walked in.

'I'm stuffed,' Angel replied, flopping down on the sofa. 'I might have to undo my jeans!' And she un-popped the top button on her low-rise J Brand jeans.

'So what am I doing with you today?' Jeanie asked.

Angel stuck out her hands. 'Nails. And I'd better have a facial, my skin is really bad at the moment.'

Jeanie walked over to Angel and considered her pretty, near-flawless skin.

'If I look really hard, I think I can see one teeny-tiny spot on your chin.'

'But look at the lines round my eyes!' Angel wailed.

'What lines? Your skin is just a little dehydrated. A facial will fix that.'

Jeanie flicked back her long glossy black hair. In defiance of the unwritten style rule that said that older women shouldn't have long hair, she was growing hers. Gemma kept teasing her that she was mutton and should have a sharp bob, but Jeanie ignored her. And actually she looked fantastic.

Jeanie grinned cheekily. 'Are you sure I can't interest you in a vajazzle while you're here?'

'Mum!' Gemma exclaimed, outraged at the suggestion.

'Oh, don't be such a prude, Gemma. Kimberly went on a training course yesterday and she's raring to get those crystals stuck on! Everyone needs a bit of sparkle in their life.'

'Not on their vajayjay!' Gemma shot back. 'It's just *so* tacky.'

'My own daughter – such a style snob. What do you say, Angel? It would make Cal's night to discover you'd had one done. Kimberly can do all sorts of shapes: love hearts, four-leaf clovers, guitars . . .'

'How about the Eiffel Tower?' Gemma said sarcastically. 'Or Elvis Presley's face?'

Jeanie pretended to take the suggestion seriously, then said, 'I think that might be stretching Kimberly's creative skills. But what about a football Angel?'

'Oh, what the hell!' she replied. 'Honey's got a play-date after school so I don't have to pick her up until six. I'll go for the love heart.'

And much later that night, she managed to give Cal a very pleasant surprise. But one which she probably wouldn't repeat as they woke up to find the bed covered in tiny crystals . . . and with Honey wanting to know what they were doing there.

Chapter 7

Tiffany sighed and looked at the clock. Another two long hours to go before she finished work. She was bored out of her mind but couldn't show it. She had managed to get a temporary job at Kara's dad's gym, Fit2Go. As soon as Douglas heard that she was looking for a job, he had offered her the receptionist's position. It was very nice of him and Tiffany was grateful, but very, very bored. She had only agreed to take on the temporary job when Kara had found out that the loathsome Gavin had frozen his membership, as she had zero wish ever to see him again. She spent her days giving the clientele marks out of ten for their sense of style, and surreptitiously flicking through *Vogue* for styling ideas while hoping that Kara – who managed the gym – would come out of the office and talk to her.

'Good evening, how are you?' Tiffany called out breezily to a forty-something woman, with an enviably toned body, whom she privately called Iron Woman. Mind you, thought Tiffany, her body damn' well should be toned, given the hours and hours the woman spent at the gym. It was one of the rules of the job that she had to say hello to everyone, and goodbye. And smile. Tiffany was fed up of smiling, especially at some of the lads who seemed to think she was giving them the come-on. She wished that instead of her nametag she could wear a badge saying: *'No, I'm not flirting with you, it's called customer service.'* And then there was Billy, her ex. This was his gym and he had taken Tiffany's new job there as a sign that she must still be interested in him and had stepped up his campaign to ask her out again. Every evening around six-thirty he would pitch up and lean on the front desk, and if he wasn't trying to talk to her, he would be looking at her longingly. What to do about Billy?

And on top of the mind-numbingly boring job, she had yet to hear from Angel. Every time her mobile rang or beeped with a text message, Tiffany hoped it might be from her. She tried to be rational and tell herself that it didn't matter whether Angel got in touch with her or not, that she had been perfectly happy before she knew Angel might be her half-sister, but she couldn't help feeling rejected. Maybe the famous celebrity Angel Summer didn't think Tiffany Taylor was an important enough person to be related to her . . .

She'd thought she was OK with this, but on this particular Friday afternoon, a full two weeks after she had tried to make contact with Angel, it had got to her.

'Hiya, Tiff.'

She looked up from the computer screen and there was Billy, looking at her expectantly. 'Got any plans for tonight?'

She shook her head. 'I'll probably have a drink with Kara.'

'Kara and Harley are going to the cinema tonight . . . so I suppose you could tag along, like a saddo goose-berry, or you could come out for dinner with me? We could go to your favourite Indian.'

Billy didn't give up. Tiffany considered him. He was looking especially cute in low-hanging jeans, showing off the top of his boxers, and a tee-shirt that revealed his muscular body, and she really didn't feel like being on her own tonight. Maybe she could have dinner with him. And all right it wasn't Nobu or Zuma or The Ivy or any of the other top restaurants Angel would go to, but the Indian he meant along Kentish Town Road was fab.

'So long as you don't think I'm going to have sex with you,' she told him bluntly, thinking back to the last time they'd met up for dinner about a month ago, which had ended up with them going to bed together. They had reached the stage in their relationship where they could say pretty much anything to each other.

A young lad was going through the turnstile. Catching what Tiffany had said, he turned round and winked at her.

She rolled her eyes. 'To clarify . . . this will be dinner as friends. And I don't mean friends with extras.'

'Sure, just friends,' Billy replied, hardly able to contain his smile. Leaning over the counter, he kissed her on the cheek. 'I'll pick you up around eight.'

By half-past ten, Billy and Tiffany had worked their way through onion bhajis, poppadoms, chicken tikka masala, a lamb rogan josh, nan breads, pilau rice, and one and a half pints of Kingfisher beer.

'Oh my God, I'm so full!' Tiffany groaned, pushing her plate away. She leant back against the burgundy mock-velvet booth. The Indian scored nul points for interior design, but the food was divine.

Billy waved the last remaining poppadom in her face. 'Sure I can't interest you in this, madam?'

'No way! I need to go and lie on my sofa.'

'You could come and lie on mine,' Billy said cheekily. 'The boys are out, and I tidied up.'

'I already told you, this is us as friends, not friends with extras,' Tiffany said. But she was weakening. It had been a while and Billy did look especially fit and she'd had a stressful couple of weeks . . . Would it be so bad to go back to his, one last time?

'Of course just as friends.' He tried unsuccessfully to hide his pleasure that she was going to come back with him. 'And you can tell me what's on your mind.'

When Billy had picked her up, she had hinted that she was worried about something, meaning the situation with Angel, and as soon as she had said it, had regretted it. 'Oh, it was nothing,' she muttered now, forgetting that he knew her better than that.

'Have you met someone else?' he asked quietly.

'Why would I be out having a curry with you on a Friday night if I'd met someone else?'

'You've got a new job?'

'Marie's having a baby.' Phew, that surely let her off the hook!

Billy had always got on well with her dad and Marie. 'That's great news, Tiff, but I don't see why it is such a big secret?' Damn, he wasn't going to be put off so easily. It probably wouldn't do any harm to tell him about Angel. She trusted him not to tell anyone. Besides, the way things were going, it seemed as if nothing was going to happen anyway.

'You remember I met my real mum a couple of months ago?'

'Oh, yeah, it didn't go too well from what you said?'

Tiffany sighed. That was an understatement. 'It was a total disaster. But she wrote to her social worker so that she could tell me . . .' She paused. It was going to sound completely mad. There they were, sitting in their local Indian, surrounded by people having a Friday-night curry, a treat at the end of a long week, and she was going to come out with this revelation. She fleetingly looked away from Billy and her attention was caught by a man sitting alone. He was staring at her, and Tiffany had a funny feeling that she had seen him before, but she couldn't think from where. He was striking-looking, with short brown hair in a buzz cut and deep brown eyes.

'Tell you what?' Billy urged her, and she looked away from the man.

'OK, you've got to promise not to tell anyone – not any of the lads.' Billy shared his student house with three other trainee teachers.

'Sure.'

Tiffany sneaked another glance at the brown-eyed man. He was reading his book now; perhaps she had imagined seeing him somewhere before.

'Tanya said that I had a half-sister.'

'Yeah? I guess it can't be that much of a surprise that you've got siblings. Your mum sounded pretty dysfunctional.'

'It's who it is. Tanya claims that my half-sister is Angel Summer.'

Billy looked suitably shocked. 'What! *The* Angel Summer who's married to Cal Bailey?' Cal was one of Billy's all-time sporting heroes. He had raised his voice in surprise and Tiffany immediately shushed him. She looked around anxiously but none of the other diners seemed to have heard.

'Yes, *that* Angel Summer, is there another one?' Tiffany couldn't help sounding sarcastic. And suddenly she realised that she didn't want to go back to Billy's flat and end up in bed with him, just because it was so easy. She wanted more than that, and every time they slept together it always gave Billy the idea that she wanted to get back with him. But, much as she liked him, he was not for her. She should really let him go. He would soon be snapped up by another woman. He was cute and kind. It wasn't his fault that she found him a little dull and a bit safe.

Tiffany's gaze was once more drawn to the brown-eyed man and this time he met her gaze and held it just a little bit longer than was polite. Wow! He was gorgeous. Tiffany was the first to look away.

'Tiff, that is awesome news! If you really are her sister, please can you introduce me to Cal Bailey? I'll do whatever you want. *Please*.' Billy reached out for her hand.

He was sweet and for an instant, as his warm hand closed over hers, she was tempted to rethink her decision not to go back to his flat. Then the good-looking stranger walked past and Tiffany found herself withdrawing her hand.

'*If* I get to meet her, then sure.'

'D'you know what?' Billy was studying her face. 'I think I can see a resemblance now, I know that Bryan'– he named one of his flatmates – 'is always saying how much like Angel you look, and I could never see it before but I can now. It's your eyes.'

'Yeah, yeah, and now you're going to say, pity I don't have Angel's other assets?'

Billy grinned. 'I would never say that, you've got great tits.'

Tiffany stood up. Time to call a halt to this conversation. 'I'm going to the Ladies. Can you ask for the bill?'

Just as she had turned down the narrow corridor, the brown-eyed man came out of the Gents. Tiffany stood to one side to let him pass, and as he walked by he looked at her again. 'Thanks,' he said in a Geordie accent.

Instantly Tiffany remembered where she had seen him before. He was the bouncer who had been working at the club the night she had met Gavin. She cringed inside at the memory of him thinking she was that wanker's girlfriend. She dashed into the Ladies, head down, determined to leave the restaurant as quickly as possible. She had thought he was giving her the eye, but instead, she realised, he must have been looking at her because he remembered her from that night. Take the shame!

By the time she returned to her table, the man had gone and Billy was keying in his pin number.

'Billy, I was going to pay half!' Tiffany protested. Usually they split the bill as neither of them had any money.

'You can treat me to a slap-up meal in some celebrity restaurant, once you've hooked up with Big Sis.'

'Yeah, sure,' Tiffany muttered. Now she was going to feel even worse about telling Billy that she wasn't going back to his place.

Outside it had started raining. Billy reached for her hand, all set to walk with her to where his car was parked. It was now or never.

'Actually, Billy, I'm going to get the bus home. I think it's best if we don't see each other like this any more. It's stopping us from meeting anyone else.' Tiffany bit her lip and pulled her biker jacket closer together, to try and keep warm. She felt terrible for saying it. A look of hurt flashed into Billy's eyes.

'But I was going to suggest we gave it another go. Come on, Tiff – we get on so well together. We know each other so well. Everyone says what a great couple we make.'

Oh, God! What was she supposed to say to that? 'I just see you as a friend now, Billy, a really good friend.'

'A friend who's been having sex with me on and off for the past six months,' he muttered.

'Yeah, but I thought we were both taking it casually.'

'Well, I wasn't. I kept thinking that you would come back to me. Can't you see that I still love you, Tiff? What a fucking loser I am!'

54

Tiffany reached out to touch him. She felt awful that Billy had misread all the times they had met up. She'd honestly had no idea he still loved her.

But Billy backed away. 'I get it now, Tiff. I won't bother you any more. Good luck with your half-sister. Perhaps you think you'll meet some flash celeb through her.'

'Oh, for God's sake, Billy! You know I don't want that. I want us to be friends.' But he was already striding away, head down, shoulders hunched.

'Please, Billy!' she called after him.

He turned back briefly. 'I'm not ready to be friends yet.' And then he started running. Should she run after him? Tiffany pushed her hair back as the rain became heavier. It was probably best to let him go, but she felt a pang of sadness. That really was it then . . .

Chapter 8

'So this is a picture of Tiffany?' Angel asked, holding up the photo of a young woman. In it Tiffany was walking along a busy street, her long brown hair lifting slightly in the breeze. She was on her mobile and smiling at something the caller was saying to her. Angel couldn't see any resemblance between her and this beautiful dark-haired girl with a fringe. Tiffany was wearing a black biker jacket, denim shorts, black tights and red Converse. She looked young and fresh-faced and not at all like a stalker-nutter. But neither had über-glam Simone, until she started changing her appearance to look like Angel.

Sean nodded. Sean Murphy was their head of security, a former soldier who Cal had hired six months ago as he had been worried that their other security guy had become a little complacent. Angel trusted Sean completely – he took his work very seriously, and was a calm, reassuring presence who made her feel safe. He was also a down-to-earth, lovely guy with a great sense of humour. Her daughter Honey already adored him, and he had quickly become an indispensable part of their family.

'D'you think she looks like me?' Angel asked Cal. The three of them were sitting in the living room.

'I do, actually. You've got the same eyes, and the same mouth.'

Angel looked at the photograph again, but she still didn't get it.

She looked over at Sean. 'So what's she like?' He had spent the last two weeks going over every inch of Tiffany Taylor's life. There was probably very little he didn't know about her.

Sean shrugged. 'She appears genuine. From my investigations, it definitely seems as if she knew nothing about being your half-sister until she received the letter from Tanya. Some of this you already know from the letter she sent you. She comes from what seems to be a happy and stable family – her dad's a carpenter, her step-mum is a teaching assistant, and she's got a much younger sister. She went to college and studied Fashion and Textiles, and she's been trying to get work as a stylist.' Sean paused. 'I'm not exactly sure what a stylist does, but I expect you know. And for the last year she has been working as a waitress. She got sacked from that job for apparently throwing pizza and wine over a customer. Now she's the receptionist at a gym.'

'Not so good at customer relations then,' Cal said dryly.

'And what's she like as a person?' Angel was curious to know.

'She's got close female friends.' That scored Tiffany points for Angel, who never trusted women who didn't get on with other women.

'She seems likeable, down-to-earth and loyal, but clearly has a temper on her, judging by the restaurant incident.' Sean frowned, as he added, 'I don't think too much of her taste in men, and she seems to get through them.'

'Oh?'

'Yeah, I realised that I'd seen her before when I

helped out a friend who needed security for a club in London. She was with a right idiot. The bloke she was with the other night didn't seem so bad, though.'

Cal grinned at Angel. 'You could give her some relationship advice – after all, you went out with that tosser boy-band singer, Mickey, before we got together.'

Mickey . . . now there was someone Angel would rather forget. Pretty, vain, and a cokehead – he had been the worst possible boyfriend choice. His boy band had long since broken up and now he appeared in various reality shows from time to time. Food seemed to have replaced coke as his drug of choice as he was always battling with his weight.

Angel shot Cal a warning look. 'Let's not go down that route, sunshine. At least none of my exes has done time in a secure psychiatric unit.'

That wiped the smile off Cal's face. 'So while we're on the subject, what's the latest on Simone Fraser?'

'She seems to be behaving herself. She's been out in Australia for the last eight months.'

'Let's hope she stays down under permanently,' Cal said with feeling. He reached out for Angel's hand and held it. Even three years on, just the mention of Simone's name sent shivers down Angel's spine and she knew Cal felt the same. Cal had wanted them to move from their large Edwardian house after Simone had broken in and tried to attack Angel. But Angel loved the house; loved its location in the heart of the Sussex countryside, surrounded by fields and well away from the prying lenses of the paps. And after an extensive security overhaul of the property, Cal had agreed they could stay.

'So what shall I do? Shall I get in touch with Tiffany?' Angel felt a mix of curiosity and apprehension about meeting her half-sister. She had reached a stage in her life when she felt happy and secure – she had her family, Cal and Honey, a close circle of friends, she got on well with her parents – and she didn't know if she wanted to rock the boat. But then again, the thought of having a half-sister was compelling . . . someone who understood what it was like to be adopted. Maybe Tiffany would be the one good thing to come out of her dysfunctional real family?

'I think you should. From what Sean says, there's a strong chance that you are related,' Cal replied. He smiled reassuringly. 'You don't have to stress about it. We can get him to arrange all the details.' He looked over at Sean. 'I think they should meet somewhere neutral, don't you? Maybe a London hotel?'

'Good idea,' Sean replied, 'I want it to be somewhere public. I would suggest somewhere like The Ritz. You could have tea and I would be at one of the other tables.' He smiled. 'You don't have to worry, Angel, I'll be watching out for you.'

She immediately felt reassured. There was something about Sean that made her feel protected. 'OK, I'll do it.'

'OMG, OMG! That is just like a plot from *Desperate Housewives!*' Jez declared when Angel told him about Tiffany. She had arranged to meet her half-sister the following day and was now having cocktails with Jez at The May Fair – the bar in the luxury hotel was one of their favourite haunts. She had held off telling him until she knew for certain that she was going to see Tiffany, well aware that he wouldn't let it drop once he heard about it. And from Jez's OTT reaction, she knew she had made the right decision. He would have driven her mad if she'd told him sooner.

'So what are you going to wear when you meet up with her? I think you should have a navy forties-style suit on, red lipstick, hair up in an elegant twist, a hat with net covering your face . . . Old movie-star style.' Jez paused. 'Oh, and a large clutch bag, plus a cigarette holder . . . maybe in mother-of-pearl.'

'I don't smoke.' Really Jez was entirely wasted as a hairdresser, with his over-active imagination.

'That's not the point – it's for the drama!'

Angel sipped her Bellini Twist. She was feeling nervous. She half-wished Jez would come with her for moral support, though knowing him he wouldn't be able to stop talking and then she would have no chance to see what Tiffany was like.

'I'm going casual, as myself, and I hope she'll be doing the same.'

'Can you imagine how she must be feeling tonight, knowing that she is going to meet you tomorrow and that you're her sister?'

'Might be. And her half-sister,' Angel corrected him.

Jez picked up the cocktail stick from his Martini glass and popped the olive in his mouth. 'You have to promise to tell me all about it?'

'Don't I always?'

And when Jez saw how anxious she was, he said, 'You'll be fine, don't worry about it. And if it doesn't work out, well, you've still got your family and friends and we all love you.'

And that was why she adored Jez – underneath all the theatrical declarations and gossipy bitchiness, he had a good heart and was a truly loyal friend.

Chapter 9

Tiffany walked past The Ritz for the second time, debating whether to go in or not. She was fifteen minutes early for her meeting with Angel and, for all her streetwise confidence, felt incredibly nervous about finally coming face to face with the famous woman who was possibly her half-sister. Kara had offered to come with her but Tiffany felt she had to do this on her own. And she still hadn't told her dad and Marie, figuring that if the meeting was a total disaster then it was best that they didn't know. She would tell them if it went well. It was a big if. She walked a little further along Piccadilly, past Green Park, dodging all the tourists, then turned round. She couldn't put it off any longer. It was time to meet Angel.

She walked into the huge hotel lobby and instantly felt self-conscious. She had never been inside such a grand place before. Sure, she had been past The Ritz enough times, usually on the bus, and had often fantasised about staying in the luxury hotel. She cautiously approached one of the hotel staff, and asked where the tearoom was. She wondered if the smartly dressed man realised that she had never stepped foot inside a five-star hotel before, and that the last one she'd stayed at had been a Travelodge. Probably he had sized her up in an instant and knew that she didn't have any money. He directed her to a luxurious and ornate room, with gold statues, whopping glittering chandeliers, tables with crisp white cloths and pretty gold chairs. Tiffany anxiously scanned the room for Angel but couldn't see her.

'I'm here to meet someone,' she said quietly to the head waiter. 'Angel Summer . . . I mean, Bailey.'

The head waiter nodded discreetly. 'Of course, mademoiselle, I will show you to your table.' He walked purposefully over to a table in the far corner of the room and pulled out a chair for Tiffany. She tried to act as if it was customary for waiters to pull out chairs for her.

'Can I get you something while you are waiting?' he asked.

A double vodka sprang to mind, but Tiffany dismissed that thought. She didn't want Angel to think she was some alkie, even though the alcohol might have given her more confidence.

'I'll just have a tea.'

'What kind of tea would mademoiselle prefer?'

All these questions! Tiffany could feel her cheeks burning with embarrassment as she looked through the bewildering list of teas arrayed on the expensive cream paper in the thick leather-bound menu. She hadn't even heard of half of them!

'I'll have English Breakfast tea, please.'

And then, thankfully, the waiter left. Tiffany looked across at the door but there was still no sign of Angel. She scrabbled through her bag for her mirror and surreptitiously checked her appearance, quickly adding another layer of lip-gloss. Her hair still looked good – which it should after the time she had spent blow drying and straightening it. She had agonised over what to wear and in the end had gone for one of her favourite outfits: a black dress with sheer sleeves from H & M, and her leopard-print heels from Office. She had thought that she looked elegant and sophisticated, but now she felt as if her clothes looked cheap and she herself totally out of place. Surveying the women at the other tables, in their expensive designer clothes, she counted at least three Chanel handbags, two Birkins, a Chloé and a Miu Miu. She kicked her own battered brown Topshop satchel under the table and then panicked that everything would have fallen out of it and had to dive under there to check that it hadn't. When she emerged from under the tablecloth, Angel was standing by the table. Typical. Talk about first impressions . . .

'Tiffany, right?'

'Oh, hi,' she said, standing up and trying to smooth down her hair and straighten her dress at the same time. She wondered whether to shake hands or kiss. Luckily Angel made that decision for her and kissed her lightly twice. Tiffany sat back down feeling completely overawed by Angel, who was even more beautiful in real life than she was on screen. Angel's long hair was honey-coloured, her skin was a light golden brown that accentuated her intensely green eyes. She looked every inch the A-list celebrity, glowing with health, success and wealth, and in true celebrity style was wearing white skinny jeans, a white cashmere jumper and a white fake-fur gilet.

Tiffany and Kara had a theory that only the very rich ever wore head to toe white as only they could afford the dry-cleaning bills. Tiffany also took in the blingtastic diamond wedding and engagement rings, the diamond bracelet, the diamond-studded Rolex. She was surprised Angel didn't need an armed guard, walking around with all those rocks on display.

'How funny. You're all in black and I'm in white,'

Angel commented. 'So this is weird, isn't it? Kind of like being on a blind date.' She picked up the menu and fiddled with it, and Tiffany realised that Angel was just as nervous as she was.

'I hope it goes better than my blind dates usually go,' she attempted to joke, and then thought, *Why the hell did I say that! It makes me sound like a total saddo who goes on loads of blind dates!*

Angel smiled. 'I'd have thought a beautiful girl like you would have them queueing up?'

'To be honest, 'I've just come out of a two-year relationship and I'm happy being single.'

'I remember how that felt. It's good to be single for a while,' Angel replied, then added, 'Are you wearing Coco Mademoiselle?'

'Yes, I always wear it, it's my signature scent.'

'That's a coincidence, it's my favourite perfume too. I've worn it since I was a teenager.'

There was a pause and as Tiffany looked at Angel she realised that their eyes and mouth were very similar. She wasn't just imagining this, caught up in the excitement of meeting someone famous.

'We've got the same eyes and mouth,' Angel said wonderingly, as if echoing her thoughts. 'Apart from Tanya, I've never met anyone I was actually related to before.'

The waiter came over to take Angel's order. Tiffany had already seen the prices and felt anxious about ordering anything else. Fortunately Angel took control and ordered them both afternoon tea.

'Oh, and shall we have a glass of champagne as well? You like champagne, don't you, Tiffany?'

Who didn't like champagne? 'Sure, thanks.' She waited until the waiter was out of earshot before saying quietly, 'I don't expect you to pay for me, Angel.'

'Don't be silly! Of course I'll pay. I suggested coming

here.' She looked around. 'Sorry it's so posh. I always feel as if I should be minding my Ps and Qs here, but I couldn't think where else to meet.' She twisted the diamond bracelet round on her wrist. 'I have to admit, I was gob-smacked to get your letter. I had no idea that I might have a sister.'

'Imagine how I felt when I got Tanya's telling me that you were mine.' Tiffany hesitated, then added, 'That's if she's telling the truth. She ended the letter by saying that you hadn't given her any money, but maybe you'd give some to me.'

Angel gave a wry smile. 'Sounds like our lovely mother. My husband Cal thought we looked similar. But I guess, to be sure, we should have a DNA test.'

Tiffany nodded. She had expected Angel to bring up the matter of a DNA test.

Angel paused. 'But, seeing you, I don't know . . . I wonder if we need to. I can so clearly see a resemblance between us . . . the way you bite your lip, the way you pull your sleeves over your hands. I'm always doing that.'

And Tiffany, who up until this meeting hadn't felt that she looked anything like Angel, could see herself as well.

'Better do it, though,' Angel added. 'Just to be sure.'

The waiter arrived with a silver trolley on which stood a layered cake-stand showing off an array of tempting finger sandwiches and exquisite miniature pastries and cakes. It looked far too perfect to eat, and besides Tiffany was so fired up about meeting Angel that food was the very last thing on her mind.

'My dad would love to see all this,' she said. 'He's so into food and cooking.'

'He brought you up, is that right?'

'He did. His relationship with Tanya was pretty much over, and then they found out she was pregnant

65

with me and so Dad stayed with her. And then, when it was obvious that she wasn't fit to look after me, he applied for full custody. He was only twenty, I really admire him for that. I mean, a lot of men of that age would have seen a baby and run.' Tiffany felt more relaxed as she talked about her dad. He was brilliant, and even if things didn't work out between her and Angel, she was so fortunate to have the family she did.

'He sounds great,' Angel replied. 'And it seems like we've both been lucky not to be brought up by our real mum. God, I used to fantasise about meeting her when I was a teenager . . . I was so sure we'd have this amazing connection.'

She broke off and Tiffany was shocked to see tears in Angel's eyes. 'Sorry,' she said, waving her hands in front of her face in a vain effort to stop them. 'It still gets to me. And it was so horrible when I did meet her. It must have been like that for you as well?'

'Exactly like you described. I was sure that I would feel something for her and that she would feel something for me, but I didn't feel anything except relief that my dad had brought me up.' Tiffany paused. 'I feel sorry for Tanya, though. Something must have happened to her, to make her like that.'

Angel looked surprised by the comment. 'Do you? I guess it's because I'm a mother, but I just think she is the most selfish woman in the world.'

'She also said sorry in the letter. Sorry to both of us for not being a proper mum. She must realise what a mess she's made of her life. It's sad, she's missed out on so much.'

Angel shook her head. 'You're obviously a much nicer person than me, because I never want to see or hear from her again.'

She reached for her champagne glass and held it up. 'Now I think we should have a toast. To us, for surviving!' Tiffany clinked her glass against Angel's and took a sip.

Sharing their experiences of Tanya broke the ice between the two women and they spent the next hour chatting about their families, what Tiffany wanted to do, and Angel's TV work. Tiffany found her so easy to talk to, there was an instant rapport. It was exactly the same when she'd first met Kara and they'd become best friends. One glass of champagne had been followed by a bottle. Every now and then Tiffany would get the urge to pinch herself to check that this was real, that here she was at The Ritz, having tea and drinking champagne with Angel Summer!

At one point Tiffany got up to go to the bathroom and felt slightly light-headed as she walked along the thickly carpeted hallway. Get a grip, she told herself, once she reached the Ladies and re-did her make-up. As she returned to the tearoom, a man sitting alone caught her attention. He seemed familiar and she realised with a jolt that it was the brown-eyed man she had seen at the Indian restaurant. Oh my God! Did *she* now have a stalker! But surely he was too fit-looking to be a weirdo. He must have women stalking him!

Tiffany stifled a hiccup as she sat down; the cham-pagne had gone straight to her head.

'You OK?' Angel asked, and put down her pink Swarovski crystal-studded BlackBerry. Kara would have killed to own a phone like that.

'I know this sounds crazy but I think I'm being stalked,' Tiffany said quietly.

'What!'

'There's a man here that I saw two weeks ago in an Indian restaurant in Kentish Town. It's a bit of a coincidence that he's here now, isn't it?' He probably knew where she lived! Tiffany was feeling thoroughly creeped out by now. But Angel didn't look at all shocked.

'Do you mean the guy sitting in the far corner?'

'Yes, but don't make it obvious that we're talking about him.'

But to Tiffany's horror, Angel waved at the man and beckoned him over. What the hell was going on?

'I know who he is, don't look so worried. He's Sean Murphy, our head of security. Sorry to freak you out, but my husband insisted we look into your background before I got in touch. He's very protective since we had an incident with a real-life stalker a few years ago. And,' Angel hesitated, 'I know this is going to sound strange, but he's here as my bodyguard.'

'Oh, right.' WTF! Just as she was thinking that she and Angel were getting on so well, Tiffany was made aware of how completely different their worlds were. And why exactly did Angel think she needed a body-guard when she was meeting her sister?

By now Sean had reached the table.

'Sean, you've been spotted, I thought you were the lean mean security machine?' Angel teased.

'With respect, it wasn't part of my plan to hide from Miss Taylor.'

He held out his hand. 'I'm Sean Murphy.'

Tiffany shook his hand. He had a very firm hand-shake and there was no denying it, he was a hottie. He looked a little like the American actor Ryan Reynolds, only more rugged, with his handsome face, chocolate-brown eyes and extremely buff body. All muscle by the look of him.

Angel called the waiter over and asked for another chair. 'Join us for a drink, Sean. I feel bad that we upset Tiffany. Order whatever you want, I'm just nipping to the loo.'

'So, how's it going?' he asked as he sat down.

'Don't you know? I'd have thought you'd have planted bugs under the table and been monitoring all our conversations,' Tiffany joked.

'I didn't think I needed to do that.'

'Did you really think Angel needed a bodyguard to meet me? What exactly did you think I would do?'

'I know it probably seems like an over-reaction to you, but she has been the victim of a stalker before. Don't take it personally.'

He was a bit serious, but maybe it was because he was being professional.

'Well, you haven't noticed my bodyguard, have you?'

He raised an eyebrow, registering that he knew she was teasing him. 'It's the sixty-something, pretending to be thirty-something, woman with the blonde bob and brown Gucci messenger bag. She might look as if a puff of wind would blow her down, but she's a black belt. She could take you. All I have to do is nod my head and she'll be right over, like a ninja.'

'Really? I'd like to see that.'

A pause. They both looked at each other. Tiffany was the first to look away. 'So, this is all a bit different from the other week in the curry house.' She gestured round at the lavishly decorated room.

'It was a good curry house, best chicken biryani I've had in ages,' Sean replied. 'You broke up with Billy then?'

Whoah! Talk about direct!

'He seemed like a sound bloke. Especially compared to that tosser in the nightclub.'

While Tiffany liked the good looks and the Geordie accent, there was something about Sean's judgemental tone that instantly put her back up. As if she needed a running commentary on her love life! And from what he'd said, she'd realised that Sean must have been watching her and Billy when they left the restaurant. Oh, God! Did that mean he had also overheard their conversation? Billy's declaration that he was still in love with Tiffany? Her own blunt reply that she thought it was only about the sex? Could it get any more embarrassing!

'That tosser in the nightclub was nothing to do with me!' she bit back. 'My friend set me up on a blind date. And for the record, it was the worst blind date I have ever been on. Not that I've been on many others. I never saw him again, except to chuck pizza and wine over him!' Now she was sounding a little *too* wound up.

'Ah, so he was the reason you got sacked? He deserved it.'

'Is there anything you don't know about me?' She was feeling at a real disadvantage, given that she knew absolutely nothing about Sean except that she remembered him saying that he had been in the army.

'I'm sure there's plenty,' he replied. And he actually smiled at her, which immediately won her over. The man was gorgeous!

Angel returned. 'I hope you've reassured Tiffany that you're not a stalker?'

Tiffany nodded.

'And now I must dash. I'm supposed to be meeting Cal at Selfridges and he's driving us back to Sussex. It's been wonderful meeting you, Tiffany and I'm sure we'll meet again soon. Let's say as soon as we've had the DNA tests done. I'll get my PA to set them up for us.' She held out her hand and signalled for the bill.

The she looked back at Tiffany. 'There's just one thing . . . I'd be so grateful if this could be kept between us for now. I'm sure you must have told someone, but I don't want the press to find out . . .' She gave a heartfelt sigh. 'I've really had enough of them picking over my life.'

'Don't worry,' Tiffany reassured her, 'I've only told two people, and I trust them not to say anything.'

The three of them left The Ritz together. Angel hugged Tiffany and again told her how brilliant it had been to meet her, and then she jumped into a taxi.

Tiffany watched the black cab pull away. Even though they didn't yet know for sure if they were sisters, she felt that nothing in her life was ever going to be the same again . . .

'What are you going to do now?' Sean asked her.

'I thought you would know my every move,' Tiffany replied, wanting to provoke a reaction from him. He was just too cool for bloody school! And even though his smile had slightly thawed her, she was still needled that he'd been digging into her life, as if she had something to hide.

'I'm guessing that you're going to meet up with your friend Kara, possibly go round to her flat, and have a debrief about your meeting with Angel over a bottle of wine?'

He really had done his research.

'Very good, Agent Murphy. And what are you going to do? Go back to your secret bunker and plan your next mission?' *Maybe a little too sarcastic . . .*

'Actually I'm off to see my daughter, so have a good night and I'll probably see you in the next week or so.'

And just as Tiffany was softening at the thought of him being a family man, Sean added, 'And please don't forget what Angel said about the press. She and her husband have been through enough.'

'You can trust me on that score! Who do you think I am? The kind of girl who does a kiss and tell? You didn't do your homework on me at all if you think that, Agent Smartarse.'

Tiffany blamed the half bottle of champagne she'd had for her coming out with 'smartarse', which probably was a bit rude, but he deserved it. And it had been a momentous afternoon. Before Sean could come out with another annoying comment, Tiffany swung her bag over her shoulder and began quickly walking along Piccadilly, looking for her bus stop. He might be good-looking, but he could do with chilling out more, and less of the telling her what to do.

Chapter 10

The following morning Tiffany was woken by her mobile ringing. It was her dad. Her very upset-sounding dad. 'Why couldn't you have told us first, Tiffany? Do you have any idea what a shock it was?'

'What are you talking about, Dad?' She reached for her watch. Eight o'clock.

'I was just out on a job and one of the lads had a copy of the *Sun*. You're on the front page.'

Tiffany sat bolt upright. 'What!'

'It says that you're Angel Summer's half-sister. Is it true, Tiffany? Marie is in a right state, worrying about what people will say to Lily-Rose at school.'

How the hell had the press found out?

'I haven't said anything to the press, Dad, and I didn't want to tell you and Marie until I knew for sure.' Tiffany quickly explained what had happened with Angel so far. She couldn't believe that her decision not to tell her parents straight away had backfired so spectacularly. She had only ever wanted to protect her family. But by the end of her explanation she was relieved that he understood her reasoning.

'Sorry, love, it was just such a shock seeing the story . . . I know you would never do anything to hurt us.'

As soon as she got off the phone, after arranging to go and see her dad that afternoon, Tiffany selected Angel's number. They had got on so well when they met. Was this going to ruin everything? She imagined how furious Angel would be that the story had got out. Tiffany simply had to let her know that she'd had nothing to do with it.

Angel's phone went straight to voice-mail and Tiffany could only leave a halting message.

She was about to switch on her laptop and look up the story online when her doorbell rang. Imagining that it was most likely the postman at this time in the morning, Tiffany grabbed her robe and put it on over her Betty Boop PJs. She ran down the three flights of stairs to the front door. She got the shock of her life when she opened the door and was confronted by a horde of photographers crowding up the path, cameras aimed right at her.

'Tiffany, is it true that you're Angel's sister?' someone yelled out.

For a second Tiffany was frozen to the spot as the cameras exploded in her face, then she slammed the door shut. Oh my God! First of all someone had quite possibly ruined any chance of her having a relationship with her sister, if Angel *was* her sister, and now she had been papped in her PJs! Without a scrap of make-up on! It reminded her of that comic scene in the film *Notting Hill*, when Hugh Grant opens the door to the paps, and then Rhys Ifans goes out and poses in his pants. But having it happen to her wasn't funny and Tiffany didn't feel at all like smiling. With a pounding heart, she went back upstairs and slammed her door shut.

There were two missed calls on her phone but they were from withheld numbers. Knowing her luck, they would be from the press. There was nothing from

Angel. Tiffany looked in the mirror. Her fringe was sticking up in all directions; eye make-up was smudged under her eyes as she hadn't bothered to take it off the night before. Panda eyes, shiny face, bedraggled hair . . . It was even worse than she had thought.

Twenty minutes later she was showered, dressed and made up, and now she had five missed calls on her mobile from unknown numbers, but still nothing from Angel. Kara had rung and left a message, but Tiffany didn't want to speak to anyone until she knew what was going on with Angel. She sent Kara's dad a text, apologising for the fact that she wouldn't be able to come to work today. She half-thought about travelling down to Brighton and calling on Angel at home, but dismissed the thought as she didn't know where Angel lived and nor did she want it to seem as if she was intruding. From the window of her studio flat she could see the front garden and it was still over-run with paps. She felt like a prisoner in her own home. There was no way she wanted to stay in, knowing that they were all milling about outside. She needed to get away.

She decided she would somehow get past the paps, take the tube to Oxford Street and hang out in the shops, before getting the train to her dad's.

She checked out the story online and groaned aloud as she read the headline: *Angel's Secret Sister Revealed!* Somehow they had managed to get hold of Tiffany's profile picture on Facebook, which showed her grinning away without a care in the world. She quickly scanned the story. There was little of substance – just the bare bones of her possibly being Angel's sister, and how she had confided in 'a friend' . . . the same friend who had told the press. Some friend then, Tiffany thought bitterly. But the article went on to talk about Tanya and her addiction, then about Angel and Cal, raking up his affair, their divorce, her relationship with

75

the baseball player. God, no wonder Angel hadn't wanted the press to find out, if this was what happened.

Her mobile rang. She frowned as she saw Billy's number flash up and was all set to ignore it, then decided to speak to him. Maybe he and his flatmates could help her get past the paparrazi?

'I'm really sorry, Tiffany,' he said as soon as she'd picked up.

'Sorry for what?' Then realisation dawned on her. 'Billy, you didn't tell the press, did you? I mean, I know you were angry with me, but that is such a shit thing to do.'

He sighed. 'No, I didn't tell them, but after I saw you I went home and got hammered and . . .' he hesitated '. . . I told Bryan.'

'Not Bryan Blabbermouth?' Billy's flatmate Bryan had a reputation for being unable to keep a secret.

'Yeah, and he admitted to me this morning that he had told some of the lads on his course, one of whom happens to be the son of a journalist. I'm really, really sorry, Tiffany.'

She knew that Billy was genuinely sorry and could hardly blame him for shooting his mouth off after they had broken up, even though it had landed her right in it. 'I believe you, and I know you didn't mean for this to happen.'

'So is Angel your sister?'

'I don't know yet, but she might well not want to have anything to do with me after this. She didn't want the press finding out.'

'Tiff, if there's anything I can do . . . I could phone her, explain what happened. It's not your fault, she can't blame you.'

'No, it's OK, Billy, I've got to handle this myself.' She didn't even want him to help her with the paps; it was best if she kept him well away.

Tiffany ended the call and wandered back over to the window. She peered out – the paps were still there. She shook back her hair and squared her shoulders. Well, so what if they were? She had done nothing wrong, nothing that she was ashamed of. She picked up her phone and called Angel once again, this time leaving a message to say that she knew who had leaked the story and that she hoped Angel would understand it wasn't something she'd wanted to happen. Then she grabbed her leather jacket, put on her Ray-Bans as worn by Kate Moss in many a pap shot, took one last look in the mirror and marched down the stairs.

Tiffany paused briefly, with her hand poised over the front door handle, listening to the paps chatting outside. Then she turned it and pushed the door open. As before, they leaped into action and started snapping away at her. But this time Tiffany didn't retreat. She continued walking down the path, doing her best to ignore the cameras being thrust in her face, the shouts, the questions. Celebrities always got into big flash cars to escape when they were being pursued, she reflected grimly as she headed down the hill to Archway tube station, the paps running behind and in front of her.

Naively she had expected them not to pursue her once they realised that she was going away from the house, but it didn't look like she was going to shake them off any time soon and she didn't want to be photographed running away from them as if she had something to be ashamed of.

Out of the corner of her eye she became aware of a sleek black car slowing down on the road next to her. A blacked-out electric window was lowered and she saw that Sean was driving. Could he be her knight in a shiny Mercedes?

'Hey, Tiffany, get in the car!'

Not hello, how are you, are you all right? Just an order. 'It's OK, I'm getting the tube, thanks.' She had no intention of being told what to do, even if it was by the sexy-looking Sean in a flash car! But the paps were seriously stressing her out. It was intimidating being pursued by a scrum of men who didn't seem like they were going to give up. At this rate she'd be trapped in the same tube carriage as them.

'We need to talk, Tiffany. Please can you get in the car?'

OK, at least he'd added 'please' this time. She may as well travel in style, and the Merc certainly beat the Northern Line plus scumbag paps. She quickly made a dash for it, and got in the car. Within seconds Sean was pulling away from the pavement and the paps. Tiffany felt like flicking them the finger, but thought it probably wasn't the best idea, as no doubt that would be the picture they'd end up using.

Sean glanced over at her, a serious expression on his face. 'I thought we agreed that you wouldn't say anything to the press? Angel's pretty upset.'

Great! So he wasn't rescuing her at all, he was giving her a telling off.

'*I* didn't tell the press. As I've already said, I told two people . . . my best friend Kara, who would never say anything, and Billy, my ex-boyfriend. Unfortunately I told him the night we finally split up. Remember that night? And when he went home he got drunk, told his flatmate, who told someone else, who told the press. So please don't give me a hard time about all this, because I'm as sorry as anyone that it has happened. I had my dad on the phone this morning, and he was upset because I hadn't even told him.' Tiffany could feel her eyes prickling with tears. It had been a horrible day so far and she certainly didn't need Sean laying into her.

'I see.'

Tiffany waited for him to apologise, but he didn't. Bloody Alpha male.

'Are you free now? I know that Angel is keen to get the DNA tests done as soon as possible. I can take you to a Harley Street clinic. The procedure doesn't take long. And I'll call Angel to let her know what happened.'

'That's fine by me,' Tiffany replied, as if it was a perfectly normal occurrence for her to be driven in a Merc to Harley Street for a DNA test. It was like a scene from a soap opera . . .

She looked out of the window as Sean expertly navigated the busy London traffic and called up Angel on his hands-free set. She was in the middle of getting ready for her TV show and so couldn't talk for long. Tiffany felt anxious all over again as Sean briefly outlined how the story had been leaked. Angel didn't seem to be saying very much, from what Tiffany could gather. She was no doubt still angry. Sean ended the call. 'She understands completely and says she'll try and call you later and that you're not to worry.'

'I'm probably not even related to her anyway,' Tiffany muttered. 'And, to be honest, if that's what the press are like, I don't know if I want to be part of it.'

Sean gave her a rare smile, reminding her again of how good-looking he was. 'Don't sound so down. We'll go to the clinic, then how about I buy you breakfast? I'm betting you haven't had any. But if you don't mind, it won't be The Ritz. My wages don't quite stretch to that.'

Two hours later, they were sitting in a café around the corner from the prestigious Harley Street, both tucking into full English breakfasts. Tiffany was starving after the adrenaline rush of the morning. The DNA test had been completely painless and quick – the nurse had simply swabbed the inside of her mouth to collect the cells – and the results would be ready in a week.

'So how come you work for Cal and Angel?' Tiffany asked, mopping up her fried egg with toast. Since Sean had found out that she hadn't leaked the story, he had been much nicer to her and they were actually having a conversation, rather than him giving her a hard time.

'A friend of mine works for them and he recommended me when I came out of the army eight months ago. I was just helping out for the opening night when you saw me at the club. Never again either! I'd rather be back in the army than face some of those drunken clubbers.' His tone was light but Tiffany noticed that his face darkened when he mentioned the army. And she didn't feel able to probe any deeper.

'You never heard anything more from that tosser?'

'That tosser' could only refer to Gavin. Tiffany shook her head. 'No, thank God!'

'Pity he got you the sack, though.'

'It would have been for something else. I'd had enough of being a waitress.'

'And how's the gym going?'

Tiffany shrugged. 'It's a job.' She sighed and added wistfully, 'But everything seems to take me further from doing what I really want to do.'

'You've got plenty of time to make it as a stylist.' He paused. 'So how would you style me then?'

Tiffany wondered if there was a trace of flirtation in his voice. Usually it was obvious when men were flirting with her, but it was exceptionally hard to tell with Mr Serious.

'I don't usually do men, but . . .' Tiffany tilted her head to one side to consider Sean. She liked his hair so short, but it could possibly be a fraction longer and still look as cute. He was wearing a battered black leather jacket that she approved of, but was ruining it with a black sweatshirt underneath, and a pair of jeans that were too nondescript and shapeless. The leather jacket said sexy and tough, the jeans and sweatshirt said safe and boring. Tiffany knew which one she preferred.

'Hmm . . . I think I'd like to rough you up at bit. Spike your hair, lose the boring sweatshirt and jeans.'

'You're not going to get me in skinny jeans.'

'No, just some that fit properly. And some black boots. You're only – what – late-twenties?'

'Twenty-eight,' Sean admitted.

'But you're dressing like someone way older!' She couldn't resist teasing him. 'One day you will be old and then you'll look back and think, Why didn't I make more of an effort when I could? Now I'm just a sad old man in bad clothes.'

Sean shrugged. 'I don't have time for clothes. They've just got to be functional and practical for work.'

'How totally boring!' Tiffany exclaimed. 'You can have such fun with clothes, and really express yourself.' She paused, curious to know the answer to her next question. 'What does your girlfriend or wife think of how you dress?'

'My ex-wife couldn't care less about how I dress. And I don't have a girlfriend.'

Ah, so he was divorced? She had thought so. And secretly she was pleased that he didn't have a girlfriend.

'How about your daughter?'

Mention of his daughter raised a smile, 'Maya doesn't mind what I wear, she's only six.'

'Oh, they start young, believe me – I was always trying to style my step-mum, and my sister is obsessed with clothes and she's only eight.'

'At the moment Maya is a bit of a tomboy, and that's

81

how I'd like it to stay. I don't want her growing up too fast.' He paused. 'It's hard, though, as I don't get to see her as much as I would like.' He changed the subject after that, asking her about her family, and Tiffany got the impression that he felt that he had revealed too much about himself and wasn't comfortable with it. She had to admit that she found him intriguing, something of a challenge. She felt a spark of excitement to be spending time with this handsome man, wanted to flirt with him, wanted him to like her. It had been a while since a man had had this effect on her. It helped put the rest of the day's events into perspective.

Nonetheless, she thought they would be going their separate ways after breakfast and was all set to head off for the tube when Sean said unexpectedly, 'I don't have to be anywhere for the rest of the day, I could give you a lift to your dad's.'

'You don't have to do that.' D'oh! Why did she say that? She would love him to give her a lift!

'It's cool. You've had a difficult morning. I like driving anyway.'

'So it's nothing to do with my charming personality?' Tiffany joked.

'Maybe.'

God, it was hard getting banter out of him! But then he smiled. Smile number three of the day, Tiffany noted, and it felt like a gift.

'You can give me some more style tips,' he said.

Was he flirting with her? It would be easier to read Sanskrit than work Sean out!

'For free? I should be charging.'

'Count it as payment in kind for the ride.'

'Oh, shit!' Tiffany exclaimed as Sean pulled up outside her parents' terraced house and she took in the sight of paps camped out on the pavement. It had never even occurred to her that the press would track down her family home.

She looked at Sean anxiously. 'My sister gets out of school in an hour, I really don't want her to see all this. And my step-mum's pregnant . . . the last thing I want is for her to be upset. What can I do?'

'I'll call some people . . . sort something out. Don't worry. First we've got to get inside. Stick close to me, and keep your head down.'

It was like preparing for battle. Tiffany put on her sunglasses again and then it was like a re-run of the morning as she and Sean pushed their way through the photographers who instantly realised who she was and started clicking away with their cameras. Thankfully there was a fairly long path up to the house and Sean made a point of closing the wrought-iron gate, and telling the paps he was quite prepared to call the police if they attempted to come through it.

Once inside he made several phone calls while Tiffany called her her dad, explaining the situation to him. They decided he would collect Marie and Lily-Rose from school, and hopefully by the time he drove them back, Sean would have some assistance.

'Cup of tea? Vodka?' Tiffany asked Sean when they'd both finished their calls. She was feeling slightly hysterical. She could see the lurking paps from the kitchen window. They really were something else.

'Hang on, I bet you never drink on duty,' she added.

'Tea would be great.' He sensed her feelings and reached out and touched her shoulder. 'Don't worry, I've got two of my lads coming over. They'll be here before your family's due back.'

He sat at the kitchen table. It had got warmer now and he had shed the leather jacket and sweatshirt and was down to a grey tee-shirt. Tiffany thought that her earlier assessment had been right; he was all muscle. She took in the curve of his biceps, his lovely muscular forearms. Phew! Perhaps she had better have a vodka.

Within an hour Sean's men had arrived, and Tiffany was feeling even more hysterical as both of them were dressed entirely in black and were huge man mountains. She had the urge to sing Will Smith's 'Men in Black', but Buster (what kind of name was that for a man? Surely that was a dog's name) and Graham didn't look like they would see the funny side. They refused her offer of a cup of tea and stood outside the front door, arms folded across their massive chests, looking menacing. At that rate, they would freak out Lily-Rose more than the paps.

'Were they in the army with you?' Tiffany asked Sean, from their vantage point in the kitchen.

'No, I met them when I came out. Not the brightest, but loyal.'

'And big . . . very big. They actually make you look quite small.' And she wanted to add, '*But I'm sure you've got better muscles*,' but resisted, as that made it sound as if she had been checking him out. And, yes, while she *had* been checking him out, she wasn't sure she wanted *him* to know that. But in spite of the bizarre situation, she realised that she was actually enjoying spending time with Sean.

She nipped off to the bathroom at one point to check on her appearance and was relieved to see that her make-up still looked good. But she added an extra layer of mascara, and put on a bit more blusher and sprayed on the final drop of Coco Mademoiselle.

By the time she was walking downstairs, her family had made it safely into the house.

'Bloody hell!' her dad exclaimed as he shrugged off his jacket and slung it on the banisters, a habit which drove Marie wild. 'I've never seen anything like it.

They're like wild beasts out there.' He caught sight of Tiffany. 'Are you OK, love?'

'I am now I know that you're all back.' She gave him a quick hug. 'Are Marie and Lily-Rose all right?'

'Yeah, they're in the kitchen with Sean.'

Marie was making him another cup of tea, while Lily-Rose was staring out of the window, fascinated by the photographers, and as Tiffany walked in she heard her step-mum say, 'Sweetie, why don't you go into the lounge and watch CBBC? I'll bring you a snack through.'

Lily-Rose was reluctant to leave until Marie bribed her with a packet of chocolate buttons. Then she turned her attention to Tiffany.

'We've been so worried about you. What an ordeal!' Marie enfolded her in a hug.

'I'm absolutely fine. I've been more worried about you and Lily-Rose.'

'No probs, babes, we had our own personal body-guard.' Marie looked over at Sean and Tiffany could have sworn that her step-mum had a glint in her eye.

'I felt all important and glam, like Whitney Houston in *The Bodyguard*, when Sean escorted us from the car.'

'Well, *please* don't sing,' Tiffany teased her, sitting down at the worn oak table opposite Sean. Marie was tone deaf but loved singing and adored belting out ballads, which cleared the room and terrified Minnie the cat.

Chris came into the kitchen. 'Will you stay for supper, Sean? It's the least we could do, to thank you for looking out for Tiffany.'

'I was just doing my job, but thanks. Supper would be great, I don't have to be in Sussex until tomorrow morning.'

'And how about a beer?' Chris continued. 'Tiffany, can you get Sean a beer? In fact, make that two, I'll have

one too. And now I have to think about what to cook.'
Chris rubbed his hands together; he loved cooking for
guests. 'How about seared salmon on a bed of
Singapore noodles?'

'Sounds good to me,' Sean replied. 'It beats the ready
meal I was going to shove in the microwave.'

'I'd have thought you would be into healthy eating.
My body is my temple kind of thing,' Tiffany commented, handing him a bottle of Bud and a glass. She
had poured herself a glass of wine.

'It's a temple I bet a lot of women wouldn't mind
worshipping at – myself included!' Marie commented,
and then clapped her hand over her mouth in embarrassment as Tiffany and Chris exchanged appalled
glances.

'I'm so sorry! It's my pregnancy hormones. I'm going
to check on Lily-Rose.' And Marie practically ran out of
the room.

'She's lived a sheltered life,' Chris joked. 'But you do
look as if you work out.'

Sean nodded, and Tiffany wondered if he was going
to mention the army. Instead he said, 'It's nice to have
a compliment from someone. I've had your eldest
daughter criticising my sense of style. It's too boring for
her apparently.'

'I wouldn't worry . . . she does that to everyone. And
I wouldn't mind, but her style isn't always on the mark.'

Tiffany glared at her dad and then looked at what she
was wearing – a flirty floral dress, toughened up with
her leather jacket and beige suede ankle boots.

'What's wrong with this? It's called fashion, Dad. You
know, the thing you were into about two thousand
years ago?' She swished her hair back. 'I'm so misunderstood by this family!'

'Well, maybe you'll be better understood by your new
family,' Chris bantered back.

He said it lightly enough but Tiffany wondered if he felt insecure about the whole Angel situation. 'No, I'm stuck with you, and that's fine by me.' She smiled at her dad, wanting to reassure him.

'Me too,' Chris replied, smiling back, then banished her and Sean out of the kitchen so he could cook in peace.

'You've got a great family,' Sean commented as he sat down on the sofa. Lily-Rose was upstairs playing and Marie was having a rest. Just as well, Tiffany thought. Who knew what else her hormonally charged step-mum would come out with...

'Yeah, I love them to bits.'

'Angel's very close to her family as well.'

'We both said how lucky we were not to be brought up by Tanya. I can't imagine how we'd have ended up if we had been.' Tiffany was sitting in her favourite chair – a comfortable scuffed brown leather armchair. She had kicked off her boots and tucked her long legs under her. She noticed that Sean was sitting up straight; he looked ready to spring into action at any moment.

'You can relax now, can't you?'

'Yes, I guess. Force of habit.' He sat back on the sofa. 'Sorry if I gave you a hard time when we first met.' He was staring right at her with those intense dark brown eyes. She could see part of a black dragon tattoo peeking out of his tee-shirt on his right shoulder. Tiffany did love a tattoo on a man's shoulder . . . well, a hot man obviously, not on some flabby fat bloke. She imagined tracing her fingers around the design, and as she stared back at him she thought that he definitely did have a body she wouldn't mind worshipping at. Whoah! She didn't even have the excuse of being pregnant.

She hastily sipped her wine then said, 'You seemed to think I was some kind of no-good slapper gold-digger when we met.'

He laughed. 'No way as bad as that! I was only doing my job, and you have to admit that a letter coming out of the blue would set alarm bells ringing.' He was actually apologising to her, but Tiffany wasn't sure that she wanted to let him off the hook so easily; she still remembered how judgemental he had been.

'Maybe you shouldn't be quite so quick to jump to conclusions about people.'

She expected him to defend himself, and was disarmed when he said, 'I'm sorry.' A pause. 'Forgive me?' And she was rewarded with another smile.

Yep, Sean Murphy was definitely a hottie . . .

Sean had to make some work phone calls after that to sort out security arrangements for the rest of the week, so Tiffany left him to it and wandered upstairs to see Lily-Rose. She ended up playing Angry Birds with her on her phone, but halfway through one level Lily-Rose suddenly stopped and said anxiously, 'If you're Angel Summer's sister, does that mean you won't be my sister any more?'

It hadn't even occurred to Tiffany that Lily-Rose would think this.

'Oh, sweetheart! Of course I'll always be your sister. Always, forever and forever.' She gave her sister a quick hug, then Lily-Rose cheered up and said, 'I'm going to whoop your ass on the next level!'

'Don't be so sure . . . and don't let Marie catch you saying that. She'll have your . . .'

'. . . guts for garters!' Lily-Rose finished with relish.

Neither Tiffany nor Lily-Rose knew what that expression meant, and Tiffany was pretty sure Lily-Rose didn't even know what garters were, but it was one of Marie's favourite expressions. Then Chris called them all to the table and the girls abandoned their game and headed downstairs.

Sean was already in the kitchen, insisting on setting the table, while Marie sat down. She still looked slightly embarrassed by her earlier comment and Tiffany thought it would probably be best not to mention it. But she would definitely store it up for future use – that was an all-time classic!

'You can come again,' Chris commented as Sean sorted out cutlery for everyone and poured out glasses of water. But if Tiffany thought that was the last moment he'd be put on the spot by a member of her family, then she was mistaken as Lily-Rose made it her mission to interrogate him with a set of random questions. Within a few minutes she had established what his favourite music was: The Killers and Elbow. His favourite animal: an orang-utan. His favourite holiday destination: Crete. *X Factor* or *Strictly*: neither. Every time Sean was about to raise his fork to his mouth, Lily-Rose would come up with yet another question.

'Let the poor man eat, Lily-Rose!' Chris exclaimed.

'Just one more,' his daughter pleaded. 'Do you have girlfriend?'

'No, not at the moment.'

'Why? What's wrong with you?'

Luckily Sean saw the funny side, and smiled. 'Where do you want to start?' A comment which was lost on Lily-Rose, who replied, 'You seem OK. Old but OK.'

And just as Tiffany was thinking that was surely the end of Lily-Rose's questions, she said, 'Tiffany hasn't got a boyfriend any more. She dumped Billy and we all really liked him. Maybe you could be her boyfriend? Unless you're gay. Daddy's second-best friend Richard is gay, and that's OK. He lives in Brighton. He always buys me ace presents. He bought me Justin Bieber.'

'Very generous of him,' Sean commented.

'Justin Bieber is her hamster,' Marie interpreted.

'So . . . are you gay?' Lily-Rose persisted.

Tiffany couldn't bring herself to look Sean in the eye, but heard him say quietly, 'No, I'm not gay.'

'Well then, you can definitely go out with . . .' But fortunately Marie intervened.

'That's enough, Lily-Rose, eat your dinner or you won't be able to go on that play-date tomorrow night.'

Another piece of blatant bribery that did the trick.

'Sorry,' Tiffany mouthed across the table to Sean.

'It's OK,' he mouthed back.

But Lily-Rose's questions had made Tiffany herself wonder if Sean could be boyfriend potential. If she could get him to loosen up more and be a little less serious . . .

They were all halfway through the meal when Sean's mobile rang. He checked the number and said, 'I'm sorry but I'm going to have to take this.' And he got up from the table and left the room, closing the door behind him.

'Can I just say, gorgeous!' Marie whispered excitedly. 'Lily-Rose is on to something. He would be a great boy-friend. Those muscles, those brown eyes . . . Strong but caring, brave and helpful around the house, *and* he's got a lovely motor.' The last comment was not serious as Marie had no interest in cars.

'I think we all know what you thought of Sean,' Chris said dryly.

'Ah, don't be insecure! You know I love you and only you. But I'm allowed to window shop, aren't I?'

Chris didn't get the chance to reply as the door opened then and Sean walked back in. 'I'm sorry to leave in the middle of dinner, but something's come up and I've got to drive to Sussex.' He had put his jacket on and looked serious.

'Is everything OK with Angel?' Tiffany asked, instantly worried for her.

'Yes, she's fine, I can't say any more than that.' He looked across at Marie and Chris and Lily-Rose. 'It was nice to meet you all. And thanks for dinner.'

Tiffany followed him out to the hall, suddenly realising that she didn't want him to go. ''Bye then,' she said at the front door. 'And thanks for helping us out today.'

'No problem. I'm sure the paps will be gone in a few hours. Any trouble, give me a call.' He handed her a card with his name and number on it.

And just as Tiffany was thinking that was it, he ducked down and kissed her on the cheek, and she felt the warmth of his lips and the graze of stubble from his face.

'Take care,' he said, opening the door.

'You too,' she replied, wondering when she would see him again and hoping it wouldn't be too long.

Chapter 11

Angel was in tears, pacing the living room. Could the day get any worse? This morning she had done a pregnancy test and it had come up negative. She had been so convinced that she was pregnant, certain that she had all the symptoms, it had been a bitter blow. Then the press had found out about Tiffany possibly being her sister and had blown the whole thing out of proportion, dragging up things from her past that she would so much rather forget. The paps had staked out the house, then followed her the whole day to and from work. She hated it when they did that. It made her feel like a hunted animal, as if she couldn't escape. She had come home, longing for peace, to be close to Cal and Honey . . . and now this.

She had been confronted by two detectives from the Met who had informed her and Cal that they had intelligence of a kidnap threat against her and Honey. A criminal they had been questioning about another crime had let the information slip.

'Come and sit down, Angel,' Cal urged her.

'Why us?' she exclaimed, spinning round to face her husband. 'Why do these horrible things keep happening to us?' God! Wasn't it enough that they'd had to cope with Simone Fraser stalking them, and threatening

Angel with a knife? She still had a recurring nightmare where Cal didn't make it in time to rescue her, and Simone stepped closer, that mad look in her eyes, the knife glinting in her hand as she thrust it into Angel over and over again . . .

While she was emotionally strung out and tearful, Cal by contrast was calm, rational, together. 'We're going to be fine,' he told her. 'Sean is going to review all our security arrangements. You and Honey will have full protection whenever you go out. There is nothing to worry about.' Now Angel did go over to him. She collapsed on the sofa next to him and he put his arms round her, holding her tight.

Sean had been silent while husband and wife reacted to the news but now he spoke. 'Cal's right, Angel, you will have round-the-clock protection. We have always taken your safety seriously. We just need to step it up a gear and be extra-vigilant.'

'Thanks,' Angel managed to say. She felt physically and emotionally drained. 'I trust you completely, Sean.' He nodded in acknowledgement, and then tactfully left the couple alone.

'See? Everything will be all right.'

'It's Honey I worry about. I don't want her childhood being ruined. It's not fair on her.'

Cal kissed his wife's head. 'It's not being ruined. She can do everything she wants to do, like any child her age. She just needs extra protection.'

Angel leaned her head on Cal's shoulder, trying to calm down.

'Anyway,' he continued, 'I thought we could do with going away for a week – just the family.'

'And our security team,' Angel added dryly.

'So I've booked a villa in Minorca. It's got its own private beach and is completely secure. And Gemma and Tony are going to come too, along with Jez and Rufus.'

'What about work? I can't just abandon the show.'

'I spoke to Oscar and he agreed it would be good for you to have a break. He's running a special diet and fitness series in your slot.'

Yet again Angel was grateful to her husband, who had done just the right thing to make her feel better.

'There's something else . . . we're going late tomorrow night.'

'What? But I haven't packed! You know how long it takes me to pack!'

Angel had been on so many foreign trips but she was still hopelessly chaotic and disorganised when it came to packing, always ended up taking far too much and didn't ever wear over half the things she took. A habit of hers which drove Cal – who was super-organised – mad.

'Yep, I do, which is why I've packed for you and Honey.'

'But you're bound to have forgotten something! I'll have to do it all over again . . .'

'Babe, anything I've forgotten we can buy out there. We're going to Minorca, not Outer Mongolia!'

Angel made to get up from the sofa to go and check what her husband had done, but he held her arm. 'You stay here and I'm going to bring you in a glass of wine and bowl of pasta and then we're going to watch a film – you can choose. And you can forget all about today.'

It was yet another of those moments when Angel wondered what she had done to deserve a man as wonderful as Cal.

'I can choose anything?' She had very different taste in films from her husband. He liked thrillers such as the *Bourne Identity* series, and while Angel appreciated the good looks of Matt Damon, she often found the plot confusing. She preferred a good rom-com. Cal wasn't keen and so usually she watched those films on a girls' night in with Gemma – not that there'd been so many of them since the arrival of Milo.

'Anything you like.'

'Anything?'

'Anything.' Cal insisted.

She smiled. Tempting as it was to make Cal watch a rom-com and see him struggle to stay awake, she would compromise. 'How about *The Hangover*?'

A look of relief on his face, Cal said, 'Are you sure you don't want to watch *27 Dresses*, *Made of Honor* or *He's Just Not That Into You*? I checked out the listings – they're all on tonight.'

'Not tonight.'

He smiled. 'I'll bring supper in.' At the doorway he paused. 'I swear everything's going to be all right, Angel.'

She wasn't sure it was, but she knew that Cal had done everything he could, so instead of voicing any further unease, she simply nodded and replied, 'I know. Love you.'

Chapter 12

Tiffany had believed, perhaps naively, that the press would have lost interest in the story by the next day. She spent the night at her parents' house. When she got up in the morning and pulled back the curtains in the tiny box room, she could still see a couple of paps lurking outside. She grabbed her dressing gown and padded downstairs to the kitchen where her dad was making Lily-Rose's packed lunch, while Marie was looking at something on her laptop and Lily-Rose was taking her time over her porridge. Her dad then fussed round Tiffany, making her tea, and scrambled eggs, even though Tiffany reminded him that she was perfectly capable of making breakfast for herself.

'I want to make sure you have something to eat before you go off to work. You had a stressful day yesterday and by the look of it –' he gestured out of the window at the paps – 'it might not be over.'

'It certainly won't be,' Marie said, and turned her laptop round. The screen showed the *Sun*'s website, dominated by a picture of Tanya, looking as rough as ever, with the headline, '*Why I Had to Give My Babies Up.*'

'Oh, God!' Tiffany groaned. 'Why did she have to do it?'

A pointless question she knew as the lure of easy money to Tanya, with her drug addiction, would have proved overwhelming. She quickly read the article where Tanya talked about how she had never wanted to lose her babies but knew that she wasn't fit to look after them. Inevitably the paper ran pictures of Angel and Cal, and there was a photograph of Tiffany coming out of her flat – thankfully not the one with her in her PJs. Tanya was also quoted as saying that Angel wanted nothing to do with her. It was so unfair, so intrusive.

'Teeth, Lily-Rose!' Marie ordered, and reluctantly the little girl got up and left the room.

'If that woman ends up dead with a needle in her arm then the press are responsible, giving someone like that money when they know exactly how she's going to spend it,' Marie said darkly. She looked over at Chris. 'Do you think there is any chance Tanya could be persuaded to go into rehab?'

He shrugged. 'I think it's too late for that.'

'What a waste of a life,' Marie said with feeling. She looked across at Tiffany. 'Are you OK, love? It's a lot to have to deal with. Why don't you phone that nice Sean and ask his advice? He was so helpful yesterday.' She smiled. 'And I think he liked you.'

'Not as much as you liked him!' Tiffany joked, remembering her step-mum's comment about Sean's body.

Marie blushed. 'I told you, that was my hormones.'

Tiffany let her off the hook. 'Anyway, I'm sure he was just doing his job.'

'No, it was more than that. He didn't have to bring you here, and he did. Go on, phone him.'

But Tiffany shook her head; she didn't want to seem like a weak little girl, who couldn't sort out her own life. She wasn't used to asking for help with anything.

'I'm fine, I don't need to involve anyone else. And I'd

better hurry up and get off to work or I'll be sacked from another job.'

'I'll give you a lift to the station. I'm not having you walk there with that bunch of animals outside,' Chris told her.

It was a nightmare journey to work. The paps crowded round as she tried to get into her dad's van. Her dad didn't want her to go to work at all after that, but Tiffany insisted. It wasn't as if she loved her job, but no way was she going to let the press dictate how she lived her life. The paps even pursued them to the station on motorbikes and surrounded the van when she got out. *For God's sake!* she wanted to shout. *Have you really nothing better to do?*

All the way in on the train Tiffany was paranoid that people recognised her from the press stories and were staring at her. She pretended to be riveted by the contents of *Grazia* but actually wasn't taking in a single word. She pulled out the card Sean had given her. Maybe she should text him to say thank you?

She reached for her phone and typed a quick message. *Thanks for yesterday, I really appreciate all you did for me and my family. Hope everything OK with you.* She hesitated at the end. Should she sign off with a kiss? She would with anyone else. It wasn't like her to be so indecisive, but it was because she cared about what Sean thought of her. She ended up going for a smiley face, and before she could change her mind pressed Send. She shoved the phone back in her bag, but couldn't resist checking it every few minutes. A big fat nothing from Agent Murphy. She was glad she hadn't left a kiss. In fact, she was actually looking forward to getting to work and putting everything else out of her mind for a few hours.

But a couple of paps were staking out the gym when

she turned up and immediately started taking pictures when they realised it was Tiffany. Arghhh! Was there no escape? She pushed through the double doors and fled into the office where Kara was already at work at her computer. She stopped what she was doing as soon as Tiffany walked in.

'Babes! Are you OK? You've been in the papers and everything. There was even a phone-in on 5 *live* about meeting up with your long-lost siblings that Harley heard where they mentioned you. You're famous! Are you going to do any interviews?'

Tiffany sat down on the chair at the next desk. She felt exhausted and the day had barely started. 'It's a nightmare, Kara. I don't want all this, I didn't choose it.'

Sensing that her friend was not sharing her excitement about suddenly being thrust into the limelight, Kara switched to sympathetic mode. She made Tiffany tell her everything that had happened, called up a couple of the personal trainers in the gym and asked them to go outside and make sure the paps didn't come in, and fetched her a coffee.

'I'm sure it will be easier once you know either way whether you and Angel are sisters. Why don't you stay with me until it's all sorted?'

Tiffany gratefully agreed. She had not been looking forward to going back to her flat and battling her way through the paps yet again. She could feel a tingling above her lip, a sure sign that a cold sore was imminent, brought on by the stress. That was all she needed: to be photographed with a huge scab on her face! She scrambled through her bag for a tube of treatment cream and saw that her phone was flashing with a message.

Agent Murphy had replied to her text: *Any time. And sorry I had to leave during dinner, tell Chris it was delicious.*

Hope you're OK and that the press aren't bothering you. Give me a shout if they are. I'm here to serve. S x.

Yay! She'd got a kiss! Suddenly things didn't seem to be quite so on top of her.

Tiffany took her coffee into the changing rooms and got into her uniform – a hot-pink polo shirt with the gym logo on the front, and black tracksuit bottoms with pink piping down the sides. Kara had designed the uniform herself, and had refused to take any of Tiffany's style tips on board. Kara's own work uniform was the polo shirt plus a pleated skirt and pink court shoes. Tiffany had told her she looked as if she was a cheerleader or about to star in a production of *Grease* as a pink lady, to no avail. Kara wanted the gym to be fun and glamorous and actually, Tiffany had to hand it to her, it did have a more fun vibe than other gyms.

She quickly sent off another text message to Sean, telling him what was happening with the paps and that she was staying with Kara. *Here to serve, Agent Murphy?* she ended cheekily. *You're so macho! x*

That's just the way I am x, he texted back.

Throughout the day, the two of them sent text messages back and forth to each other – a running commentary on what they were doing, who they had seen – each message getting ever so slightly more flirtatious.

'He must fancy you,' Kara said, when the two girls were on a break and had nipped upstairs to the coffee and juice bar.

Tiffany sipped her berry smoothie to avoid answering.

'And you fancy him, don't you? I can tell,' Kara continued. 'You've got that look when you mention his name – all dreamy-eyed – and you can't stop yourself from smiling.'

'Might do.'

'Why don't you ask him over tonight? It could be to say thank you for helping you yesterday.'

'And you could get a good old look at him!'

Kara twirled a strand of her hair and tried to act nonchalant. 'Maybe. Come on, send him a text now.'

'What if he says no?' Tiffany wasn't used to feeling so feeble around men.

'He won't. Send the text.'

Tiffany flipped through the clothes in Kara's wardrobe and despaired. She hadn't gone back to her flat and so was having to borrow something from Kara – but did her friend possess *anything* that wasn't pink or another pastel colour?

'He'll be here in a minute,' Kara commented from her position on the bed where she was painting her nails – pink.

'What am I going to wear? Everything is pink! It's just not me.' Sean's acceptance of the invitation had thrown Tiffany completely.

'Oh, for God's sake, wear my pink-checked shirt, my white skinny jeans, and pile on the eyeliner to give it some edge. I thought you were supposed to be the stylist!'

'White jeans? I'm not Liz Hurley.'

'I doubt Liz Hurley shops at New Look, which is where I got that pair. Pull yourself together.' Kara got up and stuck her head out of the door. 'It's an emergency situation, Fireman Harley. Can you pour Tiff a wine? Make it a large one.'

Grudgingly Tiff found the clothes Kara had recommended and put them on. Her friend was on the money – the pink gingham top was sexy without being slutty, and the jeans fitted perfectly. She did as Kara had suggested with her eyes, putting two swoops of eyeliner on the lids, plus lashings of mascara, and nicked some of Kara's pink blusher to give her cheeks a flush. After that she slicked gloss on to her lips. Several large sips of wine and she was feeling more relaxed, though when the doorbell rang the butterflies leaped into action. It was funny because she had been texting Sean throughout the day, but now she suddenly felt shy.

'Hiya,' she said as she opened the door to him. He looked fresh from the shower. He also looked very sexy in a black tee-shirt, jeans and leather jacket.

'Hi.' He handed her a bottle of wine, and ducked his head to kiss her on the cheek. And then it was all about introducing him to Kara and Harley, getting drinks for everyone, ordering pizza.

'I very much approve!' Kara whispered when Harley and Sean were talking.

So do I . . . Tiffany reflected, looking over at Sean. He caught her eye and smiled back. She experienced that inner glow you get when you know someone likes you. She felt as if everything around her had become sharper, brighter, better . . .

Sean was so relaxed and easy-going with her friends – there was no sign of his uptight serious side tonight. She wondered what had called him away the night before, but didn't feel she could ask him in front of everyone.

'So does she try and give you two makeovers?' Sean asked Kara and Harley.

'I'm a lost cause and she knows it,' Harley replied. 'I'm either in my uniform or in jeans.'

'Yep, I gave up on Harley a long time ago,' Tiffany replied.

'Are you suggesting I need a makeover?' Kara demanded, tonight in a pink floral playsuit, with a pink rose in her hair.

'She might look pretty in pink but she's well scary,' Tiffany warned.

'You look great,' Sean said quickly. 'And, Tiffany, I didn't think you would wear pink, but it suits you.'

'Well, enjoy it because I'm unlikely to wear it again. Tomorrow it's back to black when I go and pick up my own clothes.'

'OK,' Sean said, looking at her over his glass. 'I would offer to come with you to the flat, but I'm flying to Spain later tonight with Angel and the family.'

'Oh.' Tiffany couldn't help feeling disappointed. 'How long are you away for?'

'A week. It was a last-minute thing. I could do without it, to be honest, as I was supposed to be seeing my daughter.'

Of course then Kara had to ask him about Maya, even getting Sean to show them a picture of a pretty blue-eyed little girl with light brown hair, which left Tiffany wondering what Sean's ex-wife looked like.

'You must have missed her when you were away in the army,' Kara commented. Tiffany had to hand it to her friend, who was asking all the questions she herself would secretly have liked the answers to.

'It was one of the many reasons why I left.' Sean didn't elaborate further, and even Kara got the message that this was not something to press him on.

The pizza delivery then arrived and conversation took a lighter turn – with Sean asking Tiffany about her dad's cooking ambitions, and if she thought he should try for *MasterChef*. Tiffany had been sitting cross-legged on the floor. When she uncurled her legs to get up, she was seized with cramp. 'Ahh!' she wailed, clutching her toes. The sophisticated, sexy image was all gone in an instant as her face contorted in pain.

Sean quickly moved beside her and took over rubbing her feet. He soon managed to get rid of the cramp, and Tiffany would have been happy to have him massaging her feet all night – the man had a magic touch.

'I learned how to do reflexology,' he commented.

'Did you? I would have thought that wasn't manly enough for you.'

'Tiffany – you criticised me for jumping to conclusions about you, but it seems to me that you're guilty of doing just that with me.'

He still had his hand over her foot. Out of the corner of her eye Tiffany saw Kara beckon Harley out of the room, ostensibly to clear away the pizza debris.

'You're right, but that's the image you put out.'

'Do you have a problem with that?' he asked quietly, pressing a finger against the back of her big toe, which seemed to be releasing the tension from her shoulders. 'D'you only like metrosexual men?'

Phew! Tiffany was having difficulty in concentrating. Sean's proximity, the feel of his hands on her skin, were interfering with her ability to think straight. 'I don't have a type,' was the best she could come up with. OK, she would be brave and go for it now. 'Do you?'

He shook his head. 'Nope, I just know who I like.' He smiled at her and released her foot. 'Better now?'

'Much,' she replied, already missing his touch.

He checked his watch. 'I'm going to have to go.'

Another goodbye at the door, and a promise that he would text her. Another kiss on the cheek – frustratingly as Tiffany would gladly have kissed him properly! But he was interested, wasn't he? Maybe he just wanted to take things slowly. She could live with that, couldn't she? It was kind of old-fashioned. Romantic. Sweet.

Chapter 13

So it was official. The DNA results had come back. She was Angel's sister. Angel's agent had issued a statement to the press, stating the facts and requesting that the two of them be left in peace to come to terms with the news. Some chance of that! Tiffany thought, as she had to battle her way through the paps yet again this morning when she left the house. She was travelling down to Sussex to have Sunday lunch with Angel, Cal and their daughter. It would be the first time the two sisters had since their tea at The Ritz and Tiffany wondered how they would get on now that they knew the truth.

She got out at a small picturesque country station, complete with white wooden fences and scarlet geraniums blooming in containers. Finally summer had arrived. It had taken its time as it was mid-July, but here it was, offering up a hot cloudless day, with a bold blue sky.

Angel had promised to pick her up from the station, which was just as well as there was no such thing as a taxi rank in this tiny place. But as Tiffany stepped outside, instead of Angel there was Sean leaning against the Merc. Instantly Tiffany had an attack of butterflies. He looked so handsome, cool even, in a white tee-shirt, jeans (better fitting than his last pair) and a pair of Aviator Ray-Bans – perhaps he was sharpening up his style sense? And he was tanned from the week in Minorca.

'Hi, Sean,' she said, trying to sound casual.

'Hi, how are you?' he asked. Tiffany couldn't help feeling slightly disappointed that he didn't kiss her. Not even a kiss on the cheek.

'Good, thanks.' A comment which hardly covered her confused emotions – anxiety about meeting Angel's family and seeing her again, nervousness and excitement at coming face to face with Sean. The flirtatious texts had continued between them while he was away, but now she felt shy.

He opened the passenger door for her.

'Steady on,' Tiffany joked, 'I could get used to this life of luxury.'

'All part of the service.'

It was only a short drive to Angel's house so maybe that explained why there was no banter between them. Sean was quiet, professional. It was hard to imagine him sitting at her parents' kitchen table and answering Lily-Rose's stream of questions; harder still to imagine him in Kara's flat flirting with her. He seemed like a different man. He glanced over and said, 'I have something to tell you, which has to remain confidential.'

Sean looked so serious that Tiffany wasn't even tempted to joke that her lips were sealed. She nodded instead.

'Angel and Cal received intelligence from the police just over a week ago that there has been a kidnap threat against them. Specifically against Angel and Honey. I had to check with them first that it was OK to tell you, which is why I didn't mention it before now.'

'Oh my God! How scary. Do the police know who it is?'

'They've got a good idea, I can't say any more than that. So they've had to step up security, with round-the-clock protection. That's why I picked you up, rather than Angel. She can't go anywhere on her own at the moment.'

So it wasn't because you wanted to see me? Tiffany thought, and again there was that flare of disappointment. She had been looking forward to seeing him again, but maybe it wasn't a feeling he shared.

'I understand. You can trust me not to say anything,' she told him.

'I know.' And finally Sean smiled. OK, it was a small smile, but at least it was a smile.

He turned down a private road, past several enormous houses or rather mansions. Tiffany gazed at them, thinking of her own tiny studio flat and of her parents' small terraced house. At the end of the road, beyond a high red-brick wall with some vicious-looking spikes on top of it, and set in several acres of land, was a stunning Edwardian house. Tiffany thought it looked like the setting for a lavish TV costume drama. Her nervousness at seeing her sister again increased as Sean keyed a code into the security pad by the front gate, which slowly opened. She noticed two CCTV cameras mounted on the fence, monitoring every visitor.

An impressive drive swept up to the house, bordered with perfectly pruned shrubs. There were immaculately mown lawns, beautifully maintained flowerbeds, blazing with colour, and a flash of blue from the swimming pool. Yet again Tiffany felt as if she was entering a different world, one that she was ill equipped to deal with. She clutched her bag anxiously as Sean parked the car, and tried to joke, 'We're not in Kansas any more.'

'You'll be fine,' he said, catching sight of her slightly strained expression. 'I'll see you later.'

And there it was again, disappointment that she wouldn't be seeing him for longer.

A little girl, who must be Honey, opened the door to Tiffany. She was clearly going to be a beauty like her mother, with long dark brown curly hair framing a heart-shaped face. She had inherited her father's olive skin and stunning brown eyes.

'Hi,' Tiffany said.

The little girl looked at her solemnly then answered, 'Hi, I'm Honey.'

Tiffany stepped through the door and found herself in an impressive entrance hall lit by an enormous glittering chandelier. The hall was so vast there was room for a hot-pink velvet sofa, a mirrored glass table, a life-sized bronze sculpture of a woman which Tiffany was pretty sure was modelled on Angel, and a large Pop Art-style canvas of Angel and Cal. It still didn't look at all cluttered.

'Hiya!' Angel came racing along the corridor, dressed casually in a white Juicy Couture tracksuit and silver Havaiana flip-flops, her blonde hair worn in two plaits. Instantly Tiffany felt overdressed in her red vintage-style tea dress and high red suede sandals, but she didn't do tracksuits, not even in her own house, never mind someone else's!

Angel quickly kissed her, then said, 'Come on through to the kitchen and meet Cal. You look lovely, by the way. Sorry to be in my trackie, but I always end up slobbing out at home.'

Tiffany handed over the small bouquet of flowers she'd brought, which looked even smaller in this vast house, and tried to tell herself that it was the thought that counted. 'Pink roses . . . my favourites,' Angel said warmly.

Tiffany followed her down the elegant hallway, the

108

oyster-coloured walls of which were hung with photo-graphs of Cal, Honey and Angel. They passed a huge dining room that could seat at least forty, a spacious living room, with the largest plasma-screen TV mounted on the wall that Tiffany had ever seen, and ended up in a state-of-the-art designer kitchen/dining room, overlooking the garden, which was filled with sunshine streaming in from the French doors and the glass roof.

It was a kitchen Tiffany's dad would have absolutely loved, with its vast stainless-steel double oven, black granite work surfaces, and glossy white units. Chris was always complaining about the lack of space in their tiny kitchen, which was straight out of the seventies with its Formica surfaces, brown units and orange tiles. Now Tiffany felt particularly shy as the handsome man standing by the oven came over and introduced himself as Cal.

Like she didn't already know! She would have to have been living on the moon not to know who Cal Bailey was!

'Hi,' she said shyly as he kissed her. Cal Bailey had kissed her! Kara was going to combust with jealousy!

'It must feel a bit strange coming here,' he said, sensitive to her feelings.

'Just a bit,' Tiffany admitted. *Like the strangest thing that had ever happened to her!*

'Well, take a seat and let me get you a drink – wine, beer, water?'

Tiffany hesitated, not wanting to have an alcoholic drink unless they were.

'She'll have a glass of wine, like me, babe.' Angel replied for her. 'So come and sit down. We've got so much to talk about.'

And very quickly Tiffany stopped feeling self-conscious. Angel and Cal might be wildly famous, live in a mansion and be millionaires, but they were completely down-to-earth and friendly.

'D'you still think Tiffany looks like me?' Angel asked Cal after they'd eaten delicious mixed antipasti of roasted peppers with pesto, a green bean salad, olives and freshly baked focaccia. He admitted that he had bought it from a deli, otherwise Tiffany would have been even more impressed by him than she already was. The man had been a genius footballer, was stunning-looking, *and* he was making seafood risotto.

Cal considered Tiffany. 'Definitely. It's the eyes and the mouth. And you both wave your hands around when you're talking.'

'It's the weirdest thing, isn't it?' Angel said to Tiffany.

'It is,' she agreed.

'I always wanted a sister,' Angel said. She raised her wine glass. 'Here's to you, sister.' They clinked glasses together and smiled at each other.

'That reminds me, I've got something for you.' Angel stood up and wandered over to a tall pink dresser, where she picked up a white bag with the Chanel logo on it. 'It's just a little gift,' she said as she handed it to Tiffany.

'Oh, but I haven't got you anything.' Instantly Tiffany felt embarrassed, though she had no idea what she could have bought Angel, who could no doubt buy herself anything that she wanted.

'You brought me flowers.'

Tiffany opened up the designer bag to discover a selection of Coco Mademoiselle products: perfume, bath oil and moisturiser.

'Thank you, that's so nice of you,' she said. 'I'd just run out of my Coco Mademoiselle perfume.' She nearly added, *And I can't afford to buy any more*, but just stopped herself in time. She didn't want them to think she was angling for anything else.

110

Everyone had finished the first course by then and Cal stood up and began clearing away the plates. Instantly Tiffany got up to help.

'Can you call Sean to let him know the main course is ready? He said he was too busy to join us for starters,' Cal asked Angel.

Tiffany lowered her eyes, not wanting to let on how pleased she was about that news.

Angel reached for the house phone and made the call.

'He'll be over in five.' She stepped through the open French windows on to the terrace and stretched her arms up towards the sunshine. 'It's so hot . . . almost as hot as it was in Minorca. We should hang out by the pool after lunch.' She looked back at Tiffany. 'I can lend you a bikini, if you like.'

'Yeah, she's only got about a thousand to choose from,' Cal teased.

Angel walked back in. 'A hundred and fifty actually.'

Tiffany had two bikinis.

'What kind of saddo counts their bikinis?' Cal asked, but he was smiling at his wife.

Angel rolled her eyes. 'Claudia, the stylist, wanted to do a piece about swimwear so we ended up going through my things.' She looked over at Tiffany. 'The point is, I've got plenty to choose from.'

Thank goodness Tiffany had had a full-scale removal of body hair that morning . . . how mortifying would it have been if she hadn't? And she had painted her toe nails. In fact, she was pool ready.

She was helping Cal bring the plates over to the table when Sean walked in. 'Can I do anything?' he asked.

'Just get some beers out for us, could you?' Cal asked. 'And more wine for the ladies.'

Honey held her glass up.

'Ha-ha, very funny, Honey. Apple juice for you.'

'She's so well behaved,' Tiffany commented to Angel, marvelling at the way the five-year-old had sat so nicely at the table and eaten everything that had been put in front of her without any fuss.

Angel smiled. 'You should have seen her first thing, having an epic tantrum. So now she's on her best behaviour, otherwise we've said we won't be taking her to Disneyland Paris for her birthday.'

'Sit next to me!' Honey piped up as Sean came over to the table.

'She adores Sean,' Angel whispered. 'Which is just as well as we all see so much of each other.' She sighed, and for a moment looked anxious.

'I know Sean told you about the thing . . . we can talk about it later.' And then it seemed as if she tried to shake off the negative feeling. 'So have you forgiven him for stalking you?'

Tiffany glanced over at Sean. 'I guess, seeing as how he was so good to my family with the press. But I still think he wasn't being very clever, letting me see him that time in the restaurant and at The Ritz.' She tilted her chin up as if challenging him.

'Believe me, if I hadn't wanted you to see me, you wouldn't have,' Sean replied. 'After all, you didn't see me that time at the gym or in Tesco.'

'How can I be sure that you were following me in Tesco?'

'You bought a packet of spaghetti, a jar of pesto and a bottle of Pinot Grigio. Oh, and a packet of Jammy Dodgers.'

Well, at least it hadn't been pantie liners! She couldn't decide if Sean was teasing her or whether he was slightly annoyed that she seemed to be suggesting his skills weren't all they should be, in front of his employers. But then Cal was serving up the seafood risotto and everyone's attention turned to that and complimenting the chef.

Sean mainly talked to Cal during the meal, while Angel and Tiffany chatted. Angel wanted to know more about Tiffany's stylist ambitions. The star was so easy to talk to, Tiffany reflected, and just as she was thinking that, Angel said, 'It's funny, I don't usually make friends easily, but I feel so relaxed with you . . . as if I've known you for years.'

'I was thinking just the same!' Tiffany exclaimed. The connection that she had felt when she first met Angel was growing stronger.

The two women smiled at each other and then Angel totally floored Tiffany with her next comment. 'How would you like to come and work on the show as a stylist? We really need to shake things up, and I think you could well be the person to do it. You could work alongside Claudia. She's always moaning that she has too much to do.'

'Really?' Tiffany could hardy believe what she was hearing. It was an amazing offer.

'Yeah – I'll have to run it past the producers, but why don't you come in on Tueday and see how it all works out? We can take it from there.'

This could be Tiffany's big break, the one she had dreamed of, but she felt slightly awkward as she knew she was only getting this chance because of the connection to Angel. 'Are you sure people . . .' by that she meant the other stylist '. . . won't be put out? And think that I'm only there because of being your sister?'

Cal and Sean had overheard their exchange and Cal commented, 'Welcome to the world of showbusiness! But seriously, Angel wouldn't want you to be part of the show if she didn't rate you. You would get the job on your own merit.'

'OK, I just don't want anyone to think that I'm some

kind of free-loader. I will make it as a stylist, even without this break.' She caught Sean's eye as she came out with her feisty comment and thought he looked as if he approved of what she'd said.

Cal and Angel smiled, and she said, 'That's what I thought.'

'You sound exactly like Angel . . . stubborn and determined,' Cal added. 'And I mean that as a compliment.'

After lunch Angel took Tiffany upstairs to her dressing room. Once more Tiffany was overawed by the sheer size and luxury of the house . . . a grand wooden staircase swept up to the first floor, past walls hung with a series of vintage James Bond posters; the cream carpets were so thick she felt as if she was sinking up to her ankles in them; everywhere the paintwork gleamed freshly. Angel paused outside what was obviously Honey's room. The little girl actually slept in a white four-poster bed that was shaped like a castle! One entire wall had a mural painted on it with *Toy Story* characters, there was a beautiful wooden rocking horse, what looked like the entire collection of Sylvanian Families, complete with houses and furniture. How the other half lived . . . Lily-Rose had one family of Sylvanian hedgehogs and Marie had worked so hard to make her tiny bedroom look pretty.

Angel's dressing room was also something else. One entire wall was mirrored, floor-to-ceiling, and the other walls all had sleek white fitted wardrobes and drawers. Angel went round the room clicking open the cupboards to reveal the crystal-embellished evening dresses, the everyday dresses, shorts, mini-skirts, every variety of shoe from Converse to Jimmy Choos, and an entire two shelves devoted to her collection of UGGs. She seemed to have a pair in every colour – even silver. She also had one entire wardrobe devoted to jeans and hoodies, and another to tracksuits. 'I love my casual clothes,' she admitted.

'And here are the bikinis.' She pulled open five drawers packed with swimwear. 'Take your pick!'

Tiffany looked at the array of colours and styles. She wasn't used to having this much choice. But then her stylist instincts kicked in and, after some deliberation, she plucked out an emerald green halterneck top and matching briefs. It was best to keep it simple.

'I'm not sure if it will fit,' she commented, holding it against her. She was a 32B/C and a dress size 10, whereas Angel was at least two cup sizes larger and probably a size 8.

'Oh, it will. I think that top's too small for me anyway. I'll leave you to try a couple on. Grab anything else you want, like a kaftan or maxi-dress.'

She paused in the doorway and looked back at Tiffany. 'I'm glad you're my sister. It feels right. I guess we've got something to thank Tanya for after all.'

Tiffany smiled back at her, 'I feel the same. And I meant to say earlier, is everything OK? Sean didn't give me any details . . . you know how discreet he is.'

Angel sighed. 'I really thought we were through the bad times, but it seems as if there is always something or someone to look out for. But I'm not going to obsess. Sean has got the security in hand and I trust him completely. If I start worrying then it will take over, and I can't have that. It's bad for all of us and especially Honey, and I want to keep everything as normal as possible.' She managed to smile, 'Anyway, enough! I'll meet you by the pool.'

Tiffany waited until Angel had left the room before stripping off and trying on the bikini. The green accentuated her eyes, as she'd thought it would, and surprisingly the top fitted, as did the bikini bottoms.

Tiffany cast a very critical eye over herself as she looked in the mirror, turning this way and that. She breathed in, fiddled with the halterneck straps, slicked on a fresh layer of lip-gloss. Fleetingly she wondered if Sean would be by the pool. She just bet he looked good in trunks . . .

By the time Tiffany made it out to the stunning infinity pool surrounded by green-and-white-striped sun loungers and matching parasols, Honey was already in the water, performing an impressive front crawl.

'She's a complete water baby,' Angel commented from her position on a sun lounger. She was wearing a white bikini and could easily have been one of the Bond girls from Cal's posters. Tiffany suddenly felt self-conscious next to Angel with her effortless A-list beauty and sexy curves. She felt pale and not that interesting. Damn! she thought as she compared her pale limbs to Angel's golden-brown skin. She should have had a spray tan!

'How's the bikini?' Angel asked as Tiffany perched on the lounger next to hers.

'Fine, thanks. I just feel a bit pale next to you.'

'That's because I've been on holiday. You look good pale – it suits you. But maybe you want to borrow this?' Angel held up a bottle of sun cream that Tiffany gratefully took. There was only one thing worse than being pale and that was being sunburned.

'It's so beautiful here,' she commented, taking in the view: the garden, the orchard, the horses grazing in the fields beyond. Imagine owning all this.

'I know. We're so lucky to have it. I've always loved the countryside. I love the city too but I don't know if I could live there any more.'

'I think I'm more of a city girl but I can understand why you love it here.'

116

'You'll probably change your mind when you have children.' Angel replied.

'I'd have to get a boyfriend first!' Tiffany joked.

Angel turned to look at her. 'I can't believe you haven't got one. You're so beautiful.'

Tiffany shook her head. 'I don't think so! Anyway, to be honest, I want to concentrate on work.'

That comment raised a smile from Angel. 'Ah, but a bit of romance wouldn't hurt, would it? Is there really no one you're interested in?'

At that an image popped up in Tiffany's mind of Sean and how nice it would be if he was lying by the pool next to her. But she could hardly confess this to Angel, so she shook her head and said, 'No one at all.'

It was relaxing chatting to Angel in the sunshine and they discussed the television show. Angel wanted the women to be styled in a way that fitted their lifestyles – which was exactly what Tiffany thought. 'And it's often more about raising their self-esteem and making them feel good about themselves. So many of the women we have on are down on themselves, they hate their bodies and don't want to draw attention to them. It's sad.'

Then their conversation was cut short when Honey insisted that Tiffany get into the pool with her. It was impossible to be self-conscious when playing sharks with a five-year-old. Tiffany chased her around the pool, and the little girl squealed with delight. She was mid-game when Cal and Sean turned up.

'Honey, I hope you're not pestering our guest.' Cal said, sitting on the lounger next to Angel. 'Feel free to stop any time, Tiffany,' he added.

How typical that Sean should have turned up now when Tiffany was sure her mascara would be running down her face. And her fringe was probably all over the place.

'It's fine, honestly. I'll do five minutes more and then I'd better think about getting back to London.'

'I can give you a lift, if you like,' Sean put in.

Tiffany wiped the water from her face as she looked over at him. He was standing up, arms folded across his chest – his on-duty look. She caught another glimpse of the dragon tattoo. It was a tempting offer, but maybe he was only offering out of a sense of duty.

'It's OK, I can get the train.'

'Sean's going back to London anyway, Tiffany, and the trains will be slow. Take the lift,' Angel advised.

It would surely have been churlish to protest any more.

Sean went to brief the other security guy. So no chance to see him in his trunks, how disappointing . . . It must be the sunshine and the wine she'd had at lunchtime making her feel so frisky. Tiffany closed her eyes as she relaxed for a few minutes more on the lounger, loving the feeling of the warm sun on her skin, while Angel and Cal played with Honey in the pool. Tiffany felt as if she was in some kind of dream and any moment now she would wake up. Here she was in the grounds of a mansion, just a few feet away from the UK's most famous and photographed couple. Angel Summer, *the* Angel Summer, was her sister and Cal Bailey, *the* Cal Bailey, was her brother-in-law!

Chapter 14

The traffic was solid on the drive back to London, nose to tail on the M25. But Tiffany didn't mind because she wasn't sitting in a packed train, being forced to listen to other people's mobile phone conversations and breathe in the smell of their fast-food choices. Instead she was in a luxurious air-conditioned car that carried the expensive scent of leather. And, more importantly, she was enjoying spending time with Sean. Away from Angel and Cal, he was considerably more relaxed, back to being the Sean she felt she was getting to know.

'That was nice of you to play in the pool with Honey,' he commented as they finally turned off the M25.

'She's such a sweetheart, it was no problem.'

'So you like kids?'

Tiffany wondered if he was asking because he had a daughter and wanted to know her view on children? But most likely she was reading too much into the question. 'I'm used to them because of Lily-Rose, but yeah, I like them.' She paused. 'So when are you next seeing Maya?'

And then she cursed herself as Sean looked serious again. 'Next weekend. It's difficult with work and everything, though Cal and Angel are really understanding.'

It was clear to Tiffany that he didn't want to talk about his daughter as he turned the subject back to her, asking how she felt the day had gone.

'I think it went OK, don't you?'

A smile. 'More than OK, it's obvious that they both really liked you. And you and Angel already seem to have a strong bond.'

Tiffany appreciated his positive words because she still felt pretty overwhelmed by recent events. 'It is weird. I mean, you've seen where my family lives . . . it's like going into a different world visiting them. I keep thinking I'm going to wake up and it will all have been a dream and I'll be back to working in that pizza restaurant.'

'I'm sure it's strange for you, but for all their wealth and fame, Angel and Cal have got their feet firmly on the ground. That's why I like working for them. And it's good news about the stylist job, isn't it?'

'It's absolutely gobsmackingly brilliant!' Tiffany declared. 'I am nervous about it, though. I really don't want people to think I'm only there because of Angel.'

Another smile from him. 'I'm sure you're very talented . . . even if you were completely wrong about my style.'

Tiffany liked his teasing tone very much. She turned and looked at him. 'Sean, you have no sense of style. Well, apart from the leather jacket and Ray-Bans, and I see you have got some new jeans. You're desperately in need of a makeover. I could take you shopping . . . point out what you should be wearing. I'd be doing you a massive favour.'

'Don't be so cheeky, young lady. I'm older than you, and I've never had any complaints before about my style or lack of it.' He grinned. 'Anyway, it's what's underneath that counts.'

Tiffany smiled but couldn't think of a comeback because, yes, it was underneath that counted and she was pretty certain that Sean was doing fine in those stakes!

'I still think you could do with a makeover. How about we go shopping one day next week? Even you must get time off sometimes? You can't be on duty *all* the time.'

'OK, I'll check my schedule. And how about we seal the deal by having a drink tonight?'

Better and better! 'Sure, we could go up to a pub in Highgate that I know. I think they'll just about let you in dressed like that.'

Sean shook his head but Tiffany sensed he was enjoying the flirtatious banter as much as she was.

And the banter continued over a drink. In place of the reserved, serious Sean, Tiffany discovered someone who laughed a lot, teased her, flirted with her and made her feel brilliantly alive, as if they were both living purely in the moment. They talked trivia about their favourite TV series and films – she loved *True Blood* and *Little Miss Sunshine*, he went for *The Sopranos* and *The Shawshank Redemption*. They were serious when he asked her about Tanya and what it was like meeting her birth mother. Often Tiffany would gloss over the details to other people, but she felt she could confide in him. He seemed to understand that she felt sorry for her mum, even as she struggled to comprehend how she could have abandoned her own children. They became more flirtatious when they talked about their first kisses – hers, aged twelve, with Darren Walters, when he bit her lip; his, aged eleven with Samantha Green, who was a good two years older than him.

'What can I say? I've always liked an older woman,' Sean replied when Tiffany teased him about being a toyboy.

Damn! She hoped he liked younger women too . . .

'So, you're not seeing Billy any more? No more friends with extras?' Sean was gazing at her with those intense brown eyes of his. Did the question signal that he was interested himself? She really hoped so . . .

'Nope. We're just friends now. No extras.' She paused and sipped her wine. 'It was a mistake seeing him for so long, but I guess it was a habit. Not a very good one.'

Sean shrugged. 'We've all been there.'

And Tiffany was dying to ask, did he have a friend with extras? But felt that she couldn't without betraying quite how interested in him she was.

By now the pub had called last orders. 'Come on,' Sean said, standing up, 'I'll give you a lift home.'

'It's OK, I can walk.' She was still thinking about his friends with extras comment. When in doubt, back off.

He held out his hand. 'Don't be silly, of course I'm giving you a lift. Remember, I'm here to serve.'

Outside the temperature had dropped and Tiffany shivered in her silk dress. Sean took off his leather jacket and draped it round her shoulders. It felt like an intimate gesture and she could still feel the warmth of his body.

'See, my clothes have some uses after all,' Sean said, smiling at her.

'The jacket I like,' Tiffany replied, pulling it round her. 'I might have to keep it. But then I'd be depriving you of your one stylish item, apart from the Ray-Bans, and that would be cruel. You'd be forced to wear that totally uncool sweatshirt.'

By now they had reached the car. Sean opened the passenger door for her and said quietly, 'Like I said, it's what's underneath that counts.'

Phew! Tiffany didn't feel cold any more. Instead she was suffused with a warm glow of anticipation about what might happen next . . .

It was only a short drive to her place, during which time she decided that she was definitely going to ask Sean in for a drink and maybe something more . . . She tried to remember what state she had left her place this morning. She had been in a panic about what to wear and recalled leaving a pile of rejected outfits on the bed. With any luck she could shove them all into the wardrobe before he noticed.

Sean turned into her road, and managed to find a parking space outside her flat.

'You're so jammy!' she commented. 'If that had been me, I'd have been driving round for ages looking for somewhere to park. Is it one of your Special Agent powers to be able to park anywhere?'

But Sean didn't seem to be listening; instead he was looking over at the house.

'Is the front door usually left open?'

'Oh, someone probably forgot to close it behind them. It happens all the time. I'm sure it will all be recorded on CCTV.'

She had meant the last comment as a joke because of course the rundown house didn't have CCTV! But Sean didn't smile. Serious again. It was like going one step forward with him, two steps back. Every time she thought he was loosening up, he would retreat again.

Tiffany turned to face him. 'Thanks for the lift. D'you want to have a coffee? A glass of wine?' *Hot sex?* Because that's the way her thoughts were running now . . .

'First I want to check that everything's OK in your flat.' Super-serious now, not a hint of flirtation. And she had so wanted to kiss him! God, he was paranoid! What could be wrong?

Sean even insisted on leading the way up the stairs to the third floor – perhaps he wanted to show off his toned bum, Tiffany joked to herself as she walked behind him. Was there no part of him that wasn't toned? But the smile was wiped from her face when they reached her front door, or rather what used to be her front door as it was hanging from its hinges.

'What the hell?' Tiffany exclaimed.

But Sean held up his hand and whispered, 'Stay here, let me take a look first.'

He walked stealthily into the flat while Tiffany leaned against the wall and tried to work out what could have been taken. It wasn't as if she had anything much of value. She scrabbled around in her bag – fortunately her iPod and phone were there. Fortunately she was wearing the diamond eternity ring that had been her gran's. That just left the laptop and the TV. Bollocks! She didn't have any insurance and who knew when she would be able to replace them? She couldn't stay outside any longer; she had to see what had been taken.

She walked into the flat and froze. The place had been completely ransacked. Her clothes were strewn across the floor, it looked like some of them had been ripped, the duvet had been slashed along with the pillows, her framed *Vogue* covers had been knocked off the wall and broken, along with the framed postcards of clothes from the V&A she had collected for inspiration.

Her sandals crunched against the broken glass. It was going to take ages to put everything right. She suddenly remembered the one other piece of jewellery she owned: a Tiffany charm bracelet, a present from Marie and her dad for her eighteenth birthday, and one of her most precious possessions. She raced over to the wooden jewellery box on her dressing table. The charm bracelet was gone. Every charm on it had meant something to her; every one of them had been saved up for either by her family or by her. She would never be able to replace it. She spun round and now her gaze fell on the small plasma TV, which had been a Christmas present from her dad. The screen had been slashed. Then she saw her laptop – it had been dumped in the kitchen sink and the sink had been filled with water.

'Why would anyone do this!' she exclaimed, reaching out to pick up a photo album, the pages of which had been ripped out, though thankfully the photos were intact. She could feel her eyes brimming with tears. It felt as if someone had deliberately set out to cause her as much distress as possible. Her home had been violated and it was as if the person who did it was saying, 'We can do anything we want, you are worthless.'

'Don't touch anything.' Sean warned her. 'The police will need to fingerprint the scene.' He caught sight of the distraught expression on her face and instantly stepped over the broken glass and put his arms round her, pulling her close to him. 'You're OK, nothing's going to happen to you, I promise.' He gently tilted her face up and brushed away the tears. 'I'm going to call the police. Why don't you phone Kara and arrange to stay there tonight?'

'She's away this weekend,' Tiffany sniffed.

'You can stay with me then. There's no way you can stay here.'

Before she had discovered the break-in, Tiffany would have experienced a rush of butterflies at the thought of staying at Sean's. Now she felt exhausted, as if she'd gone ten rounds or run a marathon . . . well, a half-marathon. She supposed it was the shock. All she wanted to do was crawl into bed, pull the duvet over her and go to sleep. The day had gone from one extreme to the other and she could hardly take it all in.

The police came pretty quickly. Maybe Sean had been able to pull some strings. Once she had given a statement to a friendly male PC, he suggested she leave with Sean. There was nothing more to be done and Tiffany was longing to get out of her ruined flat. Sean arranged for someone to fix the door and then they were once again in the car, this time heading for central London. Heart FM was playing on the radio but Tiffany felt disconnected from the familiar love songs. She was still wearing Sean's jacket but even with the car's heating blasting out, she was cold.

'Why did someone do that to my flat? They took my charm bracelet but they left everything else.'

'I don't know,' Sean replied. 'The police may have some idea once they've checked the forensics. But there may be no real reason. It could easily be a random attack. Kids messing about.'

It hadn't felt like that. It felt like someone really wanted to hurt her.

Tiffany didn't know what she had been expecting Sean's place to be like but she certainly hadn't been pre-pared for the ultra-modern penthouse flat by Chelsea Bridge, with its spectacular views of the Thames. There was even an outside terrace, large enough for a table and chairs. It must have cost a fortune! Tiffany wandered over to the huge windows and took in the view – it was dark by now and London was lit up before her, with the river a black silken ribbon reflecting the lights.

'The flat belongs to Cal and Angel,' Sean said as if reading her thoughts. 'They wanted me to be located somewhere central.'

'It's lovely,' Tiffany said, moving away from the window and sitting down on one of the soft-as-butter leather sofas.

'Here, drink this, it'll make you feel better.' Sean handed her a brandy.

Tiffany didn't like brandy but still obediently took a sip, and then coughed as the liquid burned her throat.

Sean switched on the plasma-screen TV, then he was busy sorting out the spare bedroom. He did everything so efficiently, it must be his army training, she supposed, thinking of her ex-boyfriend Billy who was hopeless at anything practical. She curled up on the sofa and flicked through the channels, unable to concentrate as every few minutes she would think of her ruined possessions. She had nothing left. It felt as if all the happiness of the day had been snatched away from her.

Sean came back into the living room and held out his mobile, 'Angel wants to speak to you.' It was on the tip of Tiffany's tongue to say that she didn't want to speak to anyone, but she took the phone. Angel was full of concern for her, wanting to know if she was OK. Wearily Tiffany replied to her questions about the state of her flat and how she was feeling.

'I've got an apartment overlooking Hyde Park . . . you must move in there. I don't want you going back to that place,' Angel told her.

'It's OK, I'm sure I can stay with friends.'

'I want you to be safe and that apartment has got great security. Please Tiffany, I sort of feel responsible for what happened.' She sounded genuinely upset.

'Why do you say that? It was just a random break-in, wasn't it?'

Angel sighed. 'We're not so sure it was. It seems too much of a coincidence that it should happen after it was revealed that we are sisters. And that along with the kidnap threat . . . well, put it this way, we want to know that you are safe.'

Tiffany saw that she wouldn't be able to persuade Angel to change her mind, and she felt too exhausted to argue, so she ended up agreeing. She finished the call and flopped back on the sofa. She supposed she should phone her dad but didn't want to freak him out. It could wait until the morning.

'Can I get you something to eat?' Sean asked. 'I'm going to make a sandwich.'

Tiffany shook her head. 'I'm not hungry.'

He walked over and sat down next to her. 'You've had a shock, but it'll be OK. Angel's got a nice surprise for you tomorrow.'

'What's that?' Tiffany felt as if she was done with surprises.

Sean shook his head. 'That'll spoil it. So, what do you want to do? Watch a film? Go to bed?'

Tiffany must have been feeling subdued because she had no wish to banter back with, Is that an offer?

'I'm really tired, but I don't know if I could sleep yet.'

'How about a glass of red wine, and we'll watch a DVD?'

She nodded, just wanting someone else to make the decision for her.

Red wine after the brandy must have knocked her out because *Inception* had only been on for half an hour when Tiffany found herself falling asleep. Her head jerked up as she struggled to stay awake.

'Come on,' Sean said, 'I'll show you your room.'

He reached for her hand and practically pulled her up from the sofa. It felt as if he could easily have picked her up. He led her to the spare bedroom, which had its own en suite bathroom, and pointed out the new toothbrush.

Did he have many overnight visitors? she wondered once he had said goodnight.

Tiffany had a shower and brushed her teeth. The hot water revived her, and she found the energy to peek into the bathroom cabinet where there were two more new toothbrushes, some Nivea face wipes and a bottle of Gucci perfume. Had they been left by his ex-wife, or ex-girlfriend, or friend with extras? She used the wipes to remove the last traces of her make-up, then remembered the bag of Chanel goodies and rubbed on some of the Coco Mademoiselle body lotion to cheer herself up. Then she pulled on the tee-shirt Sean had thoughtfully left out for her and climbed into bed.

But sleep eluded her even though she was exhausted. She turned this way and that, tried to focus on all the things that made her happy, did one of her favourite tricks of creating outfits for the people she knew – a chic little black dress for pink-loving Kara; a navy-and-white polka-dot prom dress to showcase Marie's curves and get her step-mum away from her uniform of jeans. But nothing worked and Tiffany became more and more wound up. She kept thinking of her flat and of the unknown person going through her things and deliberately destroying them. Why would anyone do that? It was such a cruel act. Why hadn't they simply taken the few things of value? Why destroy everything? The questions kept going round and round in her head, on a loop. And she was still cold, chilled to the bone. Suddenly she wished Sean was with her. It had felt so good when he'd held her.

Finally she threw back the duvet and wandered into the kitchen to get a glass of water. She had the fright of her life when, just as she was running the tap, she heard Sean say, 'Are you OK?'

She spun round. He was leaning against the door-frame, dressed only in a white vest and black boxers. Even feeling as upset as she did, she still registered how good he looked . . .

'Sorry, I didn't mean to wake you. I couldn't sleep.'

'I'm not surprised, it's been a hell of a day. Why don't we talk in the lounge?'

She followed him into the room and curled up in a corner of the sofa.

'I keep thinking of my flat . . . of someone in there, wrecking all my things,' Tiffany said quietly. 'It was like someone hated me, but how can that be?' She looked at Sean, her beautiful green eyes brimming with tears.

'I don't know. It could be someone who is jealous of your connection to Angel, or it could be someone who wanted to hurt her, by hurting you.' He sighed. 'There are some nutters out there, I'm afraid.'

The tears spilled out of her eyes then, 'Today was so good . . . and then that. I feel like it's ruined everything.'

'It doesn't have to. Come on, where's the feisty, opinionated girl I was getting to know?'

'She's been crushed,' Tiffany said miserably.

'That could never happen, that's why I like you. You're tough, you'll get through this.'

He put his arm around her and Tiffany leaned against his shoulder. Suddenly she felt hyper-alert to his touch and the feel of his body against hers. She put her arms around him. He felt so good, so strong . . . she couldn't resist slipping her hands under his vest, feeling his smooth warm skin. She was crossing a line, but she couldn't stop herself. The moment seemed charged. It wasn't comforting she wanted . . . she wanted him. And it seemed as if the feeling was mutual as Sean lightly kissed her neck and then his lips touched hers. A kiss that began tenderly, slowly, built up and became deeper, hotter, more insistent . . . A kiss that said, *I want you*. And she did, so much.

They lay back on the sofa. She ran her hands down

his back, pressed her body against his and knew he was as aroused as she was. But then Sean was gently pulling away. 'I'm not sure if this is a good idea right now, after what you've been through.'

It bloody was a good idea! The best! Tiffany looked up at him. Her cheeks were flushed and her lips felt swollen from their passionate kisses. He stroked her hair, seeing that she was about to protest, 'Come on, you need to sleep. I'll stay with you.' And he lay beside her and put his arms round her. Even though Tiffany was convinced that there was no way, absolutely no way she could go to sleep, she found herself lulled by the warmth of his body. There was always the morning . . . she'd find a way of waking him up . . .

The curtains were open and both of them were bathed in the orange glow of a lit-up London. Tiffany felt suspended in time, away from everything. For the first time since the burglary, she felt protected; felt that everything was going to be all right, more than all right. She sighed and snuggled closer to Sean. Maybe a bit of deferred gratification would make the moment all the sweeter. It felt so right to be lying next to him, so close she could hear him breathing. Yes, everything was going to be all right . . .

Tiffany woke up hours later as sunshine streamed through the window. A duvet had been laid over her, but Sean was no longer beside her. She sat up feeling disorientated.

'So you're finally awake?' Sean walked into the room. Unusually for him he was dressed in a smart dark suit. He looked even more handsome in it and she was about to comment on it, and ask him teasingly if he'd had a secret makeover, but his expression stopped her. He had his serious face on again. Tiffany felt at a distinct disadvantage, sitting there in a tee-shirt. She most likely

131

looked like crap. Sean set down a cup of tea on the table next to the sofa.

'I hope it's OK but I have to take you to the new apartment within the hour, then I'm at an event all day with Angel and Cal.' He avoided looking at her and instead gazed out of the window. He was being so formal, as if they didn't know each other, as if last night hadn't happened. As if he hadn't kissed her like he meant it . . .

Tiffany was feeling more and more awkward.

'Sure,' she mumbled, 'I'll have a shower. It won't take me long to get ready.'

WTF was going on! Last night she was convinced that he had been as attracted to her as she was to him! She wasn't making it up. You couldn't make that kind of thing up. It had been the most erotic, passionate kiss of her life! Now he was behaving like a complete stranger. She quickly got dressed and put her make-up on in record time. When she emerged from the bedroom, Sean was already waiting by the front door.

'All set?' he asked.

She nodded.

'Are you warm enough? Do you want to borrow my jacket?'

Tiffany was feeling cold again, but the moment for wearing his jacket seemed to have passed. 'I'm fine,' she said. 'Are you?'

Sean avoided eye contact. 'I'm fine thanks, Tiffany. I just have a lot on at work and would appreciate it if we could get off.'

'I'm not stopping you,' she replied. And she opened the front door and marched out, feeling horribly hurt by his distant treatment of her.

Sean was silent on the drive over to the apartment. Any minute now, he'll say something, Tiffany told herself, or I should say something, ask him why he's being so standoffish. To pretend last night hadn't happened seemed ridiculous. But he didn't say anything and her courage failed her.

The luxury Hyde Park flat was stunning. In contrast to the sleek minimalism of the riverside flat, this one was like a baroque palace, thick carpets, heavy silk curtains, impressive fireplaces in the rooms, gilt-framed mirrors and pictures, chandeliers, a marble bathroom. But Tiffany couldn't focus on any of it, because she was still caught up in wondering what the hell was going on with Sean. Only when he had briefed her on the security features, handed over the keys and was about to leave did he finally mention what had happened. 'About last night . . .' He looked awkward, standing by the front door, not making eye contact.

She stared right at him, a defiant look on her face, arms folded across her chest. She was damned if she was going to say anything.

'I shouldn't have allowed it to happen.'

From the way he was talking it sounded as if she had jumped on him! Whereas she was pretty sure it had been entirely mutual. For a moment Tiffany was too shocked to speak and then she burst out with, 'You make it sound like I forced you to kiss me!' She glared at him. 'You really know how to make a girl feel good about herself.'

He shook his head. 'Of course I wanted to kiss you, you're a beautiful woman, but I shouldn't have. It was unprofessional. I shouldn't have taken advantage of you after the shock you'd had and . . .' he hesitated. 'I don't have room in my life for relationships at the moment.'

Oh, God! Tiffany sensed that she was going to cry. This was awful, toe-curlingly embarrassing. He had

133

kissed her, held her, all night, but now he was rejecting her.

Somehow she managed to hold it together. She shrugged. 'Nor do I. And thanks for doing your job so well last night.' She was aware that her voice was wobbling slightly. If he didn't get the hell out of the flat, she would lose it altogether. She was deeply hurt, but she had some pride. She wasn't going to let him see.

'It was really no big deal. And I'm not some damsel in distress, you didn't take advantage of me.'

He still could barely look her in the eye, and suddenly Tiffany wanted to hurt him as much as he had hurt her. 'Though, to be honest, I probably was a bit drunk.'

Hah! He didn't like *that* comment. Super-serious, I'm-just-not-that-into-you Sean couldn't stop himself from flinching.

She shook back her hair. 'I'm cool with everything. So you can go off to your event now. You've done your duty.' She gave a mock salute, 'Thanks again, Agent Murphy. Over and out.'

He looked at her as if he wanted to say something else but Tiffany had heard enough. 'I'm fine.' Her code for, Go right now.

He reached into his jacket pocket and pulled out an envelope, which he handed to her. It felt bulky. What now?

'This is from Angel. That surprise I told you about . . . I'd better go. Any problems, anything at all, please call me.'

Tiffany waited until she was absolutely certain he must have left the building, then she shut herself in the bathroom, sat down on the expensive marble floor, leaned against the Victorian-style bath and burst into tears.

Chapter 15

Some time later Tiffany opened the envelope and discovered it contained a thousand pounds in crisp new twenties and a note, which Angel had clearly dictated to Sean. *So sorry about what happened, Tiffany. Please accept this money and buy yourself some new clothes. Angel x.*

A thousand pounds to spend on clothes! It was unreal. And if Sean hadn't given her the monumental brush-off, Tiffany knew she would have been leaping around the room in delight. As it was, she couldn't help feeling awkward, as if she was somehow being paid off. She stuffed the money into the envelope. She would buy herself some cheap clothes and give Angel the money back.

Next, she had a phone call to make to her dad. He was stunned and upset to hear about the break-in and wanted her to move back home right away. But Tiffany managed to calm him down and reassure him that she was OK. She wasn't, but no way did she want to worry him.

'I promise I'll be fine, Dad, please. They didn't take anything of any real value. I was wearing Gran's ring.' She didn't go into the full details of how the flat was trashed nor could she bear to tell him about the loss of the Tiffany bracelet.

But her dad brought it up. 'What about your charm bracelet?'

She swallowed her tears. 'That's gone, I'm afraid.'

'Oh, well, we'll all start saving for another one. And tell that Sean to look after you or he'll have me to answer to,' her dad tried to joke, but Tiffany could tell how shaken he was.

'This apartment has got great security, honestly. CCTV and everything. I feel totally safe.' She skirted round saying Sean's name.

She then had to call Kara's dad, and tell him about the chance she had to work with Angel. He was typically sweet about it. 'Never quite saw you as a receptionist, Tiff.'

There was no point in her arguing with that, and they parted on good terms.

She quickly repaired her make-up and headed out of the flat. Within minutes she found herself walking along Old Bond Street, an incredibly posh street with many high-end designer stores. Round the corner from her flat in Archway was a pound shop, a Chinese takeaway, a fried chicken takeaway and a pawn-broker's. Here there was Yves Saint Laurent, Chanel, Dolce & Gabbana, Prada and Tiffany & Co. She stopped outside the iconic jeweller's, which always made her think of her dad as he had named her after his favourite film, *Breakfast At Tiffany's*. She wondered if she should go and buy a replacement charm bracelet with the money from Angel, but much of her joy in her original bracelet had been in the way it had been created over time.

Her mobile rang. It was Angel. For a second Tiffany hesitated, almost not wanting to speak to her. She felt too raw after what had happened with Sean, but then she took the call. It wasn't Angel's fault that she had got herself in a mess.

'I hope you're busy shopping!' Angel said. 'And make sure you get a couple of outfits you'd be happy to be filmed in.'

'Sure, will do.'

'Are you OK after last night?'

For a mad moment Tiffany thought that Angel must know about Sean, then she realised that she was talking about the burglary.

'Fine, thanks. And thanks for letting me stay in the flat. It's amazing.' She knew she sounded subdued. Angel must think she was very ungrateful.

'It's a bit OTT in its design,' Angel admitted. 'We haven't had chance to decorate yet. Just treat it like your home, put up your pictures, invite over whoever you want. I'd better go. I'll see you tomorrow . . . I'll email you the directions.' Then she added, as if she had sensed Tiffany's unease about the money, 'And *please* spend the money I gave you, I want you to have it. And if you feel funny about it, count as a down payment for your work on the show. I mean that.'

Angel was perceptive, Tiffany had to give her that, she thought as she continued along Old Bond Street. Maybe it wouldn't hurt to buy a couple of outfits, for work. She dialled up Kara's number, hoping she would have returned from her weekend away. 'Hey, are you free to meet me in town? I've got loads to tell you.'

'OMG! I don't believe it!' Kara exclaimed. The two girls were having lattes upstairs in Caffè Nero on Regent Street. 'I go away for one weekend and your whole life changes! You get offered a brilliant job, have the cash to buy yourself a brand-new wardrobe, move into a luxury pad, meet a gorgeous man and—

'Get burgled, don't forget that,' Tiffany interrupted dryly. 'And get dumped by the man before I've even gone out with him. That must be some kind of record.'

'To paraphrase Ronan Keating, "Life's a bit of roller-coaster and you've just got to ride it".'

Tiffany stuck her tongue out then said, 'I would be embarrassed to quote a Ronan Keating lyric.'

Kara shrugged. 'It seems to fit the situation. So why do you think Sean went all funny? I thought he was dead keen on you when I saw him the other week. All those looks he gave you, that sexy foot rub, the kisses.'

'And all those flirty texts he sent me . . . it doesn't make sense.' Tiffany dipped her croissant into her latte, 'He said he didn't have time for a relationship, which I'm not sure I believe. I guess he didn't like me that much, or else he's already got a girlfriend.'

Kara gave her a sympathetic look. 'I think you've got to put the bad shit behind you and focus on the good, like the job with Angel.'

Tiffany knew her friend was right, but it was hard not to brood about Sean. She couldn't help feeling hurt. She had *really* liked him and she had thought he liked her. She wasn't usually wrong about men, but it appeared she had got Sean entirely wrong.

'OK,' she replied, sounding much more optimistic than she felt. 'Let's write down what clothes I should get for the show.'

'Yay!' Kara said gleefully, and the two girls spent a very contented twenty minutes going through some ideas.

Because Angel's show was all about styling ordinary women, on fairly low budgets, Tiffany thought it was only right that she should buy her clothes from the high street. So they hit Topshop, French Connection, River Island and Miss Selfridge, then Office for shoes. Tiffany bought a tea dress, prom dress, a playsuit, a maxi-dress, a pair of jeans, a pair of shorts, a couple of cardigans, a black blazer, scarves and jewellery. She shuddered when she thought about someone rifling through her things and bought a whole new selection of underwear from M&S. She was sorely tempted to hit the designer stores but remembered her brief to keep it high street. By the end of her spree she still had £300 left and decided she would buy some clothes for Lily-Rose and baby things for Marie.

By four o'clock they were all shopped out and made their way back to Tiffany's Hyde Park apartment. 'Bit different from the Archway Road,' Kara remarked as they walked along the über-upmarket Mount Street. 'Isn't that Scott's over there?'

She pointed over to the opulent seafood restaurant, a favourite celebrity hang-out.

'Yes to both. And wait until you see the apartment,' Tiffany replied.

Kara's reaction did not disappoint. Her friend exclaimed over everything, running excitedly from room to room. 'This is awesome!' she yelled from the bathroom. 'I love those Victorian baths! And you've got gold taps and a marble floor!' She grew even more excited when she discovered the four-poster bed in the main bedroom. She hurled herself on to it and lay back and declared, 'I've always wanted a bed like this! It's like a princess bed!' And Tiffany realised this was what her own reaction should have been like, if only the burglary and weird thing with Sean hadn't happened.

'You and Harley are welcome to stay any time. In fact, why don't you stay over tonight? We could get a takeaway.' Tiffany was not looking forward to a night on her own. 'And you can have the four-poster.'

'That would be so fab! It will be like having a mini-break! I'm going to call Harley right now.'

While Kara went off to make her call, Tiffany padded around the bedroom sorting out her new clothes. She wondered if anything from her flat could be salvaged. Angel had told her to put up her own pictures, but all of them had been ruined in the break-in. She sat down on the bed and for a moment felt exhausted all over again and unable to summon any excitement for the stunning job offer and the beautiful apartment.

Kara wandered back in. 'He's going to come over around seven. And I think we should nip out to an offie – if they have such things in this posh area – to buy a bottle of champagne to celebrate your new life with.'

'I quite liked my old life,' Tiffany said gloomily. 'And I bet there won't be an offie.'

'Oh, babes!' Kara declared, sinking down on the bed next to Tiffany and putting an arm round her. 'You need to cheer up! In your old life, you didn't have a proper job – I know how much you hated working at the gym, so don't pretend. And no offence but your studio flat was horrible. It was freezing in winter and boiling in summer, and the walls were so thin you could hear your next-door neighbours having sex. *And* you were stuck in a rut with Billy. However upset you are about what happened with Sean, at least you're out of that rut. Come on!'

Tiffany managed a smile. Kara was being so sweet, trying to cheer her up, and there wasn't an ounce of jealousy in her friend. She was genuinely thrilled for Tiff.

'You're right, that flat was shit, I hated it! And the stylist job is great. And I needed to move on from Billy, and Sean obviously has issues.'

'See? All positive. Now come on, girlfriend, let's go and find some champagne or cava, depending on how much money I've got. Cava probably.'

'I'm getting this.' Tiffany reached for her bag. 'I've still got some money left over, and we are having champagne!'

*

'Oh, look,' Kara commented as they reached the entrance hall. 'You've got your own personal mail boxes . . . how cute! Why don't you see if you've got anything?'

'I doubt it,' Tiffany replied dubiously, but she found what looked like the right key on the key-ring and slotted it into the lock of the steel box with the number 5 on it. To her surprise there was an envelope inside addressed to her. She ripped it open to discover a key and a note. The note was from Sean. In spite of all her good intentions she still experienced a fluttery feeling when she saw it was from him, but as it was a completely businesslike letter, that feeling soon vanished. *Hi Tiffany, hope you are settling into your new place. Here's the key to your old flat. Best wishes, Sean.*

'Best wishes my arse!' Tiffany muttered, showing the letter to Kara. 'Could the man be any more uptight?'

'What's he supposed to say? Forget about him, Tiff. Come on, let's find that offie.'

Tiffany took a deep breath and inserted the key into the brand-new lock of the brand-new door of her studio flat. She was feeling out of breath and slightly panicky as she pushed the door open, dreading that the scene of devastation would upset her all over again. But to her surprise the flat had been completely cleaned up. The broken glass was swept away; the clothes were folded up neatly on the sofa in two piles, one for the items that were still intact, the other for the ones that had been ripped. The pictures had been stacked on the coffee table, along with the photo albums, and the broken TV and laptop had been removed. Tiffany wondered who had been responsible. It was not likely to have been the police. Could it have been Angel?

Even though there was now no sign that the flat had been burgled, Tiffany still felt nervous being there. She quickly packed a suitcase with the clothes that were OK, her books and photo albums and shoved the torn clothes into a bin bag, along with the duvet and pillows. She wanted to get out of there as soon as possible.

It was only when she was in the taxi that she called Angel to thank her for arranging to have the flat cleared.

'Don't thank me! Thank Sean. He did it. Insisted on doing it himself actually. He's such a sweetheart, isn't he? D'you have his number?'

Damn, now she would have to be in contact with Sean again. Tiffany spent a few minutes dithering about whether to phone or text him. She opted for a brief text thanking him. It was probably the coward's way out, but Tiffany felt that where she and Sean were concerned, from now on, less was more. He replied straight away to say that it had been no problem and that he hoped she was OK, and repeated his offer that she could call him if she was worried about anything. There was no kiss when he signed off.

She imagined he thought that would be unprofessional, and of course he didn't want to give her the wrong impression. Just to prove that she most certainly didn't have the wrong impression about their relationship, she didn't reply and deleted his text.

Tiffany had other, more important things on her mind right now. Tomorrow she was starting her new job so that was what she would focus on.

Chapter 16

Tiffany stood outside Angel's dressing room and tentatively knocked on the door.

'Enter!' A male voice called out. Tiffany opened the door and found herself in the middle of what seemed to be complete chaos. A very tanned blond man was rushing around brandishing a set of straighteners; Angel was standing in the middle of the room in her bra and knickers; and a very sulky-looking blonde, whom Tiffany recognised from the TV show as Claudia the stylist, was flicking through a rail of clothes, so violently that Tiffany was surprised they didn't fly off the hangers.

'Welcome to the madhouse!' Angel exclaimed, and walked over and hugged Tiffany. She was totally unselfconscious about parading around in her underwear, but then, Tiffany reasoned, if she had a body like that, she would be too. Angel's stomach was taut and toned. You would never know that she'd had a child. She had the body of a woman ten years younger.

'Let me introduce you to everyone. Jez, my hairdresser . . .' The tanned blond put down his straighteners and walked over to Tiffany. He gave her two kisses. She was getting used to this style of greeting. 'But you are too, too cute! So *bellissimo*! I love the fringe . . . love the brunette hair! Maybe you should go brunette again,' he said over his shoulder to Angel, who rolled her eyes and said, 'But, darling, I'm a natural blonde.'

'Your bush would tell a different story, if only it was there,' he quipped.

'Jez!' Angel exclaimed, but she was smiling. 'And this is Claudia.'

Claudia paused in her frenzied flicking, gave a nod and muttered, 'Hi.' Oops! Someone did not look pleased to see Tiffany. She wasn't exactly sending out welcoming vibes . . .

'And this is Darcy, my make-up artist.'

'Hiya,' Tiffany said, to a cheerful-looking redhead. She was feeling quite over-awed to find herself in a star's dressing room, in the heart of a TV studio. 'So what should I do?'

'For now, I think you should just watch and see what goes on,' Angel replied.

'And you could get some coffees,' Claudia put in, as she held up a dress to get Angel's approval. 'I'll have a skinny latte, and please make sure they use skimmed milk and not semi-skimmed. They always get it wrong, and how hard can it be!'

Angel frowned and Tiffany had the feeling that Claudia was skating on thin ice. 'Tiffany isn't here to do that, Claudia. If you're desperate for a coffee, go and get it yourself.'

Claudia slammed the dress back on the rail. 'Fine, I'll do that. Does anyone else want one?' She stood there, hands on hips, pouting. Tiffany thought she looked like a model – all long limbs and attitude. Her clothes were certainly designer – an ivory chiffon shirt, beige silk shorts that showed off her slim brown legs, and high tan wedge sandals that Tiffany adored but guessed were way out of her price range.

No one did, and Claudia flounced out of the room.

'Saucer of milk for the stylist?' Jez commented.

Angel sighed. 'She feels put out because I've asked Tiffany in to work with her. I've told her so many times that she needs to relax the style for the people on the show, but she doesn't listen to me. I think she sees herself as an "artiste", too good for day-time TV.'

Jez's comment reflected Tiffany's train of thought. 'Then why the hell have you still got her, Angel?'

Another sigh. 'I don't know. I suppose I really hate confrontation, and the producer recommended her. And—'

Jez cut her off – he must know her really well, Tiffany thought, to be so outspoken. 'And she's not right. It's your show, your shout. You've given her enough chances.'

'Well, she's on her last one.'

They stopped talking when the door opened and Claudia walked back in with her skinny latte. Tiffany wondered if she guessed they had been talking about her and would have felt sorry for Claudia if the woman hadn't kept shooting her such evil-eye looks. She watched as Claudia selected a leopard-print wrap dress for Angel in a clingy silky material which Tiffany would have steered well clear of. Was Claudia deliberately trying to make Angel look bad? Well, as bad as you could ever make someone who looked as beautiful as she did. The dress made Angel's bust look enormous, out of proportion against her slender frame. Overall it looked cheap.

Angel grimaced as she considered herself in the mirror. 'I don't know if I like it, Claudia, it doesn't seem very summery or day-time.'

Claudia curled her lip. 'Leopard-print is very now.'

'It was very autumn/winter *last* season, I thought,' Tiffany couldn't help coming out with.

That earned her a glare from Claudia. 'And you know a lot about fashion do you, Tiffany?' She pronounced 'Tiffany' very deliberately, as if mocking the name. 'Were you named after the *EastEnders* character?' she added.

'Actually, after the film. Surprised? Did you think it would be something more downmarket?' Tiffany had forgotten all about being polite and simply observing. Claudia was a bitch and a bully, and Tiffany wasn't going to sit back and be walked over by her. Tiffany always stood up to bullies. She saw Angel and Jez suppress smiles as Claudia continued to glare at her.

Tiffany continued, 'Don't you think Angel should be going for something more casual?' She turned and considered the rail of clothes, picking out a pair of tight khaki combats, a white vest, and a sheer cream blouse with a butterfly pattern. She grabbed a pair of high gold sandals. 'I think this would look summery and hip.'

'Love it!' Angel declared, while her stylist glowered in the background. 'How's Jayne getting on next-door?' she asked Claudia. 'Jayne is the woman we're styling today,' Angel explained to Tiffany.

'Fine, so long as she can stay away from the pies long enough to fit into her dress. There's only so much control underwear can do.' Claudia wrinkled her perfect little nose. 'I don't know how some women let themselves get so fat.'

Wow! That was off-the-scale bitchy! Everyone looked stunned by the comment and Tiffany wondered how Angel would reply. But she didn't get the chance as there was a knock at the door and when Angel called out, 'Come in,' a forty-something woman, dressed in a white fluffy robe, her auburn hair in Carmen rollers, marched in with a thunderous expression on her face.

'Jayne, is everything all right?' Angel asked.

'No, it bloody well isn't!' came Jayne's blunt reply, in

a strong Liverpool accent. She pointed over at Claudia. 'She keeps giving me the most God-awful clothes to wear. She's got no idea what a middle-aged woman, size 16 with a bit of a flabby stomach, would want to wear!' She pulled open the robe to reveal a black tunic dress that did absolutely nothing for her figure.

'I'm supposed to be going on a romantic date with my husband, but I look like I'm going to a funeral! And I'm not going on TV dressed like this.'

Everyone looked at Claudia, who shrugged. 'I did the best I could.' She was so arrogant!

'Well, I think we can all agree that your best isn't good enough for Jayne,' Angel said quietly, but she was clearly furious and there was a steely look of determination in her eyes. 'And I will not have the guests on my show being treated like this.' She turned to Tiffany. 'What would you want to put Jayne in?'

Talk about being put on the spot! Tiffany took a deep breath. 'First of all, I'd want to find out from Jayne herself the kind of look she is aiming for.'

'Classy and sexy. Not mutton,' Jayne replied.

Tiffany tried to block out Claudia who wore an expression of utter disdain on her face as she focused on Jayne.

'Jayne, you've got a great figure. I love your curves. So which parts of your body are you most happy with?' Tiffany asked her.

She grimaced. 'I want to say I don't like anything, but as I have to – I'd go for feet and boobs.'

'And problem areas?' Though Tiffany had already guessed the answer.

'Stomach and thighs.'

In short, she was the classic middle-aged woman.

'So I would go for a dress with a fitted waist that shows off your great boobs and skims over your problem areas, and definitely in a vibrant colour.'

Jayne nodded. 'Sounds good.'

Claudia rolled her eyes. 'Look, OK I'll go through some more outfits with Jayne. I'm sure we can find something we agree on.' She sounded so dismissive, not in any way apologetic for her previus poor work.

'That won't be necessary, Tiffany is going to do it,' Angel told her.

'Oh, yeah?' Now Claudia had more passion in her voice. 'And what the fuck does *she* know about styling anyone?'

'We'll find out, but I trust her and I've stopped trusting you.' Angel paused. 'I've always wanted to do this, but it's never been the right time . . . until now.' She raised her hand and pointed her finger.

'Claudia, you're fired!'

It was Claudia's turn to look stunned. She tossed back her expensively highlighted hair and spat back, 'I've had plenty of other offers, you know. *Dazed and Confused, Wallpaper* . . . all sorts of cutting-edge publications that I expect you haven't even heard of are very, *very* interested in me. I don't need this.'

Angel shrugged. 'Great, because we don't want you.'

Claudia stood frozen to the spot with shock. Even though she had been incredibly rude, she clearly hadn't expected Angel to stick to her guns.

Jez clapped his hands. 'Off you trot then, Claudia. I'll call the production assistant and let her know you'll be dropping off your security pass.'

Claudia grabbed her tan Mulberrry Bayswater bag and beige leather biker jacket and whisked out of the room, slamming the door behind her.

'What a drama!' Jez declared. 'I love it! She totally deserved to go. And I happen to know that money is no object to Claudia – her daddy bought her a bijou flat in Chelsea and he gives her an allowance. She probably just used the money she earned on the show to buy her handbags. Do you know how much those Mulberry bags cost? She has at least six of them. And that jacket was well over a grand . . .'

Angel pushed him playfully in the shoulder. 'He is a terror, but I love him to bits.' She frowned and looked over at Tiffany. 'OK, babe, this is going to be you in at the deep end. You've got half an hour to style Jayne.' She looked at their makeover guest, 'Is that OK with you?'

'Absolutely! I can't wait.'

'Great. Can I just have a quick word with Tiffany and then she'll be right with you.'

'Sure thing.' Jayne headed out of the room, and paused at the door to say, 'Angel Summer, you kick ass!'

Everyone laughed.

Tiffany was tempted to follow Jayne out of the door and keep on walking. She hadn't expected this on her first day! She felt a sudden urge to run all the way back to her boring but safe job at the gym, where all she was expected to do was be nice and smile.

Angel smiled warmly at her. 'You can do this, I know you can.'

'So I'll appear on the show today?' Tiffany asked, nerves kicking in.

Angel nodded. 'You'll be brilliant. I'll get Jez to do your hair and Darcy to do your make-up. Remember, we're styling Jayne who's a mum of three and works part-time in care home. The film inserts have been recorded, so all you need to do is to come up with her outfit for a special night out with her husband.' She hesitated. 'I was going to think about this some more, but I guess we'll just have to wing it. How would you feel if we also talked about us being sisters? Everyone knows because of the press story, so we may as well put our side across. And Jessica and Matthew' – she named the hosts of the day-time TV show – 'will be very sympathetic.'

The morning had just got a whole lot weirder. Tiffany took a deep breath. 'So long as I can tell my dad and step-mum first, and you do most of the talking on air.'

'Absolutely, call them now. But I'm sure you'll be OK when we're live.'

Tiffany wished she had Angel's confidence. But there was no time to obsess about anything. She quickly called her dad, who was very nearly speechless that his little girl was going to be on TV and told him to let Kara know. And then she knocked on the door to the next-door dressing room. It was time to start styling Jayne.

'Hiya, again,' Tiffany said breezily as she walked in, trying to sound like a confident stylist who knew what they were doing and not like a quivering jelly.

Jayne was sitting still while a young male make-up artist, with enviably groomed eyebrows, was smoothing foundation on to her skin.

'Hiya, I'm so glad I've got you!' Jayne beamed at her. 'That Claudia was a poisonous witch! Every time she saw me in my underwear I knew that she was thinking, "What a fat old bag! I'm never going to look like that." I felt like saying, "I've had three kids and I can't afford a personal trainer. This is what real women look like!"

'I'll give her some credit, she did find me some jeans that fitted and were flattering, and didn't give me a whacking great muffin top,' Jayne admitted. 'But the black tunic? I like wearing black but she might as well have put me in a bin bag! I want something special. It's my wedding anniversary at the end of the month and we're going on a mini-break. I'd love to wear something to make my husband go "Wow".' She sighed. 'My mum died two years ago and I felt so down I didn't care about my appearance. Our marriage went through a rough patch . . . But I want to put all that behind me, for the sake of my family.'

Tiffany got up from her chair and hugged Jayne. 'I understand. I promise, I want you to look and feel sensational.'

Jayne smiled. 'I can already tell that you're a whole lot nicer than Claudia. Much prettier too. She looked as if she had a poker stuck up her arse! Thought she was far too good for the likes of me.'

'She thought she was too good for the likes of anyone!' Tiffany replied, and then got down to work.

She flicked through the rack of clothes, weighing up each garment. The stand-out item for her was a halterneck dress, with a fitted waist and full skirt, in a beautiful shade of coral. The halterneck would show off a hint of cleavage, the fitted cut would emphasis Jayne's waist and skim over the problem tummy and the full skirt would hang below her knees, so covering up any thigh issues. The warm colour would flatter her pale skin.

Tiffany held up the dress. 'Cinderella, you are going to the ball!'

'Isn't the colour a bit too bright? I don't want to look like mutton. And what about my bingo wings?' Jayne waved them above her head. 'They have to be covered up! I don't want to scare people.'

Damn, this was going to be harder than Tiffany had realised.

'Jayne, black is *so* boring. This coral will make you glow. If you're worried about your arms, you can put on a sheer gold wrap.' She saved the best bit till last as she held up a pair of gorgeous gold strappy sandals. 'And these shoes will set it all off perfectly and show off your very pretty feet.'

The shoes seemed to weaken Jayne's resolve slightly. 'I suppose I could at least try it on . . .'

'When your hair and make-up is finished. I want you to get the full effect.'

Twenty minutes later, Jayne's hair and make-up were done to perfection and Tiffany was able to persuade her to try on the dress. As she had predicted the design flattered Jayne's hour-glass figure. She watched Jayne considering her reflection in the mirror, then carefully placed the sheer gold wrap around her shoulders. 'Personally I don't think you need it, but if you feel insecure about your arms, it's there.'

'I love it!' Jayne declared, looking bowled over by the sight of her new self. 'I absolutely love it!'

In fact everyone loved it, including Angel, who, after she'd seen Jayne, hugged Tiffany and said, 'You did good. Now get yourself into my dressing room, it's time for *your* makeover.'

Tiffany had been so caught up in getting Jayne ready, she had almost forgotten that she herself was going to be on TV. Instantly her stomach lurched with nerves. She clutched Angel's arm. 'Can we talk about what I'm going to say?'

'Of course. We've still got an hour.'

Forty minutes later Tiffany and Angel had run through the kinds of things she needed to say – both of them wanted to steer clear of saying anything about Tanya. Jez had trimmed Tiffany's fringe and made her usually sleek brunette hair look even sleeker. Darcy had emphasised her green eyes with shades of gold and bronze, and given her ruby-red lips. She had changed from her skinny jeans into a cute black-and-pink rose-patterned dress from Topshop, teamed with black shoe boots and bare legs.

'You look divine,' Jez declared. 'Love the look . . . kind of Daisy Lowe rock chick . . . and it's great that it's all high street and affordable for our viewers. Madam Claudia only ever wore designer.'

'D'you think so? Say I get all sweaty? I don't want to be on *Harry Hill's TV Burp* with Sweatiest Armpits of the week!'

Jez put his hands on his hips. 'Now come on, young lady. This is your big break. Would you really rather be back serving pizzas? Or saying "Have a nice day" to gym bunnies? You go out there and shine, shine, shine! And if you can't do it for yourself, do it for Jayne next-door who's a mass of nerves but is doing it anyway – and has already stripped off to her underwear for the TV cameras.'

Then he took pity on Tiffany and came over and gave her a hug. God! All this hugging and emotion, it was exhausting.

'You'll be great, I promise. I have a feeling you'll be a natural in front of the cameras.'

'How come you're so good at analysing everyone?' Tiffany asked, marvelling at the way he seemed so certain about *everything*.

Jez sighed theatrically. 'Years and years and years of listening to my clients. I'm part hairdresser, part psychologist, part confessor.'

'And don't forget part drama queen,' Angel quipped as she walked into the room. She smiled at Tiffany. 'Ready? It's time to go.'

Tiffany sat on the comfortable blue sofa next to Angel, barely able to bring herself to look out at the array of TV cameras zoomed in on the set. The studio lights were fiercely hot. At this rate she would find herself on *Harry Hill's TV Burp* as person with the shiniest face of the week.

Jessica, a bubbly blonde – Tiffany supposed you couldn't be a miserable and sarcastic day-time TV presenter – and Matthew, middle-aged, conventionally and unthreateningly handsome, were both very welcoming. But Tiffany felt like a rabbit caught in the headlights, knowing that any second now she would be on live TV. Angel reached out and squeezed her hand. 'Don't worry. Just enjoy it. We'll go out and have lunch afterwards.'

Tiffany had been far too nervous to have any breakfast. Her mouth felt dry and she reached for the glass of water, aware that her hand was shaking. Was it too late to say that she'd changed her mind?

But then the adverts finished and the show's bright and breezy sig tune cut in, and Jessica and Matthew were beaming their perfect white smiles at the camera as they introduced Angel's Makeover.

'And it's a special one today, isn't it, Angel, as you've been joined by a certain someone?' More smiles from Jessica, flashing her whiter than white teeth.

'It is. I'd like to introduce my sister Tiffany who has helped with today's styling. And as the press has already reported, our big news is that we've just discovered we are in fact sisters.'

Cue intrigued but sympathetic looks from Jessica and Matthew.

'It's an incredible story, isn't it?' Jessica gushed.

'So, Tiffany, how did you feel when you found out that you were Angel's sister?' That from Matthew, along with a concerned, sympathetic, you-can-tell-me-everything look.

Oh, God! Now she had to speak. 'Um . . . of course, it was a bit of a shock.' Tiffany was aware how wobbly her voice sounded. 'I had no idea I even had a sister, let alone a celebrity one.'

Angel helped her out. 'But once we met – even though we didn't know for certain we were sisters because we hadn't had the DNA test – we really hit it off. We even discovered we were wearing the same perfume, Coco Mademoiselle.' She smiled at Tiffany.

154

'It's great discovering that I have a sister.'

'Well, we'll be talking more about your bombshell news after your makeover slot. So who's had the treatment today?'

And now Tiffany started to relax as Angel talked about Jayne and introduced the film clips. She knew what she wanted to say. And when Jessica asked her about the style choices that had been made for Jayne, Tiffany was able to give an eloquent answer about why certain garments had been chosen and how important it was to boost Jayne's self-esteem and find the clothes that suited her lifestyle. She realised that she could do this. And, more to the point, she was enjoying herself.

The highlight had to be when Jayne came on wearing the coral dress and looking gorgeous. And what thrilled Tiffany more than anything was that not only did the dress look great but Jayne was obviously delighted with her appearance and loving the reaction from the audience, who were cheering and clapping her as she made her grand entrance.

'Jez was right, you are a natural in front of the camera!' Angel told her as they walked off the set together. 'I can't believe it was the first time you've ever done that. It took me ages to stop being wooden, even after a load of media training. And I still think there's room for improvement.'

Tiffany was pretty sure that Angel was simply being nice, but it was good to know that she had not disgraced herself or let her sister down. But it turned out everyone on the show was delighted with her too.

'You rock, Tiff!' Jez declared when she and Angel walked into the dressing room. 'Is it OK if I call you Tiff?'

'Everyone does except my dad.' And Sean, but she didn't mention his name.

There was a quick debrief about the following day's filming and then they were free to go for lunch. As Tiffany walked out of the production meeting, she bumped into Sean and felt a whoosh of butterflies inside her as his arm brushed against hers.

For a second Sean looked as surprised to see her as she was to see him, but he quickly composed himself. 'Congratulations, I thought you did really well.'

Angel overheard him and draped her arm round Tiffany's shoulders, 'She was fab, wasn't she? Can you drop us off at Locatelli's? We're going to have a celebration lunch. You're welcome to join us.'

'Thank you but I have some calls to make, so it's best if I don't.'

Tiffany felt a mix of relief and disappointment. Sean walked ahead of the three of them to the car and she soon discovered that Jez shared her disappointment,

'Sean Murphy, the enigma continues . . . I just can't figure him out at all! It's doing my head in. He's so damned inscrutable. Why will he never come out for lunch with us?' he whispered.

'Perhaps he doesn't like you,' Angel teased him.

'Or maybe he wouldn't be able to control himself if he spent too long in my company,' Jez pouted.

Angel winked at Tiffany. 'Your gaydar's off. Sean is straight. But maybe he'd make an exception for you, Jez.'

'What do you think of him, Tiff?' he demanded. 'Isn't he divinely hot?'

Tiffany had been trying to suppress all thoughts of Sean, not entirely successfully. She had dreamed of him the night before – a passionate, erotic dream that made her long for him even while she was furious with him for rejecting her.

She shrugged, 'He's OK, if you like that kind of thing. I get the feeling there's not much to him beyond his looks.'

'But what looks they are!' Jez enthused.

And then an image of Sean lying beside her on the sofa, dressed only in a vest and boxers, flashed throughTiffany's mind. 'Hmm,' she muttered, and was relieved when they reached the car.

Jez sat in the front of the Merc. Tiffany was directly behind Sean, which meant she inadvertently kept catching his eye in the rear-view mirror, every time she looked over at Jez.

'So, Miss Taylor, what else do I need to know about you?' he demanded. 'Are you gay, straight, bisexual, single, attached?'

'He doesn't beat about the bush, does he?' Tiffany complained to Angel, very aware that Sean was listening. How could he not be?

'Come on! Give me the bare bones now, then I can have all the juicy details over lunch.'

Tiffany rolled her eyes. 'I'm straight and single. There – are you satisfied?' She was looking across at Jez but her eyes strayed to the mirror to see Sean looking at her.

'Happy being single or on the lookout?'

'Very happy being single.' She had better nip Jez's questions in the bud. It was mortifying having to answer in front of Sean I'm-just-not-that-into-you Murphy.

Jez sighed. 'I don't know if anyone is *happy* being single.' An idea seemed to occur to him and he suddenly exclaimed, 'Angel, you'll have to set Tiff up with some hot young thing. It's your thirtieth birthday party at the end of July. That'll be the perfect event for finding someone for her.'

'Thanks for reminding me I'm thirty, Jez!' Angel scolded. 'I won't remind you of the hissy fit you threw when you hit the big three oh.'

'But, darling, I don't know what you're talking about. I'm only twenty-nine.'

'For the last four years,' Angel joked.

'Delusional!' Jez looked back at them, then added, 'You're thirty and fab-u-lous. Anyway thirty is the new twenty, and forty is the new thirty.'

'And I don't need anyone to set me up, thanks, Jez,' Tiffany put in. 'Like I said, I'm perfectly happy being single.'

'Bet you change your mind when you see some of the hotties Cal knows,' Jez challenged her.

Tiffany looked at Angel and raised her eyebrows. 'Does he never give up?'

'Never,' Angel replied.

And then Jez directed his attention to Sean. 'So have you got a girlfriend, Sean?'

Tiffany pretended to be fascinated by the view out of the window, but she was hanging on every word.

'No.'

'Happy being single?' Jez persisted. 'Or on the lookout?'

He really didn't give up. And Tiffany couldn't resist looking in the mirror once more where Sean stared back at her for a moment, his expression impossible to read, before he replied, 'I'm happy, thanks.'

And Tiffany felt like saying, *Yeah, Sean, we all get the message, don't worry.*

Jez folded his arms. 'What happened to romance? Passion? Happy being single? Pah! So boring.'

He turned back to Tiffany. 'I'm pinning my hopes on you, Tiff. You're going to meet someone gorgeous at Angel's party, I know it.'

'So now you're a clairvoyant as well as a hairdresser, psychologist, confessor and drama queen?' Tiffany teased him.

'I just know that you will meet someone,' he

persisted. 'I've got very good antennae for these things. In fact, I'm going to go through the guest list with Angel and make sure you're sitting next to someone truly scrumptious.'

Tiffany remembered once more how humiliating it was when Sean had told her he wasn't interested. Instead of telling Jez not to bother, she replied, 'OK, but only if they're truly scrumptious.'

And then she made sure she was staring out of the window, as if Sean's reaction was of absolutely no interest to her whatsoever.

Jez clapped his hands together. 'Now we're talking, sister!'

Chapter 17

For the next two weeks Tiffany felt as if her life was on fast forward. She had never been so busy. She appeared on Angel's makeover show twice a week, and when she wasn't on that, she was filming inserts for the show, sourcing clothes, and talking to the women with Angel about what image they wanted to be given. On top of that the tabloids, celeb magazines and chat shows were all fascinated by her and she was inundated with interview requests. But so far Tiffany had turned them all down. She didn't want Angel to think that she was trading on being her sister, and the truth was she wasn't interested in being famous. She wanted to be known for being a good stylist, not to be famous just because she happened to be a celebrity's sister. The stylist work was everything she had ever dreamed of. The only down-side was that it was hard keeping up with her friends and her family.

When she was finally able to ask them over for Sunday lunch they were completely taken aback by the lavish, luxurious apartment. At first Marie and Chris moved around cautiously as if they were in a museum and couldn't touch anything, while Lily-Rose tore around checking everything out.

'Relax!' Tiffany ordered her dad, who was perched

uncomfortably on the edge of the sofa. 'You're not going to break anything.'

'I wouldn't be so sure,' Marie replied as Lily-Rose danced around the living room, pausing to balance on one leg by the black marble fireplace and look at herself in the mirror. Marie rubbed her hands over her baby bump – now at five months, she was really showing. Tiffany thought her step-mum looked pale and tired, and there were dark circles under her eyes. She hoped Marie was taking it easy, though knowing her she probably wasn't.

They chatted about how Tiffany's new job was going and Chris and Marie seemed so proud of her.

'You look gorgeous as well, love, all glossy and sleek, like the girls in the magazines,' Marie told her.

Tiffany laughed. 'I do have to make more of an effort with my grooming. Look at my nails.' She held out her hands, showing off a perfect French manicure. 'They're almost as good as yours.'

Marie, who was not at all a vain woman and hardly wore any make-up, loved having well-manicured nails. And given that she spent so much time doing arts and crafts with small children, this was no mean achievement.

'Very ladylike,' she commented, then sighed. 'But mine have gone to pot, I've been too tired to do them.' She held up her hands and Tiffany saw that the pale pink nail varnish was chipped and her cuticles were uneven. It was really out of character. She must be feeling rough.

'How about after lunch I give you a manicure? I could give you a pedicure as well, if you like? I bet you haven't been able to do your feet either.'

Marie shook her head. 'You don't have to do that, it's your day off.' She managed a smile, 'You've been giving middle-aged women makeovers all week. My nails don't matter.'

161

'I'd like to. And I'm going to.'

'Can I have one too?' Lily-Rose asked hopefully.

Tiffany looked at Marie to check if it was OK.

Marie nodded. 'You can, but we'll have to take the varnish off before school tomorrow.'

Chris stood up, rubbing his hands together.

'D'you want one too, Dad?' Tiffany teased him.

'I was going to suggest that you do Marie's nails now and I'll crack on with lunch.' As usual Chris was itching to get into the kitchen. He was the world's worst dinner guest. Tiffany knew from past experience that if she refused his offer, he would only be sitting there thinking about how much better he could have cooked the food.

'Dad, I was supposed to be cooking you lunch!' Tiffany exclaimed, sounding outraged when in fact she had suspected this might happen and so had left the veg, gravy, and apple crumble for him to do.

'I find it relaxing and it would be nice for Marie to have a bit of pampering.' He leaned down and planted a kiss on his wife's head. 'She's been a bit rundown. I keep asking her to take some time off work, but she won't.'

'I'm fine, Chris, and I have to go to work. If I'm not there, the school can't afford to get anyone else in. You know how hard things are at the moment.'

Chris raised his eyebrows. 'You've got to think of yourself as well, and the baby.' It was clearly a bone of contention. But Marie waved her hand at him to end it and said jokingly, 'Get into the kitchen and cook my dinner!'

'Shall I come and show you where everything is?' Tiffany asked.

'Don't bother, I reckon I've got a better chance of finding things – have you actually cooked anything since you've been here?' he replied.

How well her dad knew her! Tiffany shook her head.

'Nope. Just Marmite on toast. Oh, and I did have a jacket potato with tuna and mayo once.'

Chris went off to the kitchen, shaking his head.

'So have you seen any more of the gorgeous Sean?' Marie asked as Tiffany got down to work. Marie really had been neglecting her nails – they were in a terrible state.

She shrugged, not wanting to give too much away. 'I see him at work. He's basically Angel's full-time bodyguard.'

'Lucky her!' Marie said. 'Not only does she have the handsome Cal Bailey, she's got sexy Sean too.' She paused and smiled at Tiffany. 'But I reckon he really liked you. He was so kind that day, and I saw the way he couldn't keep his eyes off you. You know how much I liked Billy, but Sean seems to have so much more about him. He would be your equal, not someone you could wrap round your finger.'

Tiffany snorted, 'Marie, I love you dearly but you are deluded! Sean was just doing his job. He takes it *very* seriously. I don't think anything else matters to him.' Oops! She'd sounded a little bitter. She'd better watch that or Marie would pick up on it.

'But he didn't have to tidy up your flat after the break-in, and he did. I think he's lovely.'

'Well, you can think it all you like. Nothing is going to happen between us.' And to deflect Marie's attention away from what was still a rather sensitive subject, Tiffany held up two bottles of nail varnish: 'Rebel Red or Peach Daiquiri?'

Lunch was a great success; Chris basked in everyone's compliments for his 'unbeatable' roast potatoes and 'sublime' apple crumble. Marie seemed more relaxed, and it was lovely for Tiffany being able to catch up with her family.

'We're so proud of you,' Marie said as they hugged goodbye.

'I'll second that,' Chris added. 'In spite of everything that's happened, you've kept your head screwed on. I always knew you would. Just make sure you phone us a little bit more.'

Tiffany bit her lip. She felt bad that she had been neglecting them all lately. 'I promise.' She turned to Marie. 'And you've got to promise to take it easier . . . Dad's right.'

Marie rolled her eyes. 'I'd forgotten how bossy you are.' But then she smiled and said, 'I'll do my best.'

Spending time with her family on Sunday had felt so normal – albeit in a luxury flat – that Tiffany was struck again the following day by how much her life had changed. She met up with Angel in a designer boutique on New Bond Street, along with the film crew from the TV show.

Today the two women were going to be filmed tracking down their perfect dresses for Angel's thirtieth birthday party. It had been Oscar the director's idea to bring a bit of glamour to the makeovers.

'I love our older ladies,' he had told Angel and Tiffany, in a production meeting, 'but I think we could do with a bit of a change and your party is the perfect excuse.'

Tiffany just bet he was itching to get some more glamorous shots of Angel, ideally in her underwear. She had overheard him commenting to Robbie, one of the assistant directors, before the meeting, that there were only 'so many shots of the older lady in Spanx that a man could take'. Angel was not a woman who would ever have any need of control underwear.

Tiffany hadn't been at all sure that she herself wanted to be the centre of attention, but Angel had

164

persuaded her, saying it would be fun. Now, as she was trying on an exquisite midnight blue strapless evening dress, she had to agree. She had never worn such a glamorous dress before. She felt as if she was off to the Oscars ceremony – this dress definitely had red-carpet status.

'I feel like such a lady!' she declared to Angel, as she surveyed her reflection in the mirror, turning this way and that, and enjoying the feel of the cool silk swishing against her skin.

'You look beautiful,' Angel told her. She sighed as she looked down at the white silk dress with a crystal-studded neckline that she was wearing. 'Are you sure I don't look a bit mutton?'

Tiffany burst out laughing. 'You look amazing! And you're only thirty! How can that be mutton?' It was astonishing to realise that someone as beautiful as Angel could be as insecure as any other woman. But maybe that's what made her such a sympathetic and likeable person; she genuinely didn't realise how beautiful she was.

'But how about you try something different on? I've seen lots of pictures of you wearing similar dresses and I don't think you need all that sparkle,' Tiffany advised her.

'OK.' Angel shrugged. 'Find me something different . . . you're the stylist.'

And Tiffany spent a very happy hour finding the perfect dress for Angel. The film crew, of course, loved it, as they got to film plenty of footage of Angel parading around in beautiful dresses. They would have tried to get in the changing room too, given half the chance, but Angel said no, very firmly. Oscar wanted Tiffany to try on more dresses but she had set her heart on the midnight blue dress and wanted to stick to her resolution of not giving too much away. She was back in her skinny jeans, a cute red shirt tied at the waist and ballerina pumps.

'This is the one!' Tiffany held up an exquisite one-shoulder silk crêpe evening dress, the colour of champagne. It had a long split at the front and had a built-in corset, but absolutely no embellishments.

'Really?' Angel asked dubiously. 'But it's so plain.'

'Exactly! It will show you off perfectly. It's like when-ever Angelina Jolie wears a dress on the red carpet . . . it is always simple. Beautifully designed, but simple. *That's* the look we should be going for with you. All you need is a pair of pale gold sandals – and some diamond earrings. I'm sure you have a pair of those?'

'Several,' Angel admitted. 'But I hardly ever wear them.'

She took the dress off to the fitting room while Tiffany turned to the camera and said, 'I hope I'm right!'

She need not have worried. When Angel emerged everyone stopped in their tracks. The cut of the dress emphasised her slender figure and enviable curves, the colour of the silk set off her skin and gave it a golden glow. And because it was such a simple design you just saw Angel, stunning, beautiful Angel.

'Well, what's the verdict?' she asked, looking rather self-conscious as everyone was staring at her.

'It's the one,' Tiffany told her.

'I've really missed you!' Tiffany declared that evening, pouring Kara another glass of Pinot Grigio. The two girls were meeting at a little bar off Regent Street and were already on to their second bottle.

'I've missed you too, but I get my fix of you by watching the show,' Kara told her.

Tiffany shook her head. 'It's not the same.' She was feeling more than a little drunk, the roller-coaster past few weeks seemed to be catching up with her. And she couldn't admit to anyone other than Kara how it was affecting her to keep seeing Sean. She couldn't stop thinking about him; she realised that she had an almighty crush on him. It just showed that the old saying had a lot of truth in it: treat them mean, keep them keen. He had told her that he wasn't interested and now she couldn't stop thinking about him. Today when she had tried on the evening dress her first thought had been, *I wonder what Sean will think of me in it?* She was clearly a hopeless case...

'So come on, we've talked about everything else, the show, Angel, your family . . . and you haven't mentioned Sean at all. Is there nothing to tell?' her friend insisted.

God, Kara knew her so well! Tiffany picked up her glass, moodily swirled the wine around in it, then put it back down. 'There's nothing to tell from his point of view. Sometimes I think he might be looking at me, but that's probably me being completely deluded!' She took a sip of her wine. 'The trouble is, I still really like him. I still think he's gorgeous. So sexy, even though his dress sense isn't so hot and he's *so* serious.' She grimaced. 'And, of course, the big one . . . he's not interested in me at all.'

'I bet he is, but feels he can't get involved with you because of his work. And Angel and Cal would probably feel odd about him seeing you because of your connection to her.'

Tiffany groaned. 'How can I stop obsessing about him?'

'Maybe you will meet someone gorgeous at Angel's thirtieth. Forget about Sean, there are so many good things happening in your life right now.'

Tiffany was about to say that was easier said than done when two lads approached their table, their gazes fixed on her. Instinctively she lowered her head. She wasn't used to being recognised and didn't know that she liked it.

'You're Angel Summer's sister, aren't you?' The one with the stripy shirt and acne addressed her. Hmm, spots and stripes . . . a fashion no-no. Tiffany considered pointing it out to him, then reconsidered. He had a hard-looking face. She shook her head. 'People are always thinking that, but I'm not.'

'Well, you look just like her,' the other lad, dressed in a white Fred Perry shirt, put in.

'It's her,' Stripy Shirt said. 'I don't know why she's being so stuck up. It's not like she's a real celeb.'

'Oh, piss off!' Kara told them. 'We're not bothering you.'

'Another stuck-up cow.' That from Stripy Spotty. He held up his camera phone and took a picture, which outraged Kara.

'I'd like to hear you say that if my boyfriend was here, you pair of total twats!' Kara was getting carried away, forgetting that the reassuringly strongly built Harley was not in fact here.

Tiffany was just wondering how they would be able to make a rapid exit when a thick-set doorman came over. 'Are these gentlemen bothering you?'

The doorman had clocked Tiffany when she had arrived. Perhaps there were some advantages to being known.

'A bit,' she replied. 'But we're going, thanks.' And she grabbed her jacket and bag, and made Kara do the same.

'But there's half a bottle left,' her friend declared.

'You can have a glass at my place,' Tiffany whispered, anxious to get the hell out of there. The two lads were giving her and Kara the evil eye.

Outside the doorman saw them safely into a taxi, but

Tiffany didn't feel relaxed until they had driven off and she was certain the two lads weren't following.

'Are you going to come in?' she asked her friend as the taxi pulled up outside the Hyde Park apartment block.

Kara stifled a yawn. 'D'you mind if I don't? I'm knackered, and I think I drank too much.'

'Not at all, babe, I'll call you tomorrow.' Tiffany quickly hugged her friend and handed the cabbie a £20 note, in spite of Kara's protests that she would pay.

Tiffany had the shock of her life when she opened the door to the block of flats and discovered Sean sitting on the stairs.

'What's going on?'

'Your alarm was set off earlier tonight. I got an alert and came by to check everything was OK.'

Tiffany felt a flash of panic, as she thought back to her previous flat being burgled.

'And everything *is* OK,' Sean reassured her. 'I've checked round the flat. It was a false alarm.' He smiled. 'Do you never check your phone? I left you a couple of messages.'

'Sorry, I was out having a drink with Kara. The bar was really noisy.'

Sean stood up. 'I'll go then. I just wanted to let you know what had gone on.'

Tiffany bit her lip. 'Would you mind coming up to the flat and checking round the rooms once more? I know that sounds silly but I'd feel better if you did.'

As soon as she'd made her request she regretted it. Maybe Sean would think that she was planning on trying to make a move. 'I mean, I don't want you to stay or anything,' she added hastily.

'Of course,' he replied, and quickly walked up the stairs, taking them two at a time.

Tiffany stayed close to him as he went from room to room, but everything seemed to be in its usual place. Nothing had been disturbed and it didn't look as if anyone had been in the flat.

'OK?' Sean asked at the front door.

'Thanks for doing that.'

'I can stay longer if you want, have a cup of tea?'

She was tempted. Maybe if they spent some time on their own together she could break through his reserve, but finally she shook her head. 'Nope, I'm going to crash.' She checked her watch. 'I've got to be up in six hours.'

He grinned. 'Me too. I'll see you tomorrow, Tiffany. Any worries, anything at all, then call me.' He reached into his pocket and took out a card. 'And here are the numbers of the other security guys, just in case you can't get hold of me for whatever reason.'

'Thanks,' Tiffany repeated, and with that Sean was gone. Maybe the card with the other numbers was a hint that he didn't want her to contact him. Oh, God knows!

Sean was simply doing his job, she told herself when she got into bed. He was on duty so he had received the alarm signal. It might just as easily have been one of his colleagues. Tiffany only represented work to him. But how she wished that wasn't so! Especially at 3 a.m. when she still couldn't sleep and wanted nothing more than to feel the reassurance of his strong arms around her.

Chapter 18

Angel's thirtieth was being held in a huge marquee in the grounds of her house. Tiffany arrived late-afternoon to find a whirlwind of activity in progress. Caterers were busy setting up in the kitchen, florists were arranging elegant bouquets at every table: chandeliers and spotlights were being rigged in the marquee, and fairy lights were being hung on the trees outside. The dominant colour was pink, even down to the marquee itself with its carpet and chandeliers. Kara would have absolutely loved it, Tiffany thought, as she had a sneaky peek into the marquee.

'Stylish enough for you?' It was Sean. She hadn't even noticed him approach. Walking stealthily was no doubt another of his special-agent skills.

'It's a pink paradise. I'm surprised Angel isn't making all you security guys dress up in pink suits.' Tiffany tried to keep her tone light, but being around Sean always unsettled her, made her realise that she still wasn't over him.

'Black, always black.'

'Lucky for you. Pink really isn't your colour.'

Sean gave the smallest of smiles. He took off his sun-glasses and Tiffany was struck by the exhaustion etched into his face. There were dark circles under his eyes and it looked as if he hadn't had a good night's sleep in ages. She was torn between feeling sympathetic because his work was no doubt full on when there was such a big event, and thinking he had chosen his work over everything else and would have to live with the consequences.

'Well, I must go and get ready and drink champagne . . . you know how it is. Have fun yourself, Agent Murphy,' she said brightly, and instantly regretted sounding so flippant. She was almost tempted to turn back and make up for the remark. But she didn't.

Upstairs in the house the bedrooms had been turned over to guests preparing for the party. Wafts of different perfumes floated through the air, mixed with the smells of hairspray and nail varnish. Conversations competed against the sound of hairdryers. Getting ready for such an A-list event, Tiffany reflected, was a full-on operation. She was all set to go to her guest room when Angel called out from her bedroom, 'Hey, Tiff, come and get ready in here.'

Tiffany walked in to the vast master suite, where everything was white – white walls, white furniture, white bed linen. The only colour came from a stunning canvas aerial photograph of the vivid green and turquoise Indian Ocean, dotted with emerald green islands edged with white sand beaches. Clearly Cal had put his foot down and vetoed pink in here. Angel was sitting in front of her pretty Venetian glass dressing-table mirror, dressed in a white robe, while Jez worked on her hair.

'God, updos are so hard! I've been at it for hours!' he moaned through a mouthful of hairpins.

'Worth it, though,' Tiffany replied, perching on the end of the bed. 'It will look stunning with the dress. Real old-school glamour.'

'Yes, and now *please* can I have a glass of champagne? I'm gasping,' Jez declared, as he inserted the final hairpin. 'And *please* don't tell me you want yours put up as well? I love you, Tiff, but I don't think I can go on. Angel is so high-maintenance! The woman's drained me.'

'Told you he was a drama queen,' she said, smiling.

'I can do it myself, Jez, thanks. And champagne is coming up.'

Tiffany poured out three glasses and handed theirs to Jez and Angel.

'Happy birthday, Angel,' she said, clinking glasses. And then she got out the present she had bought for her sister and shyly handed it over. It was a belated present as Angel's actual birthday was in May. Tiffany had spent ages wondering what to get her and then she had found it: a diamante angel's wings necklace from Butler & Wilson. OK, it wasn't made of real diamonds, but it was very pretty.

Angel opened the box and exclaimed in genuine delight, 'I love it! Thank you, Tiff. Oh, and I have something for you too.'

She held up a shoe box. Not just any old shoe box, but the Holy Grail of shoe boxes – a Louboutin shoe box.

'I was in the store the other day and saw these. I thought you might like them.'

Might like them! What was not to like about the iconic shoes?
Tiffany looked at her. 'Really?'

'Really.'

Tiffany felt like all her birthdays and Christmases had come at once as she opened the box and discovered the beautiful shoes nestling in red tissue paper. A pair of amethyst patent pumps, with a five-and-a-half-inch heel and the iconic scarlet soles.

'We thought the amethyst was edgier than the black,'

173

Jez put in. 'Now come on, Cinders, put them on. We've got a ball to go to!'

Tiffany did as she was told. The shoes were so gorgeous that frankly she would have been perfectly happy to look at herself wearing them in the mirror all night. Well, maybe not all night, just a couple of hours . . . Even though the heels were so high, the platform made them slightly easier to walk in. They were the most expensive things she had ever worn, apart from the dress. But even as she admired herself in them, she couldn't help feeling a pang of guilt when she thought of her family – the shoes probably cost the same as her dad's monthly mortgage payment, and last time she had seen her parents, Marie was commenting on how expensive Lily-Rose's school shoes were – and she was talking about *Clarks* . . .

'Your feet were made for them!' Jez exclaimed, and Tiffany tried to shake off the feelings of guilt.

'Thanks, Angel, that's so generous of you.'

'You're very welcome,' Angel told her.

The three of them gossiped and giggled for the next hour as they all got ready. Tiffany gave Jez a manicure, which perked him up, and he painted her nails a vampy red to go with the midnight blue dress. It felt so relaxed in Angel's bedroom that Tiffany almost forgot about the big party ahead of her. She left the bedroom rather reluctantly, worrying about mixing with so many people she didn't know.

'Hey, don't look so nervous,' Angel told her, sensing her unease, 'Jez has got strict instructions to look after you. And I have put you next to the most gorgeous man for dinner.'

'Ooh, yes!' Jez put in. 'Raul Garcia, the Brazilian Formula One racing driver. He puts the *phoar* into Formula One, I can tell you!'

174

'Yeah, yeah.' Tiffany was sure they were taking the piss. Raul indeed, the gorgeous racing driver she had never heard of – not that she followed Formula One. But it didn't sound plausible. She was probably sitting next to some fat old bloke with halitosis no one else wanted to sit next to.

The three of them walked arm-in-arm into the kitchen and found Sean and Cal chatting together at the kitchen table. But they broke off when the trio entered the room.

'You all look amazing,' Cal said, standing up. 'Will I do?' He was devastatingly handsome in a black tuxedo.

'Perfect,' Angel said, putting her arms round her husband. 'And what do you think of my dress? Tiffany chose it for me.'

'I love it.' Cal dropped a kiss on her neck. The couple seemed to be more in love than ever, and while of course being happy for them, Tiffany felt a pang of longing as she wondered if she would ever have that kind of relationship with anyone.

'And doesn't Tiffany look beautiful?' Angel addressed the two men.

'Stunning,' Cal replied. Tiffany almost held her breath, wondering if Sean would speak.

'Yes, she does,' he said quietly, and for a second their eyes met before he turned away. All the time she had been getting ready, she had been thinking of Sean, had wanted him to be impressed. He had probably just said it to be polite. All part of his job, make the boss's sister feel good . . .

Angel then became caught up with greeting her guests. Jez linked arms with Tiffany and they strolled through the grounds and into the marquee together. There they found Rufus, Jez's husband, talking to Gemma. Tiffany was a little wary of Gemma, who in

175

contrast to Angel's other friends and family had been quite cool with her. Tiffany had felt that perhaps Gemma didn't trust her. But tonight she seemed more relaxed, maybe it was the champagne she was drinking, and the two women quickly fell into conversation about their favourite designers. Gemma was full of praise for Tiffany's work on the show.

From time to time Tiffany scanned the marquee. In spite of everything, she couldn't help hoping for another glimpse of Sean. She didn't see him but caught the eye of an extremely handsome man who smiled broadly at her. For a moment Tiffany was uncertain if the smile was intended for her and checked over her shoulder, but there was no one else there. The smile had indeed been meant for her. She smiled back shyly.

And then it was time to take their places at the elegant dinner tables. Tiffany clutched Jez's arm as they checked the seating plan.

'You will rescue me if the person next to me is really boring, won't you?' she whispered, but not quietly enough. She had been overheard by the handsome man whose eye she had caught earlier.

'I promise you, he will do his very best not to be boring.' He had a slight accent, and Tiffany thought he was most probably Spanish.

'How can you be so sure?'

'Because the man is me.'

Wow! Wow! Wow! He certainly wasn't the fat, balding relative she had been anticipating. He was quite possibly the best-looking man Tiffany had ever spoken to.

'You should believe me in future,' Jez commented. 'Tiffany, this is Raul Garcia. Raul, this is Tiffany Taylor, Angel's sister.'

Raul took her hand and raised it to his lips. 'Of course, I thought as much. You're the only woman in the room able to compete with Angel.'

Half of Tiffany wanted to giggle because he was so over the top, but the other half was mesmerised by his good looks. She didn't think she had ever seen a man with such a handsome face. He resembled the stunning male model David Gandy, with his sculpted cheekbones, sensual mouth and olive skin.

She stifled the smile. 'That's nice of you to say but not true.'

'It certainly is true, but we have all night to argue. Shall we go to our table?'

He held out his arm for Tiffany to take. Jez winked at her and mouthed, 'Go, girl!'

Once they reached the table, Raul pulled out the chair for her like a perfect gentleman. The first few minutes were taken up with introductions to the other guests on the table – Jez and Rufus were opposite, and there were also two couples in their thirties. Tiffany recognised both the men as being former footballers. Candy, a pretty blonde in her twenties, was sitting next to Tiffany, and her husband, Liam Miller, who played for Liverpool, was beside Raul. Candy was heavily pregnant and very chatty.

'He's gorgeous!' she whispered when Raul was talking to Liam. 'Is he single?'

'No idea,' Tiffany whispered back. 'But I agree with your first comment.'

'Get in there is my advice,' Candy said cheekily.

'What are you ladies talking about?' Raul asked.

'Oh, Candy was just telling me about when her baby's due,' Tiffany said quickly, but by the smile on Raul's face she thought he knew exactly what they'd been talking about.

He then got caught up talking to Liam again and

Candy wasted no time in firing off questions at Tiffany – she could give Lily-Rose a run for her money!

'So you had no idea until two months ago that Angel was your sister?'

Tiffany nodded. 'I know it seems incredible, but it's true.'

'And how do you feel about it all?' She paused. 'Sorry, I'm dead nosy, you don't have to answer. I've only got a few weeks before the baby's due and I'm bored out of my mind! I can't do any of the things I usually like doing.'

'She means shopping and going to the gym,' Liam put in dryly.

Candy pretended to look offended then laughed. 'Actually I've been doing a lot of shopping online – I am a WAG after all, I have to shop, it's in my DNA – but before you think that's all I do, I also co-own a children's clothes boutique.' She shook back her long blonde hair. 'I am a businesswoman. I don't know why Lord Sugar doesn't ask me to go on *The Apprentice*, I'd be ace at giving advice.'

Eye roll from Liam. 'You keep buying all the stock from the boutique for the baby, so I don't exactly think you're going to be making a profit any time soon.'

'Ignore him,' Candy said. 'He's got no idea.' But she smiled lovingly at her husband. Across the table Jez had his arm round Rufus, and everywhere she looked it seemed to Tiffany that she was surrounded by happy couples.

'Is Candy ever going to stop monopolising you?' Raul murmured during a brief lull in her stream of conversation. 'I have many things I want to ask you.'

But he was prevented from asking anything as at that moment Cal stood up, signalling that it was time for him to make a birthday toast. The guests obligingly fell silent.

'Thanks to everyone for coming tonight. It's not every day that my wife turns' – Cal pretend to cough – 'twenty-nine. She ordered me to say that!'

Tiffany looked over at Angel who was laughing at her husband.

'Seriously, I am the luckiest man in the world to be married to Angel, who is getting more beautiful with every year that goes by. And this is going to sound corny, but I don't care – beautiful not just in her looks, but as a person.' He reached for her hand. 'I have learned that as long as we're together, nothing else matters. She is the love of my life and always will be.' Cal brought her hand to his lips as the guests let out a collective 'Ahhh.'

Now Tiffany's gaze strayed to the far corner of the marquee where she saw Sean standing guard. She wondered what he thought when he heard Cal talking about his relationship with Angel. Did he feel that there was something missing from his own life? Or was he immune to such feelings?

'It's very romantic, isn't it?' Raul whispered. 'They have such love for each other.'

Tiffany nodded, not quite trusting herself to speak. She still felt bruised by what had happened with Sean. Hearing Cal's declarations of love, and being sur- rounded by all these couples, was making her feel insecure and conspicuous – as if she was the only single person there tonight.

Thankfully Cal kept his speech short and sweet and it was then time to raise a toast to the birthday girl. But Angel wanted her say as well. She stood up. 'You all know that I hate making speeches, I'm rubbish at it, but I wanted to thank Cal for arranging my party . . . and of course for being the best husband in the world.' More 'Ahhhs' and cheers from the guests, especially when she blew him a kiss. 'And I also wanted

179

to say thanks to my sister Tiffany,' Angel added, looking over at her. 'It's been brilliant getting to know her, and I'm so glad we found each other. So I wanted to give a toast to her.' She raised her glass. 'To Tiffany.'

Tiffany could feel herself blushing as some two hundred people all said her name and looked at her. Her blush deepened when Raul whispered, 'To getting to know the beautiful Tiffany.'

And then the waiting staff marched in with the starters – where Cal's Italian roots were evident in the choice of prawn and courgette risotto.

'Lovely, lovely ciabatta!' Candy declared, looking longingly at the bread basket. She picked up a slice of bread and dipped it in the dish of olive oil. 'That is one of the many good things about being pregnant, I can eat whatever I like! Hello, carbs! Come to Mamma!'

'You still look really slim,' Tiffany replied, taking in her slender arms and neat baby bump.

'No way! I'm a right porker!'

'Just don't get obsessed with losing the baby weight,' Liam put in. 'I like you with more curves.'

Eye roll from Candy this time. 'Men always say that, but I never believe them, do you? We're going to St Barts after Christmas and I have got to be back in my bikini. I mean, *hello*, do you know any fat WAGs?' She lowered her voice so only Tiffany heard. 'I've already booked my personal trainer. Six weeks after I've had the baby, it's Bikini Bootcamp for me.' Candy looked very sweet with her blonde curls and dimples in her cheeks but she clearly had a will of steel.

Raul had been listening. He commented, 'It's curves every time for me. No man wants a woman without curves. We Latin men especially.'

Tiffany was aware of him looking at her appreciatively as he spoke and she was sneakily glad that she had chosen a dress that showcased her own curves. Across the table Jez witnessed the look and winked knowingly at her. Could he be any more unsubtle!

The conversation then turned to Raul's racing career as Liam was apparently a huge fan and wanted to know how the season was going.

Raul shrugged. 'Monte Carlo was good, I came first. But the real test will be Monza in September.'

Tiffany exchanged glances with Candy at the mention of Monte Carlo. It sounded so glamorous!

'I've got an apartment in Monte Carlo. You are all welcome to stay, any time. It's a good place to relax,' Raul added. Once more his gaze lingered on Tiffany. Again she fought the urge to laugh. Her last holiday had been a dirt-cheap package to Crete on easyJet, where she and Kara stayed in a dodgy apartment where the walls were so thin they could hear the lads next door taking a pee. And Kara had freaked when she had found a cockroach under the bed. Somehow Tiffany doubted the budget airline flew to Monte Carlo – people who went there probably chartered their own jets!

'Or come out to Itay and see me at Monza. I could arrange VIP tickets for all of you to watch the race in September.'

'That would be awesome, mate!' Liam exclaimed. Cindy glared at him. In his excitement he had forgotten a certain important date that was coming up.

'What?' he asked in all innocence. 'The shopping is bound to be fantastic there and you love Italian food.' Thereby digging himself into an even deeper hole.

Somehow Candy managed to say through gritted teeth, 'You won't be going anywhere, Liam, as I will be about to give birth to your son! Remember, that life-changing event that's coming up soon?'

Liam looked slightly shamefaced as he mumbled, 'Sorry. I knew that.'

While he and Candy had a whispered domestic, Raul said, 'You should come out, Tiffany, I think you would like it very much.'

She didn't doubt that for a second, but she didn't want to seem like the kind of girl who would do anything to go somewhere glamorous. She wasn't some bimbo free-loader; she had a career. She was an independent woman.

'It's nice of you to ask me, Raul, but I don't have any holiday coming up.'

'You could just come for a night then.' He wasn't going to give up that easily. 'It's a very short flight.'

'I am really very busy,' Tiffany persisted, enjoying the fact that this divinely handsome man was making a play for her.

Raul narrowed his dark brown eyes. 'You know what they say? All work and no play is not good for you. You should make time to play, Tiffany.'

Across the table Jez was so obviously eavesdropping on their conversation that Tiffany couldn't resist drawing him into the conversation. 'Have you ever been to Monte Carlo, Jez?'

Jez pretended at first that he hadn't heard her; that he was busy talking to Rufus. He might be an outstanding hairdresser but he was a rubbish actor! Tiffany repeated her question.

'Monte Carlo? Oh, no!' Jez exclaimed. 'But I have absolutely always wanted to go. Have you need of my tonsorial services, Raul?'

He looked a little confused. 'I am sorry, Jez, but I am straight. Women are my thing. I don't mean to be rude. Thank you for your offer, I am sure you are very good at . . . er . . . administering those . . . er . . . services.'

Clearly Raul thought 'tonsorial' meant something naughty! And Tiffany thought it was very sweet of him to be so polite.

'Jez is being a show-off,' she interpreted. 'Tonsorial means hairdressing.'

Relief replaced confusion. 'I thought he was offering to give me a blow job!'

The entire table erupted into raucous laughter. 'You should be so lucky!' Jez pouted. 'I'm a married man! And my lips and heart and everything else belong to him and him alone!'

'My sincerest apologies.' Raul bowed his head at Jez and blew him a kiss, much to everyone's delight.

'I forgive you,' Jez declared. 'So long as I get an invite one day to that Monte Carlo apartment.'

'Of course. You could always accompany Tiffany when she finally has some free time.' Raul flashed a smile at her.

Tiffany had started out the night thinking that Raul was nothing more than a *very* pretty face, but she was warming to him more and more. He was funny and warm and generous. And it was absolutely lovely basking in the glow of his attention. He might well be like this with every attractive girl he met, but she didn't care. It was a much-needed confidence boost. Fleetingly she thought of her last flirtation – with Sean – and how that had ended up. But she shrugged off the memory; she wasn't going to ruin the evening by negative thoughts.

And so her flirtation with Raul continued over dinner. He wanted to know all about the job she cared so much about, and he told her about his family – he had four elder sisters. No wonder he was so at ease around women. His father was English and he had spent his childhood in the UK before moving to Brazil aged thirteen, when his parents divorced, hence his impeccable English. His grandfather had been a famous Brazilian racing driver and had inspired Raul to follow in his footsteps. From the age of seven he had known that he wanted to become a driver too. While Tiffany was no fan of racing, she was attracted by Raul's obvious passion and commitment to his sport. But she still couldn't resist teasing him.

'So it's true to say that you were very driven?'

'I *am* very driven. I like to work hard and play hard.' He looked at her meaningfully. Tiffany just bet he did . . .

After dinner he leaned closer to her and whispered, 'I'm bored of being surrounded by all these people. Let's go and have a drink, just you and me.'

The other guests were also getting up and circulating, while the tables were cleared away for the dancing, so Tiffany figured it was OK. Once again she caught Jez's eye as she got up, and was rewarded with another wink. Raul put his arm round her as they walked over to the chill-out area of the marquee, where there were bright pink – what else? – velvet sofas to relax on.

'So your boyfriend won't mind when you tell him that you talked to me all night?' Raul asked as they sat down together.

Tiffany shook her head. 'Actually I don't have a boyfriend.'

'How can that be possible?' he demanded. It was outrageous flirtation, but Tiffany was loving the attention. She smiled.

'So what about your girlfriend . . . will she mind?'

Raul shrugged. 'I don't have a girlfriend.'

Yeah, right! He probably had several women on the go at once. One for every Grand Prix location.

'How can that be possible?' she teased. And was rewarded with a knowing look.

'I haven't found the right woman.' He paused, and his voice seemed to grow huskier when he spoke again. 'Not until now, maybe.'

Tiffany burst out laughing. 'You are shameless, Raul! I don't believe you!'

He pretended to be hurt, but there was a mischievous look in his eyes as he declared, 'You are trampling over my feelings, Tiffany, breaking my heart!'

'OK, I'm sorry, I guess that's not the reaction you normally receive from women.'

'I think you've got the wrong idea about me. You are stereotyping me as a playboy, when really I am a slave to my sport. I practically live like a monk.' His mouth twitched as if he was trying to contain a smile.

'Sure you do,' Tiffany replied, and then they both laughed.

'You're like a breath of fresh air,' Raul declared as he leaned back on the sofa. 'I'm so bored of women hanging on my every word. You are more of a challenge.' And he ran his hand lightly down her arm. Even though Tiffany was perfectly aware of what a player he was, she still shivered in anticipation. The man was so gorgeous!

'Am I?' she murmured, looking at him from under her lashes. Her most provocative look.

'I like challenges,' he replied, and leaning towards her, lightly kissed her on the lips.

He pulled back. 'Mmm, that was nice, maybe you're softening towards me.'

Tiffany most certainly was and she realised that she very much wanted him to kiss her again.

Raul checked his watch. A very expensive, diamond-studded watch, she noticed; she imagined everything about Raul was expensive.

'We could slip away . . . go back to my place? I am sure your sister wouldn't mind.' Now he was giving her what she was sure was *his* most provocative stare – his brown eyes seemed to smoulder and she could have sworn his pupils had dilated as if he was mesmerised by her. He'd had so much practice in seducing women, he could probably dilate his pupils to order. He lightly caressed her arm again, and even knowing that she would be just another notch on a very overcrowded bed post, she was still tempted . . . Bad girl, Tiffany!

'To your monk-like cell?' she asked.

'To my four-storey house in Richmond overlooking the river.'

'Only four storeys?' Tiffany turned her nose up. 'It must be so pokey. That's much smaller than I'm used to.'

'Nothing else will be, I guarantee,' murmured Raul. Then he caught her eye and they both laughed again. She liked the fact that he didn't take himself too seriously.

'I hope you don't use that line on other women,' she said.

Raul sighed. 'Sometimes I think they only care about the size of my bank balance and how much publicity they can get for themselves by being seen with me.'

'Oh, poor misunderstood baby!'

'You are teasing me too badly, Tiffany. Really, I can't take any more unless you tell me you are going to come back with me?'

She pretended to consider the offer, then said, 'Nope.'

A heartfelt sigh escaped him. 'Well, at least come and dance with me.' And he stood up and reached for her hand.

Tiffany was aware of people staring at them as they wove their way through the guests and on to the dance floor. Raul was such a big star – a hero to so many men because of his sporting prowess and a major heart throb

186

to women because of his stunning looks. They passed Sean on one of his security patrols and his eyes met Tiffany's fleetingly. She saw the look of disapproval he gave her when he noticed her holding Raul's hand. What was his problem? Like he cared about what she did! He had made that perfectly plain. She tilted her chin defiantly and moved closer to Raul, sending out the message that, yes, she was with him. And when they hit the dance floor, she deliberately danced in a flirtatious way, looking only at Raul, focusing all her attention on him.

Angel had wanted music from the last three decades and Tiffany and Raul found themselves in the eighties as they strutted their stuff to Wham!, trying to outdo each other with the most outrageous moves. She had thought Raul would be so full of himself that he would never want to do anything silly, but he was throwing himself around, mouthing along with the words, not caring how ridiculous he looked. He scored points for that.

They danced energetically to Wham!'s 'Wake Me Up Before You Go-Go', Blondie's 'Heart of Glass' and Human League's 'Don't You Want Me?' *I think I do*, Tiffany thought as Raul moved closer to her. They had eyes only for each other, and were out of breath and hot, so when Raul suggested they go for a drink outside, she readily agreed.

He took two glasses of champagne from a passing waiter. Outside the marquee several guests were milling around smoking. Raul walked past them to a secluded bench with an arch of roses over it that seemed made for a romantic moment. The night had grown cooler and Tiffany shivered in her silk evening dress. Raul took off his jacket and slipped it over her shoulders, in a move she was certain he would have made many, many times before. But she appreciated the gesture. The jacket was warm from his body and yet again there was the thrill of getting close to him. An image of her night with Sean flashed into in her mind. He had lent her his leather jacket . . . but she tried to suppress the thought. She wasn't going to let it spoil the fun she was having here and now.

'Cheers!' Raul held up his glass. 'Here's to getting to know each other better.'

She clinked her glass against his.

'So, are you free for dinner on Monday night?' he asked, treating her to another of his smouldering stares.

'I'll have to check my itinerary, I might be filming,' Tiffany lied, knowing perfectly well that she was free.

'You are making me work so hard, Tiffany,' he groaned.

'It's good for you. No one should have everything their own way all the time.' She paused. 'Only some of it.' And she leaned forward and lightly kissed him on the lips.

But if she thought she was going to get away with a playful kiss then she was mistaken. Raul took the champagne glass out of her hand and put it on the ground, then he drew her towards him and kissed her again. This time it was a passionate, I-want-you kiss that took her breath away.

Tiffany closed her eyes and for a fleeting second another image came into her head: of kissing Sean. She opened her eyes. Reality check. She was kissing Raul Garcia. What more could a girl want? And angry with herself for giving any head space to Sean, she kissed Raul back with a renewed intensity.

'God, Tiffany, we could be so good together,' he murmured when they broke off for air. He traced one finger around her lips. 'What a beautiful mouth you have.' He kissed her neck. 'Beautiful everything actually.' And now his caresses became more searching. He slid a hand under her silk skirt, inching it along her thigh, all the while kissing her neck, her lips. Tiffany pressed her knees together – no way did she want him to think she was easy. But the delicate, teasing caresses were weakening her resolve and she allowed his hands to continue their exploration, to lightly caress her inner thighs and to move higher still . . . And just as she was thinking she really should stop him right now, before she got completely carried away, a torch was shone directly at them, dazzling her in its beam.

WTF! She pulled away from Raul and smoothed down her skirt, then held up her hand to shield her eyes as the owner of the torch continued to shine it at them. It was one of the security guards.

'What are you doing, my friend?' Raul demanded. 'We are guests at the party, surely you can see that?'

'Just doing my security rounds, sir,' the guard said evenly. 'Sorry to have disturbed you. I'll leave you to it. But just to make you aware, there are CCTV cameras trained on the grounds.'

God, did that mean that someone had been watching them? The thought creeped Tiffany out completely, and it had certainly dampened her desire. It seemed to have the same effect on Raul because once the guard had left, he suggested they should return to the marquee.

Once inside, Tiffany nipped to the loo. She checked out her appearance in the mirror. She didn't look bad. If anything, better than ever. The embrace and the cool air had brought a flush to her cheeks and a sparkle to her eyes. She strutted out of the bathroom, still with Raul's black jacket draped around her shoulders, and ran slap bang into Sean.

'I see you're enjoying yourself, Tiffany,' he commented quietly. He sounded in control as ever, but she wondered if there was a slight edge to his voice.

'I am very much, thank you.' The jacket slipped off one of her shoulders and she pulled it back on. 'How's your night going?' *Not as good as mine, I bet,* she felt like adding.

Sean ignored her question.

'You do know about Raul Garcia's reputation, don't you? He's a player, always with a different woman on the go. I didn't think you were like that, Tiffany.'

For God's sake! Now he sounded like her dad. 'Yes, Sean, I know exactly the kind of man Raul is, but it's cool with me. I know where I stand with him, which is more than I can say for some other men I've met recently.' Oops! She didn't mean to sound bitter. She'd wanted to come across like a woman who knew what she wanted; she tried again.

'It's just a bit of fun. You know what fun means, Agent Murphy? No, of course you don't. Everything is serious, serious, serious with you.' She seemed to be having some difficulty in getting her words out clearly. She pointed her finger at him and swayed slightly, and suddenly she realised that she was a little drunk. Hardly surprising after the number of glasses of champagne she'd had. That was the trouble with champagne, it slipped down treacherously easily.

Sean reached out to steady her. 'I don't want you to get hurt, that's all.'

Instantly Tiffany felt defensive. 'I'm not going to get hurt by Raul.' She shook off Sean's hand and glared at him. 'Haven't you got security rounds to make and more couples to spy on with your CCTV? Or maybe that's how you get your fun.' She probably shouldn't have said that. Blame the champagne, blame Sean for winding her up – *again*.

He looked exasperated. 'That wasn't me, Tiffany.' But she was already marching away, trying her hardest to walk straight.

The party wound to a close quite soon after that. Raul left after stealing another kiss and a promise that Tiffany would meet him on Monday night. As far as she was concerned she had nothing to lose. By 3 a.m. she was drinking tea and tucking into peanut butter on toast with Angel in the kitchen.

Both women had kicked off their heels and put hoodies over their evening dresses. Tiffany was sobering up now, and regretting her outburst to Sean.

'You looked like you were getting on very well with Raul,' Angel commented and grinned at her. 'Aren't you glad that I arranged for you to sit next to him? And Jez told me he's asked you on a date.'

'Yeah, but don't worry, I'm not going to make a fool of myself. We're just going to have dinner.'

'And the rest,' Angel muttered, arching an eyebrow. 'That man is dangerously good-looking.' She paused. 'OMG! I sound like your mum!'

'My step-mum maybe, I can't imagine Tanya caring, can you? She'd be too busy calculating what he was worth.'

'What are you two gossiping about?' Cal walked in through the French windows, followed by Sean.

Tiffany lowered her eyes, feeling embarrassed about their earlier fall-out.

'I was giving Tiffany some sisterly advice about Raul and, quite rightly, she was telling me that she was perfectly capable of looking after herself.' Angel yawned and stretched, 'Well, I'm off to bed. I'm an old lady now, I can't take these late nights any more.'

'Is it hard being twenty-nine again?' Cal teased, putting his arms around his wife.

'Probably not as hard as being thirty-nine,' she bantered back.

'Right, that's it!' Cal replied, and in one fluid movement he picked Angel up from the chair. 'I might be old, but there's plenty of life in me yet.'

'So I can see,' she said, curling her arms round his neck as she looked adoringly into his eyes. And after saying goodnight, Cal whisked his wife upstairs in his arms. Sometimes, Tiffany thought, they could be annoyingly perfect with their PDAs, but you had to love them.

She managed to look over at Sean. The rational part of her wanted to offer him a cup of tea, be civilised, make up for her outburst, while her emotions said, *Get the hell out of there!* But she was just about to put the kettle on when Sean said, 'Goodnight, Tiffany. You'd better have a glass of water and some Paracetamol before you go to bed, the amount you've had tonight.'

Sean wasn't annoyingly perfect, he was just annoying! Tiffany leaped out of her chair. 'I'm *not* drunk! Just because I flirted with a man does not make me drunk! Any woman would want to flirt with Raul Garcia. And d'you know what? It felt good. *He* made me feel good. Which was a change from some men making me feel like total shit!' There she went again, giving too much away. Stop it!

And before Sean could come out with another of his annoying replies, she grabbed her mug of tea and marched upstairs to bed.

Chapter 19

Jez was even more excited about Tiffany's dinner date with Raul than she was, when she told him about it on Monday morning.

'OMG! I bet he is going to take you somewhere utterly divine. It's the start of a whirlwind romance, I can just feel it!' He paused for breath, while Tiffany exchanged eye rolls with Angel.

'He was totally taken with you,' Jez started up again. 'You obviously intrigued him because you're not one of the super-rich socialites he usually hangs out with. You're not some thick rich girl who knows nothing about real life.'

'Are you trying to say that I'm common, Jez?' Tiffany teased.

'Not at all! You're a passionate, independent woman!'

Any minute now Jez would channel Beyoncé and burst into song . . .

'Have you been doing your homework on Raul? I Googled him and Formula One. I had no idea drivers had to be such amazing athletes, but I'm telling you, if you do get up close and personal, you are in for a treat – they have to work out all the time. They have to be incredibly strong. Apparently driving in a race needs the same endurance as running a marathon . . . who knew? I thought they just got in the car and turned the ignition, but it seems their bodies are as finely tuned as their motors!'

There was a small cough from Angel, and she looked at her watch.

'Jez, I'm on air in twenty minutes. D'you think you could possibly talk and work at the same time? I'm sure Eden Haywood doesn't get this treatment from you.' She named a wildly successful British pop star who was another of Jez's clients.

'Eden is touring in Europe so I haven't seen her for the last four months,' Jez said huffily. 'And I'm a consummate professional. *Of course* I can talk and work at the same time, I thrive under pressure.' He reached for the straighteners and began expertly running them through Angel's hair. But Angel had only been teasing him and Jez couldn't stay silent for long.

After less than five minutes he couldn't stop himself from coming out with another comment. 'So where do you stand on sex on a first date?'

Angel and Tiffany burst out laughing. 'Against the wall?' Tiffany teased. 'Isn't it really hard to balance otherwise?'

'Hah! You didn't answer my question and I'm a hairdresser! I have a right to know these things, it's written in my contract. And my advice would be not to give it up for Mr Garcia on the first date. Nothing like a bit of deferred gratification to keep a man on his toes. He'll want you all the more if you make him wait.'

'Is that what happened with you and Rufus then?' Tiffany asked.

'Get real! We had one drink and then it was straight back to mine and straight to bed where we—'

Angel cut across him. 'OK, thanks, Jez. We get the picture.'

'All night long,' he got in. 'So come on, Tiff. To shag or not to shag . . . that is the question.'

Tiffany had quickly learned that with Jez there was pretty much no subject he considered off limits. 'I'll have to see how the evening goes,' she said coyly, knowing that he would be infuriated by her not coming out with a straight answer. But the truth was, she really didn't know. She had never slept with a man on a first date before; she'd always wanted to wait a while, to get to know them better. Then again, she had never gone out with a drop dead gorgeous Formula One racing driver before. Perhaps different rules would apply . . .

Jez glared at her and was about to interrogate her further when there was a knock at the door and Sean came in. What perfect timing! Not! Tiffany pretended to be checking through the show's running order. She hadn't seen him since the party and even though the prospect of a date with Raul was intriguing, the man she had mainly been thinking about was Sean . . . damn him.

'Ah, you can give us the straight male perspective on the question,' Jez declared gleefully, while Tiffany wanted to put her hands over her ears. This was so embarrassing!

'Sex on a first date or not? I think no, Tiffany won't say, so what about you, Sean?'

Tiffany couldn't stop herself from glancing up at Sean, who was in a black shirt and black jeans today. His dress sense seemed to have improved lately. She wondered if he had a new girlfriend giving him some tips.

He shook his head. 'I'm a gentleman, Jez, I would never kiss and tell.'

'I'll take that as a yes then,' Jez said cheekily. He really never did give up.

Sean talked to Angel about security arrangements for

195

the rest of the day while Tiffany pretended that she needed to get something from the dressing room next door. She didn't think she was up to any more of Jez's questions. By the time she returned, Sean had gone and it was time for Angel and herself to make their way to the studio.

Tiffany was feeling increasingly confident about being on TV. She had a really good on-screen working relationship with Angel and the two hosts of the morning show. In fact, she often forgot about the cameras, as it felt much more like a conversation between friends. And she absolutely adored the styling parts of the job. To be able to take a woman who was stuck in style rut, or worse a style disaster, and give them a new wardrobe which boosted their self-esteem felt like such a privilege. The salary she received didn't hurt either. Tiffany had never earned so much money. It was probably a drop in the ocean compared to what other celebrity stylists made, but to her it represented a fortune. She actually had money in her bank account, had paid off her credit cards and overdraft, even had a savings account. It was a world away from the life she had led before she met Angel. She felt incredibly grateful for that.

'Another great show, Tiff!' Angel declared as the two of them packed up their things in the dressing room later. 'D'you want a lift anywhere? Sean's supposed to be driving me back to Sussex but I'm sure we can make a detour.'

Sit in the car with Sean after Jez's sex question? No way! 'I'll get a taxi, thanks. I'm meeting Kara for lunch.'

'And a bit of shopping? Maybe to buy the perfect date outfit?' Angel teased her.

'Maybe,' Tiffany conceded, knowing that after lunch

she was hotfooting it to French Connection with Kara, where she had her eye on a cute white prom dress. She reached for her jacket then paused. 'I'm also going to write to Tanya.'

Angel stopped what she was doing. She looked shocked. 'Why would you do that? I didn't think you wanted anything to do with her?'

Tiffany had been meaning to talk to Angel about their mother for a while. Ever since she had first met Angel she had harboured a wish to see Tanya again, but somehow the timing had never seemed right. But today, when everything seemed to be going so well for her and she had so much to be grateful for, she wanted to open up to her sister.

'I wanted to thank her for putting us in touch with each other.'

Angel frowned. 'It's the very least she could do, isn't it? After totally failing to be a mother to us.'

'Maybe it wasn't all her fault,' Tiffany suggested.

'What? Someone forced her to abandon us and be a heroin addict? She chose drugs over her own babies. I don't want anything to do with her. I vowed that after I met her. Please tell me you're not going to give her any money? She'll never stop asking you if you do, and you'll only be funding her addiction.'

That was exactly what Tiffany was planning on doing. She was also going to suggest that Tanya went into rehab and was going to offer to help in whatever way she could. But it didn't seem like a good idea to share this with Angel now.

'I'm sorry, Angel, I didn't mean to upset you. I suppose I feel so lucky, with everything that's happened to me.'

Her sister shook her head. 'No, I didn't mean to snap. Talking about Tanya is always like opening a wound that I think has healed.' She managed a smile.

'You must do whatever you think is right. It's not up to me to tell you. Anyway, you must get going. Buy that outfit and enjoy your date!'

Tiffany didn't feel that they had sufficiently discussed Tanya, but it seemed as if Angel thought the subject was closed. Her hard-line opinion of Tanya didn't alter Tiffany's own feeling that she wanted to do something for her mother, however small.

Tiffany paced her apartment, checking out her appearance in the many mirrors around the flat. The sleeveless white dress was a perfect fit. Nipped in at the waist with a short flared skirt, it showed off her figure but wasn't at all slutty. She'd tied her hair back into a sleek ponytail – sophisticated, not Croydon face lift. She'd gone for dark eyes, with bronze eye shadow and lashings of mascara, and her favourite Mac lip-gloss in red. She completed the outfit with her prized Louboutins and a silver necklace with stars on it.

'This is just a bit of fun,' she told herself. 'Nothing to stress about.'

Her doorbell rang, and checking the security screen she saw Raul. Wow! She had almost forgotten how stunning he was. He looked like a movie star, hands in his jacket pockets, with that air of confidence of some-one who always got his own way. *We'll have to see about that, Mr Garcia*, she thought to herself.

'I'll be right down,' she told him, reaching for her bag.

Outside Raul was leaning against a silver Aston Martin convertible. Tiffany's ex-boyfriend Billy had had an ancient Fiat Panda, which always smelled of Doritos. There wasn't really any comparison. 'Nice car,' Tiffany commented, as Raul greeted her with a kiss on each cheek. 'If you're trying to impress me, it's working.'

'I promise you, this is just the beginning,' he replied, holding the door open for her, his eyes doing the smouldering thing.

As she walked by him, he lightly touched her arm and said, 'You look beautiful.'

And even though Tiffany had promised herself that she would be on high alert for any corny chat-up lines, ready to crush Raul with her sharp wit, she found herself murmuring, 'Thank you.' The combination of the gorgeous man and the luxury car was rather bewitching. She even managed to get into the car and sit down gracefully, as if she was quite used to getting in and out of motors that cost over a hundred thousand pounds.

Raul drove expertly and at some speed. Tiffany felt as if she was in a movie, driving through central London, with the wind blowing through her hair (thank God for the ponytail otherwise her hair would have ended up in a right state), the roar of the powerful engine, the handsome man beside her at the wheel. She was expecting him to pull up outside an expensive restaurant so it was a surprise when he turned into the multi-storey car park on Brewer Street in Soho.

'I thought you'd have a valet parking your car,' she commented as the barrier lifted.

'I'm not too posh to park.'

'Very funny. So where are we going?'

'One of my favourite restaurants, I always come here when I'm in London.'

Raul held her hand as they walked through Soho and ended up on Dean Street. Tiffany was aware of people staring at them, no doubt recognising Raul.

'Is it strange, having people look at you all the time?' she commented.

'They're staring at you because you're so beautiful.'

OK, he was off. Tiffany swiped a punch at his arm.

'Stop it! I never know if you really mean what you're saying, when you come out with things like that, or whether it's all part of the Raul Garcia seduction technique.'

'Of course I mean what I say to you! Always. I would never lie.'

'Hmm.' Tiffany didn't believe a word.

'So here we are.' Raul stopped outside an intimate-looking restaurant. Again he had confounded her as she had expected somewhere incredibly posh, where she wouldn't have had a clue what to do with her cutlery and would feel out of place. But this, although clearly a very good restaurant, wasn't terrifyingly out of her league. The other diners, sitting at tables with snowy white cloths on them, all looked like normal working Londoners and not as if they had just stepped off a private jet. The maître d' approached and showed them to a candlelit table. Raul ordered two glasses of champagne.

Tiffany looked around her. 'I like it here,' she commented.

Raul smiled at her. 'I knew you would, I didn't think you would be the kind of woman who was only interested in going somewhere because of its status. And you have to promise me that you will eat? I don't think I can have another meal with a woman who doesn't eat the food but pushes it around on her plate as if it is toxic.'

'I'm bloody starving! I've only had half a tuna sand-wich and a packet of Monster Munch, so there's no chance of that!' Tiffany took a wholemeal roll from the basket offered by the waiter.

Raul frowned. 'Monster Munch?'

He really did move in different circles from her.

'Oh, they're sort of crisps. Bright orange, like fangs.' She paused to slather butter on her bread. 'I don't suppose your supermodels or actresses would eat Monster Munch.' She too had Googled Raul. He'd been out with two supermodels – one American, one Brazilian – and an actress. 'So am I your bit of rough, guv'nor?' She deliberately put on a cockney accent.

Raul frowned. 'Of course not! How can you say that? Especially when you look so elegant.' He leaned forward. 'Yet very sexy in that dress.' He paused. 'You are different from my exes, though, and that is precisely why I like you.'

It could just be that Raul was after some novelty after his string of beautiful and no doubt high-maintenance girlfriends, Tiffany reflected over dinner – a very delicious grilled sea bream for her and roast duck for him. And was there anything wrong with that? Wasn't she drawn to him precisely because he was so different from any other man she had known, and specifically different from Sean? Raul was witty, charming, very easy to talk to, and with those good looks . . . why shouldn't she enjoy herself with him? She had a feeling that her heart wouldn't be in any danger.

'So do you want to have dessert here? Or we could go back to my house and have champagne and strawberries dipped in chocolate.'

That smouldering look again. It was definitely working on Tiffany. She was extremely tempted to go back, and it wasn't for the offer of champagne or strawberries dipped in chocolate. Raul was so sexy . . . and the looks he had been giving her were weakening her resolve to make him wait . . .

'I know this never happens to you, Raul, but actually tonight I need to go home alone. I have such an early start tomorrow,' she forced herself to say and even managed to throw in a fake yawn.

'Come over to my house for dinner on Thursday – I promise I'll get you to bed early.' A naughty grin.

Tiffany shook her head. 'You really don't give up, do you?'

'Never,' Raul replied. 'Not when the stakes are so high.'

Half an hour later he pulled up outside her apartment.

'Well, thank you for a lovely dinner,' Tiffany said, unfastening her seat belt and facing him. 'And next time I will pay.' Raul had insisted on paying tonight, in spite of her request that they should split the bill.

'It really was my pleasure,' he replied.

'So . . . goodnight.' She leaned over, intending to go for a quick kiss. But Raul pulled her to him and kissed her deeply, a sensuous, suggestive kiss, which triggered a chain reaction of desire within her and many questions. *Did she really want the night to end now? So what if she slept with him after the first date? If he could kiss as well as this, everything else was bound to be good . . . It had been a long time since she'd slept with anyone, didn't she deserve this? . . . Did she have any condoms?*

But somehow, even though her body was saying yes, she held fast to her resolution. She broke off the kiss. 'Goodnight, Raul.'

He raised an eyebrow as if to say, Really? After that kiss? Then sighed and said, 'Thursday then. I'll text you the address.'

Chapter 20

The following morning Tiffany found herself slap bang in the middle of another media storm as the *Sun* ran pictures of her with Raul under the headline, *Angel's Little Sister Gets in Pole Position!* Some pap had snatched a picture of her and Raul as they walked together through Soho. Kara saw the story first and phoned to tell her in a state of high excitement. 'You're a sleb in your own right now!' she exclaimed. 'It's wicked!'

'Pole position!' Tiffany wailed. 'That is *so* tacky. I've only been on one date with him, and I don't want everyone knowing about my private life. It's meant to be private!'

'Just chill, it doesn't matter. It's a bit of fun,' Kara told her, and then demanded a rundown of the previous night's events. Tiffany cheered up as she recounted the details. She had enjoyed herself with Raul.

But it was no fun leaving the house and discovering a scrum of paps outside again. It was getting to be a familiar and unwelcome scenario. Tiffany reached for her sunglasses, put her head down and tried to march purposefully through the photographers towards the road. God! Where was a taxi when you needed one? A succession of unavailable black cabs sailed past her. And then a black Merc pulled up, the window lowered – this really was *déjà vu* – and Sean called out, 'Need a lift?'

Tiffany didn't need to be asked again.

'Thanks,' she said gratefully, slamming the door on the photographers who were still shouting out her name and pushing and shoving each other in their desperation to get a picture.

'I saw the papers this morning and figured you might need a lift to work.' Sean was in super-serious mode. 'I thought Raul probably wouldn't get up this early.'

He seemed to be implying that she had left Raul lying in bed – *in her bed*! He was doing his judgemental number and Tiffany could do without it.

'He's hardly going to drive from Richmond to the West End, is he?'

'I see.' A beat. 'So how was your night?'

Ooh, wasn't that rather a personal question from Sean I-can't-have-anything-to-do-with-you Murphy?

It was on the tip of Tiffany's tongue to say, *None of your business!* Instead, she replied, 'Very good, thanks. How was yours?'

She'd only been in Sean's company a matter of minutes and he was already winding her up with his questions.

'Fine, thanks.' A pause. 'So do you think you'll be seeing Raul Garcia again?'

Why was he asking her about Raul? What did he care? Tiffany fiddled impatiently with her scarf. 'Yes. Is this the end of the interrogation? Because I'm knackered and I'm going to shut my eyes.'

The cheek! The bare-faced, blatant cheek of Sean asking her about her private life when he always deflected any personal questions and hid behind his 'I'm just doing my job' mantra.

Sean didn't say another word to her for the rest of the journey.

*

204

Tiffany walked into the dressing room to discover that Jez had of course seen the article and pinned it up on the wall, a love heart drawn around the photograph in bright red lipstick. 'Tiffany and Raul, sitting in the tree, k-i-s-s-i-n-g,' he chanted, then winked. 'And the rest! You, my darling, are now officially a sleb.'

She had to introduce him to Kara – they would get on brilliantly.

'You've got the celebrity boyfriend, the TV job, you've been papped more than once. They'll be asking you to go on *I'm A Celebrity . . . Get Me Out of Here!* next. And how about appearing on *The Graham Norton Show*? I love him. You have to promise to introduce me to him if you do.'

Tiffany slumped down on one of the chairs. 'I don't want to go on any shows. I just want to get on with my job.' She picked at her nails, chipping off a fragment of coral-coloured varnish. Bugger! Now she would have to re-do them.

'Welcome to my world,' Angel replied, from the chair next to her. She turned and smiled at Tiffany, 'Are you OK, babe?'

She shrugged. 'Yes and no. I don't want paps outside my flat or taking pictures of me when I'm out.' Even as she said it, she realised yet again how much her life had changed. This last sentence was not something she ever would have come out with three months ago.

'I understand, and it will die down. But I think you might need to get an agent to field all the press stuff. I was going to suggest my agent Susie. She's very good.'

'See, you really are a celeb now you've got an agent!' Jez exclaimed.

Eye roll from Tiffany. 'I haven't got one – I'm thinking about getting one.'

'Oh, get one! It's the celebrity must-have accessory. Like a Chanel bag, a ridiculous tattoo quotation on your body that no one understands, and an addiction to something . . . but preferably not food as that's not sexy. Though you if you did start porking out to deal with the fame, you could always go on *Celebrity Fat Camp* and then bring out a fitness DVD . . .'

Tiffany's phone rang, a merciful release from Jez's stream of consciousness on celebrity. It was Raul. 'Tiffany, my PR has just phoned me about the news-paper – are you OK? The press haven't been bothering you, have they?'

He sounded concerned for her – it was sweet of him. Tiffany could feel some of the stress ease. A photograph of her and Raul in the papers was hardly the end of the world. She looked at the picture Jez had pinned up on the wall. At least it was a good photograph.

'The paps were outside this morning, but Sean picked me up.'

'Who's Sean?' Tiffany detected a note of jealousy. She rather liked that.

'He's Angel's head of security. He was just doing his job.' *And giving me a hard time.*

'OK. Well, if you ever find yourself in that situation again, give me a ring and I'll be right over. And I will arrange to have a driver pick you up on Thursday. He is skilled in getting past the paparazzi.'

'I was going to get the train.' Tiffany wasn't sure if she liked people arranging her life for her. She was used to her independence.

'Please let me do this for you?'

It seemed rude not to say yes.

Raul lowered his voice and she could just imagine his pupils dilating as he continued, 'And I am counting the hours until I see you again. I can't stop thinking about you and that kiss . . . You have the softest lips I've ever kissed.'

Phew! Tiffany felt all hot thinking about it, and didn't

206

even want to retort that he should know, after all the women he'd kissed.

'Raul?' Angel asked as soon as Tiffany ended the call.

'He was just checking I was OK.' She could hardly keep the grin off her face.

'He's very smitten, isn't he, kitten? See? It paid off, not shagging him on the first date.' Jez , naturally.

'Might have. But how do you know that I didn't?' Tiffany teased him.

'A woman of mystery! I like it! Did you?'

Tiffany shook her head, laughing.

After the show Angel arranged a meeting for Tiffany with her agent. Sean drove them to Soho. Angel, of course, had no idea that there had ever been anything between Tiffany and Sean so she chatted away about Raul, wanting to know what he was like, asking Tiffany what she thought of him. Just the sort of questions any sister would ask, but Tiffany felt uncomfortable having it with Sean there – silent, serious Sean.

'Jez said that Raul asked you to go to Italy. That would be awesome, wouldn't it?'

'I'll be working, so I doubt I can go.'

Angel smiled. 'It would be for a weekend, you wouldn't need any time off. Just imagine it – the glamour of the place, watching the race – it would be so exciting. And Raul is so handsome. And he really likes you.' She paused. 'You like him too, don't you?'

Not this conversation in front of Sean! 'Sure, but I'm just going to see how it goes.'

Thankfully Angel didn't have Jez's terrier-like habit of trying to extract information about every single aspect of her love life, so Tiffany was spared any further questions on Raul.

'I meant to ask, did you send Tanya the letter?'

Tiffany had been so caught up in her Raul

infatuation that she had done nothing about it. She felt a pang of guilt. 'No, but I will.'

'Well, let me know how you get on and if she replies.' Angel looked serious. 'I can't imagine what she'll have to say for herself, though.'

Then it was clear that she didn't want to carry on talking about Tanya as she reached for her crystal-encrusted phone and began checking through her messages. Tiffany looked up and caught Sean's eye in the rear-view mirror. As usual she couldn't read his expression. Their former flirtatious banter seemed to belong to another lifetime.

Susie was an extremely competent, no-nonsense straight-talking thirty-something woman. Tiffany clocked and approved of her white designer trouser suit, and black suede Jimmy Choos. As Susie revealed her game plan for dealing with the press, Tiffany registered that she was in the presence of an expert and felt some of the anxiety leave her. She readily agreed Susie should represent her, which meant that from now on Susie would handle the press, and put out any statements when they were needed.

'And we should also talk about your career,' she said once they had dealt with the question of the press.

'It's going OK, isn't it?' Tiffany replied. 'I mean, only three months ago I was was a waitress and now I'm on day-time TV.'

'Darling, you've done brilliantly, but you need to work at your profile. I think we should set up a series of interviews with the celeb mags . . . maybe with a view to you getting your own column. You're the perfect demographic for those mags. You're young, beautiful, sassy. Frankly they should be chewing my arm off to get to you.'

Tiffany looked anxiously over at Angel. 'I'm not sure.

I don't want to trade off Angel's name and talk about her. I only want to talk about my job.'

Susie gave her a slightly sceptical look, as if she couldn't quite believe that Tiffany would turn such an opportunity down.

'I think you should do it,' Angel told her. 'I know you're not going to use me to get famous, but it's fine to give them something – like how well we get on. And they're bound to want to ask you about your private life.'

'Ah, yes, Raul Garcia!' Susie's eyes lit up. 'He's a keeper. If you ever get tired of him, do send him my way!' She gave a dirty laugh. 'Just kidding, I'm very happy with my Eduardo – got to love the Latin man, haven't you?' She quickly snapped out of it and got back to business. 'So how about I make some calls and see if we can set you up with some interviews?'

When Tiffany still hesitated, Angel stepped in. 'Do it, Tiffany. It will also be a good way of raising the show's profile, so everyone will be happy.' She smiled. 'I've been so lucky with my own career I'd love to be able to help you out. And before you say that you want to get there under your own steam, I'm doing it because you're talented.'

Tiffany looked over at Susie. 'OK then, make the calls.'

Susie got an instant and positive response from the mags and Tiffany found herself booked in to do three interviews and shoots – the first of which was going to be on Thursday, her day off from filming the show. Angel must have thought she was doing her a favour when she told Tiffany that she had arranged for Sean to take her to the shoots and stay with her. 'I'm going to be at home with Cal so he's all yours,' she'd said brightly when she'd called Tiffany.

'Are you sure you don't need him?'

'No, we've got two other guys with us and I want you to have the best. That way the paps won't bother you.'

Tiffany couldn't face being alone with Sean in the car and getting the same judgemental treatment from him again, so she called Kara who managed to wangle a day off work – luckily Kara's dad was the most easy-going boss where his daughter was concerned. Then she phoned Sean. Tiffany just bet he was surprised to see her name flash up, but she got straight to the point. 'Listen, you don't need to take me to the shoot on Thursday. Kara's going to come with me and we'll get taxis.'

'Angel did ask me to check that you were OK . . .'

'I am.' She paused. 'To be honest, it would make me feel on edge if you were around.'

'Oh?'

Did she really have to spell everything out for him?

'If you must know, I could do without your comments about my private life. I'm free to do whatever I want and see whoever I want!' Now she sounded like a petulant little girl, but so be it.

A pause, and Tiffany wondered if Sean was going to tell her what he really thought or hide behind his job. 'No problem. I'll let Angel know that this is your decision.'

Sean was so infuriatingly calm – it made her want to stick out her tongue and stamp her feet and throw a massive hissy fit!

Tiffany looked up at the white stucco four-storey Regency house in open-mouthed admiration. Raul's Richmond mansion was even grander than Angel's country house. She thanked his driver, Luis, half wondering if she should tip him, and walked up the stone steps to the imposing front door. It was painted an elegant pale green, flanked by white pillars with elaborate scrolls at the top that reminded her of a wedding cake. She rang the bell, fiddling with the straps of her red maxi-dress while she waited. She had gone for a casual, summery look and hoped she'd made the right call.

Raul opened the door, casually dressed in a white shirt and beige linen trousers. He was barefoot. He even had beautifully pedicured feet, whereas she'd only given hers a quick pumice in the shower this morning.

'Welcome to my house, Tiffany,' he said, after kissing her on the lips. 'I hope you find everything to your satisfaction.'

Why did everything he said make her think of sex? Of writhing on the bed with him, limbs entwined . . . although, at all costs, she must remember to keep her hard-skinned feet away from his baby-soft ones! He would never recover from the shock.

She stepped into a huge hallway, with a black-and-white marble floor. A dining room lay to one side and a living room to the other. Either Raul had just moved in or his taste was minimalist in the extreme as there was hardly any furniture visible. She followed him along a corridor and down some steps into a vast, ultra-modern kitchen. It had aubergine-coloured units and a massive Pop Art painting of a racing car dominating one entire wall.

'Would Dom Perignon be OK for you?'

Raul held up the distinctively squat dark green bottle. This was a champagne Tiffany had never tasted before. Its hefty price tag had seen to that. She stared at him, wondering if he was teasing her.

'That would be lovely. I guess you haven't got any vintage Cristal?'

Raul walked over to an industrial-sized silver fridge and opened it. Where most people's fridges held everyday items, Raul's seemed to be full only of

211

champagne and wine. 'I've got Cristal, Laurent Perrier or Krug.'

'The Dom Perignon is fine,' Tiffany said quickly, adding, 'But where do you put your milk?'

Raul obliged by opening what looked like a cupboard on the outside, to reveal a very well-stocked fridge. He gave a wry smile. 'Anything else you want to see in the kitchen? My tray of organic vegetables . . . my spice rack? Or shall we go through to the garden?'

'Garden sounds good to me.'

It was hard to believe that they were still virtually in London as they sat down in Raul's outdoor paradise, surrounded by a magnolia tree, huge exotic-looking grasses and an elegant water feature, except of course for every now and then when the planes flew overhead to and from Heathrow. 'I'm used to them,' Raul told her. 'I quite like it . . . makes me feel connected.'

He had laid out a delicious picnic of breads, olives, tapas, strawberries – except Tiffany had a suspicion that he'd done no such thing, it had probably been done by one of his many staff.

She sipped her champagne, enjoying the sensation of the bubbles exploding in her mouth. The Dom Perignon was divine. Raul had ruined her. She was never, ever going to be able to drink cheap wine again!

'So, any thoughts about Italy? I'm due there in two weeks' time. You know I would love it if you flew out.'

'Like I said, I'll have to check my work schedule.'

Raul smiled. 'I'm sure that your sister isn't such a slave driver that she never lets you have time off. And you can think of it as work-related, as research . . . you can check out all the styles in Italy.'

Tiffany laughed. 'All the styles of the über-über-rich? I don't think I'm going to be replicating their look on the show. We don't cater for women who have several grand to blow on a handbag, on a regular basis.'

'OK, well, couldn't you just come for my sake?' He reached out, took her hand and kissed it, giving her the smouldering look. 'It would mean so much to me.'

Even though the touch of his lips on her skin set off a delicious tingle of anticipation, Tiffany persisted in playing it cool. 'Don't you need to concentrate before a race and not have any distractions?'

'Pah! I always drive better when I'm happy.' He gave a cheeky grin.

More champagne flowed, they ate some of the picnic, but all the while Tiffany was aware of him sitting opposite her, and wondering what was going to happen next. It came quicker than she had anticipated when Raul pushed his plate to the side and leaned forward on his elbows, 'So, would you like to try out my hot tub? I've just had it installed and need an expert opinion.'

Tiffany burst out laughing. 'That is the worst chat-up line I have ever heard! And you've already come out with some corkers.'

'But it's true! I'll show you the receipt. It's brand new. What do you say? Champagne, hot tub, a beautiful girl. It's an irresistible combination.'

She wrinkled her nose. 'Don't you think it's kind of tacky?'

'You haven't seen my hot tub yet.' He stood up, and reached for her hand. 'Come see and then you can judge.'

Tiffany allowed him to lead her to a secluded part of the garden. The hot tub was surrounded by weeping willows, and under a wooden gazebo with vines trailing over it. The area was discreetly lit and had an intimate, but definitely not tacky, feel.

Her gaze fell on another bottle of champagne chilling in a silver ice bucket. Raul had everything all planned out. A small part of her wanted to resist but she was won over by the fun, the glamour, the brazen seduction of it. Why not enjoy the moment?

Raul looked at her. 'So?'

'I don't have a swimming costume.'

'I promise I won't look.'

'Turn around then. And no peeping!' Tiffany ordered. Only when she was sure his back was turned did she step out of her maxi-dress. She toyed with the idea of keeping on her underwear then thought, What the hell? and unclipped her bra and slipped off her briefs. Then she stepped into the pleasantly warm hot tub and sat on the wooden bench. But this wouldn't do at all! The still water offered a perfect view of her naked body.

'How do I switch this thing on?'

'There's a button by the side of the tub.'

She pressed it and the water began bubbling away furiously, conveniently preserving her modesty.

'OK, I'm ready.'

Raul turned round and smiled at her. 'Close your eyes, Tiffany, I'm coming in.'

Tiffany did as she was told, then couldn't resist peeking at the very moment that Raul walked over to the hot tub completely naked. And what a fine figure of a man he was, with his muscular chest, well-defined abs and a rather lovely-looking—

'Tiffany! You cheated and I didn't!' Raul exclaimed, catching her out but making no attempt to cover himself up.

'I'm no lady, didn't you know?' she said, grinning, as she watched him pour out two glasses of champagne before getting into the tub. Check that out! Hot man in a hot tub . . . and didn't he just know it!

Raul handed her a glass of champagne, then sat down next to her. 'Now we are here, what's your verdict?'

Tiffany sipped her drink. 'I admit that it's very nice. All of it.' She looked at him under her lashes and licked her lips provocatively. God, the hot tub was making her behave like some kind of porn star!

'I'm glad you like it, I want only to please you.'

And then it was as if they both decided that they would not play games any longer. They put their glasses down and, moving closer together, found each other's lips, kissing hungrily while their hands carried out their own explorations under the bubbles. Raul's body felt every bit as good as it looked. He returned the favour, with smooth practised caresses that were tantalisingly arousing. It had been a while since her last encounter with Billy, and Sean . . . no, she wasn't going to go there. She surely deserved the mind-blowing orgasm that was undoubtedly coming her way.

Raul pulled her on to his lap but no way was she going any further without a condom, however turned on she was. 'Beautiful Tiffany,' he murmured as he kissed her breasts. Tiffany shut her eyes as she revelled in the sheer pleasure of feeling this handsome man beneath her . . . but something made her open them again and she yelped in surprise when she saw Luis, the driver, standing by the hot tub. Immediately she slid off Raul's lap and wrapped her arms protectively over her body.

'What the hell's going on?' Raul demanded, turning round.

Luis spoke. 'I'm terribly sorry to disturb you, sir, but there is an urgent phone call for you.'

'Can't it wait?' Raul exclaimed.

'I'm afraid not, sir, it's your mother.' He coughed. 'Your sister is in a bit of trouble again.'

Raul muttered what had to be a Portuguese swear word, then gestured to Luis to bring over a robe.

'I'm sorry, Tiffany, I have to take this call, but I

shouldn't be long.' He blew her a kiss as he put on the robe, but he was as deflated as Tiffany felt, by the look of it.

She stayed in the hot tub for the next few minutes, finishing her champagne, but the moment for getting naughty in the tub seemed to have passed and she felt silly and self-conscious waiting for Raul to return. She hauled herself out of the tub and quickly dried off, dressed and walked back into the house. She paused to look at some photographs on the wall in the hallway: pictures of Raul as a boy with his sisters, at the race track as a young man, hanging out on a yacht with a group of lads – he really did come from a different world to her. But one in particular held her gaze: a silver-framed photograph of Raul with his arm round a beautiful dark-haired woman with cheekbones to die for and sensuous lips like Angelina Jolie's. Tiffany recognised her as being one of the supermodels Raul had gone out with. Now why was her photograph still up on his wall?

Luis came out of the kitchen and saw what she was looking at.

'This is Holly Beech, isn't it? Raul's ex-girlfriend.' Except maybe she wasn't that ex.

Luis looked awkward. 'I am sorry, I was meant to remove it. Mr Garcia did ask me to.'

Tiffany didn't want to get him into trouble.

'It's no problem, I won't say anything.' But she couldn't help wondering whether Raul still had feelings for the beautiful Holly.

'And I'm afraid Mr Garcia is still on the phone and fears that he will be otherwise engaged for the rest of the night. He has asked me to drive you home. He will call you later.'

Tiffany wondered what on earth could be so urgent that Raul couldn't even say goodbye to her. She looked questioningly at Luis. 'It's a family matter, Miss Taylor. I am sure Mr Garcia will be able to fill you in, but for now he cannot be disturbed. Shall we go?'

It was definitely not the ending to the night that Tiffany had been expecting. And it was only half-past eight! She felt totally wired, not at all keen on returning to an empty flat albeit a luxury one. As Luis drove her back into central London, she got straight on her iPhone and texted Jez and Kara to see if they fancied going clubbing. Both said yes and agreed to meet at the Hyde Park flat for champagne first. It would be Sainsbury's own-brand, but, hey, she could live with that . . .

Chapter 21

Tiffany was loving being out with her friends – as she had expected, Kara and Jez hit it off straight away. They gossiped, danced and drank cocktails; gossiped, danced, drank more cocktails. She had swapped the maxi for black skinny jeans and an off-the-shoulder white tee-shirt with a black-and-white picture of Debbie Harry circa 1986. Her gorgeous Louboutins completed the look. She tousled her hair, went big on the eyeliner and false lashes.

Tiffany deliberately didn't look at her phone, because she couldn't help feeling slightly put out by what had happened. She would have been very surprised if Raul had handed out that sort of treatment to his two supermodels and the actress. Maybe he thought he could get away with it with Tiffany. She wasn't super or A-list enough. But hadn't she deserved some kind of explanation before Luis whisked her away? And, yes, possibly she was being over-sensitive, but after Sean that wasn't surprising . . .

'Ooh, that footballer can't keep his eyes off you,' Jez exclaimed as they collapsed on the blood-red leather sofas. 'He's been past here twice, checking you out.'

'He plays for Chelsea, doesn't he?' Kara put in, a

footie fan herself, though she supported West Ham.

Tiffany sipped her strawberry Mojito and shrugged. 'I don't know, but shouldn't he be looking for someone more WAG-like than me? Are you sure he wasn't checking you out, Kara?' Her friend was wearing a gold sequined mini-skirt and black strapless top.

Tiffany crossed her legs and swung her left leg, admiring the shiny Louboutin. So much prettier and more reliable than a man. Every time she thought back to earlier that evening, straddling Raul in the hot tub, a wave of embarrassment, mixed with desire, swept over her.

'I think I might dedicate myself to shoes and fashion and forget all about men,' she declared.

'You don't mean that! And I bet Raul has left loads of messages on your phone. I'm sure he was just as gutted as you about what happened.' This from Kara. The three friends had already dissected the night's events, with both Kara and Jez putting a sympathetic spin on what had happened. Jez had gone off on one and said that it sounded like a great Country and Western song, and then proceeded to sing, 'Oh, my man gone done and left me in a hot tub, and the bubbling, fragrant water can't hide my pain. Did I do something awful to provoke his disdain?' He would have gone on with several choruses if Tiffany hadn't threatened him with physical violence.

One of the men who was with the footballer stopped by them at that point. 'Hi. My friend wondered if you and your friends would like to join him for a drink in the VIP area?'

Tiffany smiled. 'Can't your friend speak for himself?'

'He's a bit shy,' the man admitted.

It was on the tip of Tiffany's tongue to say that if he was trying to procure her for his friend then she was not interested, but Kara was so thrilled to be asked into the VIP area that Tiffany thought it would be mean not to at least have a drink and say hello.

'OK,' she said nonchalantly, getting up from the sofa. 'Lead the way.'

They ended up in a very exclusive part of the club – The Dom Perignon Room, which had walls and leather sofas as green as the bottle holding the champagne Tiffany had drunk earlier that night. The footballer was sitting at a table in an intimate alcove. He stood up when Tiffany and her friends approached.

Tiffany put him at around her own age. He was mixed race, good-looking, with a shaved head and diamond studs in both ears. Tiffany clocked the black silk shirt and leather trousers. Good-looking as he undoubtedly was, he was so not her type. And he might have the body for leather trousers, but that didn't mean he should wear them. Frankly no one should. Whenever she saw anyone wearing leather trousers she only ever thought how hot they must be, and that was hot as in sweaty. The friend, who they discovered was called Gerry, introduced everyone to the footballer then manoeuvred them all into position so that Tiffany was sitting next to the young man. Hilariously she realised that Gerry hadn't bothered to tell them the footballer's name, clearly expecting they would all know who he was. A waiter came over with two bottles of champagne – Dom Perignon, naturally. She was definitely never going to be able to drink cheap wine again . . .

'Thanks for coming over,' the footballer said quietly. He had a strong Manchester accent. 'I've seen you on TV, you're really good.' Tiffany smiled at him; he was cute with adorably long eyelashes that would be the envy of most women. He didn't seem like the kind of footballer who would shag you and then shaft you with a super-injunction . . . but appearances were often deceptive. She leaned closer to him. 'And I would say that I've seen you play football, but,' she shrugged, 'the beautiful game is not for me.'

'No way! I bet you don't say that to Cal Bailey!'

This was awkward. He knew exactly who she was, and she didn't have a clue who he was.

'I do actually.' Then she 'fessed up, 'No, you're right, I pretend that I love football. I even read up on what the offside rule means before I met him. Cal Bailey is an icon.'

The footballer raised his eyebrows. 'But you have no problem telling me that you don't like football?'

Tiffany had obviously had one too many drinks because she wasn't thinking straight. She screwed up her face. 'Sorry, it's been a bit of a long night. Will you accept my apology?'

'A beautiful girl like you? No problem.' He smiled at her then and Tiffany had to admit that the night was looking up. Absolutely nothing was going to happen between her and the footballer, but it was flattering to have two handsome men pursuing her in less than twenty-four hours, even if one had left her on her own in a hot tub. Jez was right, it did sound like a corny Country and Western song . . .

'So what is the offside rule?' The footballer scored for having a sense of humour.

'Well, der! I thought you would know that!' Tiffany teased. 'But let me explain and it will really help out your game . . .' She arranged the glasses and the champagne bottles and proceeded to demonstrate the offside rule.

'You're funny,' the footballer told her.

'Funny ha-ha or funny peculiar?'

'Funny I like you.' He was staring at her.

Yeah, whoever you are.

They talked some more – the footballer told her

about how he had recently moved to London to play for Chelsea, and that he was really missing his friends and family. And girlfriend? Tiffany wondered. He was bound to have a WAG attached to him. Was there any such thing as a single premiership footballer? Tiffany told him about working on the TV show and a little bit about what it was like when she'd found out Angel was her sister. He became sweetly flirtatious, and Tiffany wondered if she should tell him about Raul. Then again, tell him what? *I'm sort of seeing this guy who has just abandoned me in a hot tub?* She bet that kind of thing never happened to Angel.

By now it was after two and Tiffany realised that she was starving – the few mouthfuls of tapas had not hit the spot – and so when the footballer suggested they all go to Balans in Soho, the restaurant and bar on Old Compton Street, Tiffany was well up for it, as were Jez and Kara. Tiffany had been having such a good time that she had completely forgotten who hung round outside London nightclubs frequented by celebrities, but as she and the footballer stepped outside, the paps leaped into action, dazzling her with their flashes. No wonder celebs wore shades at night! No one ever had a bad photograph of themselves taken with sunglasses on, whereas God only knows what she was going to look like. The footballer put a protective arm around her as the paps crowded round, while Gerry muscled ahead to the black Range Rover.

'God, I don't know how you bear it!' Tiffany exclaimed, as Gerry shut the door on the photographers and she sank back in the leather seat.

The footballer shrugged, 'Occupational hazard. You must know that by now. I'm used to it.'

'Hmm, I don't think I'll ever get used to it.'

A full English breakfast later, Tiffany was starting to

sober up and wonder if she had done the right thing in hanging out with the footballer. She hadn't wanted to give him the impression that she was interested – other than being friendly. Whereas the footballer seemed more than friendly now. He had sat next to her at Balans, rested his arm on the back of her chair, addressed all his comments to her. She had also checked her phone and seen that she had five missed calls and a text from Raul and now she was itching to see what he had to say for himself.

'So, can I get your number?' the footballer asked. 'Just in case I need to check that offside rule with you some time . . . or to ask you out for dinner?'

Was this the moment she revealed that she may or may not be seeing Raul? Tiffany bottled it. 'Sure.' She reeled off her number. 'Send me a text and then I'll have your number too. And now I'm going to have to go. I'm filming at midday and really need to get some sleep. Or Darcy, my make-up artist, will have to pile on the make-up with a Black and Decker.'

'OK, funny girl, I'll text you', the footballer replied. And he reached out for her hand, brought it to his lips and kissed it.

'What a gentleman!' Jez declared in the cab on the way back to Hyde Park. 'He's like the acceptable face of a young footballer. I mean, he didn't ask you and Kara for a threesome, or film you performing a lewd sex act on him which he then posted on his Twitter account.'

'He was very sweet,' Tiffany admitted. 'Whoever the hell he was.'

Kara stared at her, eyes wide in astonishment. 'You mean, you still didn't find out his name? I'll Google him.' She reached for her phone.

'I sort of like not knowing his name, it adds to his air of mystery,' Tiffany mused, reaching for her own phone. Now she accessed the text from Raul. *Tiffany, please call me when you get this, it doesn't matter how late, I want to explain and apologise. Believe me when I say that events were entirely out of my hands. Yours Raul xx*

It seemed sincere enough. Next she replayed her voice-mail message from him, another plea for her to call him, no matter how late. And at that moment her phone vibrated with a message. *Hey Tiffany, good 2 meet u tonite. How about dinner Saturday nite? Xxx*

'And I *still* don't know what his name is!' Tiffany exclaimed, after she'd read out the text. Then her phone rang. It was Raul.

'Someone's in demand,' Jez commented wryly. Tiffany didn't answer the call and switched her phone to silent.

'Got him! His name is Andy Lloyd.' Kara triumphantly held up her phone.

'I think I prefer to think of him as the footballer,' Tiffany replied.

'Whatever he's called, he's well lush,' Kara said. 'Then again, so is Raul.'

'Oh, poor Tiff! Torn between a premiership footballer and Formula One racing driver!' Jez replied, 'I feel a song coming on.' And he launched into: 'Torn between two sportsmen, both of them are hot, one drives for Ferrari, the other one's got a yacht.'

Tiffany made a cutting signal under her neck. Anything but Jez's warbles! 'Do you want me to tell Rufus that you ate an entire English breakfast, all of Andy's fries and a banoffee pie tonight?' Jez was supposed to be on a low-carbs diet. In the short time that Tiffany had known him, Jez had been on at least three diets. He always blew them.

'You wouldn't!' he protested. 'You know what that means for me – he'll make me go running with him and I.CAN'T.RUN. It's not in my genetic make-up. I would never have been a hunter gatherer, I would have been back at the cave making it look nice and doing my hair.'

Tiffany folded her arms. 'Well then, don't sing.'

'Spoilsport,' Jez muttered.

'So what *are* you going to do about Raul and Andy?' Kara asked.

Tiffany stifled a yawn. 'Nothing right now. I'll see how I feel in the morning.'

'Perhaps you'd better toss a coin for them,' Jez said cheekily.

Tiffany shot him a warning look. 'I will tell.'

Jez blew her a kiss.

Tiffany's phone rang at ten the following morning, rousing her from a very deep sleep. Blearily she took the call from Susie. 'Andy Lloyd and Raul Garcia! In one night? Isn't that a teeny bit greedy, Tiffany?'

'What?' Tiffany sat up clutching her head. Her mouth felt horribly dry. She was dehydrated and hungover.

'I've had a call from one of my press contacts wanting the low-down on you and Andy Lloyd. Apparently you couldn't keep your hands off each other last night.'

'Yeah, right, and other tabloid clichés,' Tiffany said sarcastically. 'Yes, I met Andy Lloyd at Movida, but it was all completely innocent. Not that I should have to justify myself anyway!'

'Shame, and there was I thinking you were following in big sis's footsteps and falling for a footballer. What do you want me to say then?'

Tiffany sighed and ran her hands through her hair. 'Do we have to say anything?' She couldn't help feeling that anything she came out with would only be used against her.

'No problem, I can just say we decline to comment.' A pause. 'So what is happening with Raul?'

225

Tiffany liked Susie, and admired her professionally, but she wasn't at all sure that she wanted to confide in her. 'I don't know. Let's just say the night didn't go quite to plan.'

'Oh, well. I've got some news that might cheer you up – I've had a bite from a celeb mag about you having your own weekly style column. The money's not great – we're only talking about a grand.'

'A month?'

'A week. And if they got you for that it would be a complete bargain, so I'm pushing for one and a half K.'

It was another of those surreal moments for Tiffany. This new life, so far away from her old one . . .

After the call she dragged herself off to the shower. Jez and Kara had already left for work. As she had breakfast (muesli and yoghurt to make up for the alcohol and English breakfast blow-out) she toyed with the idea of calling Raul. But every time she picked up her phone, she found herself putting it back down as she remembered how embarrassing it had been to wind up in the hot tub on her own. Beyond cringey! How could he have done that to her? She got dressed, careful to avoid wearing anything she had been filmed in before as she and Angel were interviewing one of their guests today in the Covent Garden studio flat the TV show rented.

Outside the flat the paps were out in force. They had clearly already heard about her meeting with Andy Lloyd, unless they were still there because of Raul. She shook back her hair, sunglasses firmly in place, a neutral, I-don't-even-see you expression on her face, and walked through them. And in a lucky break a taxi went past with its light on and Tiffany hailed it.

*

As she walked up the stairs to the top-floor flat she came face to face with Sean who was running down them. He had his super-serious expression on. Don't say that he already knew about Andy!

'Absolutely nothing happened,' she declared bolshily. 'Before you start giving me one of your legendary hard times.'

'What?'

'Between me and Andy Lloyd.' But even as she came out with it, Tiffany realised that Sean looked distracted and clearly didn't know what the hell she was talking about.

'I've got to go,' he told her.

'Is everything OK?' she called after him, as he raced down the stairs, immediately thinking of the kidnap threat.

'My daughter's in hospital.' And with that he opened the front door and stepped outside, slamming the door shut before Tiffany had a chance to ask him what had happened.

Shit! How shallow and stupid of her to think that everything was about her. It was this mad celebrity world. Poor, poor Sean. She quickly ran upstairs to the flat, anxious to see if Angel knew any more about Maya.

Darcy was already working on Angel's make-up when Tiffany rushed in. She didn't waste time on hellos. 'Angel, do you know what's wrong with Sean's daughter? I've just seen him and he told me she was in hospital.'

'She had an asthma attack, a bad one, poor darling.'

Tiffany sat down next to her. 'I didn't even know she had asthma.'

'She was out at a picnic trip for a friend's birthday when it happened so I think it was all pretty scary. And it's horrible for Sean, being so far away. But he should be there within two hours. She's in a hospital in

Cambridge.' Angel smiled at her. 'I'm sure she'll be fine, it's not the first time it's happened.'

'But she might not be. People die from bad asthma attacks don't they?' And suddenly Tiffany burst into tears. She didn't know what had come over her but she couldn't stop.

Instantly Angel put her arms round her. 'Hey, Tiff, I'm sure she'll be OK.'

'I'm sorry, I just feel so bad for her and I guess I'm thinking how I would feel if it was Lily-Rose. And, God, I haven't seen my family for ages. And when Sean looked all serious, I thought it was because he was judging me for being out with that footballer when all the time he was distraught about his daughter. And I don't even know why I chatted to the footballer . . . he probably thinks I'm interested in him and I'm not . . . and I don't want people to think I'm some kind of fame-hungry slag.' Her words were tumbling over each other in a rush. 'I'm sorry.'

Angel looked at her with concern. 'I'm sorry too, Tiff, I thought you were handling all the fame stuff and Raul so well.' She paused. 'Sorry . . . what footballer? I thought you were seeing Raul last night.'

Tiffany sighed. 'I was.' And then gave a quick rundown of what had happened in the last twenty-four hours, ending with, 'So you could say I've had an eventful time.'

'Yes, but you haven't done anything wrong, nothing to be ashamed of. Talking to someone isn't leading them on, and it sounds like you just had fun. Don't be so hard on yourself, Tiff.' Angel hugged her again. 'So much has changed for you and you need time to take it all in. I should have realised that myself. Why don't you take the day off and go and see your parents? It sounds like you could do with a break.'

Tiffany shook her head, and attempted to wipe away

her tears. 'No, I'll be fine, honestly. I'll go and see them after we've finished filming. And if Sean gets in touch with you, you will let me know how his daughter is, won't you?'

Angel promised and Tiffany managed to put on a brave face as she was filmed interviewing Nadine, a single mum from Margate who had lost a staggering five stone and had no idea how to dress for her new figure. No one watching Tiffany, as she smiled and chatted away, would have realised that she felt so emotional and anxious for Sean. They were halfway through filming when Angel received a text from him saying that he was with Maya and she was much better and should be discharged from hospital by the end of the day.

'That's so typical of him,' Angel commented, scrolling through the text. 'He's offering to come back to work tomorrow night. But I'm giving him the rest of the week off, whether he likes it or not.'

Tiffany felt weak with relief. She sent her own message to him, *So glad that Maya is OK. Take care x.*

And then she had another message to send – this time to Andy. *Thanx for the dinner invitation, my life's a bit complicated right now, so I'm afraid I can't make it. You're a lovely guy. Hope u soon feel settled in London, Tiffany x.* It felt like the right thing to do. As for Raul? She still didn't feel like speaking to him and he hadn't called back again. Perhaps that flirtation was over. Right now she felt like she needed time out. Her parents' cosy home offered the perfect escape.

Chapter 22

'Wow, you look about ready to pop!' Tiffany exclaimed as a very heavily pregnant Marie opened the door to her later that day. 'Are you sure you're not having twins?'

'I would roll my eyes but I haven't got the energy,' Marie retorted. 'I've still got over six weeks to go. And FYI that's what everyone's been saying.'

'Sorry.' Tiffany gave her step-mum a kiss. 'It's my day for being insensitive.'

'You never are, Tiff. Come into the kitchen, you look done in.'

Tiffany followed Marie into the kitchen where her dad and Lily-Rose were chopping up vegetables for a stir-fry. It was all so normal. Just what she needed. Chris put the knife down and hugged his daughter. 'We're honoured to see you, Tiffany. Don't you have a Formula One racing driver to flirt with?'

She had given her dad a brief rundown of what had been going on, omitting certain details such as the hot tub.

'Ha-ha, Dad,' Tiffany replied, ruffling her sister's hair.

'Don't be mean. Can't you see how exhausted Tiff looks?' Marie put in.

'I was only teasing! Sorry, Tiffany.'

'It's OK. I am feeling a bit knackered, to be honest.'

'You two go into the living room, and I'll bring through a carrot, orange and ginger juice for each of you. It's a great pick-me-up,' Chris said.

Tiffany pulled a face.

'It's actually nicer than it sounds,' Marie told her.

'It's not!' Lily-Rose shouted.

They settled in the living room. Tiffany curled up on her favourite armchair, Marie lay on the sofa, legs propped up on cushions, which was supposed to ease the fluid retention she was suffering in her legs. 'I've seen elephants with slimmer ankles than me,' she said mournfully.

'They'll go down once you've had the baby.'

'They'd better. My ankles were one of my best features. I don't want to end up with the curse of cankles.'

Tiffany checked her phone and there was a text from Sean. *Maya much better thanks. See you soon. I didn't realise I gave you a hard time. Sorry x*

'Message from Raul?' Marie enquired.

'It's from Sean, letting me know his daughter is OK.'

'And are you OK? You seemed so upset on the phone when you rang earlier.'

'Yeah, I am. I think it maybe all got a bit too much.' She smiled at Marie. 'Honestly, I feel so much better. Seeing you and Dad is just what I needed.'

'And getting the text from Sean, judging by the smile on your face?'

'Oh, I'm just relieved that his little girl is better,' Tiffany replied, realising that her step-mum was right, and not wanting to admit it. She couldn't still have feelings for Sean, could she? What kind of masochist was she!

*

231

On Saturday morning there was a small piece in the *Mirror* about her being seen leaving the nightclub with Andy Lloyd and inevitably a couple of paps appeared outside her family house. They were like parasites, Tiffany thought to herself, only able to feed off everybody else's lives. She did her best to ignore them and spent the weekend chilling out with her family: taking Lily-Rose to her dance and drama classes on Saturday to give her parents a break; helping her dad paint the box room pale yellow, which Marie decided was gender neutral as she hadn't wanted to find out whether she was having a boy or a girl; watching *Dr Who* and *Harry Hill's TV Burp* with Lily-Rose. She offered to babysit to give Marie and Chris a chance to go out, but Marie was too exhausted, so Tiffany and Chris watched *Carlito's Way* again, one of her dad's favourite films. On Sunday she went bowling with Lily-Rose and Chris and had one of her dad's stupendous roasts.

Andy sent a text saying that he understood, but she should text him if she ever fancied dinner. Tiffany had to smile, she couldn't imagine him staying single for long. There was nothing from Raul, but that was hardly surprising seeing as she had not replied to any of his texts or messages. By Sunday night Tiffany was feeling altogether more grounded. And then Raul turned up in his silver Aston Martin.

Tiffany and Lily-Rose were on Wii Dance when the doorbell rang. Chris went to answer it and returned with Raul, who was carrying an enormous bunch of pink lilies. Chris, who was an avid follower of Formula One, was completely star struck to find himself in the presence of a sporting hero while Tiffany was mortified to be caught out dancing to Mika's 'Big Girls (You Are Beautiful)' by the gorgeous Raul, even if she was still cross with him. She should have been glammed up to the max, with perfect make-up, so she could have looked all sultry and unattainable, instead of appearing slightly sweaty, with barely a scrap of make-up on.

'Tiffany, I'm so sorry to intrude like this but I had to see you,' Raul said, while Chris and Lily-Rose stared at him. Any minute now Lily-Rose would come out with her list of questions, and Marie would come in and make an inappropriate comment about Raul's body. Her two worlds were colliding! And she wasn't prepared for it. Mika was still singing about big girls being beautiful in the background. Tiffany put down the Wii remote. She had to get out of there. 'OK, let's go outside.' She started walking out of the living room, followed by Raul who was still clutching the flowers.

'Can I get you anything to eat?' Chris asked hopefully. 'Anything to drink?'

'No, thank you,' Raul replied.

Tiffany marched out into the garden and stood on the patio, hands on hips, ready for battle.

'These are for you.' Raul moved forward to try and give the bouquet to her, but when Tiffany's arms remained folded he put it down on the table.

'Welcome to my world,' she said. 'As you can see, we haven't got round to installing the hot tub yet, but apparently Asda do a great inflatable one. And I don't think you'll find any Dom Perignon in the fridge, Tesco's Pinot Grigio is as good as it gets here. And Daddy had to let the butler go, which is why he answered the door to you himself.' She sounded sarcastic and spiky, which was fine by her as she felt sarcastic and spiky!

'I like Pinot Grigio,' Raul replied. He stepped forward. 'Tiffany, I am so sorry about abandoning you the other night.'

'Yep, well, don't worry about me, I had a great time clubbing.'

233

'So I saw.'

Tiffany was not going to explain herself to him. 'So what was so important? Phone call to Holly Beech? I saw her picture at your house. Are you sure she's your ex?'

He sighed and ran a hand through his hair and for a moment looked uncertain, even vulnerable, not at all the confident Raul she'd thought he was. 'I'm sure she's my ex. The truth is my youngest sister has been battling an alcohol addiction for many years. We all thought she was doing OK but the other night she got arrested for drink driving and became abusive to the police officer and ended up in jail. The reason I had to leave you was to help my mother arrange bail for her and a place in rehab. It took a while.'

'Oh.' Now Tiffany felt awful for being so rude. 'I'm sorry.'

'No, I am sorry. I should have told you what was going on, but I was right in the middle of it. Please, Tiffany, give me another chance.' He lowered his voice. 'Before the phone call we seemed to be getting on very well.'

An image flashed through her mind of Raul caressing her naked body, of her touching his. Yes, they had been getting on very well . . .

'But it's more than a physical connection. I really like you, Tiffany. Very much. And I think we could be good together.'

There was no denying it, Raul was a total charmer. And it was working. Tiffany was thawing. 'I like you too, Raul.'

He smiled, a sexy, lazy smile, a cat that nearly got the cream smile, 'So can I drive you back to London? We could go out for dinner or go back to my place?'

Tempting, very tempting. But it had been a roller-coaster few days, and Tiffany didn't know if she was quite ready to plunge back into that life.

'I'm going to stay here tonight.'

'But you will see me again?'

She nodded. And now Raul moved towards her and put his arms round her. 'I'm not leaving until you tell me when.' Dipping his head, he kissed her lightly on the lips. Tiffany would have been more than happy for the kiss to deepen, but at that moment her dad came out into the garden, which kind of killed the moment. Perhaps she and Raul were destined never to go any further. Immediately she sprung away from him.

'Sorry!' Chris called out. 'Just came to see if you guys wanted anything.'

'We're fine thanks, Dad. In fact, Raul has to get back now.'

'I do?'

'You do,' Tiffany said firmly. She needed to keep her two worlds apart for just one more night, then she would feel strong enough to return to her new life. Also tonight she was finally going to sit down and write to Tanya, something she had been putting off for far too long.

Four days later Tiffany was in a panic about what to wear to the premiere of the latest Johnny Depp film, to which Raul had invited her. The words 'premiere' and 'Johnny Depp' kept exploding in her head like fireworks. What the hell should she wear! She was a stylist, for God's sake! She had to look sensational on the red carpet, nothing less would do. And Raul was used to going to these events with frigging supermodels! How could she compete?

Usually Tiffany had a very clear idea about how she wanted to look, but right now as she sat on her bed with Angel, who was also coming to the premiere, she felt as if her fashion mojo had completely deserted her. It didn't help that it was very hot – around 28° in London, and even now in the early-evening, it was still boiling – so all her stylish LBDs were completely wrong and she would melt in anything that wasn't in a thin floaty material. Nothing she tried on seemed right.

'Just relax, Tiff, and wear something you feel happy in. You must have an outfit like that.' Angel looked cool and calm in a white maxi-dress, her long hair down and held back by a white flower clip at the side. 'What about that?' She pointed at a yellow lace strapless prom-style dress. 'Didn't you say the other day that lace is very now?'

Tiffany selected the dress from the rail. It had been an impulse buy a couple of weeks ago that she had completely forgotten about. She held it against her and looked in the mirror. Against her tan the dress looked fresh and summery. And she had the perfect accessories to go with it – a pearl necklace and matching bracelet, and a pair of leg-lengthening nude platform slingbacks, not Louboutins but they still looked good. And she liked the fact that her outfit was made up of high-street brands.

She quickly changed into the dress. 'What do you think?' she asked Angel.

'Fabulous.'

'Are you sure it looks OK?'

'Yes, yes! Now quickly do your make-up, Cal and Raul will be here in a minute.' She smiled at Tiffany. 'I'm glad you made it up with Raul. He's very taken with you. Cal saw him at some charity event the other night and apparently he could not stop talking about you.'

'I think it's my novelty value. Maybe he's just tired of supermodels and wants a bit of rough.'

Angel shook her head disbelievingly. 'Don't be so down on yourself. You're a beautiful and talented woman and Raul should count himself lucky to see you.'

Tiffany paused in putting on red lipstick to say, 'Thanks, Angel, I appreciate you saying that.'

She shrugged. 'What else are big sisters for? Now, I'm going to open some fizz and we can have a quick glass before the men get here.'

She was just returning with two glasses of champagne when the doorbell rang. 'I'll get it,' she called out. 'Oh, hiya, Sean,' Tiffany heard her say, 'I'll just buzz you in.'

Tiffany wasn't prepared for this; she had assumed that Cal would be driving them. She hadn't seen Sean since his daughter was taken ill. She had thought of him, though, hoping that Maya was OK, and that he was . . .

Angel breezed back into the bedroom with the champagne. 'Here you go.' She clinked her glass against Tiffany's. 'Cheers. Your first red carpet outing! Enjoy!'

Tiffany heard the front door open and Sean walk into the flat.

'Hi,' he called out. 'Where would you like me to wait?'

Tiffany felt awful hearing him ask that, like some kind of servant. 'Wherever you like,' she called back. 'And help yourself to a drink.'

Angel remained in the bedroom, talking to her, though Tiffany was itching to see Sean. Then the men arrived and, while Angel let them in, Tiffany nipped into the kitchen where Sean was sitting at the table, checking his phone. He looked up when she walked in and she was struck again by his good looks.

'Hi, Sean, how's Maya?'

'Much better, thanks. It's just one of those things we all have to live with. How are you?'

'Good, thanks. Yeah, everything's fine. Work . . . everything.' Tiffany was babbling, and she felt self-conscious standing in front of him in her party dress, holding a glass of champagne. There was a glass of tap water in front of Sean.

237

'And you're seeing Raul Garcia tonight?'

'Yep.' Tiffany could hear the men walking into the flat. 'And hopefully Johnny Depp. He's one of my all-time favourites. I love him in whatever he's in . . . *What's Eating Gilbert Grape*, brilliant. *Donnie Brasco*, fantastic. *Pirates of the Caribbean*, long but good.' There she went, babbling again.

'Well, don't let me keep you from your guests.'

He sounded so formal and distant, talking to her out of politeness. And she had wanted to be friendly, to prove that there was no hard feeling on her side. But the same couldn't be said about him . . .

'Um . . . I'd better go and say hi. See you later, Sean.'

Raul and Cal were standing by the fireplace chatting when Tiffany walked into the living room. Both men looked staggeringly handsome in black tie, confident, wealthy, masters of their universe. Again she felt bad thinking about Sean having to wait in the kitchen.

'Tiffany, you look beautiful . . . a cool sorbet for this hot night,' Raul declared, in his typical over-the-top way, walking over and kissing her on both cheeks. 'Missed you,' he whispered.

'And I have a bone to pick with you, Miss Taylor,' he continued. 'You always make yourself out to be some kind of working-class heroine and yet here you are, living in the lap of luxury in one of the most desirable parts of London!'

'Well, first, it doesn't actually belong to me. And second, I still don't have a hot tub. And I am guessing your suit is bespoke.' She pulled back his sleeve. 'You're wearing an Omega watch. Your shoes look handmade. Whereas my entire outfit comes to less than two hundred quid.'

'And yet you make it look priceless.'

She caught Cal and Angel smiling at each other knowingly as if to say, Look at those two flirting.

The four of them drank champagne and chatted. Raul and Cal knew each other fairly well and so conversation flowed easily. But all the time they sat in the living room, Tiffany kept thinking about Sean. Raul was gorgeous, charismatic, charming, very sexy. But Tiffany missed the banter she'd once experienced with Sean. When it was time to leave she gathered up the champagne glasses and went into the kitchen, determined to have one last crack at getting him to loosen up.

'Ready to go?' Sean asked, standing up.

'Sorry to keep you waiting, I hope you weren't too bored.'

'Nope, I was fine, just texting a friend.'

And something in his tone instantly made Tiffany wonder if that friend was female and might even be a girlfriend. And she couldn't stop a hot stab of jealousy, and instead of continuing the conversation didn't say another word but marched out of the room.

'My friend, couldn't you drive a little faster? We're running late and we have to get these ladies on that red carpet.' Raul was speaking to Sean as he drove them around Hyde Park Corner.

Tiffany felt mortified that Raul didn't even know Sean's name, nor did she like his tone – that of a man used to addressing staff. In spite of her own awkward exchange with Sean in the kitchen, she couldn't help feeling protective towards him . . .

'I don't want to break the speed limit, Mr Garcia. We will be there on time, I can assure you.'

'I'm glad you are so confident! At this rate we'll only catch the end credits. And you will have to face the wrath of Tiffany for preventing her from seeing the great Johnny,' Raul persisted.

'Sean always gets us everywhere on time, Raul,' Cal

intervened. 'He's the best head of security and best driver we've ever had.'

At least Cal had noticed Raul's tone and was doing something about it.

Tiffany glanced at Sean in the mirror. Ultra-serious, jaw clenched, eyes unreadable behind the Aviator Ray-Bans, but she bet he was pissed off. Who wouldn't be? Raul draped his arm round Tiffany. 'So, we have been invited to the party afterwards or we can go for dinner?'

'Can I see how I feel after the film?' Tiffany wasn't ready to give in to Raul's suggestions so easily after his off-hand treatment of Sean.

For a second Raul looked slightly taken aback, then he said, 'Of course. As you wish.'

But Tiffany's resolve to keep him waiting was blown out of the water by Angel's next comment. 'Are you going to see your girlfriend while we're at the film, Sean?'

'I am if that's OK.'

Tiffany stared at Sean in the mirror. He had a girl-friend! Since when?

'She's called Erin, isn't she? Honey told me that she was a nanny. It must be hard to get time off together,' Angel continued, blissfully unaware that Tiffany was seething with jealousy.

Sean had a girlfriend! So he had found space in his life for Erin when he claimed to have none for her. Why was she wasting her time even worrying about his feelings! She was such an idiot!

She turned to Raul and put her hand on his thigh. Leaning closer to him, she murmured, 'Let's have dinner afterwards.'

'It's a pity we can't skip the film,' he whispered back.

'But you know how much I love Johnny!'

'Don't say that, you make me horribly jealous.' Raul

kissed her neck and Tiffany turned to him and kissed him on the lips.

They were so caught up in each other that they hadn't realised the car had pulled up outside the cinema.

'Come on, you two!' Cal said as he and Angel waited by the door.

Tiffany quickly stepped out of the car, mindful of keeping her legs together and her skirt pulled down. She had seen too many shots of celebrities showing off too much thigh or worse as the paps tried to get ever-more intimate photographs. Not that she saw herself as a celebrity, but the tabloids seemed to think she was . . .

Sean was holding the door open for them, the perfect chauffeur. 'Thanks,' she said as she passed him, barely giving him a second glance, while Raul patted him on the shoulder and thanked him for getting them there on time. Now Tiffany didn't care that Raul sounded patronising because Sean was with Erin. What did Erin have that she didn't? And then she had to put all thoughts of Sean out of her head as Raul took her hand and they began walking up the red carpet.

Crowds were gathered behind the crash barriers, calling out the names of the people they could see – Tiffany even heard her own name, along with those of Cal, Angel and Raul – and all the while cameras were clicking away. The red carpet was floodlit, and spot-lights were trained up into the night sky from the cinema's grand entrance. Tiffany felt as if she was starring in her own film as she smiled away and prayed that her dress didn't slip down in some wardrobe malfunction. Lady Gaga might be able to pull off the exposed nipples look and not bat a false eyelash, but Tiffany knew she would never have lived it down.

As they reached the entrance the photographers appealed to Cal and Angel to pose together, followed by

Raul and Tiffany. She tried to remember what she'd read about the best way to be photographed on the red carpet – weren't you supposed to put one leg slightly forward, which apparently made you look thinner? Who knows? All she knew was that she really wanted to get inside, away from all the cameras.

'Well done, little sis!' Angel declared once they were inside the foyer, 'You survived your first red carpet! Jez will be so proud when I tell him. You were so much more confident than I ever was. I was like a jelly!'

'I had all of you with me,' Tiffany replied. 'So it was no biggie. Anyway, they're not interested in me! They only want pictures of you lot.'

'Oh, yeah?' Angel raised an eyebrow as a style journalist from *heat* approached Tiffany to ask her what label she was wearing.

As they all took their seats in the auditorium, Tiffany craned her neck trying to star spot, while Raul, Angel and Cal were completely oblivious. She supposed that they were the ones who were used to being spotted and they had been to these events many, many times before. She was hugely excited when she managed to catch a glimpse of Johnny Depp, who was dressed in one of the quirky outfits – a beret, waistcoat and brown pinstriped trousers – that only he could have got away with. Then there were all the usual suspects from various reality shows but even spotting them was entertaining, seeing what they were wearing, how much flesh they were flaunting without actually being naked, how intense their fake tans were – everything from golden brown to Orangina; she was only surprised some of them didn't glow in the dark as the lights dimmed.

In spite of the presence of the lovely Johnny, and having Raul by her side, the film was only so-so and not good enough to stop Tiffany's attention from wandering. She kept thinking about Sean, wondering where he was and what he was doing with Erin. Were they having dinner? Had they gone back to his place? Were they in bed? Was Erin tracing her fingers around the dragon tattoo after they'd made love? No, no, no! This wouldn't do at all. She felt as if her sympathy for him when his daughter was unwell had allowed all her feelings for him to rise to the surface again – feelings which she'd thought she had buried. The fact that he was now seeing Erin only added an extra intensity to the mix. She sneaked a glance at Raul. He was so handsome with his perfect features and gorgeous olive skin. Yes, she should focus on him, on the here and now. Not what might have been with Sean but never was going to be. He was with Erin; she was with Raul.

Chapter 23

'Tiffany, are you awake? I have to go to training now.'
It was Raul speaking.

Tiffany opened her eyes, to see him leaning over her,
freshly showered and dressed in jeans and a pink shirt,
with navy blue deck shoes. Hmm, she might have to say
something about those shoes and that shirt . . . it wasn't
exactly edgy. But then nothing about Raul was edgy; he
was sophisticated, slick, and expensive.

'So, my angel, you can sleep all you like, it's only half-
past six, and then Luis can make you some breakfast.'

Mindful that her breath might not be as minty fresh
as his, Tiffany mumbled, 'Thanks.'

In rom-coms, the morning after the night before
always showed couples kissing passionately, without that
all-important trip to the bathroom to freshen up. But
this was not a film, and Tiffany knew that her breath
must smell of garlic from dinner the night before. If she
kissed Raul now she would probably asphyxiate him. He
maybe had the same thought as he dropped a kiss on
her head and said, 'I'll call you later. Sweet dreams.'

Tiffany snuggled back down under the duvet, needing time to process last night's events. After the film she
and Raul had gone for dinner at Nobu, a flirtatious,
suggestive, will we, won't we time. As it turned out – we

will . . . They had gone back to his house and picked up where they had left off from the week before, though thankfully not in the hot tub. Tiffany didn't know if she would ever want to get into a hot tub again. It was no surprise to discover that Raul was a skilful, practised lover who knew how to please a woman . . . but Tiffany had to admit to being slightly disappointed that when it came to other things, it was all over rather too quickly for her liking. Somewhat prematurely. Somehow she would have thought Raul had more stamina . . . but maybe she shouldn't be so quick to judge. It was their first time together after all and he had pleased her in other ways, very much . . .

She fell back to sleep for another hour and then it was a mad dash to get back to her flat to change before going to the studio. Turning up in last night's dress would have been too much of a giveaway. But of course Jez had her number and wanted to know every detail. Well, as much as she would let on.

'It was very nice,' she finally admitted under his intense interrogation. She was only surprised he didn't shine a spotlight into her eyes to get her to blab.

'Nice! Wasn't it passionate, sensual, erotic? Didn't the earth move?'

'It was and, yes, it did.' In *parts*, she nearly added. 'But I'm not going to tell you any more than that.'

'Spoilsport!' Jez stuck out his tongue, 'At least let me know if he had a big cock or not?'

Tiffany rolled her eyes. 'You're so coarse, Jez!'

'Just give him something,' Angel advised, 'or he'll never let up.'

'OK then, yes, he had a massive wanger! I'm surprised it's not in the *Guinness Book of Records*.'

'Lucky you!' Jez replied. 'So a red carpet moment, dinner at Nobu and then a good seeing to. What more could anyone possibly want?'

245

For it to have lasted a little bit longer . . . a thought Tiffany did not voice. 'And now, I must get on with my work!' She got up and left the dressing room. As she was about to go and talk to the contributor in the next dressing room, she saw Sean walking along the corridor towards her, with Tammy, one of the PAs, who was holding an enormous bouquet of flowers.

'These are for you.' Tammy handed them over. 'Is it your birthday or something?'

Tiffany shook her head.

'Well, somebody loves you! Is it that lush racing driver? Lucky you!' she exclaimed, and then rushed off to her next task.

Tiffany felt herself blush as she thought she might as well have a Post-it stuck to her forehead, reading, *I have just shagged Raul Garcia.*

'Hi, Sean,' she said, trying to sound casual.

'Morning, Tiffany, nice flowers.'

She looked at him. He was wearing jeans and a blue-and-white checked shirt, the sleeves rolled up, showing off his tanned forearms, and despite herself the thought came unbidden into her head that Sean looked like a man who had staying power. *Oh, for God's sake, stop obsessing about him!* she told herself as she went into the dressing room. *If he has got staying power then it's all for Erin.* But even as she tried to tell herself that, another thought popped up. *Lucky Erin.*

Believing Sean to be with Erin, Tiffany threw herself into her romance with Raul, figuring why shouldn't she have some fun? Raul was the perfect boyfriend . . . entertaining, flirtatious, attentive, very sexy. But there was a 'but' lurking in there and it was this: they had spent five more nights together and the sex seemed to be missing something, a magic ingredient to make it zing. It was too much like sex by numbers, and Raul's

246

performance was still disappointingly quick. And there was the other thing. The minute they'd finished, he would practically leap up and go and shower.

Tiffany was all in favour of personal hygiene, but at the same time she loved that moment after sex when you lay in each other's arms, sweaty and satisfied. Raul's hasty showering made her feel as if she had contaminated him. She liked her men a bit more earthy and, well, manly. She knew that Jez would have a view on it, but wasn't ready to share the information with him. And everything else was so good, it seemed mean-spirited to concentrate on the two things that weren't quite right.

And work was just brilliant. Susie had managed to land her the style column in a weekly celeb mag for the astonishing sum of one and a half grand a week. Tiffany was determined to put the money to good use and give some to her dad and Marie . . . and to pay for Tanya to go into rehab, not that she had heard back from her. She resolved to leave it another week and then go and see her mother again and put the offer to her, face to face.

If only she could get over her feelings for Sean, then everything in her life would be pretty much perfect. But every time she saw him, he got under her skin and needled her. Like today, for instance, when she was on her way out of the TV studios and saw him chatting to a young blonde woman in reception. Was she Erin? Tiffany waved at the pair of them, while giving the young woman a surreptitious once-over. Sure she was pretty and slim, but was she any prettier than Tiffany? She registered the warm smile on Sean's face as he chatted to the woman. He never smiled like that for her any more . . . And somehow telling herself that she was going on an amazing date with Raul that night couldn't cut it. She felt in a bad mood all the way home.

Tonight was the first time she was going to meet some of his friends and teammates as they were going to a summer ball organised by Ferrari, for whom Raul raced. She had been all set to wear the midnight blue evening gown but Jez had pointed out that it wouldn't do for Raul to see her wearing the same dress she had worn to Angel's birthday party. Tiffany didn't think that it was a problem but even Angel had intervened and had lent her one of her own evening dresses – a simply stunning red dress by Valentino which she'd had altered to fit Tiffany – along with a pair of breath-taking diamond earrings. Jez was round at her flat now, putting her hair into an elegant updo. Tiffany had wanted to wear her hair down but Jez had overruled her and was busy with the tongs and hairspray. And as the hairstyle took shape, Tiffany had to admit that it was the perfect look for the dress.

'So given that you're about to swan off to a ball with the most handsome man in racing, wearing couture and dripping in diamonds, I have to say that you don't seem that excited.'

'I am too!' Tiffany exclaimed, not wanting to admit that seeing Sean with the woman who might be Erin had taken some of the spring out of her step. Realising that she didn't sound convincing, she added, 'I'm a bit nervous actually. I won't know anyone except Raul and I bet everyone will be' – she put on an upper-class accent – 'frightfully posh.'

That didn't wash with Jez. 'Raul won't leave your side, I can guarantee it, so just enjoy yourself. There, all done.'

Tiffany surveyed herself in the mirror, and even by her hyper-critical standards she had to admit that she looked good. Mind you, the dress was a show-stopper, a vivid scarlet that seemed to glow when you looked at it, as well as being beautifully designed to show off her figure. And then there was no more time to fuss as Raul arrived.

'Tiffany,' he exclaimed as she got into the car beside him. Luis was driving. 'You look exquisite.' He took one of her hands and kissed it.

'But you're missing something.'

She looked at him blankly. He held up a distinctive blue bag from Tiffany & Co. and swung it to and fro from the string handle, as if hypnotising her.

'Wow! For me! Really?'

He nodded as he handed it over. Tiffany hesitated a second before opening the bag and pulling out a blue box. It felt heavy. Inside she discovered a sensational diamond bracelet – five rows of glittering diamonds set in white gold. 'Wow,' she repeated. It must have cost a fortune.

'Put it on then.'

She slipped it on to her wrist. It was the perfect accessory to the dress and diamond earrings.

'You shouldn't have,' she said quietly, feeling slightly overawed by his generosity.

Raul smiled. 'Tiffany, I want to buy you lovely things. Compared to some of the other women I have been out with, you do not seem to think that the world revolves around money. I have plenty of it and even if my racing career ends, my family has more. So, enjoy. You were born to wear diamonds.'

Tiffany kissed him lightly on the lips. She knew that none of her friends would understand but she felt funny about accepting the bracelet. It was too much. Maybe if she was head over heels in love with Raul she would have felt differently, but she wasn't.

The car pulled up outside The Dorchester. 'Don't look so nervous,' Raul told her. 'We're here to smile and be nice to the sponsors. And then we can go back to my place. You look beautiful in that dress, but' – he lowered his voice – 'I cannot wait to get you out of it.' He caught sight of her rolling her eyes. 'What? Too smooth for you?'

Tiffany still teased him about the way he spoke to her. She sometimes felt in danger of being swept up by his world of wealth and sophistication and needed to hold on to reality.

She nodded.

'How about I rip it off you?'

She couldn't see it somehow . . .

'Nope, it's Angel's dress and vintage Valentino.'

'Understood. I will unzip it with caution.'

He held her hand as they walked into the lobby of the five-star hotel where they were directed to the ball-room. Men were in black tie, women were in vividly coloured evening dresses. Everywhere Tiffany looked she could see diamonds and other precious jewels catching the light and sparkling. She took the glass of champagne offered to her by a waiter.

A young man approached them, hand outstretched. 'Raul, how are you?'

Raul turned to Tiffany. 'This is Charlie Beaufort-Black, one of the team's PRs. Charlie, this is Tiffany Taylor, my girlfriend.'

'Lovely to meet you,' Charlie gushed, in exactly the kind of frightfully posh accent Tiffany would expect from someone with that double-barrelled name. 'And I think you may have met my fiancée before.' He could have come straight from the set of *Made In Chelsea*.

Tiffany couldn't imagine where the Hooray Henry thought she might have met any fiancée of his, but she smiled politely. 'Oh?'

'Yah, her name's Claudia.'

Please, *please* let it not be Claudia the bitch stylist. Tiffany rarely used that word against another woman, but Claudia deserved it. Worse actually . . . But Tiffany prayed in vain as Claudia the bitch stylist approached them. 'Raul, how divine to see you again,' she purred.

Claudia was dressed in a slinky gold dress that very few women would have been able to get away with, but she carried off effortlessly. She wore clinking gold bangles on her slim brown arms and a gold band around her head. She looked beautiful, rich and privileged. 'And Tiffany . . . lovely to see you again.' She still said 'Tiffany' with that slightly mocking air she remembered from their previous encounter.

Tiffany was sure that the loathing she felt for Claudia was entirely reciprocated, but the two women air-kissed and smiled at each other. And Tiffany wondered how long Claudia would keep up the friendly façade. After all, Tiffany had been instrumental in getting her fired! But thankfully Raul spotted his agent and one of his closest friends, Bruno Cabassi, and whisked her away to meet him.

During dinner Tiffany and Raul were sitting well away from Claudia and Charlie. Tiffany was actually enjoying herself – so far everyone she had been introduced to was charming – and Raul kept her close to him, as if he couldn't bear to be parted from her. It was only when she went to the Ladies that she came face to face with Claudia, who was checking her appearance in the mirror. Tiffany was about to go past her but Claudia stepped forward, blocking her way.

'I hear you've landed a style column. Congrats.'

Tiffany waited for the sting in the tail.

'So now you can give all those chavvy readers some style tips. Good luck with that! They certainly need them.'

God, she was a stuck-up bitch!

'Actually, Claudia, I think you'll find that chav has become quite an offensive word, especially when used by someone like you. You need to move with the times.

251

You're talking about people who haven't had your advantages . . . who don't have your money. So who are you exactly to look down on them?'

Claudia shook back her mane of blonde hair. 'One is born with style. You either have it,' she paused to look dismissively at Tiffany, 'or you don't. Mind you, you have struck lucky with Raul. I guess you make a change from all those supermodels he usually dates. But don't expect it to last. You're most likely his summer fling. He'll start lining someone else up for winter fairly soon. I can't imagine that he'll be keen to introduce you to Mummy. She's very high up in Brazilian society.'

Tiffany pretended to stifle a yawn; there was no way she was going to rise to Claudia's bait. 'If you've finished, I'd really like to go to the lavatory. Or is it loo or toilet? I can't remember what you posh people say.'

Claudia looked furious that Tiffany wasn't going to be riled, but stood aside to let her past. Thankfully she was gone when Tiffany emerged from the cubicle. But although she had appeared to shrug off Claudia's barbed words, she couldn't help but be upset by the encounter. She wasn't used to people being so foul to her and looking down on her, and Claudia had mentioned the one thing that made her insecure in her relationship with Raul – namely that she was a novelty to him. *He's a novelty to me too*, she tried to tell herself. But the truth was she had never been a fling sort of girl . . . Fortunately Raul suggested they leave soon afterwards, which Tiffany was very happy to do.

'So how was that for you?' Raul asked some time later, after he had carefully unzipped the red dress, when they had made love and it should have been a perfect end to the night. But Tiffany still felt as if there was something missing, a connection that wasn't being made between them . . . It was on the tip of her tongue

252

to say '*Quite nice*', which was ridiculous as it made her sound as if she was describing a biscuit! 'Fantastic,' she murmured, wondering if there was something wrong with *her*.

'Good,' Raul replied, kissing her on the lips. 'And now I have to sleep, I have to be up early for training.' And sure enough he switched the light off and turned over and seemed to go straight to sleep.

Tiffany, on the other hand, was wide awake. Claudia's words kept swirling around in her head. She quietly got out of bed, retrieved her underwear, slipped on a tee-shirt of Raul's that carried the scent of his expensive citrus aftershave, and went downstairs. She made herself a cup of tea and curled up on one of the silver velvet sofas. She switched on the vast plasma TV and started mindlessly watching *The Hills*. The champagne had given her a headache and she felt slightly blue.

She realised that she hadn't checked her phone all night – there were bound to be texts from Kara and Jez wanting to know how she had got on. She retrieved it from her bag and switched it on. There were ten missed calls from her dad. *Oh my God!* Panic coursed through her as she instantly feared there must be something wrong. She hit voice-mail. Marie had been rushed into hospital after going into premature labour. Tiffany tried calling her dad but his phone was switched off. She was about to dash upstairs and get dressed when the doorbell rang. Who the hell could it be? It was after 4 a.m.

Cautiously she approached the front door and looked through the spy hole. To her astonishment, she saw Sean standing on the doorstep. Tiffany quickly unlocked the door. He got straight to the point,

'Your dad called me because Marie's in hospital and he couldn't get hold of you. I can take you to see them.'

'I had my phone switched off . . . I didn't realise.' Her eyes filled with tears. 'Did Dad tell you how she was? And the baby?'

Sean shook his head. 'Just that he'd like you to be there.'

'I can't bear it if anything's happened to them.' Tiffany's voice cracked with emotion. Sean stepped towards her and put his arms round her, and for a moment she clung to him. Even in the midst of feeling distraught she registered how good it felt to be close to him.

He gently pulled away. 'Get dressed and I'll meet you in the car.'

They were quiet on the drive, the silence broken every now and then by Sean asking her if she was OK. 'Not really,' she told him after the third time he'd asked. 'I feel awful that Dad couldn't get hold of me. I don't know why I didn't check my phone. It was stupid of me.' She'd had no choice but to put the red evening dress back on, having no other clothes with her.

'Well, you had a big night out, so it's not surprising.'

Tiffany was too strung out to be sure if Sean was being patronising or not, and his next comment showed that perhaps he wasn't as he glanced at her and said, 'Don't beat yourself up about it. We'll be there soon.'

Tiffany felt as if she was in a nightmare as she raced into the hospital, while Sean parked the car. She left her shoes in the car and ran barefoot all the way to the Obstetrics ward. *Please be OK, Marie, please, please, please*, beat out a rhythm in her head as she ran. And then she was standing outside the security door to the ward and praying so hard. She was buzzed in, and could hardly get her words out as she asked the midwife on duty where Marie was. There was a horrible moment when the midwife consulted a chart and Tiffany was convinced that she was going to tell her that Marie was dead. But then she directed her to a side room. Chris was sitting by his wife's bedside, Marie appeared to be asleep and there was no sign of the baby. Tiffany tentatively opened the door and walked in.

'Dad,' she whispered.

He turned round, looking exhausted and red-eyed. 'Tiffany, thank God you're here!' He stood up and hugged her tight.

'How's Marie and . . .' She just couldn't say 'the baby'.

'She's lost a lot of blood and had to have a transfusion, but she should be fine. The baby's in special care. We have a little girl. She's in an incubator as she needs help with her breathing, but she's going to be OK. She's a tough one, just like her mother.'

'Oh, Dad, I was so worried.' Tiffany hadn't cried until now, but she couldn't stop the tears from falling.

'I didn't mean to worry you with all the calls and then sending Sean, I just needed you to be here because there was a minute it looked as if things weren't going to be OK. But they are, Tiffany, they really are.'

She sat down for a while, catching her breath, trying to calm herself. Eventually Chris told her, 'You should go and let Sean know. And thank him from us.'

Tiffany tracked him down in the car park where he was sitting in the Merc. She tapped on the window and he got out of the car. 'They're OK. Thank you so much, Sean.'

He ran a hand over his head. 'What a relief.'

She thought about how much he must dread hospitals because of his experience with his daughter; the frantic rush to get here must have triggered painful memories.

'Thank you,' she said again and, stepping forward, kissed him on the cheek. And then everything seemed to happen very quickly as Sean caught her in his arms and kissed her back. And whoah! What a kiss, soft at first . . . then gaining in intensity, and Tiffany couldn't think about anything other than how good this felt. She curled her arms round his neck, pressing her body into his. God, she wanted him so much, felt waves of desire building up inside her. She wanted to shower kisses on him, rip off his clothes. And it wasn't one-sided. Sean's arms were around her, pulling her close to him. Both of them seemed caught up in their passion for each other. She didn't care that anyone could see them . . . This was what she had wanted for so long . . .

But the kiss was shattered by the ringing of his mobile phone. Sean pulled away. 'I'm sorry, I'll have to take this.'

Reality forced its way back. What was she doing? She was with Raul; Sean with Erin. This was completely mad! Any second now Sean would turn round and reject her all over again, talk about how unprofessional it was. She couldn't go through that a second time.

Mumbling another, 'Thanks,' Tiffany sprinted into the hospital and didn't look back.

Chapter 24

Angel was in a panic. It was six in the morning and Tiffany had just called her to give her the news about her step-mum and the baby. She had said that she would come in and do the show, in true trouper style, but it was clear to Angel that she was exhausted. 'No way! Take the day off. I'll clear it with Oscar. Now go and have a rest, and give that new sister of yours a kiss from me.'

She knew she had made the right decision in letting Tiff have time off, but God knows how they were going to fill the slot. She could talk round the outfits a little bit, but not as expertly as Tiff. And she didn't feel that great herself. She sighed. The show had to go on.

Oscar was not well pleased about her decision, but then Angel had a spur-of-the-moment brainwave when she thought about having Jez on the sofa with her for a special on hair. They could get a couple of models in and he could talk them through some styles. Oscar agreed and then there was Jez to convince, or rather calm down as he went off into orbit with excitement, and then moaned that she should have given him more warning so he could have got a spray tan and had his roots done.

'That's showbusiness,' Cal told her as she filled him in on what was going on over breakfast.

'I could do without it,' Angel muttered. Cal had made her muesli with yoghurt, but unusually for her she no appetite. The cereal tasted like cardboard.

'Are you OK?' he asked, sitting down opposite her.

'I don't feel great, I'm probably just tired.'

'Well, take it easy, and I'll pick you up after the show. We can have lunch. How about The Ivy?'

It was only when Angel was in the car and Sean was driving her to London that she realised her period was late – four days late to be precise – and she was never late. 'Sean, I've got to stop at a chemist right now!' she exclaimed.

'Just as soon as we get off the M25,' he told her.

She looked out of the window, and realised they were still on the motorway, 'Oh, yeah, sorry, I'm a bit distracted.' Could she be pregnant? She did feel tired, and she had a weird metal taste in her mouth that she was sure she'd had when she was pregnant with Honey.

She tried to gather her thoughts, not wanting to get her hopes up too much – she knew how bad the crash could be if it turned out to be a false alarm. 'Cal said you drove Tiff to the hospital last night. Thanks so much for doing that.'

'I was glad to. Her dad called me because he couldn't get hold of her. And I guessed that she would be staying at Mr Garcia's. She left her shoes in the car, would you be able to give them back to her?'

'Of course, and it was very good of you, Sean. I'm sure Tiffany really appreciates it.'

'Well, I didn't think Mr Garcia would be up to driving anywhere.'

There was a definite edge to Sean's voice that Angel picked up on, distracted though she was. 'Don't you like Raul?' It was unusual for Sean to voice a personal opinion.

'I don't have a problem with him. If Tiffany's happy, that's all that counts.'

It didn't sound as if he meant it, though.

'And what girl wouldn't be happy to be going out with him?' Angel commented.

'Because he's rich and successful?' Sean said flatly.

'I was thinking more that he was so good-looking and charming. I think Tiffany is enjoying the attention but I don't think his money's an issue for her. If anything, I reckon that would put her off. She's very proud where money is concerned. But as you say, so long as she's happy then that's all that matters.'

They fell silent after that, only talking when Sean pointed out a chemist and pulled over and Angel dashed inside to buy a pregnancy test. She bought five. However accurate they were, she was never able to trust just one. She just hoped that no one had spotted her making her purchases; she could do without something so private becoming public knowledge.

As soon as they arrived at the studio Angel dashed to the loo. She couldn't bear to wait another second to find out whether she was pregnant or not. She'd done these tests so many times over the years but she still made herself read the instructions and followed them to the letter. Then she could only wait. She stared at the white plastic stick, willing a cross to appear that would indicate a yes. Almost instantly she could see a faint outline forming! It deepened to dark blue. Yes! Yes! Yes! She wanted to shout out with happiness but was mindful of being in a public place. She had to let Cal know before anyone else found out.

'I'm pregnant!' she whispered into the phone as soon as he picked up.

'You are? That is fantastic, brilliant news! See, I told you we just had to be patient.'

'And have loads of sex.'

'And did you have a problem with that?'

'Nope. And it's lucky we did because who knows when I'll next feel like it?' she teased. Then she was serious again as she was caught up by emotion. 'Oh, Cal, this is just the best news ever! I was beginning to think it wasn't going to happen for us.'

There was complete chaos in the dressing room when she walked in, as Jez was busy doing his own hair and getting in Darcy's way. Angel let it all wash over her. She felt totally serene and, she suddenly realised, very sick. She dashed back into the Ladies and threw up. She smiled grimly as she looked at herself in the mirror. Just another fourteen weeks of morning sickness to endure, if her pregnancy with Honey was anything to go by . . .

Somehow they muddled through the show, with Angel taking up more of Tiffany's role, talking about the style choices, and Jez demonstrating three different summer hairstyles: beachy hair, festival hair and party hair. Angel was usually hyper-alert when she was on TV, but today could feel herself day-dreaming when the camera wasn't on her. She was having a baby! Everything else seemed to pale into insignificance.

'Well, what's your verdict?' Jez demanded as soon as they came off air and walked back to the dressing room.

Angel looked at him blankly, still caught up in her own news.

'On my performance,' he prompted.

Oops! Hell had no fury like Jez not praised. 'You were brilliant,' she quickly assured him. 'Fantastic. We must do it again. I'll see if Oscar can make it a regular slot. And now I have to meet Cal.'

'But I thought we'd have a proper debrief and go through everything,' Jez said, a little sulkily. And Angel realised that she was going to have to tell him her news or risk upsetting him. She linked arms with him. 'I need to tell you something, but it is a secret, though of course you can tell Rufus.'

He nodded.

'I'm pregnant,' she whispered.

Jez looked as if he was about to let out a whoop of joy. He knew how much she wanted another baby. Angel put her finger over her lips.

'*Mamma mia!* That is joyous tidings. Who's the daddy?' he teased. Angel slapped him on the bum.

'Oh, harder, please, I like it!'

An eye roll from Angel, and then she blew him a kiss as she hurried off to meet the daddy.

'To us!' Cal declared holding up his glass of champagne and clinking it against Angel's fizzy mineral water. He reached out for her hand. They were so lucky, Angel thought. She still remembered the dark time when it had looked as if she might never be with Cal again and how lost she'd felt without him, even as she had tried to pretend to herself that she wanted to be with Ethan . . . Cal was the one, there was no other man for her.

'What are you thinking?'

Angel never liked mentioning Ethan's name. While she and Cal had moved on, he didn't like to be reminded of the man she had nearly married . . . nor did she like being reminded of Madeleine, the beautiful French model Cal had seen while she was with Ethan. They'd both had to work hard to let go of the past.

'Just that I'm so thankful we're together.'

'Me too.'

They were quiet for a moment as the waiter carefully placed their plates in front of them – Angel had gone for a simple dish of potato gnocchi, while Cal had roast chicken. Usually she'd have had fish and chips. But she may as well forget about eating anything like that until the morning sickness passed.

Cal waited until the waiter was out of earshot before continuing, 'I've some other good news as well. The police called me this morning to say that they've arrested someone they're convinced was behind the kidnap plot. They can't go into any details because the case is very sensitive and connected to another one about to go to trial. But they think we can let down our guard.'

'That is a relief.' Although Angel had put on a brave face and carried on with her life as normal, the kidnap threat had always been in the back of her mind.

'I'm still keeping up the security for you and Honey, but I don't think we need to be quite so obsessive. I've already told Sean that he's to take a month off. Apart from the time when Maya was ill, he's taken no holiday at all.'

'Poor Sean, I've noticed how knackered he's been looking lately. He's such a hero, isn't he? Always helping people out. He drove Tiff to see her step-mum in hospital last night and then he was back to take me to work.'

'Yeah, the guy definitely needs a break. He's one of those people who is always looking out for others, but seems to forget about himself.'

Angel picked at the gnocchi. She had no appetite. 'I know what you mean. He's very protective of Tiff.'

'He's very protective of all of us, it's his job.'

'Maybe.' Angel wasn't so sure, and wondered if Sean perhaps had feelings for Tiff that went beyond his work. In so many ways she would rather see her sister with someone like him. She felt rather responsible for setting Tiffany up with Raul. She liked him, but couldn't help wondering how serious he was about Tiffany. She really didn't want her sister to get hurt.

Chapter 25

Tiffany would have been interested to hear Angel's thoughts on Sean because even now, a full week after the dash to the hospital, she could not stop thinking about him. Specifically that kiss, the memory of which burned into her, as if it had been branded on to her soul. It had been even more intense than their first kiss all those months ago . . . She kept having to remind herself that it was just a kiss. *Just* a kiss? Who was she kidding? Just the best kiss of her life, a part of her acknowledged, while the rational part tried its best to squash that thought. It was too dangerous, too intoxicating, too bloody overwhelming, far too sexy . . . because here she was watching Marie holding tiny, perfect baby Faith, and still thinking about it! Its intensity took her breath away and she couldn't quite believe that it had finished with her running away and Sean letting her go. It had seemed like the beginning of something . . .

She'd had one text from him since, asking if the baby was OK, but not a word about the kiss. Hadn't it meant anything to him at all? She knew that he'd been given a month off work. He must be spending time with his daughter and with Erin. He'd probably end up marrying her. Maya would be a flower girl . . .

Tiffany had replied that the baby was doing great. She didn't mention the kiss either.

She forced herself back to the present, and focused on Faith. 'She's so beautiful!' she exclaimed. And in truth she was, with her peachy skin and perfect features.

'She is, isn't she?' Marie looked exhausted, but was glowing as well; she seemed to radiate happiness and love. 'I know I should put her down in her cot as she'll get used to being held all the time, but I don't want to. I keep thinking of her being on her own in that incubator in special care.' It had been a traumatic week for Marie and Chris but finally Faith was out of hospital. Tiffany had dashed over after the show to see her.

'Can I get you anything?' she asked. 'Tea, hot chocolate, pint of Guinness?' Marie had to watch her iron intake after the transfusion.

'I'm fine. Your dad's busy cooking up some iron-rich feast. Tell me how it goes in the real world, and what you've been up to? I feel like I've been in a bubble, worrying about Faith. I don't even know what day it is!'

Tiffany had not been up to much except being anxious about Marie and Faith, and obsessing about Sean's kiss. Raul was away in France on some pro-motional tour. Her relationship/fling/whatever she was having with him seemed to belong to another life . . . She hadn't seen him since the night of the ball. She couldn't imagine kissing him again after that kiss with Sean.

'It's Wednesday and I've just been working.' She was about to add the one really exciting piece of news, that Angel was pregnant, but stopped herself in time as her sister had asked her not to say anything to anyone until she was over sixteen weeks pregnant and had had all the tests to check that the baby was OK.

Marie laughed. 'You make it sound as if you've been

doing something really boring, like working at a check-out, instead of appearing on TV!' She scrabbled around on the sofa and held up a copy of *Glamour Now!* and waved it. 'Plus having your own column!'

'I know, I guess my mind has been on you and the baby. And realising what matters most to me.'

'And how about Raul? Have you seen much of him? Has he whisked you off to any amazing places lately?'

'He's been away and I'm supposed to be flying over to Italy to meet him at the weekend and watch the race. It's the Italian Grand Prix. But I'm not sure if I should go.'

Marie looked at her as if she was bonkers. 'Why on earth not!'

Tiffany shrugged. 'I don't want to be away at the moment.' Since the night Marie had been rushed into hospital, Tiffany had been haunted by thoughts of what might have happened . . . And she kept berating herself for having had her phone switched off. She didn't want to voice her anxieties, but her step-mum knew her too well.

'We're all fine,' she said gently. 'Nothing's going to happen. Go to Italy and have a great time. And then you can tell me all about it, I don't get out much, I need the distraction. Well, not all of it! Seriously, you mustn't worry about us, Tiff.'

'I'll think about it.' She knew that she should be excited about the trip – all her friends were, Kara and Jez, even Angel – but there was Sean and that *kiss*. And even if she told herself simply to enjoy whatever she had going with Raul, Claudia's words kept coming back to her. Soon it would be autumn. Would that be when she passed her sell-by date for Raul?

Then there was Tanya. Seeing Marie with her daughter triggered all kinds of feelings in Tiffany about her mother – feelings of hurt and rejection all over again . . . and yet she still felt compassion for her. Tanya must have held her and Angel in her arms, just as Marie held Faith. She must have loved her babies, and then to lose them . . . Tiffany couldn't believe that their mother didn't feel the loss, whatever Angel thought. She still hadn't heard anything from Tanya, but she couldn't let it go. She had to see her, offer her the chance of rehab. Tanya had abandoned her but something tugged at Tiffany, stopping her from doing the same to her mother.

She was dealing with all these thoughts on her own, as she felt there was no way she could confide in her dad and Marie, they were so caught up with the new baby and with Lily-Rose, and Angel had made it clear that she didn't want to have anything to do with Tanya. Tiffany couldn't imagine confiding in Raul. Even though he had a sister with an addiction, somehow she couldn't see him having any conception of Tanya's ruined life . . . The one person she thought probably would understand was Sean. But she could hardly tell him.

She stayed for an early supper with her family and then headed back to London where she was supremely glad when Kara called in on her way home from the hairdresser's. It was the first time Tiffany had seen her friend in a week and she was desperate to confide in her about Sean and the kiss. But first of all she had to give a full account of the birth of her sister. Kara cooed over the pictures of baby Faith and wanted to know every detail of the birth. While a lot of women who hadn't had children avoided hearing any stories about that, for fear of putting themselves off for life, Kara adored hearing them. Nothing fazed her. Once she had got the low-down, her attention turned to Raul and the trip to Italy.

'Have you started packing yet? You're going to need so many different outfits. You know what amazing dressers Italian women are. And say Claudia the bitch stylist is there – you don't want to be outshone by her.'

Tiffany shrugged. 'I'm only there for a weekend. I thought I'd just take a couple of dresses for the evening and my shorts and a skirt for the day.'

Kara wrinkled her nose. 'You're going to be in the VIP area. You've got to dress to impress.'

Another shrug. 'I'll never be able to compete with those wealthy women. I want to be me.'

'Yeah, but you want to be the best you, don't you?'

'I suppose.' Just the thought of it all exhausted her.

'Don't you want to go, babe?'

If she didn't tell Kara about Sean she would scream! Everything else felt like a distraction. 'I kissed Sean,' Tiffany blurted out.

Kara's expression was suitably shocked. 'But I didn't even think you liked him any more?'

'I didn't think he liked me. It just happened.'

'Chemistry,' Kara said wisely. 'That's what you've got between you.'

Tiffany reached for one of the cushions and hugged it. 'It's doing my head in! I can't stop thinking about it. But I've heard nothing from him since. What is it about him? He can give me a look or a kiss and then I'm all over the place. Whereas he's probably being all manly and together with Erin.'

'Babes, two words – Raul and Italy.'

'I know, I know, I'm obviously losing it . . . Maybe I shouldn't go?'

''Course you should!'

Kara was right, wasn't she? Tiffany couldn't be so stupid as to throw away the chance of a relationship with this great guy, all because she had kissed Sean . . . could she? She'd got over it the first time it had happened, she'd get over it again.

*

Tiffany had never flown first-class before and was rather regretful that the flight to Milan was so short, with barely time for her to make the most of the free champagne and the delicious food that bore no resemblance to the plastic-tasting economy airline food she was used to. From Milan she had another short flight to the closest airport to Monza, where the Italian Grand Prix was being held. Knowing practically zilch about the Grand Prix, and with Raul never seeming to want to talk about his sport, she'd had a quick Google and discovered that the track at Monza – Autodromo Nazionale di Monza – was the fastest circuit on the Formula One calendar. The drivers had to do 53 laps – just over 300 kilometres – and the race would probably last a couple of hours.

Luis was there to whisk her straight to the hotel in a blacked-out Alpha Romeo. Tiffany was booked in to the penthouse suite with Raul. It felt strange being in the luxurious rooms without him, almost as if she was trespassing on his space. They had only known each other just over a month and Tiffany didn't feel that their relationship had progressed emotionally beyond their first encounter. They flirted with each other, but it didn't seem to go any deeper than that, and she didn't know if it ever could.

She wandered around unpacking her clothes, opening wardrobes, looking at his clothes. She paused and picked up a shirt. It was an expensive, freshly laundered petrol blue Dolce & Gabbana one. She felt curiously disconnected from him. Was she Raul's girlfriend? Was Raul her boyfriend? They were something to each other, but were they that?

She was still wondering when she arrived at the track. Luis led her straight to the Ferrari team's area. The spectators were already in place, and Tiffany drank in the atmosphere of the crowds, the feeling of anticipation, the noise, the bright sunlight reflecting on the gleaming racing cars. *I'm meeting Raul Garcia, my boyfriend*, she thought to herself. But it still didn't sound right.

Raul was already wearing his team jumpsuit in bold red, the names of his sponsors emblazoned across it. He was surrounded by people who were all vying for his attention, but as soon as he saw Tiffany he walked over to her.

'Tiffany, beautiful Tiffany.' He put his arms around her and kissed her. 'Have you missed me?'

Honestly? No. ''Course. Very much.' She had hardly thought about him. And now, he was as handsome as ever, but where was the excitement at seeing him again? Where were the butterflies?

'So what have you been doing?'

'Oh, filming . . . seeing my parents and new sister.' *Kissing another man.*

'What have you been up to?' *Must show interest in hot boyfriend.*

'Training, training, training. You find me in the peak of physical and mental perfection. And once the race is over, I will be all yours.' He gave her his smouldering look.

Nope, still no butterflies.

'But now I must focus. Wish me luck! Charlie and Claudia will look after you.'

Oh, great . . . Tiffany glanced to the side and there was Claudia the bitch stylist with Hooray Henry. She kissed Raul and hugged him, trying to act like the perfect adoring girlfriend, knowing that Claudia's beady eyes were on her.

'Well, hello there, like some champagne?' Charlie asked.

Champagne might be the only way to get through this . . .

'Thanks,' she replied, taking the glass he offered.

'First time at a race?'

She nodded. 'Yep.'

'Don't worry. Raul is in top form, he's tipped to do well.'

Claudia stepped forward, looking stunning in a turquoise jumpsuit, slashed practically to the navel. Tiffany could only imagine that she herself would look like a smurf in such an outfit.

'It's a tough one for Raul, though, because of Jonas,' Claudia drawled.

'It's always tough, isn't it?' Tiffany replied, wondering what Claudia was up to. She was bound to be point-scoring in some devious, snide way.

'With Holly here to watch Jonas.' Claudia spoke as if addressing a small child, a half-smile playing on her glossed lips.

'You mean, Holly Beech?' *See, I do know about Raul's exes*. But apparently she didn't know everything as Tiffany was floored by Claudia's next comment.

'Then I expect that Raul must have told you they were engaged? It was all very hush-hush, the media didn't know.' Claudia gave a patronising, knowing smile. 'Poor Raul was devastated when she broke it off, five months ago, and went off with Jonas. It makes the race very personal for him, as you can imagine. She's over there. I expect she's about to go off to the Mercedes area, she shouldn't really be here.'

In spite of being shocked by the revelation, Tiffany tried to keep her expression neutral as Claudia nodded in the direction of a tall, dark-haired woman. Holly was talking to another woman who could have been a supermodel herself. At that very moment Raul walked past them. Tiffany watched as the two ex-lovers looked at each other. In that brief glance Tiffany thought

270

she saw longing in each of them. They didn't seem like ex-lovers . . .

Questions collided inside Tiffany's mind. Why hadn't Raul told her he had been engaged to Holly, and that she was seeing a fellow driver? And, more to the point, why hadn't he told her that he was still in love with Holly . . . because that's what the look in his eyes told her? Tiffany didn't want to stay with Claudia and Charlie. As she scanned the room for someone she recognised from the ball, she caught sight of Bruno, and went off to talk to him.

'Ah, Tiffany, you're here. Raul must be so relieved.' He waved his arms around. 'What do you think of it all? It's exciting, isn't it?' Bruno smiled warmly at her, clearly expecting her to share his enthusiasm.

'Very.' Tiffany tucked her hair behind her ears. 'I have to ask you something.' She hesitated and looked behind her to check that the loathsome Claudia was not in earshot. 'How does Raul feel about Holly Beech?'

Immediately Bruno's cheerful expression vanished. 'Oh. You know about Holly?'

'Only that she was engaged to Raul.' She sighed. 'I wish he'd told me. He always made out his past relationships weren't serious. I feel a fool for coming out here. What am I? The reserve until he finds someone else as beautiful as Holly?' Now it was her turn to gesture round the room. 'Well, he can take his pick can't he?'

Tiffany had never seen so many beautiful women in one room – all stunning, with perfect figures and long silky hair. She suddenly felt very upset with Raul, as if he had broken some unwritten agreement between them. They were supposed to be having fun. Finding herself slap bang in the middle of his past relationship was not fun.

'Hey, don't get upset. You are beautiful, Tiffany, and

271

Raul adores you. Really, you have made him very happy. He'd been very down until he met you.'

'I wish I could go,' she said miserably. And indeed she wanted nothing more than to get away from all these people, this world that she didn't feel part of.

'Please don't. It would upset Raul greatly. He needs to know that you are here for him.'

She sighed, and reluctantly agreed to stay.

'Come, let's go and find a good position. The race is going to be starting soon.'

Tiffany allowed Bruno to steer her to the front of the pit wall. The drivers were lined up on the starting grid, some twenty or so cars. She could see Raul flanked by two blonde Grid Girls posing away for photographs. She tried to cheer herself up by thinking how glad she was that she didn't have to wear their outfit of bright red skin-tight Lycra shorts and a matching Lycra cropped top. It didn't exactly seem as if they'd been chosen for their intellectual assets . . .

And then the grid cleared of people as the engines started. The noise was staggeringly loud, a snarling, whining sound that had always made Tiffany clear the room when her dad watched the Grand Prix on TV, but being here was entirely different and in spite of what she had just learned about Raul, she too felt the excitement and tension.

'It's a warm-up or formation lap first,' Bruno told her. She stood on tiptoe, watching the cars take their position on the grid, looking out for Raul in the tomato-red Ferrari, the distinctive yellow badge with the rearing black horse on its side. She could just see his green, blue and red helmet. *Go, Raul*, she urged him silently.

And after the formation lap came the real thing. The tension seemed to ratchet up. Tiffany watched as the five traffic lights above the starting line glowed red, one after another, and then they all went off to signal the start of the race. Bruno acted as her personal commentator, explaining what was going on, where Raul was, the pit stops, the tyre changes. A huge plasma screen showed the race, along with two smaller screens relaying the images from the camera in Raul's helmet. Right from the start Jonas led, or was in pole position, but Raul seemed to be doing all he could to close the gap.

There was a gasp from the room as Raul overtook to gain second place. It was nail-bitingly tense, watching him trying to push forward and get past Jonas. What must he be thinking? Tiffany wondered. Not only was Jonas running away with the race but he was with the woman Raul loved. Or was Raul able to blank out all thoughts, focus only on what he was doing? But however hard he tried, it was destined to be Jonas's race. The black and gold car streaked across the finish line in first place.

'Do you mind if I don't come to the dinner tonight?' Tiffany said quietly. They were back at the hotel. She was perched on the double bed; Raul had just come off the phone to his mother. He seemed very down after the race, which was only to be expected, but now Tiffany knew it wasn't just about that. They had hugged and kissed but once more she felt as if their embrace lacked that vital ingredient – passion.

He frowned. 'Why not?'

Tiffany sighed. 'Why didn't you tell me you were engaged to Holly and that she was with Jonas? I felt such an idiot when Claudia told me.'

'I'm sorry, but what is there to tell? She left me. People leave people all the time. I'm over it.'

He didn't sound like the usual happy-go-lucky Raul today. He sounded broken. Tiffany didn't even feel angry with him, just sad, for him and for herself.

'I don't think you are over it,' she said gently, suddenly feeling very old and very wise. 'I think you still love her.'

She expected him to deny it, but instead he came over and sat next to her, 'I don't know what I think any more. This entire year felt like a kind of punishment until I met you.'

'But I can't make it go away, Raul. You should tell Holly how you feel.'

'What makes you think she would want to know? She's with Jonas – the winner in every way.'

He stood up, 'Come on, we should go to dinner. People will wonder where we are.'

'Why? So you can walk in with me and act like you don't care about Holly? Show that you're on to the next one? You were engaged to her, you must have really loved her. And I saw the way she looked at you . . . I think she loves you still.'

Raul sat back down, and put his head in his hands. 'I did really love her.' He paused. 'I do really love her. I am sorry, Tiffany. You are right.' When he looked up again, his eyes were wet with tears.

She put an arm around him. 'Then promise me you will do something about it? Tell her, Raul.'

She felt nothing but friendship now for this handsome man. He turned and hugged her tight. 'How did you get to be so wise, so young?' He kissed her forehead. 'I will try not to be offended that you don't seem too upset about us.' He put his hands on her shoulders and looked at her. 'Ah, of course! You're in love with someone else . . . that's how you know exactly how I feel!'

Raul was more perceptive than she had given him credit for. But Tiffany still tried to deflect the comment, and shook her head. She would admit to an intense crush on Sean, but that was as far as it went, wasn't it?

Raul narrowed his eyes. 'I don't believe you.'

She sighed. It would be a relief to say it out loud. 'Actually there is someone, but he doesn't care about me.'

'I don't believe that for a second! Who is this man? I will go and tell him to get his act together. He is a fool! Love is all that matters!'

She shook her head. 'There is nothing you can do, Raul.'

He reached for the bottle of champagne. 'I finally got you vintage Cristal,' he said, pouring them each a glass. He held his up, 'To friendship with you, Tiffany. I will always be there if you need me.' He gave his naughty smile, 'And we could always be friends with extras?'

Tiffany punched him lightly on the arm. 'Nope, we couldn't. But friends, yes.' And she smiled back at him.

Chapter 26

It was bliss to be back in London and getting ready for the show on Monday. Tiffany felt very at home in her cosy dressing room, with its battered brown leather sofa, the over-the-top purple velvet chairs with gold legs which Jez had brought in from his salon, the ideas board on the wall where she pinned up pictures of clothes that caught her eye. This was her kind of place now, and she was with Angel and Jez who were her kind of people; she felt she could truly be herself with them. She had parted from Raul on very good terms. She had a strong suspicion that the next time she heard from him, he would tell her that he was reunited with Holly. She didn't feel any regret about her fling with him coming to an end. Instead it felt great to be single. Perhaps now she would finally be able to talk to Sean and find out what he really thought of her.

'You could always give that footballer Andy Lloyd a ring,' Jez suggested as Tiffany flicked through her ideas folder. They had a production meeting after the show and she needed to prepare for it. 'I bet he'd be well up for seeing you.' *Lovely Jez, but so completely off the mark . . .*

She looked across at Angel, who arched an eyebrow and said, 'Jez doesn't get it that actually you might want to be single for a while.'

He gave one of his theatrical shudders. 'Only because *I* hated being single so much. And I don't want to panic you, Tiff, but we're only two months away from Christmas. And who wants to be single at Christmas? That is the saddest time to be on your lonesome . . . except for New Year, waiting for all those couples to finish exchanging kisses on the stroke of midnight, before they turn to you. Sad, single, lonely you.'

When Jez went off on one, he went off big-time.

'Shall I shoot myself now?' Tiffany protested. 'It's only the middle of September – I'm still wearing sandals and a summer dress! We're more than three months away from Christmas.'

Jez shook his head. 'You're in denial, sweet cheeks. As soon as the first of December hits, that's when Christmas officially starts – it's about the run-up, the parties, the anticipation, as much as the day itself.'

'Jez has got a thing about Christmas, Tiff,' Angel explained, unnecessarily.

'I don't just want a White Christmas . . . I want a perfect one! I want to be with my nearest and dearest, eating lovely food, drinking lovely wine, watching festive movies. I want chestnuts roasting on an open fire, I want to walk in a winter wonderland, I want carol singers decking the hall with boughs of holly! I want figgy fucking pudding! And so would you if you'd had the crap Christmases I'd had when I was growing up. My mum and dad divorced when I was five and they always argued so bitterly about who was going to have me and my brother in the run-up that it ruined it. I just wanted it to be over.'

Usually Tiffany would have teased anyone for being so over the top about Christmas, but this was one of those rare moments when Jez let his guard down, stopped being the camp entertainer and showed a glimpse of a more emotional and vulnerable man. So instead she gave him a big hug. 'I love Christmas as well, Jez. But I will survive it if I'm single.'

'But imagine what present you'll get if you do go out with Andy Lloyd. Have you seen the size of his packet? He looks like a man who could fill a girl's stocking *and some*.' The jokey Jez was back.

Tiffany punched him playfully on the shoulder. 'Ouch!' he yelped. 'That's my cutting arm! I'll sue!'

He went off to get coffees after that, leaving Tiffany and Angel alone for the first time that morning.

'Are you really OK about Raul?' Angel asked tentatively. 'I thought you were getting on so well together.'

'We were, kind of, except he's in love with someone else!' *And so am I.* 'We had fun, but that's as far as it went. There are no hard feelings at all. In fact, I hope we'll be friends.'

Angel was looking at her, faintly awestruck. 'Wow, little sis, you are so grown up and sorted! I was nothing like you at your age. You seem so sussed.'

If only Angel knew . . . Tiffany smiled. 'Anyway, how are you feeling?' She noticed that her sister looked unusually pale.

Angel grimaced. 'I'm OK apart from this morning sickness. I can hardly eat anything except dry toast and Marmite. It's so typical that the one time I could really pig out and not worry, I physically can't do it!

'When you've gone public with the news I thought we could do an item on maternity clothes, especially what to wear during the winter. I think it's easier in summer as you can just wear maxi-dresses.' Tiffany raised an eyebrow. 'I mean normal women, of course, because I bet you don't show for ages.' She remembered seeing pictures of Angel wearing what looked like regular jeans when she was heavily pregnant with Honey.

Angel patted her non-existent stomach. 'I'm bound to with this baby as it's my second. But, yes, maternity clothes are a good idea, and we should start planning the Christmas shows, looking at party outfits. And you should get some great invites.'

'Ah, but what could beat the Mamma Mia Christmas party last year where evil Vera tried to seduce all the good-looking waiters, but then had to make do with horrible Vincent the chef. One of the waitresses caught them shagging in the kitchen. She said she would never forget the sight of Vincent's bare pimply bum pumping away. And they were on the work surface! It was very unhygienic.'

'Gross! Don't make me throw up again.' Angel paused. 'You know, Jez has got me thinking . . . I know it's only September, but how would you feel about coming to my house for Christmas? Rufus and Jez are going to be there – I had to ask them in May, would you believe? I think it would be really special if we could be together, for our first Christmas as sisters.'

Tiffany hadn't thought that far ahead and had been assuming that she would be spending it with her family. 'That sounds wonderful, but I'll have to run it by my dad and Marie – I've always gone home for Christmas before.'

'Sure, understood, it's only Jez wittering on that's made me think of it.'

As if on cue he returned with the coffees. 'Wittering on? I never witter on! I make pertinent, interesting comments about life, relationships, hair and popular culture.'

'And men's dicks,' Angel said cheekily.

Jez tossed back his head. 'You know how to lower the tone, don't you, Mrs Bailey!' He sighed as he popped the lid off his latte. 'Anyway, I hardly know what to do with myself since Angel let my crush go on extended leave. Honestly, it was so lovely coming to work and seeing the boy with the dragon tattoo, it really brightened up my day. Colin, the new security guy, is cute-ish but not in the same league as Sean.'

Instantly Tiffany stopped flicking through *Elle*. 'Has Sean left?'

'Not left, but we thought he could do with a break and he's going to be working for one of Cal's former Chelsea teammates who now plays for LA Galaxy.'

'In LA, America?' Tiffany said quietly, hardly believing this turn of events.

'The clue is in the title, sweetie. And there is only one LA.' That from Jez.

'He's coming back just before Christmas, but we thought it would be a good opportunity for him. It's been so intense here these last six months. Poor bloke's in danger of burning out.'

'What about his daughter?' Maybe she shouldn't be appearing quite so interested in what Angel's body-guard was doing, but Tiffany couldn't help it. She had been longing to see Sean, to find out where she stood now that she was single, after *that kiss*. To learn that he wasn't even going to be in the same country seemed too cruel.

'He'll be flying back quite regularly with the player's family, so I don't think he'll see any less of his daughter.' Angel smiled. 'So are you sorted for today?'

'Absolutely,' Tiffany replied, feeling all over the place. But perhaps she needed to get the message once and for all – Sean wasn't interested. He had taken this job in LA without a thought for her. Their kiss was just a kiss, however good. Maybe the defences had been down for both of them and it had overtaken them. Just because the kiss had been so good, didn't mean that it actually meant anything. Oh, who was she fooling? The thought of not seeing Sean again was unbearable!

Tiffany picked up her phone, not wanting to talk about him any more. It was too difficult putting on an act that she didn't care. She checked her messages for something to do. There were texts from Kara, asking if she was free to meet up that night and Marie had sent her a cute picture of baby Faith. Nothing from Sean about his big news.

All Bar One on Villiers Street, just by the Thames, was packed with people winding down after work, but Kara had managed to secure a table by the window. She was reading a magazine when Tiffany arrived, but quickly shoved it in her bag. 'Tiff! Are you OK?' Kara hugged her. 'I feel like it's all my fault because I said you should go to Italy.'

Bless Kara for being such a sweetie. Tiffany sat down. 'I'm fine about Raul. I know I went out with him for all the wrong reasons – I wanted to forget about Sean, and I was flattered.' She held up her hands. 'It was my fault and I'm cool about it.' She found it ironic that people were so hung up about Raul when all the time it was Sean she cared about. 'Any chance of a glass of wine?'

Kara obliged by picking up the bottle of house champagne from the ice bucket. This was not their usual drink when they came here – that was Pinot Grigio, as Sean would know. God, why did everything remind her of him!

'And we're celebrating what exactly?' Tiffany asked, but then she caught sight of the pretty diamond engagement ring on Kara's slim finger. Question answered.

'Oh, wow! You're engaged! That is so brilliant!' She leaped up and gave her friend a hug.

'You don't mind?' Kara asked anxiously, when Tiffany sat down again.

'Why should I? Oh, what? Because my love life is so crap! 'Course not, Kara! What kind of friend do you think I am? Now come on, I want to hear all about the proposal. And I'm guessing that was a wedding magazine you hid in your bag?'

Kara didn't need any further encouragement and filled her in on the details. They'd gone for a walk and Harley had proposed at the top of Parliament Hill fields, with its great view of London, actually going down on one knee. Kara hadn't been expecting it at all. It all sounded very romantic . . .

'And I want you to be my maid of honour and help me choose the dress. I want something classic. But no way are you going to upstage me with your sexy bum, the way Pippa Middleton, her royal hotness, did to her sis!' Kara grinned. 'Perhaps I'll have the bridesmaids in pink or maybe violet . . . something flouncy and bum-concealing.'

'Of course I'll be your maid of honour, and of course I'll help you choose the dress, but no way are you putting me in pink or violet.' Tiffany clapped her hands together. 'Yay! I get to plan the hen party!'

They happily discussed dresses, dissected the highs and lows of weddings they'd gone to. Highs included the beautiful church wedding Chris and Marie had had; lows when a friend's dad got off with one of the bridesmaids in full view of his wife.

It was after midnight when Tiffany arrived home and it was only then that she checked her phone. There was a message from Sean. She felt quite breathless just seeing his name . . . for a second she stared at the first line of the message, feeling that what it went on to say would really matter.

Hi, Tiffany, hope you're OK. Angel told me about Raul . . . sorry. I'm in LA for the next two months but you can always call/ text me. I hope we can be friends. Sx

Friends? Outraged, Tiffany threw her phone on the bed. Friends! She didn't want to be friends with Sean Murphy. Her feelings for him went way beyond friendship. She hadn't had a friend yet she wanted to kiss like she wanted to kiss Sean . . . and so much more! This actually felt worse than the time he'd kissed her and told her he couldn't get involved with her, all those months ago. At least then she had felt there had been some sort of regret about it from him. But now he seemed to have drawn a line under everything that had gone on between them and moved on, leaving her stuck with her hopeless longing for him. This sucked big-time. Tiffany couldn't even bring herself to reply.

After a night when she drank too much wine, listened to Adele's haunting love songs on a loop, and brooded about Sean, the next day Tiffany was determined to get her act together. She had never let a man affect her the way Sean had, and enough was enough. She had a brilliant career, fantastic friends and family, and yet instead of focusing on that, she was obsessing about a man, thousands of miles away, who clearly didn't give a flying fuck about her, except as 'friends'. Not even friends with extras . . . Just friends. It felt like the worst-ever consolation prize.

And in the process of getting herself together Tiffany realised that it had been several weeks since she had sent the letter to Tanya and she still hadn't heard from her. She'd had these grand schemes about helping her mother and what had she done about them? Nothing. She wasn't filming today and she wasn't going to pro-crastinate any longer. She was going to see Tanya.

Could there be a more depressing place to live? she wondered as she hurried through the council estate to her mum's tower block. A children's playground was the only splash of colour amongst the grey concrete, along with the graffiti gang tags sprayed on the walls. She hesitated at the lifts, wondering if she should take the stairs, but her mum's flat was on the fifteenth floor so reluctantly Tiffany got in the lift, which inevitably stank of piss. When the doors slid open she stepped out, trying to remember which end of the corridor her mum's flat was. Now it was coming back to her. Number 55 had a rust-coloured door that reminded her of dried blood, with a black iron gate in front of it.

Tiffany rang the bell, which didn't seem to be working, and then tried knocking, squeezing her hand through the iron bars. No reply. She kneeled down and pushed open the letterbox.

'Hello, Tanya,' she called out. 'It's Tiffany, are you there?'

Nothing. She called again.

The front door of the neighbouring flat opened and she heard a male voice say, 'She's in hospital.'

Tiffany swung round to see a middle-aged man, dressed in a grey hoodie and sweatpants, his belly bulging out over the top.

'D'you know what happened?'

He shrugged, 'Got beat up by her boyfriend.'

'Is she all right?'

Another shrug.

'Which hospital?

'Lewisham, I think.'

Muttering a hurried 'thanks', Tiffany ran to the lifts.

Tanya had looked rough when Tiffany met her all those months ago. She looked even worse now. One eye was barely able to open, a huge purple-black bruise surrounding it; there was a deep cut on her forehead, and her arm was in a sling. She was also pitifully thin.

Tiffany sat down by the side of the bed, wondering what to say to this wreck of a woman, her mother.

Tanya moved her cracked lips and tried to speak. Tiffany leaned forward to hear her better.

'Sorry,' Tanya rasped. 'I told him I was getting off the gear, after I got your letter. That's when he hit me.'

Tiffany felt sick; this had all been her fault.

'I'm so sorry,' she whispered back, 'I never meant for this to happen. I wanted to help you.' She reached out and lightly touched Tanya's fingers, careful to avoid the drip attached to her hand.

'You don't have to say sorry to me,' her mother managed to get out. 'I'm going to do it . . .' Her voice trailed off, and her eyelids flickered. She was clearly too exhausted to carry on.

For a few minutes Tiffany sat there on the hard, royal blue plastic chair, in a daze. A young Asian nurse walked briskly up to the bed. She smiled cheerfully at Tiffany as she checked the drip and Tanya's pulse.

'Are you her daughter? I recognise you from the pictures.'

Tiffany looked at her blankly. Did the nurse mean from TV or the magazine?

She pointed out a small battered photo album with a white and gold plastic cover, lying on the bedside locker. 'The pictures in there. She was holding it when she was brought in. We could hardly get it out of her hands. She must really love you guys.' The nurse smiled again and walked off.

Tiffany slowly reached out for the photo album. She opened it up and there was a picture of a very young-looking and very pretty Tanya, holding a baby in her arms. *Angel, 3 days old* was printed underneath in wobbly blue biro. Tiffany turned over the page and there was a picture of a chubby-cheeked toddler, who had to be Angel. Another picture – this time of a baby boy lying in his cot in a blue stripy sleep suit. There were no other pictures of him. Then a picture of Tiffany as a baby, clearly only a few hours old, lying in Tanya's arms. Chris was there, too, and both of them were smiling.

There were more pictures from Tiffany's childhood – as a toddler playing in a sandpit; her first day at school in her navy blue jumper and pleated skirt; learning to rollerskate; running out of the sea in a scarlet polka-dot swimsuit, grinning away and showing off her gap-toothed smile as she'd just lost her two front baby teeth. The last one showed her heading off to her school prom aged sixteen, dressed in a black strapless dress and looking self-conscious. Tiffany realised her dad must have sent the pictures to Tanya over the years; it was the only explanation. Then there were also news-paper cuttings about Angel and Tiffany carefully tucked into the plastic wallet at the back of the album, along with three baby wristbands, worn by them in the hospital, giving their date and time of birth, sex and weight. The baby boy was called Matthew. What had become of him? Tiffany wondered.

'Are you all right?' She looked up to see a young male doctor standing by the bed and realised that she was crying.

She brushed away the tears. 'Yes.' She tried to pull herself together. 'I need to talk to someone about Tanya and what happens next. She wants to go to rehab, and I'll pay, whatever it takes.'

'She has to want to go to make it work, you do know that?' the doctor said gently, clearly not wanting to trigger a hysterical outburst.

'Oh, she wants to go,' Tiffany said with conviction. 'That's why she ended up here. I know she can get better. She just needs help.' She suddenly remembered something her gran, her dad's mum, had been fond of saying. *There's a light that shines in the darkest place*. Hope. There was hope. Tanya had taken the first step. She wanted to go to rehab, she wanted to change her life. And Tiffany was going to help her.

*

When she returned home she called Angel to give her the news, hoping that she would want to go and see Tanya in hospital. 'She had pictures of us,' she told her sister. 'It was obvious that they were her most important possessions.' And it looks like we've got a half-brother. He's called Matthew.'

'I've always said God knows how many children that woman gave away. And a picture is hardly a substitute for the real thing, is it?' Angel snapped back, surprising Tiffany by her cold tone.

'I know, but she wants to try and get off the drugs now.'

'Bit late in the day, isn't it? She must think you're going to give her money. I told you what would happen.'

'No, I think she's serious about rehab.'

'Even if she does manage it, which I doubt very much, does she seriously think I want to see her, or that I would let her within a hundred miles of Honey?'

Angel was usually so easy-going and warm it was a shock to hear her speaking like this.

'I don't think she expects anything,' Tiffany said quietly. 'Look, I don't want us to fall out about this, so I won't talk to you about her any more.'

'That's probably for the best,' Angel replied. 'I don't have room in my life for Tanya and that's her fault, not mine. In fact, I don't want to hear anything more about her. I'll see you at the studio tomorrow.' And she put the phone down.

Whoah! Tiffany hadn't been expecting that reaction. But it didn't lessen her determination to help her mum.

Chapter 27

In the weeks that followed, Tiffany stuck to her resolution to get on with her life and not allow herself to waste time thinking about Sean. Easier said than done, of course. She was very disciplined at work, but at home when she was alone it was harder and she had moments of intense longing for him and definitely not as a friend . . . But she was busier than ever, with filming the show and writing her column. And on top of that she and Angel had come up with the idea of launching their own clothing and jewellery range online and she was working on plans for that, as well as sourcing suppliers.

Tanya went into rehab and was due to stay there for at least four months. Tiffany exchanged emails with her mum, as Tanya had asked her not to visit until she had completed the programme, and through the emails she was starting to gain an insight into her mum and her life. She'd been abandoned by her own mother when she was five and been taken into care. By the time she was fifteen she'd had thirty different foster carers; it was all too easy to see how drugs became her escape. She had always wanted to keep her children but had never managed it. Matthew had been taken away from her by social services when he was just hours old. He had never got in touch with her. Tiffany said nothing of this to Angel, and her sister never mentioned Tanya.

After a mild autumn, winter had arrived and London looked like a scene from a snow globe. Tiffany adored the snow. Sure, it made getting around difficult, but it was so pretty and she felt like a big kid every time she went outside and saw the frozen white layer on the flash cars parked on her street. She couldn't resist scooping it off and making snowballs. She loved the change in seasons, loved being in the capital city at this time of year, seeing the lights go up and the festive window displays. She went ice-skating with Kara and Jez on the picturesque ice rink outside Somerset House; took Lily-Rose to the Winter Wonderland at Hyde Park; actually enjoyed Christmas shopping as she finally had some money. And Angel was right, she did get invited to some great parties.

Take tonight when she was due at the TV channel's Christmas party at a West End club. It was fancy dress and she and Jez were getting ready at her flat and having a blast. They were dancing around her bedroom to The Black Eyed Peas', 'I Gotta a Feeling' and making inroads into a bottle of champagne. Tiffany was going as a Christmas angel in a white tutu and silver glittery wings. She wasn't at all sure about the outfit; the skirt was very short and the bodice very low-cut.

'I'm meant to be a Christmas angel, not a porno angel,' she grumbled to Jez as she tried to tug the skirt over her bum, then realised that had the effect of giving her even more cleavage.

'Oh, shut up! At least you're not wearing what I am!' Jez was going as an elf and wearing the most extraordinary skimpy green velvet playsuit, teamed with red tights and pointy green shoes, which made Tiffany want to giggle every time she looked at him.

'It's just as well I'm not on the pull,' he added. 'It would be practically impossible to get lucky in this.'

'Unless you met someone with an elf fetish.'

'Whereas you look hot to trot in that outfit. It's not too late to get yourself a boyfriend for Christmas . . .'

Tiffany ignored him, and carefully glued on her silver false eyelashes. There was no point in being subtle; she may as well go for it.

'We're going to have such a good time at Angel's at Christmas, I cannot wait! I'm so glad you're coming. I'm really hoping we get snowed in,' Jez declared, flopping down on the bed. Tiffany was definitely spending Christmas with Angel as Marie and Chris were going to Marie's mum.

'I don't mind being snowed in for a day, but any longer and don't you think we might all go a bit mad? Haven't you seen *The Shining*?'

Jez dismissed her comment. 'We can play charades and watch films, Cal can cook, Rufus could do some workouts with us, I can try out some new hairstyles on you girls . . . what's not to love?' He looked at his watch. 'Come along, Tiff, hurry up and get ready! We've got to get this party started!'

Tiffany was in the mood for letting her hair down at the club. She knew all the people working on the show now, and happily chatted away to everyone from Tammy the PA to Jessica and Matthew the presenters. And then she and Jez hit the dance floor and danced wildly to a succession of Christmas hits: 'Fairy Tale of New York', 'Merry Christmas, Everybody', 'I Wish It Could Be Christmas Every Day' . . . the cheesier the better. Every now and then she'd catch a glimpse of Angel, looking radiant. The morning sickness had finally ended and now she had a glow about her and the tiniest of baby bumps.

After a marathon dancing session Tiffany and Jez headed back to their table. 'Ouch, my feet are killing me!' Tiffany complained, kicking off her heels and reaching for her champagne glass. She'd lost track of how much she'd had to drink. But, hey, it was Christmas and she just about felt in control. It wasn't as if she was going to break into the office and photocopy her bum, and there was no one she wanted to snog and would then regret snogging in the morning. No one here anyway.

Suddenly Jez grabbed her arm. 'At last he's back!' he shouted over 'All I want for Christmas Is You'.

Tiffany looked at him blankly.

'My boy with the dragon tattoo!'

Did he mean who she thought he did? Instantly butterflies and champagne clashed . . . and Tiffany didn't know which was the most intoxicating . . .

'Come on, let's go and welcome back Mr LA!'

No way. Tiffany wasn't ready to come face to face with Sean. She needed to compose herself, sober up, get a grip . . .

'I'm going to the Ladies.' Tiffany shook off Jez's hand and picked up her shoes.

What a sight she looked in the mirror! Her bra strap had slipped halfway down her arm, her tights were laddered, and her mascara had smudged. The silver eye make-up that Jez assured her was great now made her look like a drag queen, and one false eyelash was hanging off. Quickly Tiffany worked to get her act together, brushed her hair, removed the fake lashes, re-did her make-up. Then she suddenly felt giddy and leaned against the basin. Say Erin was here as well? As far as she knew the two of them were still an item. Seeing them together would ruin Tiffany's night . . . and her Christmas.

291

She eased her aching feet back into her heels and walked out of the Ladies, putting on an act that she was fine, but feeling light-headed and jittery. Out of the corner of her eye she saw Jez beckon her over to the table where he was sitting with Angel, Cal, and yes, it definitely was him, *Sean*. He was in a dark suit and Tiffany felt even more foolish in her fancy dress.

She pretended she hadn't noticed and went and sat with Oscar (dressed as a snowman) and a cute young assisant director called Robbie (dressed as Rudolph). She made sure she was sitting with her back to Jez and his party, drank more champagne, chatted away and tried to ignore her racing heart and the memory of the last time she had seen Sean . . . and that kiss.

By now she was feeling pretty drunk; she was getting that spinny-headed feeling, which didn't improve when Oscar left and Robbie suggested they have some tequila shots at the bar. Through her drunken haze Tiffany registered two things. 1. that it probably wasn't a good idea, and 2. Robbie seemed have taken a bit of a shine to her. She based 2. on all the meaningful looks he kept giving her, and by the way he was sitting so close to her, hanging on her every word.

'Great idea!' she exclaimed and leaped out of her seat, wobbling precariously in her heels. Robbie put his arm around her and they walked – she hoped she walked, most likely she staggered – to the bar, where they both perched on bar stools. It took Tiffany two attempts actually to get on hers.

Three shots later and the drunken haze had turned into a drunken fog, but she drew the line at licking salt from Robbie's hand before downing the shots, which was what he suggested.

'Oscar tells me you've got a really cool place. It must be awesome to live so centrally.'

Was he hinting that he wanted to come back? Dream on, Rudolph.

'Well, it's not actually mine, it's Angel's.' Tiffany was having difficulty getting the words out. The third shot had been a shot too far. She was also having difficulty focusing. She squinted. There seemed to be two Robbies talking to her.

He grinned. 'Good to be so well connected, I guess. Another shot?' Two Robbies held up two glasses.

'I think she's had enough.' Sean had joined them.

'Who are you, mate? Her dad? The night's only just getting started, Grandpa.'

What the hell! Tiffany turned and looked at Sean. 'He's right, I'll decide when I've had enough.' At least she thought that's what she'd said, but judging by the look on Sean's face, it hadn't come out quite like that. 'And what about saying hello? Isn't that what friends are supposed to do? I haven't seen you for over two months but how typical – the first thing you say to me is a criticism!'

She jabbed her finger at him and nearly fell off her stool. Sean reached out to steady her.

The two Robbies seemed to realise that Tiffany and Sean had issues and slunk away.

Sean sat down on the stool next to Tiffany and slid a glass of water in front of her. 'Get this down you, you'll thank me for it.'

Tiffany pursed her lips. 'No, I'm going to have another shot.' She waved her hand in the direction of the barman, but just as he was coming over, Jez appeared. 'Tiffany Taylor, I think it's high time we got you to bed.'

'Ooh, what an offer – a threesome with a gay elf who fancies the pants off the boy with the dragon tattoo, and the boy with the dragon tattoo who just wants to be friends.' *Shit, did she really say that?*

'I wanna another shot! It's Christmas! I won't be told what to do by an elf and a control freak!'

Sean nodded at Jez and the two of them put their arms round Tiffany and lifted her off the stool.

From then on everything became a series of disconnected images flashing through her head. Sean putting her coat round her, and leading her to the taxi while she continued to protest. Sitting down next to Jez in the taxi and then leaning against him, head on his shoulder, wanting very much to stop the spinny feeling and go to sleep. Closing her eyes.

Jez shook her awake. 'Tiff, we're at your place. Come on, I can't carry you upstairs. I'm a gay elf, remember, not a fireman!'

Tiffany managed to open her eyes and stagger upstairs to her flat, where all she could do was kick off her shoes, wriggle out of the angel wings, slip out of her dress and collapse on the bed. She vaguely heard Jez urging her to drink some water, and telling her that she was a terrible slut for not taking off her make-up, and then she passed out.

It was extremely fortunate that she wasn't filming the next day as she woke up with a shocking hangover. Her head was pounding, and she kept thinking she was going to be sick. But the physical symptoms weren't the worst of it . . . The worst of it was remembering that she had seen Sean. She had seen him and had been vile to him, not that he didn't deserve it . . . he did deserve it for his 'let's be friends' comment. But she wanted to have the moral high ground. Not for him to have seen her drunk, dressed as a slutty angel. She might just as well have photo-copied her bum. And she had a vague recollection of saying something appalling to Jez . . .

She pulled the duvet over her head, and let the feeling of shame wash over her. It was only around four that she was finally able to drag herself out of bed and the first thing she did was phone Jez. She had an apology to make.

'I can't quite remember what I said, but I know it wasn't good. And I'm sorry, Jez.'

'Oh, enough already! It was funny and also intriguing. What did you mean when you said that Sean only wanted to be friends? Is there history between you two that I don't know about?'

Tiffany was too hungover to be able to lie convincingly. 'You could say that, but as I said, he only wants to be friends.'

'Now hold it right there, missy! If you are going to be divulging the details of your relationship with the boy with the dragon tattoo, I have to see you face to face. Get yourself in a taxi up to mine and I'll take you out for egg and chips. It is the only reliable cure for a hangover.'

An hour later they were sitting in a café just off Islington's Upper Street. Jez had insisted Tiffany should eat before she told him anything. Now she was sipping a strong cup of sweet tea and finally feeling human again.

'So?'

'What?' Tiffany played dumb.

'I didn't just ask you here to watch you to eat two fried eggs, bacon, beans and chips, and two slices of white toast.'

She could do without the rundown of what she'd just eaten . . .

'There's nothing much to tell.'

Jez scowled. She wasn't going to get away with not saying anything.

'OK, I admit it, I've fancied Sean for ages, but he doesn't feel the same way about me.'

Jez held up a hand. 'Now hold on there, I want full and frank disclosure.'

In a way it was a relief to tell him about her feelings for Sean. Jez had quickly become such a good friend it had felt strange keeping this secret from him. 'But he just wants to be friends,' Tiffany rounded off her story. 'Just friends.'

'I'm not so sure . . . he's always been very protective of you. Take last night. He didn't have to rescue you from Rudolph the Randy Reindeer, but he did.'

'He would just see that as doing his job. He wouldn't want me to cause any problems for Angel. Anyway, he's got a girlfriend. Erin.'

'I don't even know if he's seeing her any more. And maybe he only started going out with her when you got together with Raul . . .'

'I got together with Raul because Sean said he wasn't interested, that he didn't have room in his life for a relationship, and because he thought it was unprofessional!' Tiffany had raised her voice during this outburst and half the diners stopped eating their fry-ups, riveted by the exchange.

'As if Angel would mind! I know how much she likes and respects Sean. God, the man's an idiot. Then again, I can just imagine him being all manly and self-sacrificing. Wanting you, but not letting himself . . .' Jez got a dreamy look in his eyes.

Tiffany clicked her fingers to get him back to the present. 'So what do I do?'

'For once, I have absolutely no idea. But I'm sure I'll think of something.'

Tiffany did not share his optimism.

Back home she curled up on the sofa and watched *The Holiday*, needing complete escape. And clearly some kind of release as she was still crying when her phone rang. Raul. Why was he calling her now? They had exchanged a few texts since September. After asking her how she was, and how work was going, he paused.

'I wanted to tell you something.' He sounded slightly nervous.

It was a no-brainer. 'You're engaged to Holly?'

'How did you know?'

'Lucky guess. Congratulations. I'm really happy for you.' And she genuinely was.

'Thank you, Tiffany. I wanted to let you know before the press finds out. And tell me, have you got together with the one you love?'

She sighed, 'No, but it's OK. I'm sure I'll get over him.'

'Ah, Tiffany, so good at giving at advice to other people. Don't you think it's time you took a leaf out of your own book and told him how you feel? What do you have to lose?'

But Tiffany couldn't imagine telling Sean how she felt. He had rejected her once and she wasn't going back for more punishment. No, come January, her New Year's resolution was to forget all about Sean Murphy.

Chapter 28

'I have got some major goss for you!' Jez declared. Angel had just finished filming the show and she and Jez were alone in the dressing room. Tiffany had dashed off to meet one of the contributors.

Angel knew of old that Jez had a tendency to exaggerate and she probably wouldn't even have heard of the people concerned. 'Oh, yeah?' She was mentally going through the list of all the Christmas presents she still needed to buy and was planning a trip to Selfridges to try and get something for Cal. Though what did you buy the man who had everything?

'Tiffany is in love with Sean. And I am pretty sure that he is in love with her!' Now that was major! Jez had Angel's full attention.

'How do you know?' She felt slightly put out that Jez knew something about her sister that she didn't.

'Well, maybe love is over-stating it, but they definitely have feelings for each other.' And Jez quickly filled her in on everything he knew. He felt OK doing this as Tiffany hadn't sworn him to secrecy.

'Who'd have thought it?' Angel mused. 'But I've often wondered if Sean did have feelings for Tiff – he's always very protective of her, and he hated it when she was seeing Raul. He didn't have a good word to say about the guy. And Tiffany never seemed that into Raul . . .' She clapped her hands together in delight. 'This is so romantic!' She was a sucker for a love story.

'It's not that romantic,' Jez said dryly, 'seeing as neither of them is going to admit it to the other. They're both stubborn, especially Sean. And he's all hung up on the idea that it would be unprofessional.'

'God, I can just imagine Cal being like that! D' you remember how he didn't want to get involved with me at first because I was his best friend's sister? The hours I spent longing for that man! Jez, we have to do something.'

They were both silent for a moment then he said, 'Got it! We can be like Santa's little helpers and grant them their Christmas wish.'

'Please don't wear that elf outfit again . . . How do you propose we do that?'

'Tiffany is coming to yours for Christmas, isn't she? And didn't you say that you had invited Sean for Christmas Eve and Christmas Day?'

'They're hardly going to hit it off together with all of us there. Especially you, Jez, you're so unsubtle.'

'How about you ask them to arrive a few days before Christmas, and then you could go away somewhere, leaving the two of them alone in the house?'

'But how are we going to make sure they stay there?'

'You could say to Sean that you're worried about Tiffany and want him to look out for her.'

'Then he'll go into his "I can't do anything about my feelings, I'm a professional".'

'Bugger, you're right. This matchmaking is harder than I thought it would be. I guess all we can do is get them together, and set the scene. The rest is up to them.

Angel had certainly gone for it with the Christmas

decorations – more was more. There were flashing fairy lights in the shrubs lining the drive, an illuminated Santa and his reindeer and sleigh climbing one side of the house, shooting star lights on the other, and a gigantic model of a snowman by the front door, which changed colour from white, to blue, to pink. Tiffany just bet the snobby neighbours loved all the flashing lights and models. It didn't exactly scream tasteful. But it was fun, it was festive, and she adored her sister for being so over the top.

She rang the bell and Angel opened the front door. She looked glowing in a huge black fake-fur hat and matching cape, jeans, and silver UGGs.

'Tiff, the plans have changed! Cal and I are taking Honey off to this amazing Winter Wonderland in Edinburgh to see Father Christmas. It's a last-minute thing, we just couldn't resist it – she's so excited. You don't mind being here on your own, do you? Well, you won't be on your own as Sean will be here too. Cal's made supper for you both, and there's a bottle of champagne in the fridge. Help yourself to anything else you want. We'll be back late tomorrow night.'

Sean was going to be here with her?

'Is Sean's girlfriend staying as well?' Talk about putting a downer on her Christmas. Tiffany was tempted to get a taxi back to the station.

'Oh, no,' Angel beamed at her, 'just Sean.'

Just Sean, who she hadn't seen since the night of the Christmas party. Just Sean, who only wanted to be friends . . .

'And he's staying here for Christmas. Didn't I tell you?'

No, she hadn't! Tiffany would have remembered that!

She followed Angel into the hall which was dominated by the most enormous Christmas tree she had ever seen, hung with a dazzling array of glittering baubles: stars, snowflakes, snowmen, fairies, candy

300

sticks, plus Honey's own decorations, a wonky star with sequins and a paper angel (pink, naturally; Honey obviously knew her mother well), along with multi-coloured flashing fairy lights. Less a Christmas tree, more a disco tree. It was sensory overload. There was a scent of pine needles, which instantly made Tiffany think of her dad and Marie and Lily-Rose, and their far more modest tree.

'Believe it or not, I wanted to go for a tasteful colour scheme in silver and gold, not pink for a change, but Cal and Honey got there first. And you can blame them for the Santa and snowman outside. We've already had a letter from one of the neighbours accusing us of lowering the tone. Honestly! Where's their Christmas spirit?' Angel stopped and looked at her sister. 'Everything OK with you?' she carried on. 'You look great by the way. Are you using a different foundation?'

No idea! Maybe it was the mention of Sean's name . . .

Angel was too busy rifling through her bag to check she had the plane tickets to pursue the matter. And after a hasty goodbye, she, Cal and Honey were off on their festive adventure.

This was weird, Tiffany reflected as she carried her suitcase up to the guest bedroom. She wondered where Sean was going to be sleeping. And where he was. Just the thought of seeing him was making her nervous. How was she going to feel when they came face to face?

An hour later, when it was already dark at four o'clock, he arrived. Tiffany was in the kitchen making a cup of tea when he walked in. He was wrapped up against the cold in a black coat and sheepskin aviator hat.

'Hi, Tiffany.' He seemed surprised to find her alone. *As surprised as she was to find herself alone with him.* 'Where is everyone?'

'They've gone away for a night; some last-minute

301

trip. They'll be back tomorrow night. I don't know why they didn't tell me, I'd have stayed up in London.' She was having difficulty making eye contact.

'It is strange they didn't tell us.'

Strange or unfortunate because he was deprived of more time with Erin?

'Oh, well,' he added, 'you'll just have to put up with me.'

Tiffany managed to look up at his face and Sean was actually smiling. He was probably just being polite. Well, she wasn't going to hang around while he made small talk and was nice to the boss's sister.

'I'm going to get on with wrapping up some presents.' And she took her mug of tea and marched upstairs. Honestly! This was a great start to her Christmas holiday. *Not.*

She wrapped up all her presents – a gorgeous red Swarovski crystal clutch bag in the shape of a pair of lips for Angel; the original poster of *Diamonds Are Forever* for Cal – the only Bond film poster he was missing. She'd spent a lot of money on Cal and Angel but she figured she hadn't paid them rent, so it was a way of saying thank you. She'd bought Honey a Hello Kitty suitcase; for Jez a midnight blue velvet Alexander McQueen scarf; and for Rufus a wok, which sounded boring but apparently was what he wanted. And nothing, she realised, for Sean, as she hadn't even known he would be here! She'd have to nip to the shops one last time. Though quite what she would get him . . .

Tiffany flopped down on the bed and checked her messages. Nothing. She texted Jez, asking him if he'd known that she was going to be alone with Sean. He didn't reply, which was unlike Jez as he was constantly checking his messages.

There was a knock at the door. She quickly sat up and smoothed down her hair. 'Come in.'

Sean opened the door. 'I've lit a fire in the living room and wondered if you wanted to have a glass of wine? That's if you're not on the wagon after the party.' He smiled. His second of the day, it must be some kind of record for him. And it had been a very long time since Sean had bantered with her. Maybe he felt he could because he had the security of knowing he was with Erin?

Tiffany frowned. 'No, I'm not on the wagon. I wasn't *that* bad.'

'You were quite bad. I think you might have mentioned a threesome,' Sean teased. *Yes, teased her. What was going on!*

Her threesome comment still had the power to embarrass her, and she was uncomfortably aware of her cheeks flushing. 'You must have imagined it.' She got up off the bed.

'I promise you, I didn't. And coming from someone with that angel outfit on, it was quite an offer.'

She was standing in front of him without her heels on. He towered over her and she had a sudden longing to throw her arms around him, to bury her face in his shoulder. Who was she kidding? She wanted to do so much more than that.

'I'll have that glass of wine if it's going,' she said primly. 'Just give me five minutes.' *Talk about sending out the wrong message!*

'Wine coming right up. I've checked and there's no randy reindeers to make me jealous.'

He was definitely flirting!

She waited until he'd left before hastily brushing her hair and putting on another layer of mascara, and spraying on some Coco Mademoiselle.

This is a drink between friends, she told herself as she looked in the mirror. Just friends . . .

*

The living room looked very cosy and inviting with a fire flickering in the fireplace, and Sean had lit candles on the mantelpiece. There was a smaller, slightly more tasteful Christmas tree in the corner and the fairy lights glowed off and on. Tiffany sat at one end of the sofa and sipped her red wine. Sean sat at the other. It suddenly felt very intimate, almost like a date. Or was it her imagination, reading a deeper meaning where there was none? Where Sean was concerned, she felt her intuition had deserted her.

'Why aren't you spending Christmas with your girl-friend?' Tiffany came straight out with her question.

'I don't have a girlfriend.' A pause. 'We broke up just before I came back from LA.'

'Oh, I'm sorry.' *She wasn't.*

'I saw that Raul Garcia got engaged. Are you OK about that?'

'I'm totally, one hundred percent completely OK about it. I'm happy for him. He's a good bloke. Just not for me.'

'I thought you liked him. He had everything going for him.'

Was that a teeny-tiny note of jealousy she could detect in his tone?

'He did, but we just didn't have a connection.' A pause, then: 'Why did you break up with Erin?'

'Probably similar reasons to you and Raul. And she could tell that I was thinking about someone else.'

Tiffany held her breath.

'Oh?' She wasn't going to make this easy for him. 'Who's that then?'

Now Sean was gazing at her. 'Do you seriously not know? It's you Tiffany. I can't stop thinking about you. And now I've finally got the chance to tell you how I feel.'

'As your friend?'

'No. I don't want to be your friend. That was such a stupid thing to say.'

One slip and she felt he would be lost to her, this man, this gorgeous, infuriating, kind, sexy man with whom she had fallen in love. He would go. And she'd be lost. She knew that now.

He moved closer to her, 'Tiffany, I need to know. Is there any chance you might feel the same about me?'

The butterflies were fluttering wildly inside her as she struggled with her emotions. Desire, longing, fear that it was all going to go wrong again . . . The moment seemed to require a leap of faith. She reached out and lightly touched his face. 'Of course I feel the same way. You idiot!'

'Who are you calling an idiot!' And in one fluid movement he took her in his arms and kissed her.

She curled her arms around his neck as she kissed him back. Such a soft, gentle kiss at first, as if they were unsure of each other and of themselves. And then the kiss became deeper as they let their passion go. Sparks of lust were exploding inside her at the feel of him against her.

'D'you think maybe we could go upstairs?' she murmured, when they caught their breath. She gestured at the CCTV camera in the corner of the room.

'Don't worry. I disabled it. But yes, upstairs would be good.'

He shut the bedroom door behind them and they practically fell on the bed together, tugging off each other's clothes. He kissed her again, deep, hard, hungry kisses that made her burn for him, then she was slipping off his boxers, caressing him, thrilling at the feel of his body against hers and didn't think she had ever been this turned on . . . she was longing for him to touch her, longing to touch him. She slid her hands under his tee-shirt, felt his smooth, warm skin. He felt so good, just as she'd remembered. Strong, solid, warm . . . She kissed the dragon tattoo, wanted to kiss every part of him. She couldn't get enough of him.

He pushed her tee-shirt up, caressed her breasts. She gasped as his lips took over, sucking and kissing her nipples in a way which turned her on so much, and then he was caressing her between her legs, where she was already melting, circling, teasing her.

'You're so beautiful,' he murmured, 'I want you so much.'

He touched her slowly, sensuously, as if he had all the time in the world and wanted only to please her. She surrendered to his touch, gasping as the exquisite waves of orgasm rocked through her. She ran her hands over his muscular chest, his rock-hard abs, dared to go lower.

It was his turn to gasp as she touched him. All she wanted to do was please, pleasure, this beautiful man. She had never felt so powerful . . . but then he pulled her back to him, and she lay down, knowing what he wanted . . . what they both wanted . . . and it was every bit as a good as she had anticipated. Oh, yes, Sean had staying power. She felt connected, close, caught up in him . . . every movement of their bodies bringing them closer . . . until he came and called out her name.

'No regrets?' Tiffany said afterwards.

'Only that I was stupid enough to say I couldn't see you months ago.' He lay back on the pillow. 'If only you knew how much I've wanted you all this time! What it was like seeing you with Raul . . .' He pulled her on top of him, so that they were gazing into each other's eyes. 'I've wanted you for so long. I didn't want to admit it, I thought it would go away, but it didn't.'

'What? Even when you saw me in the nightclub with

that wanker?' she teased, when all the while she was thrilled by his declaration.

'Even then I fancied you like crazy, I just couldn't believe you were with him.'

Tiffany didn't want to bring up anything serious, just wanted to revel in lying next to Sean, but she knew she had to. 'What are we going to do about Angel and your job?'

Sean lightly stroked her hair. 'Tell her the truth. And if she wants me to resign, I will. I'll get another job, I know that now. I'm thinking about starting my own business, have been for a while.' He grinned. 'Anyway, you're a famous TV star, I could be your kept man.'

'No way! I don't want any free-loaders.'

Sean rolled over so she was underneath him. 'Not even ones who will be your sex slave and do whatever you want?' He dipped his head down to kiss her neck, her breasts, and kept going . . .

'Hmm, I suppose I could find an opening.' Sean definitely had staying power.

Later they lay in each other's arms, totally blissed out.

'This is the best Christmas present ever,' Tiffany told him, reaching for his hand. *Now, he'll tell me that he loves me!* She had never cared in the past whether her boyfriends told her they loved her or not. She had never been in love with them, so it hadn't mattered. When they had told her that they were in love with her, she had always replied that she loved them, it seemed the right thing to do, but she never had been in love. And it seemed as if she might be about to get her wish as Sean said, 'Tiffany, I've got something to tell you.'

But whatever that something was would have to wait as the electricity suddenly went off, plunging the room into darkness, lit only by the moonlight and by the flickering candles.

Instantly Sean got up and pulled on his jeans and jumper. 'It's probably the decorations tripping the system,' he told her. 'I'll just go and check outside.' And when he saw Tiffany was all set to follow him, he said, 'Stay inside and keep warm, I won't be long.'

For a few minutes Tiffany did as she was told, but when Sean didn't come straight back, she started to feel anxious. She slipped on her clothes and walked cautiously out of the room.

'Sean, are you there?' she called out in the pitch-black hallway. No reply. He must still be outside.

Everything's fine, she told herself. *The house is completely secure.* She had to feel her way along the corridor and down the stairs, but once she reached the kitchen the windows let in moonlight. She shivered. Sean had left the French windows open. *Where was he?*

There was a pair of Angel's UGG boots by the door and Tiffany slipped them on, along with her aviator jacket. If Kara could only see her now, wearing UGGs which she had vowed she never would. The temperature seemed to have plummeted; it was freezing. Perhaps it would be a White Christmas, she told herself, trying to stay calm. She stepped outside. Already a hard frost was setting in. Her breath came out in white clouds.

'Sean!' she shouted. 'Where are you?'

Again, there was no reply. The only sound was the gravel crunching under her boots. The drive curved to the right and when Tiffany turned the corner she saw there was something lying on the path. Oh, God! Not something, someone! She sprinted over. It was Sean, lying face down.

She kneeled beside him. 'Sean, it's me, Tiffany. Can you hear me?'

She quickly took off her jacket and laid it over him. He groaned and tried to move. Tiffany could see blood coming from a wound on the side of his head.

'You have to get out of here,' he managed to say.

'I'm not leaving you.' She reached for her mobile in her jacket pocket. 'I'm calling an ambulance right now.'

'No, call the police.'

She glanced behind her; there was no one there. With any luck the burglars, because surely that's who they were, would be inside.

'Operator, which service?' asked a female voice.

Tiffany didn't reply. A man wearing a black ski mask had a gun pointed straight at her.

'Hang up now, and drop your phone!'

She did as she was told. The man grabbed her and pulled her roughly back into the house.

'We can't leave Sean outside . . . it's too cold . . . he could die.' Right now Tiffany wasn't at all scared for herself. Getting Sean somewhere safe was all she could think of.

'Shut up! Don't tell us what to do.'

He pushed her into the kitchen where there were two other masked men.

'Found her outside, looking for lover boy.' He pulled a length of rope from his jacket pocket and bound Tiffany's hands together in front of her.

Tiffany was sure his voice sounded familiar, he had an accent – maybe from Manchester? Where had she heard it before?

'Please can we bring him inside? She winced as he knotted the rope tightly.

'Shut up, unless you want me to gag you as well.'

'I could think of a way of shutting her up,' one of the men said, and laughed. 'She's almost as fit as Angel. I've always wanted to have her. Her sister could be the next best thing.'

Fear gripped Tiffany as she realised how completely powerless she was.

But the man who had grabbed her told the other one to shut up. Then tied a scarf over her eyes.

'She stays with me. Bring him in from outside as well. Lock him in the living room.'

It was a nightmare that she couldn't get out of. Tiffany tried to stay calm, tried to block out the panic that was threatening to take over. So long as she was with this man, she would be OK. He was a burglar; he wasn't interested in her. And Sean would be OK, if he could just hold on. *Be strong*, she found herself praying, for herself and for Sean.

The man marched her through the house and upstairs to what she guessed was Angel's bedroom. He made her sit on the floor while he rifled through Angel's dressing table. Tiffany remembered Cal was always nagging Angel to put her jewellery in the safe and her reply that she would. But she never got round to it. By the sound of it the burglar was finding plenty of it. Tiffany tried fiddling with the knots but it was hopeless, they had been tied too tightly.

'Get up!' He grabbed her. 'Ground floor for laptops – hopefully with some saucy snaps of the celebrity couple with a high resale value, TVs, music systems and cameras.' He said it sarcastically, like a lift operator in a department store. 'You can stay put with lover boy.'

He thrust her into the living room without taking off her blindfold.

'Sean? Where are you?'

'Tiffany, thank God. Are you OK?'

'I can't see and my hands are tied.'

'I'm on the sofa.'

His voice sounded so weak. Tiffany edged forward cautiously, trying to remember where the furniture was in the room. She winced as she bumped into the glass coffee table and bruised her hip. And then she reached the sofa.

'I'm here,' Sean managed to say. 'Sit down and I'll take off the blindfold.'

He struggled to undo the knot.

'Oh my God!' she exclaimed as soon as it was off. The room was dark but she could see blood was still flowing from the wound on Sean's head. He struggled to sit up.

'No, stay still. Tell me what I can do?'

'Let me untie your hands first.' But his own were shaking and Tiffany was terrified that he would lose more blood if he exerted himself. And then he seemed to lose consciousness.

'Stay with me, Sean,' she pleaded. 'You're going to be OK. The burglars will be gone soon and then I'll call an ambulance . . .'

His eyes flickered open. 'Tiffany, I have to tell you—'

'Don't speak, please. You're going to be OK, I promise.'

He closed his eyes again, as if unable even to sustain the effort of keeping them open.

Tiffany lost all track of time as she talked to him about Maya, and how his daughter must be looking forward to Christmas and to seeing him. And then about her own feelings for him, and finally found herself blurting out, 'Sean, be OK, *please*. I love you.'

No response. She was so focused on him that she hadn't realised the door had opened.

'What a lovely couple you make,' said the man with the Manchester accent, 'but I'm afraid we've got to break you up. One of my men had the good idea of taking you with us, Tiffany, and seeing how much your sister thinks you're worth; it being Christmas, she'll probably be feeling extra-generous.'

'Please, we've got to get an ambulance for Sean!' Tiffany exclaimed.

'Oh, we'll do that later,' the man said breezily. 'Now

311

come with me, or I'll let Buzz get his hands on you. Not his real name, of course. I'm not that stupid.'

He took Tiffany's arm, and even though she knew it was pointless she still tried to shake him off. He squeezed so tightly she gasped in pain.

'Leave her alone!' Sean struggled to sit up and the man roughly shoved him back down.

Events became a sickening blur as the man retied her blindfold then dragged her out of the house and into the freezing night air. She heard a van's door being opened then she was shoved inside. When the door was slammed shut behind her and she heard the engine start, she curled up in a ball and gave in to the tears.

Tiffany did not let herself cry for long. Think, focus, be strong, she told herself, as a kind of mantra. Sitting at the front of the van, the men turned the radio up high so she couldn't hear their voices. Cheery Christmas numbers were blaring out. 'Last Christmas I Gave You My Heart' . . . 'All I Want For Christmas Is You.' *It's true Sean, all I want for Christmas is you* . . . Oh, God, would he be all right? Only concern for him stopped Tiffany from despairing entirely about her own situation.

The van pulled up. It sounded as if it was being driven into a garage. Focus – how long had they been driving for? Tiffany went through the songs that she'd heard. It must be at least half an hour, so they were likely to be about thirty miles away. Manchester man pulled her out of the van. 'No calling out, no funny business, or you get the gag.'

She nodded. He led her up several flights of stairs. Focus – what could she smell? Air freshener and fried food.

He opened a door and pushed her in.

'My hands are really hurting,' she said plaintively. 'Please could you untie them?'

312

'OK, but don't try anything or I'll let Buzz come up and see you. And he's no gentleman, as you've heard.'

He undid the knots and for a moment Tiffany couldn't feel her hands, then it was agony as the blood flowed into them once more.

'I'll be back.' Manchester man had put on a ridiculous Schwarzenegger accent. God, that was an annoying habit. He seemed to have an accent for every occasion. It was sparking off a memory – she had heard someone do just this, but where?

Tiffany fumbled to pull off the blindfold and saw that she was in a tiny attic room with a single bed. She rushed over to the window and tried to open it. It was locked. She peered out. The house opposite was dark, and below her was a concrete yard where the bins were kept. She reckoned she was probably three storeys up. Hopeless to think about breaking the window and climbing out, she was more likely to break her neck. There was a tiny en suite with a shower and a loo, individually wrapped soap and miniature shampoo. She must be in some kind of B & B. Maybe she should try screaming for help. But somehow she doubted help would come, and she shuddered as she thought of a visit from Buzz.

She looked at herself in the mirror – her face was tear-stained and streaked with mascara. *And it's supposed to be waterproof, I'm not getting that again*, she tried to cheer herself up. She checked her watch. It was after midnight.

She jumped as the door opened.

'Here's Johnny!' Now Manchester man was imitating Jack Nicholson in *The Shining*. He sat on the bed, an incongruous sight in the cosy bedroom in his black ski mask and entirely black outfit. 'We need to send big sis a picture, tug at her heart strings.' He held up his camera phone. 'Say cheese.'

313

He took a series of pictures, then added, 'And now let's hear a plea from you.'

Tiffany shook her head; she wasn't going to do everything she was told to.

'Do it and I'll call that ambulance you want. If you won't, then . . .' He shrugged.'

Tiffany took a deep breath. 'Angel, I'm sorry I don't know where I am or who I'm with. They burgled the house and attacked Sean. It doesn't matter about me, but please call an ambulance for him.' She bit her lip. 'I'm worried he's not going to make it.' She had vowed to be strong but couldn't stop the tears from falling now.

Manchester man lowered the phone.

'Like the tears, nice touch.' He got up. 'I'm off to send this and then I'll bring you some tea. No hard feelings. When someone has as much as Angel and Cal, it's only fair to have a bit of a redistribution.'

As the door shut, Tiffany realised who Manchester man was. It was Colin, one of the security guards. No wonder he'd been able to get into the house! She'd always thought he was OK. How wrong could you be?

She pulled a thin duvet with a design of white daisies on it around her. She didn't know if it made her situation better or worse that he was involved. She checked her watch again, desperate to keep track of time. Forty minutes later the door was unlocked and Colin brought in a tray with a bowl of tomato soup, plate of bread and butter and a cup of tea.

'You've gone more upmarket since you found out Angel was your sis, I expect, but this is all we have on offer. No sushi, no caviar, no foie gras.'

If this was a film, and she was Lara Croft, Tiffany imagined that she would have hurled the soup in his face and legged it out of the room and to freedom. But three storeys up, she didn't rate her chances of getting very far.

'I haven't heard from Angel yet, I expect she's digesting the news.' Colin paused in the doorway. 'I'll keep you posted.'

'Did you call an ambulance for Sean?'

'He's a tough one, he'll be OK.'

'He was losing so much blood . . . please call.'

'OK, OK, being as how it's nearly Christmas, I already did.'

Tiffany had expected she would feel like pushing the tray away and not touching anything those bastards had made her. Instead her survival instinct kicked in and she ravenously crammed the bread into her mouth, wishing there was more, and drank the soup. Then she stood up and went and listened by the door. She couldn't hear anything. She tried the lock. Nothing doing there. She returned to her position on the bed, pulling the duvet round her to keep warm. She must have been at the house for over two hours. Would Angel have got the message by now? And what would she do about it? At least she could call an ambulance for Sean. Tiffany still wasn't convinced that Colin had. Every time she thought of Sean, panic threatened to overtake her.

Be OK, be OK, she pleaded. *All I want for Christmas is you.*

Chapter 29

Angel opened her eyes and looked round the hotel room. She'd been deeply asleep but something had woken her. Her gaze fell on the phone on the bedside table; the red light was flashing. Sleepily she reached for it and saw she had a voice-mail message and a text.

She opened the text message first and was confronted with a picture of a terrified-looking Tiffany in a room Angel didn't recognise. An icy trickle of terror inched down her spine as she accessed her voice-mail and heard Tiffany's anguished tones.

'Oh my God! Cal, wake up!' She shook her husband's shoulder.

'Is everything OK? Is it the baby?' he asked, quickly surfacing from sleep.

Angel instinctively laid her hand over her baby bump. 'No, no, it's Tiffany . . . I think she's been kidnapped and Sean's been injured. What do we do?'

Typically, even faced with such a crisis, Cal remained calm. He listened to the message himself and then checked Angel's text and saw that there was a further message from the kidnappers, demanding half a million pounds and warning them not to go to the police.

'If we knew Sean was OK, then I would think about doing just that, but we don't know how seriously he's been hurt. We have to call the police. They'll know how to handle this. Agreed?'

Angel nodded, too consumed with panic and fear for her sister to be able to think straight. And there was guilt too. She had been responsible for getting Tiffany and Sean together at the house . . . if anything happened to them now it would be her fault. She thought of the plan she had hatched with Jez, pretending to be flying to Edinburgh when instead she, Cal and Honey had checked in to the Mandarin Oriental in London and spent the time taking Honey ice-skating, going to see Father Christmas at Harrods, doing some last-minute shopping and having spa treatments. She could still smell the essential oils on her skin . . . But now, instead of relaxing her, the smell of geranium and lavender was a reminder that while she was being pampered, Tiffany was being kidnapped.

Within the hour Angel, Cal and Honey had checked out of the hotel and were driving back to Sussex to meet the police. Sean had been taken to hospital with a head injury, but his condition was not thought to be serious. Honey had fallen back to sleep and was tucked up under a duvet, and Cal had suggested that Angel try and sleep as well, but she was far too anxious. She sat in the passenger seat biting her nails, a habit she was supposed to have ditched years ago. What was happening to Tiffany now? Was she OK? Was she hurt? The thought of anyone harming her sister was unbearable.

'It's not your fault this has happened,' Cal said quietly.

'It is! I shouldn't have got them in this situation.'

'I promise you it's not.' He reached for her hand and

squeezed it tightly. 'Tiffany and Sean are both strong characters.'

Angel could only hope that Cal was right.

Before going home they dropped Honey off at Angel's parents. Cal wanted Angel to stay with them too but there was no way she was going to do that. She called Jez and asked him and Rufus to travel down, knowing that she needed her friends around her. They had expected that Sean would still be in the hospital so it was a shock to find that he had discharged himself and was back at the house, along with a whole team of police officers taking forensic evidence.

'What are you doing here, Sean?' Angel exclaimed, walking over to him and taking in the stitches at the side of his head and the livid bruise on his forehead. He was sitting at the table, hunched over his laptop.

Angel glanced at the screen and saw that he was looking at footage from the CCTV cameras in the house. He had paused the film at the moment a masked man was tying Tiffany's hands together. Angel flinched at the image of her sister looking so vulnerable and afraid.

'Shouldn't you be in hospital?' she said to him.

Sean couldn't drag his eyes away from the screen. 'There are things I have to do.' He pointed at the masked man. 'I'm sure I recognise him. What do you think?'

Angel looked at the man. It was impossible to see anything distinctive as the mask covered his entire face as well as his hair. She shook her head. 'I've no idea who he is.'

She watched as Sean pressed Play and continued to stare intently at the grainy black-and-white images.

'Sean, shouldn't you be in hospital?' she repeated.

'I'm OK, they ran a CAT scan and it was clear. It

doesn't matter about me anyway. Have you any news at all of Tiffany?' He was ashen-faced with worry.

'Nothing now,' Angel replied, her eyes filling with tears as she thought of how terrified her sister must be.

'I should have protected her,' Sean said quietly. 'I let her down . . . failed her when she most needed me.'

Angel's heart went out to him then, and she hugged him. 'You didn't,' she told him. 'If anything, it was my fault for trying to get the pair of you together and leaving you alone in the house.'

Cal intervened, 'Stop beating yourselves up. The police reckon that the burglars took Tiffany on the spur of the moment. They think they're pretty amateurish. We're definitely going to find her.'

'God, I hope so! I couldn't live with myself if anything happened to Tiffany.'

And with that heartfelt comment Angel realised that Sean's feelings for her sister ran far deeper than they had guessed.

She looked at him, seeing the anguish in his eyes. 'You love her, don't you?'

He nodded. 'Yes, I do.'

And suddenly Angel felt a new surge of determination. 'Well, we'd better get our girl back then, hadn't we? So you can tell her. You will tell her, won't you?'

'I'm not going to waste any more time,' Sean replied with conviction.

Cal insisted they should all sit down while he made tea for everyone. Angel didn't especially want a cup of tea but it felt good to have something to do while they waited for news. For a few minutes they sat around the table in silence. Sean continued to go through the footage and Angel cupped her hands round the mug to keep warm.

'My sister's a pretty amazing person, isn't she?' she said finally. 'I thought that, when we met, it would be all about her learning how to live in my world, but it turns out I've had so much more to learn from her.'

Cal looked at her. 'What do you mean, babe?'

'I've been thinking about how she's been able to forgive Tanya and even feel sympathy for her. Tiffany paid for her to go into rehab, did you know that, Sean?'

He shook his head, without taking his eyes away from the screen. 'It doesn't surprise me.'

Angel took a deep breath. 'Well, I'm going to take a leaf out of Tiffany's book. When she gets back, I want to go and see Tanya with her. Life's too short to hate anyone.'

'I think it would be amazing if you could do that,' Cal told her.

Suddenly Sean slammed his hand down on the table and exclaimed, 'I know who it is! It's Colin Mason.'

Angel and Cal both got out of their seats and looked at the screen. 'How can you be so sure?' Angel asked, failing to see anything that would identify the man.

'He's got a way of rubbing his hands together that I remember. It's him! I know it.'

At that moment, one of the detectives, a woman called DCI Wayne to whom Angel had taken an instant liking for her calm, no-nonsense attitude, walked into the kitchen. Sean immediately filled her in on his suspicion.

'We'll get on to it straight away,' the DCI replied. 'I also wanted to check with you whether Tiffany had her mobile phone here? We've been through all her things and can't seem to locate one.'

'Yes, she does, I'd just given her a new one – it's a customised BlackBerry – with black-and-white crystals as she said my pink one was too girlie for her. I know she had it with her as I saw it in her bag just before I left.'

'Could you let me have the number?'

Angel was about to check on her own phone but Sean beat her to it, reeling it off.

'Do you think she's got the phone on her?' Angel asked.

'I doubt she's got it but maybe one of the burglars took it. And we're hoping that they may have left it switched on.'

Angel looked puzzled and DCI Wayne added, 'If it is switched on then we'll be able to pinpoint where Tiffany is.'

Angel glanced over at Sean and it was clear that he was thinking exactly the same as her.

Do it then! What are you waiting for?

Chapter 30

Tiffany must have fallen asleep, but she woke up suddenly when the door was unlocked again. Immediately she sat up, pulling the duvet round her. She was expecting Colin so it was a shock when Buzz walked in. She recognised him by his stocky build and the smell of cheap aftershave. He sat on the bed and Tiffany hugged her knees to her protectively. Now she could smell alcohol on his breath. She felt a prickling of fear.

'I've seen you on telly but you're much prettier in real life.'

'Where's the other one?' Tiffany asked, trying to hide the panic she felt at being alone with Buzz.

'Busy. Why, do you like him more?' He moved closer.

Keep him talking, Tiffany told herself, needing to play for time.

'No, I just wondered what he was doing, that's all. What's your name then? Because it's not really Buzz is it?'

A mean laugh from him. 'I'm not going to tell you my name! Do you think I'm stupid?'

Tiffany shook her head and wondered if there was any chance she could make a run for it. Buzz seemed to fill the room with his bulk; she couldn't see how she could possibly escape him.

'What time is it?' she asked, desperate to hold him in conversation.

He shrugged. 'Around nine.'

God! She'd been there all night . . .

'It's Christmas Eve tomorrow, I'd really like to be back with my family.'

'Ah, poor Tiffany. If big sis pays up then 'course you will be.'

He reached out and tried to touch her face; she reared back.

'Don't touch me!' she hissed.

'Or what? No one's going to hear you. It's just you and me.' He laughed and tried to grab hold of her. Tiffany kicked out, but he was too strong for her. He ripped off the duvet and pinned her to the bed. She struggled with all her might, tried to claw his face through the mask. He was yanking her top up, trying to force down her jeans. *No, no, no! This cannot be happening to me!* She struggled more furiously; he retaliated by slapping her hard round the face. And just as Tiffany had given up all hope, the door burst open.

'Give me a break, mate!' Buzz exclaimed, rolling off Tiffany. She looked over, expecting to see the masked man. Instead there was Sean. He didn't hesitate for a second but charged into the room and punched her attacker hard in the stomach. The room was suddenly full of armed police, two of whom grabbed Buzz and handcuffed him.

'Did he hurt you?' Sean asked urgently, reaching for Tiffany. She clung on to him.

'No,' she whispered. 'No.' She didn't want to go down the route of what could have happened. 'Your head?'

'I'm tougher than I look. Come on, let's get you out of here.'

*

'Are you awake?'

Tiffany opened her eyes to find Sean sitting on the edge of the bed. He was dressed, had shaved, and seemed to have suffered no ill effects from the blow to his head, whereas Tiffany felt exhausted and drained of energy.

'What time is it?' she asked, wincing in the bright light streaming into the room.

'Three o'clock'

She struggled to sit up. 'It's so bright in here.'

'That's because it snowed a couple of hours ago and settled.'

A White Christmas.

Sean reached out and stroked her hair. 'How are you?'

'I feel so weak.'

'I'm not surprised – you had a terrible ordeal.' He hesitated. 'I'm so sorry that I couldn't protect you, Tiffany.'

Typical Sean! 'You'd been knocked out. It wasn't your fault. And you were there when I needed you most.' She reached for his hand and held on to it.

'Everyone's downstairs, dying to see you.'

Tiffany closed her eyes, not sure she was up to dealing with so many people. She felt Sean lift the duvet and slip into bed beside her. He put his arms around her. 'But you don't have to see anyone you don't want to. We can stay up here. Just you and me.'

Tiffany rested her head against his chest. It was tempting, but she felt she had to pull herself together. 'I want to get up. I want to forget about what happened.'

The nightmare, the raw fear she had felt for Sean, the terror when Buzz had attacked her; then the door being broken down and Sean rescuing her. Afterwards the police, the statements, being comforted by her

324

sister. Apparently the break-in was a last-minute plan of Colin's, triggered when he had found out that Angel and Cal wouldn't be keeping him on when Sean returned. That figured; it had felt to Tiffany as if the robbery was personal. It was a simple slip-up by Buzz that had led the police to the B & B in Shoreham – a small town along the coast from Brighton. He hadn't been able to resist taking Tiffany's Swarovski crystal-studded BlackBerry, and he had left it switched on, enabling the police to track the GPS signal. If he hadn't done that . . . Tiffany dreaded to think how they would have found her. If they would have found her. But, no, she wouldn't think of that now. Not with Sean's arms around her.

So much in her life had changed for the good. Now Angel and Cal knew about her and Sean, and apparently were fine about it . . . more than fine. Angel and Jez had revealed early this morning that they were the ones who had arranged for Tiffany and Sean to find themselves alone together in the house, and so their relationship was well and truly out in the open.

Angel, Cal, Rufus and Jez were sitting round the kitchen table when Tiffany and Sean walked into the room. All traces of the burglary had been cleared away. The table was dominated by an arrangement of mince pies, Stollen cakes, satsumas, a chocolate log and a mountain of nuts. Pride of place was occupied by a home-made Christmas cake with an exceptionally camp-looking Santa holding court over a snowman and elf in the middle of the white icing. The cake was obviously Jez's contribution. A saucepan of mulled wine was simmering on the stove, filling the kitchen with the spicy aroma of cloves. 'I Saw Mommy Kissing Santa Claus' was playing on the stereo. Clearly Jez's mission to have the perfect Christmas had begun.

'Here she is!' he declared as soon as he saw Tiffany. He immediately leaped up to enfold her in a tight hug. 'How are you feeling, sweetie?'

'Much better, thanks,' she replied. She didn't admit that she also felt quite overwhelmed.

Angel hugged her next.

'Thank God you're OK now, Tiff,' she said, her voice breaking with emotion.

Jez clapped his hands together. 'Come and sit down, and have something to eat. I'm turning all domestic goddess. Have you noticed my cake?'

Tiffany nodded, searching for the right word to describe it. 'It's very . . . festive.' And she couldn't resist adding, 'Is Santa propositioning the other two?'

'Tut-tut, lowering the tone, Miss Taylor. You're obviously feeling better.'

He pulled out his iPhone and checked something. 'Right. Eat, drink and be merry because then we can go for a walk in the snow, make snow angels, have some more mulled wine, and watch a choice of movies: *It's A Wonderful Life* – a timeless classic – or *Love Actually*, if you need something modern and in colour. I prefer a classic myself, but I'm open to persuasion. Then it's champagne and canapés and a game of charades.'

Tiffany's head was spinning. Sean put his arm round her. Tiffany liked the gesture. She leaned against him while he said, 'Actually, I'm going to make Tiffany some scrambled eggs and take it from there.'

'Jez wants the perfect country Christmas. He's got it all mapped out, literally, on his iPhone,' Rufus put in.

'I did tell you how I felt about Christmas!' Jez pouted.

'So absolutely no pressure at all then,' Tiffany teased, adding, 'I will come for a walk. I think the fresh air will be good for me.'

'Great! Wear something photogenic for the pics as they'll all be going on Facebook. I'm going to get my Cossack hat.' Jez nipped out of the room.

Angel rolled her eyes at Tiffany. 'I'm sure he'll calm down *eventually*.'

Angel and Cal then set off to pick up Honey from her parents'. Tiffany wandered over to the French windows and looked out at the snow. It was as if it had wiped away all traces of last night's terrifying events, turning the garden into a winter wonderland. The lawn was an untouched blanket of white, perfectly ready for Jez to make his snow angel; the trees looked like delicate sculptures. It was beautiful. Everything was going to be all right . . .

She turned back to find that Sean had set a plate of scrambled eggs on the table – they almost looked as good as the ones her dad made – and a mug of hot chocolate.

'It's got brandy in it – I think we could both do with getting slowly drunk.'

'I'm not sure that's on Jez's list until later,' Tiffany replied, putting her arms round him.

'What's not on my list?' Jez overheard as he walked back into the room looking very dapper in a silver fake-fur Cossack hat and floor-length grey coat. And he was holding a matching fake-fur muff.

Tiffany burst out laughing. 'I bet that's the first time you've got your hands on a nice muff.'

'You definitely are feeling better!' Jez shot back.

Tiffany polished off her scrambled eggs and the hot chocolate; the brandy made her feel pleasantly relaxed. Sean was looking at her. She put a hand to her mouth. 'Have I got something there?'

'No, I just like looking at you,' he said quietly. Then he turned to Jez and Rufus.

'Actually I don't think Tiffany is up to a walk just yet.

So would it be OK if you guys went on your own? I think she needs a rest.'

Tiffany was about to protest that she was fine when Sean winked at her and it was clear that a rest was not what he had in mind at all.

She pretended to yawn. 'Yes, I'm exhausted. I'll see you in a couple of hours.'

Jez arched an eyebrow. 'Sean could always come with us.'

'I was kidnapped, you know, Jez, I need him with me.'

'You win,' Jez conceded. 'But don't think you're getting out of charades.'

They giggled all the way upstairs to the guest bedroom, where Sean shut and locked the door. 'Now get into bed, you look like you need a good rest.'

She grinned. 'Yes, I need a really good rest.'

Tiffany trailed her fingers over the dragon tattoo. Making love to Sean, she had felt she was banishing the terrifying experiences of the night before.

'Are you happy to be with me?' he asked.

'I'm *so* happy!' Tiffany replied. 'So deliriously, wonderfully happy! I couldn't be happier! What about you?'

'Very.'

'That's it? I've opened my heart to you and told you how I feel – and I just get back "very"! Could do better, Agent Murphy!' She made to get up.

'Where are you going?'

'To get my tee-shirt.'

'No way. I want to see your beautiful body.' Sean propped himself up on one elbow and considered her, where she lay on the pillow, her hair fanned out behind her. 'I'm not as good at expressing myself as you. I know I keep things inside, locked away. But it doesn't mean I don't feel them. And last night, when those men had taken you . . . oh God, Tiffany. I felt like I was being ripped up inside. And there's something else I have to tell you.' A beat. She waited, almost holding her breath. Would this be the moment that he told her he loved her?

'Maybe it's too soon to be telling you this, but I don't care, I can't wait. I love you, Tiffany. I love you like I've never loved anyone before.'

Wow! He loved her! Sean loved her! Tiffany wanted to jump up and down with delight, wanted to cartwheel across the room, wanted to shout out with happiness; she settled for, 'I love you too.'

'I know,' he whispered. 'You told me that night. It's what kept me going.'

They curled up together, needing to be close, reluctant to get up. But by seven o'clock Jez had clearly decided that they'd had a good enough rest. He knocked on the door.

'Champagne and canapés are now being served in the living room.'

'We'll come in a while, Jez,' Sean called back.

'Haven't you had a good *rest* by now?' Judging by his tone of voice, Jez had seen straight through Sean's pretence that Tiffany was tired.

'You can never have too much!' Tiffany shouted.

'I'm coming in!' Jez opened the door, while Tiffany shrieked and pulled the duvet over her and Sean.

Jez stood in the doorway, hands on hips. 'You two have got to come downstairs and thank me and Angel for getting you together! We were like Santa's little helpers. God knows when the pair of you would have got round to revealing your true feelings otherwise.'

Sean sat up. 'Do you seriously think I wouldn't have got together with the woman I love? It might have taken me a little longer, but I would have got there.'

Tiffany waited for Jez to come back with one of his put-downs. Instead he got that dreamy look in his eyes at the sight of Sean's muscular chest, and said, 'He is *so* manly!'

'He is, isn't he?' Tiffany replied, pulling Sean back down beside her. 'Shut the door behind you.'

Chapter 31

Tiffany snuggled up to a sleeping Sean. It was Christmas Eve morning and she couldn't quite believe that she was here, lying next to the man she was in love with. She'd thought this would never happen.

Last night they'd drunk champagne and Cal and Rufus had cooked a delicious lasagne; both men were great cooks. They had thwarted Jez's charades plans because everyone wanted to talk, but had promised him they would play on Christmas Day instead. In spite of what had happened to Tiffany it had been such a joyful time. She'd had a shocking, terrifying experience, but she didn't want to let it overwhelm her, didn't want to feel like a victim . . . And all the time she felt an inner glow of happiness because Sean loved her!

He stirred next to her. She kissed his shoulder, trailed her fingers over his rock-hard abs. She was still getting to know his body. She couldn't get enough of him. Last night they had made love again, but she was ready for more . . .

'What's the time?' he said sleepily.

'Nine. We don't have to be anywhere yet according to Jez's schedule.' She carried on caressing him, enjoying the knowledge that she was turning him on.

But Sean was sitting up. 'I've got to get something!'

He leaped out of bed, scrambling for his clothes.

'Hey!' Tiffany said, sitting up herself. 'I need you here!'

He blew her a kiss. 'I'll be back as soon as I can.'

Tiffany felt as sulky as Jez when he didn't get his own way.

Downstairs Angel was already dressed and having breakfast with Honey. 'Sleep OK?' she asked with a smile.

Tiffany had hardly slept at all, not that she was complaining.

'Hmm,' she replied, sitting at the table and helping herself to a slice of toast. Outside the snow hadn't yet melted and she could see the snowman that Cal and Honey had built, wearing Jez's Cossack hat. She doubted that was part of his plan . . .

'I'm going to get some last-minute presents in Brighton, if you want to come with me.' Angel smiled. 'I thought you might want to get something for Sean?'

Tiffany had completely forgotten that she didn't have a present for him. 'God, yes! Let me get dressed and I'll be right with you.'

What to get Sean? She agonised over her decision as she quickly showered and got dressed. And then just as they were driving into Brighton, it came to her. A new leather jacket. She'd noticed that the one he owned had a rip under the arm. And she quite wanted his old leather jacket for herself . . .

'Did you send Tanya a present?' Angel asked unexpectedly. She hadn't mentioned their mother at all for the last couple of months.

Tiffany hesitated, wondering if Angel would give her a hard time when she admitted that she had. 'I gave her an iPod. She really likes listening to music.'

She waited for Angel to snap back that Tanya would

probably end up selling it. But no, instead there was another question. 'What does she like listening to?'

'A mix, I think. Kylie, Adele, The Feeling, U2.'

'And how's she getting on in rehab?'

'Really well. She's got two more months and after that I'm hoping she'll live somewhere near her sister in Guildford. She's talking about going to college, getting some qualifications.'

'That's great.' Angel paused. 'I'm really glad you helped her, Tiff. I know I didn't have it in me.'

'I'm sure you could have.'

But Angel shook her head. 'No, I didn't. So all credit to you.'

They arranged to meet in an hour's time after their shopping. Tiffany headed straight for a men's designer boutique recommended by Angel, who naturally knew all the boutiques in Brighton. And there she found the perfect gift – a gorgeous chocolate-brown distressed leather jacket. She had never spent so much money on a present before, never spent so much money on anything for herself! But she figured, what was the point of earning money if she couldn't treat the people she loved? And she knew it was going to look so sexy on Sean.

Her sister seemed a little distracted when she met up with Tiffany again, but she put that down to it being Christmas Eve and all the last-minute arrangements there were to make. And Tiffany was more than happy not to talk, just be lost in her own thoughts about Sean. They were some ten miles away from the house when Angel suddenly took an unexpected turning, taking them in a different direction.

'Have you got to do something else?' Tiffany asked.

'I thought we could call in and see Tanya. I've got a present for her.'

'Really? I mean, is that a good idea?'

'I called the clinic and they're OK about it. They've told her to expect us. I know I said I didn't want anything to do with her, but I have been thinking about her. It's funny, I thought I could shut down all my feelings for her, but I can't. You're been such an inspiration to me, Tiff. I've seen from you that it is possible to forgive. I do want to forgive her.'

'I think it would be so good if you could,' Tiffany said quietly.

The clinic was an imposing grey-stone country house, set in several acres of garden. 'Seems OK, doesn't it?' Angel said as they got out of the car. Tiffany could tell that her sister was very nervous, and linked arms with her as they approached the building.

Inside, a friendly male nurse signed them in and showed them to a cosy café that looked out over the gardens, telling them that he would let Tanya know they had arrived. Angel fumbled in her bag and pulled out a gift-wrapped box from Links the jeweller's. 'I got her a necklace. It's very simple . . . I didn't know what else to choose.'

Tiffany had never seen her sister seem so unsure of herself.

The male nurse returned with a slim woman who was unrecognisable from the Tanya Tiffany had first met. Gone were the gaunt cheeks and glazed expression, the lank hair. The woman standing before them, in jeans and a red jumper, was thin but pretty. Her hair looked freshly washed. She also looked very nervous and tugged the sleeves of her jumper over her hands, a habit both Tiffany and Angel shared.

'Hi,' she said shyly. 'Nice to see you both.'

'Hi, Tanya,' Tiffany said, getting up and giving her a quick hug.

Angel didn't say anything and didn't move.

Tanya sat down at the table. 'Would you like anything to drink? There's a self-service machine, the coffee isn't too bad.'

'I'll get them,' Tiffany said, figuring her sister might need some time alone with Tanya. 'Coffees all round?'

By the time she returned Angel was showing Tiffany pictures of Honey on her phone.

'She's beautiful. Just her like her mum.' Tanya smiled shyly at Angel. It was only when she did that you realised what kind of life she'd led as her teeth were badly discoloured.

'Just like her dad,' Angel replied.

'And when's the baby due? I read about it in the paper. I'm very happy for you.'

'May, just before my birthday.'

'Lovely time of year to have a baby,' Tanya said brightly, but Tiffany could see she was struggling to contain her emotions. 'I'm glad you've come. I wanted to say sorry . . . for everything really. For not being a mum to you when you were kids, and then when you came and found me, not being a mum then either. I'll never forgive myself, but I am trying to change. I wanted to for such a long time, but I could never do it.'

She looked over at Tiffany. 'And then, when you sent me that letter, I thought, this is it, this is my last chance and I've got to take it.' She paused and continued, 'Thank you, Tiffany.'

Angel put her arm round her sister. 'She's pretty special, isn't she? I thought I had it all sussed out . . . that I never wanted to see you, that I hated you. And it's taken Tiffany to make me realise that I don't hate you. I hate what you did, but I don't hate you.'

By now all three women were in tears. They talked for a while longer about how Tanya was getting on in rehab and her plans for the future.

'I could help get you set up in your own place,' Angel suggested. She was full of surprises today. But Tanya shook her head.

'No, I'm going to do this myself. But just to have seen you both has meant so much to me.'

'And we'll see you again,' Angel said quietly.

Tanya nodded, too overcome to speak.

Back at the house everyone was in the kitchen drinking hot chocolate. Sean came straight over to Tiffany and hugged her. She very much liked this new side of him, where he wasn't afraid to show his feelings.

'Cal told me where you both went. Are you OK?'

She nodded and leaned against him. She thought she'd had a roller-coaster year, but the last three days had given her some of the greatest highs and lows of her life.

Jez waved his phone around. 'We are so off my schedule! First of all Tiff goes and gets kidnapped, which definitely wasn't part of my festive plans, then you guys go off for this emotional family reunion. In fact, the only thing that's gone according to plan is Tiff and Sean finally getting together.'

'We should have a toast,' Cal declared. 'Let's open the champagne.'

'It's supposed to be mulled wine and mince pies time! Champagne is for Christmas morning!' Jez protested. But he was overruled as Cal cracked open the champagne and everyone went into the living room and curled up by the fire. No one felt like playing charades. As Jez was forced to admit, 'Who needs the drama? We've had enough already!'

Honey put out a glass of wine and a mince pie for Father Christmas and a carrot for Rudolph, after being assured by Angel that even though the fire was burning now, by the time Santa came down the chimney it would have gone out. And if it hadn't, well, he would use his magic powers to put it out . . .

By midnight Tiffany and Sean were in bed. It felt like the most perfect Christmas present ever to be lying next to him.

'You do know that I'll never be able to afford a house like this?' Sean said.

He was so paranoid! Tiffany shook her head at him. 'I'm not with you because of how much money you have. And who says I even want a house like this? There's such a thing as too big! I love you, remember. And everything doesn't have to be perfect. We're together, that's what matters.'

She was rewarded with a smile. 'OK, sorry, I suppose I still can't believe you would want to be with me.'

'Believe it,' Tiffany replied. And then she showed him exactly how much she wanted to be with him . . .

In the morning, before they went downstairs and joined everyone, they exchanged presents. Sean handed her a blue Tiffany bag, and she was overwhelmed when she opened it and discovered a charm bracelet, exactly like the one which had been stolen but with one addition, a diamond love heart charm. 'How did you know which ones to get?'

'I spoke to your dad. I wanted to give it to you even before we met up here. I bought the love heart charm yesterday in London.'

It was such a romantic present, she suddenly felt as if hers didn't match up. But as Sean ripped open the paper and pulled the jacket on, Tiffany changed her mind. She had been spot on with the fit and the colour, and he looked every bit as sexy as she'd predicted.

'So am I cool enough for you now?' he demanded, shoving his hands into the jacket pockets.

'You might want to put some trousers on with it!'

Tiffany teased as he stood before her in his boxers. 'And anyway, didn't you once say it's what's underneath that counts?' She hooked her finger into the waistband of his boxers and pulled him towards her. 'And I'd like to test that theory out right now.'

They were getting close to testing it out when there was a hammering on the door. 'OMG! It snowed in the night . . . we're snowed in! We're surrounded by a winter wonderland!' It was Jez, of course.

Tiffany got out of bed and tiptoed to the door where she turned the key.

'What are you doing? Aren't you going to come downstairs? We've got presents to open and games to play!'

'All in good time, Jez,' she replied, running back to bed.

KATIE'S AMAZING BOOK SIGNING!

Not quite a world record, but a fantastic day was had by all at the O2 Academy in Leeds on 27 july 2011.

"It is always exciting when one of my new books is released and this time it was extra special. Thank you so much to everyone who came along to support me. It was a really brilliant day and I loved every minute. My fans really are the best and as a way of saying thank you I have put all your names in the book over the next two pages!"

Katie Price
x

MELANIE DELVES KATIE NORMIE MELISSA NORMIE NATALIE ENGLISH JOHN SMITH
MEGAN ALLAN JADE CLIFTON MICHAELA CASH TANISHA PRITCHARD NAMY NEVISON
JESS GUY FIONA YOUNG LIAM O'BRIEN AMY LOUISE THOMPSON SANILAMA REBECCA
SPRANGLE MORGAN WHEELER ABBIE LUMB BECKY NICHOLS OLIVIA ATMARTON
KRISTINA HICKS JOSHUA CHADBURN DANIEL NORMAN TONI LLEWELLYN GEORGE JANNEY
DIANE HUNT LUCY HESSE CHARLOTTE RIDDELL ALBERT HARDING SARAH PREECE
STEPH HOLROYD SOPHIE MORELLI AIMEE BEALES AMILEE HALL FIONNUALA FLYNN PHIL
ROTHWELL DANVINNIA JACQUES REBEKAH WATSON HAYLEY FERDINAND EMILY WILLIAMS
MELISSA BLAKEY DANIELLE NORTON LIAM NORMINGTON JESS MAIRE SAMANTHA BENNETT SAIF
SHAHIDI ELLIE MCCULLOCH NICOLE YATES LAURA WOODHOUSE SUZANA ZERIAVOVA PAIGE
ROBSON CHLOE HUNT AGATHA SPINK HANNAH NORMAN NATALIE AYRES TARA MOLYNEAUX
EMMY MCCOMISH TIGER REND ASHLEIGH RUTTLEDGE DANIELLE BROWN BEN BREWER ROSS
CRABTREE NICOLA FOX MARIA SPARK FLORENTYNA SMITH RACHEL WOOLFORD JAMES BURRISS
JESSICA   GREGORY   JESSICA   SKILLINGTON   LOUISE VICKERS   RACHEL   FLANAGAN

MEGAN COLEMAN DANIELLE HODSON LAURA SIMPSON LOUISE | RILEY EVIE NAYLOR MELISSA RUDDOCK
MEGAN INGRAM DECLAN PAYNE REBECCA PAYNE LAURA WALKER | KATY WALKER HAILEY MCBEIGH JESSICA
WILLMER KENNEDY HARRIS RACHEL HARRIS LAUREN LHARTLEY | ELLIE DAVIES EMIKA DAVIES NICOL DAVIES
KAREN FENTON ELLIE JOBSON CHLOE RUSSELL JADE | SKYRIPAK ANTONIA HOWKER GEORGIA LUNN
ABBIE DOBSWORTH KATIE CARLISLE RACHAEL GRIMES | MOLLIE MONTGOMERY TRACEY TURNER
JO MATTHEWS CORRIE WELLS LAURA CULLEN ASHLEIGH | RHODES NICOLE ROURKE   JESS CASEY
GEORGIA   WARD   CHLOE MINTO MICHAELLE MINTO ZOE | WATKINS NATALIE LINNEY SARAH PALKA CHLOE
ANDREWS-BLIGH   CHANTELLE   WORRALL | HAYLEY ANDERSON KAYLEIGH SMITH LANA HALL
LINSEY   WILDBORE   N A T A L I E | WELLER ANGHARAD GREEN EMILY MOHUN GRACE
HODGSON   ELLIOT | MINLER JADE GARRITY LAYLA JADE ANDERSON
LAURA BOWERMAN JANE | ALLAN NICOLA INGLEDEW STACEY WOODMAN
EMILY   KNOTT   LEAH | JOHNSON CLAIRE SMEDLEY PARIS BROOKS BILLY
ROCHE LAYLA PHILLIPS ALEX | BODROZIC CRUISE ADAMS TEO ADAMS ANN-
MARIS FREEMAN KELLY MOSS | JAMES BAKER DANIELLE NICHOLSON
EMILY   WILDBORE   STEPHANIE | WELLER SIOBHAN BYRNE
ABBIE WALLIS BRONWYN WHEELER | S A M A N T H A
CLEE   DAWN   NICHOLS   REBECCA | HANDLEY
DANIELLE DURHAM MAE COLEMAN VANESSA | M A S S E Y
STEPH MASSEY JUNE PHEASBY KATIE WALKER | EMMA JONES SARAH
BROOKS   RACHEL THOMAS REBECCA | HORROCKS NATASHA LINNEY
SRAH BLAY EMMA MONEY EMMA BENNETT | STACEY   RANKIN   KARA   DAWSON
STEPHANIE SHEARD ALANNAH BASZYNSKI | MERCEDES   JASKOLKA   HANNAH   O'BRIEN
JESSICA   HAMILTON   MELISSA | PENGELLY   MELANIE   COPLEY   VICTORIA
STEVENSON EMILY RAMSDEN | CLARE VICARS PAIGE WORTHINGTON KAYLEIGH
WARD   JESSICA   ALLAN | IOANNE BEEVOR NAOMI JONES SHANNON
ELLIOTT   ZOE   DAVEY | KISS SMITH KARRAN SIMPSON LAURA PERRY
CHARLOTTE   BOWDEN   SOPHIE | BOWDEN DENISE BOWLES MARY LAMBETH DALE
WHITEHEAD   LAUREN   STRAKER   ROSS | NORMIE SHAUNI BURROW ALEX COFFEY STACEY
L O C K W O O D   SHANNON   WOODHOUSE | IODIE MINGHELLA JANE HEY ASHLEIGH
KING   TASMIN   WILLIAMS   SAFFRON   WILLIAMS | CHARLOTTE   CORNTHWAITE   GEMMA
WELLS KIMBERLEY HOULSTON REBECCA JOHNSON KATIE | WARREN   JESSICA   STONEHOUSE
GEMMA HUME MEGAN SMITH APRILE ROGAN POPPY ROGAN | JORDAN   YOUNG   KATHRYN   SINCLAIR
AFTON MCHARG LYNSEY BROWN GRACE GARDINER JOSEPH | PALMER   BETHANY   FELMING   KATY
FULLER TRACEY COUGILL BECKY GREENWOOD HOLLY BEECH | CLAIRE MORGAN AMY ESTELLE KAYLEIGH
BRADSHAW LUCY BARKER KELLY BARKER CRAIG CAPP ANTHONY | SNITH CLAIRE SPENCER WENDY EVANS

BELINDA DIAS HOLLY MCALLISTER EMILY LONGBOTTOM EVE LENDHILL   CHARLOTTE   HEWARD
BRODIE TIMSON AIMEE JONES JAKE STEWART ELOISE WATSON KIM PENROSE YASMIN CHALKLEY
JULES CROFT JULIE RUSHTON SHANNON HOULSTON AMANDA BAKER NATASHA SMITH KATIE
WEAVER EMILY SYNNOTT JOANNA MATHESON CHARLOTTE MATHESON SHANEELAH KHAN
SARAH COTTON JACK RICHARDS HOLLY CHRISTIAN LEWIS BRAMLEY TOM FOX CHRISTINA
CEEARA PRICE SAM FROST EMMA RAWLINS STEFANIE CLARKE STEPHANIE BIANCHI ABBIE
PILLING JAZZ RAMSBOTTOM SARAH JACKSON KARLIE BROOKES LUCY CORREIA LIVVY
BALL ABBY MAGEE JOHANNA BADHAMS CHELSEA COLLINS PAULINE SHARP SARAH FROST
SAMMY MAUNDRILL DANIEL RUSTON LIBBY LEE INDRE OLIVE NATALIE FAULKNER HANNAH
TARPEY JESSICA BRAME NATHAN THURSFIELD EMMA HOWELL LAURA BELCHER KAYLEIGH
MARSHALL GEORGIE CULLERTON LISA GREENWOOD LAYLA GIBSON JAYE FERNEYHOUGH
CHARLOTTE SWITHENBANK AIMEE BAKER ANNIE-LOUISE HIRD SHARRON BROWN MOLLY
HOULSTON ANDY SMITH VICKY BOULTON JESSICA PEACOCK LEAH HARPER SHARON
HARTLEY NATASHA LANDREGAN ANTHONY SMITH ASHLIE HALL OLIVER JOHNSON MICHELLE
BIRKIN CHARLOTTE BURNELL STACEY KNUTSEN AMY JEFFERY JESSICA FINLAY JESSICA
O'HANLON JESS BOYES CHANEL KEANE KAYLEIGH JESSOP LOUISE HARPER EMILY HARPER
MARIE HARPER MEGAN HACKFORD JESSICA SWALES RACHNA BHAGANI JESS BIOLETTI
LINDA BIOLETTI JAKE O'SHEA LAUREN MCQUEEN BIANCA HEILIG ANNALISE DONNELLY
KELLY SWAILES AMBER HUDSON YVONNE MILLARD KEELEY TERRY KAREN BOULTWOOD

VICKY SAUNDERS MEGAN BOYES AMY KILLBURN BETH WILKINSON ERICA STYLES
DONNA WAIN MEGAN IBBOTSON NATALIE ADAMS LAURA MCCONNACHIE ZOE CARR
NICOLA HAGUE NATALIE COOLLEDGE KEREN GOFF MELISSA JEFFERY JOANN TUNSTALL
BECKI SPURR MOHAMMED HUSSNAIN HANIF MICHAEL GIBBONS JESS NORTH BETHANIE
GRUNDELL CARY ELLIS EMMA SYKES RACHEL SKINNER AMY WILLIAMSON MANDY
HRINTCHUK TAYLOR-ROSE MITCHELL MEGAN PICKERING LUCY MILNES SHAUNIE
LAMMING LYNDSEY TOWLER MICHAELA HONEYBAUME JESS WHITEHEAD CHARLOTTE FIELDER
EMILY SMITHIES KATIE HARKER BETH BARLOW LAUREN KOCADAG TET CONNEALLY LUCY GHAI LISA
SEWELL JOANNE BOWMAN CHELSEA DECOSTA ANN BOWMAN BUFFY-JANE KYLE JADE WARDELL
NIKKI WARDELL APRIL TAYLOR HEIDI BROCKLEHURST MELISSA HARVEY NATALIE BRAIN
KIM HEPWORTH KATIE HESTER LEANNE ANDREWS EMMA MARIE WALTON LUCY MATTHEWS
THERESA SPINK MATTY CARTWRIGHT DAWN CAMARA ELLIE-MAE FULLARD KAIAH BEEBY
DEMI REGAN LOUBI SKINNER NICOLA GLOVER LAURA HUTT JESSYCA CUELHO JESSICA
MARSDEN CHARLOTTE ATKIN BILLIE MARSHALL DANIELLE LAMMING MELISSA GUY MOLLY
CHARNLEY MADELINE ORME RACHAEL HALE ASHLEY PRITCHARD MORGAN PRITCHARD
BETHANY HEALY IZZY WOODS LAUREN NAYLOR EMILY BEADSWORTH LINSEY DUFFY AMY
SWAIN VICKI MORREY AIMEE BRANNAN SHAYLEY GARTH
EMMA GRAHAME LAUREN MCCAFFERY
JAMES MCCAFFERTY SARAH-JANE HOWARTH LINDA
HOFMANN DANIELLA HEARN JOANNE CANNON GEORGIA
WEATHERS FRANKIE LLOYD HAYLEY MACKOWSKI JESSICA
VERNON SABRINA HARRISON LINDA WHITE FLORENCE WHITE SOPHIE CHRISTIANSEN
LUCY CHRISTIANSEN HANNAH STANLEY EVIE ENGLISH STEPHANIE HAZLEGREAVES HANNAH
WEBB JESSICA MAWE KATIE MEAGER JODIE MEAGER RAEESAH MUSA BETH BROWN
CHARLOTTE HARLEY JODIE MAKINSON GRETTA WALSH-BALSHAW MICHELLE CLAVEN
SIMONE MORRISON MICHAELA WHITCOMBE INDIA GADD SADIE MALKIN CHLOE
TODD GEMMA SAWYER JAMIE SAWYER ROSIE BEARDSWORTH GEORGINA SHAW AMELIA
SHAW GARETH SHAW ANGELA THOMPSON A L I C E THOMPSON MORGAN RABET KIRSTY HOLLEY SHAE
FARQUHARSON MOLLY JOHNSON ROXANNE SCOTT SOPHIE DIXON ASHLEIGH GOWLAND ISOBEL RAYNER HOLLIE TAYLOR
SIMON DUFFY LAUREN WALKER ABIGAIL MAKINSON JILLIAN NORTH LAUREN STIRK ROSIE STOCKS LORNA STOCKS JACQUELINE
BUCK MCKULL CELASCHI PABLO DAVID SUSAN MORGAN NIKKI PRIEDITIS ALISON SIDDONS MIA LORRYMAN BEKEH RENNISON LINZI
O'TOOLE TAZER HIGGINS MILLIE SULLIVAN AMBER SULLIVAN HAYLEY CROOT MEGAN CROOT DEBBIE TAYLOR SUE WAITE-PULLAN
ALEX YOUNGER LAUREN BETTY HOWARD LYNSEY DAVIES LINDSAY BUCKHAM ALICE HEYWOOD HELEN COGAN BEN BROOK EMILY MINSKIP
HAYLEE JONES RUTH PEVERALL GRAZIELLA RESTAINO RUTH MADDISON ALLY BULMER IAN SMITH JOANNE LLOYD JILL CROOT SARAH BUCKHAM NAOMI
CLAYTON LAURIE LAMB BETHANY LAMB CHLOE GODFREY CHARLOTTE KEENAN BRITNEY HINSLEY EMMA WETHERILL NATALIE MEISTER BIANCA COWARD
COURTNEY POWERS EMMA-LOUISE COUPLAND HOLLIE PEDERSEN CLAIRE HODGSON HANNAH LEA KRISTINA BANKS JOANNE
BRAITHWAITE CERYS GILES ELLIE WILSON JENNIFER HAMILTON KATIE HOLFORD ROSIE JOHNSON BETH MEEK KIRSTY TORDOFF IZZY
ETHERINGTON GRACE KENWORTHY BECKY GREGSON EMMA THWAITE CHERELLE HUDSON LAUREN SLATER OLIVIA WILSON CHLOE
REYNOLDS LANA-BETH MORGAN REBEKAH DARMANN LUCY KENWORTHY ANNA-MARIE BAHRA KATRINA BELL JESSICA DOBSON
WALLACE DUROW LAURA RONEY JANET WOOD CLAIRE SCULL GEORGIA JOHNSON RACHEL MEADE WILL
MORRISON EILISH CULLEN GEORGIA BENTLEY RACHEL SENENIUK NICOLA ROSENDALE KIRBYLEA ROSENDALE
KENZI ROSENDALE AALIYAH ROTHERY CHANELLE CROOKE GAIL ROTHERY SARAH RONEY STEPH SIMPSON
DAVID MCGEOWN JAMES STUBLEY LARISSA KEEBLE CORAL BYRNE SAM SLACK CLARE MADDEN ALICIA
SWAIN MICHELLE BENTLEY AMY MILLER GEMMA MURTAGH APRIL SMITH CHARLOTTE MALONEY JESSICA
BENNETT VICTORIA LOWRY BESS FENN JULIA BOSOMWORTH NATALIE HOY KATIE
WADE DANIELLE PEARCE LYDIA SPENCER STACEY HOLDSWORTH CLAUDIA HARDMAN
JESSICA HARRIS KATE SMITH JOANNE KENNEDY JODIE SMITH REBECCA
VALENTINE EMMA SKELTON D O N N A WOODHEAD OLIVIA ELLIS
LAUREN DACK HELEN COLCLOUGH SAMANTHA MURRAY
HOLLY WHARTON NIKKI ARMITAGE BIANCA MARSHALL ABBY
OLMYORD EM SHELDON MELISSA EARNSHAW JASON MULDOON
JADE HRINTCHUK LEIGHANNE ROWLANDS LUCY
W I L S O N ELEANOR BAKER LAURA RUSSELL
L I V V Y TISO PAGAN SUNMAN ARABELLA
WHITE LAURA- ELISE WHITTALL RACHEL MAWE
EMALEIGH SIMESON PAULA MELLOR CATHERINE
HAMILTON ARCHIE HAMILTON- EDWARDS GEORGIA
SPENDLOVE SARAH WOMACK TARA MCLEOD LAUREN
COOPER STACEY SUMMERFIELD GEMMA KEEBLE CLAIRE
WARD KERRIE CHRURCH L U C Y M O R R I S O N - C H I L D S
EMILY WOAN NICOLA SWAIN DULCIE CLOSE ROSIE STEVENS AMY
STEVENS OLIVIA SIZER LIZZIE HARRISON TAMSIN FENN STEPHANIE SMITH CRAIG
SCOTT ANDREW WADC HANNAH WATSON KIRSTY EMANNUEL MALIKA SALLERI JAMIE-
LEIGH ROBERTS KAITLYN BUCK GRACE MARTIN LILY MARTIN MCKELL DAVID KIRSTEN
CROARKIN DANIELLA GRICE DANIELLA PARK DANNY CODY SARAH OLIVER ALEX
OLIVER GRAHAM HALL GRACE WALKER SAMANTHA JANE PRESTON NATALIE OLSEN JULIE
WADEMAN MOLLY KENTON KASEY HARTNEY BETHANY PEARSON CHELSEA STEELE KIRA
POLLARD ABBIE OLIVER NICOLA HARNEY ALICIA HARNEY NATALIE LYTHGOE RUTH IRWIN

The Comeback Girl

By Katie Price

Once upon a time, Eden had it all; she was one of the most successful young singers in the UK, and the darling of the pop industry. Life couldn't have been better. But just two years after a sell-out tour, Eden is regarded as a has-been, better known for her drinking and the kiss-and-tell stories that a string of men have sold to the papers.

Desperate to get back in the big time, Eden begins recording a new album with songwriter Jack Steele, a man who drives her crazy for all the wrong reasons. But when she's asked to be a judge on the TV talent show *Band Ambition*, it's just the break she needs, and she's determined not to mess it up. So falling in love with Stevie, a contestant on the show, is probably not a very good idea. But Eden has always followed her heart, and she is sure that Stevie is 'the one'.

But is Eden setting herself up for another fall?

'Glam, glitz, gorgeous people . . . so Jordan!' *Woman*

'A real insight into the celebrity world' *OK!*

'Brilliantly bitchy' *New!*

Century · London

Angel

Katie Price

A sparkling and sexy tale of glamour modelling, romance and the treacherous promises of fame.

When Angel is discovered by a model agent, her life changes for ever. Young, beautiful and sexy, she seems destined for a successful career and, very quickly, the glitzy world of celebrity fame and riches becomes her new home.

But then she meets Mickey, the lead singer of a boy band, who is as irresistible as he is dangerous, and Angel realises that a rising star can just as quickly fall . . .

'The perfect sexy summer read' *heat*

'A page-turner . . . it is brilliant. Genuinely amusing and readable. This summer, every beach will be polka-dotted with its neon pink covers' *Evening Standard*

'The perfect post-modern fairy tale' *Glamour*

arrow books

Angel Uncovered

By Katie Price

Angel Summer looks as if she has found her happy ever after. She's married to the love of her life, sexy footballer Cal, they have a beautiful baby girl and Angel is Britain's top glamour model. But all is not as it seems and there is heartache in store.

When Cal is transferred to AC Milan, Angel feels isolated being so far away from her family and friends instead of embracing the WAG lifestyle of designer shopping and pampering. Surrounded by beautiful people, will Angel and Cal pull together or will they turn elsewhere to seek comfort? Angel's worst nightmares come to life when an old flame of Cal's comes back on the scene and suddenly Angel is fighting to save her marriage, and herself . . .

'Glam, glitz, gorgeous people . . . so Jordan!' *Woman*

'A real insight into the celebrity world' *OK!*

'Brilliantly bitchy' *New!*

arrow books

Paradise

Katie Price

It's six months since beautiful model Angel Summer found herself having to choose between a life with Ethan Turner, the laid-back Californian baseball player, or giving her marriage to football star Cal Bailey another go. Her friends and family were stunned when she picked Ethan, but it looks like Angel made the right decision: Ethan loves her and she loves him.

But nothing is perfect. Ethan has secrets in his past that could threaten their relationship and when he faces financial ruin the couple are forced to star in a reality TV show about their life together. Despite everything, though, Angel is convinced that Ethan is the man for her. So why can't she stop thinking about Cal?

As the tabloids have always been quick to point out, the path of true love has never run smoothly for our sexy celebrity, and when her dad falls dangerously ill Angel rushes back to England to be by his bedside, throwing her and Cal back together. But Ethan loves her, Cal has a girlfriend, and Angel has made her choice. It's too late to go back now . . . isn't it?

'A fabulous guilty holiday pleasure' *Heat*

'Peppered with cutting asides and a directness you can only imagine coming from Katie Price, it's a fun, blisteringly paced yet fluffy novel.' *Cosmopolitan*

arrow books

Crystal

Katie Price

A glittering and sexy story of passion and betrayal and one woman's search for true love.

Crystal is beautiful, talented and ambitious. All her life she has dreamed of making it as a singer. After years of trying to break into the music industry her chance finally comes when her girl band enters a TV reality show contest.

But Crystal has a secret. She's fallen for the wrong man and this one mistake could cost her everything – her friendships, her fame and her chance of ever finding love again . . .

'*Crystal* is charming. Gloriously infectious' *Evening Standard*

'Peppered with cutting asides and a directness you can only imagine coming from Katie Price, it's a fun, blisteringly paced yet fluffy novel.' *Cosmopolitan*

'Passion-filled' *heat*

'Fun and full of excitement. A feisty tale of friendship, love and fame that's bound to be a bestseller' *Woman*

arrow books

Sapphire

Katie Price

Sapphire Jones doesn't believe in relationships any more – not since she caught her husband in bed with another woman. Now Sapphire only sees men on her terms, which is why her current lover is younger than her, good-looking, doesn't place any emotional demands on her (so far, fingers crossed) and is great in bed. What more does a girl need?

Sapphire puts all her passion into running her own business – a high-end lingerie and hen-weekend company. She is doing well and life seems pretty good until she meets a very handsome, charming businessman who seems more than a match for Sapphire. Then things go badly wrong at the hen party she has planned for a soap star and tabloid darling. The evening is one that everyone will be talking about for all the wrong reasons, and Sapphire faces front-page headlines all of her own . . .

Suddenly her business is in jeopardy, her well-controlled private life is falling apart, and in the middle of all this Sapphire realises that she is not immune to love after all, but has she left it too late?

'An incredibly addictive read' *heat*

'Fun and full of excitement. A feisty tale of friendship, love and fame that's bound to be a bestseller' *Woman*

arrow books